THE

Forgotten Kingdom

ALSO BY SIGNE PIKE

The Lost Queen

*Faery Tale: One Woman's Search
for Enchantment in a Modern World*

THE
Forgotten
Kingdom

☙ A NOVEL ❧

SIGNE PIKE

ATRIA BOOKS

New York   London   Toronto   Sydney   New Delhi

ATRIA
BOOKS

An Imprint of Simon & Schuster, Inc.
1230 Avenue of the Americas
New York, NY 10020

First Atria Books hardcover edition September 2020

ATRIA BOOKS and colophon are trademarks of Simon & Schuster, Inc.

For information about special discounts for bulk purchases,
please contact Simon & Schuster Special Sales at
1-866-506-1949 or business@simonandschuster.com.

The Simon & Schuster Speakers Bureau can bring authors to your live event. For
more information or to book an event, contact the Simon & Schuster Speakers
Bureau at 1-866-248-3049 or visit our website at www.simonspeakers.com.

Interior design by Jill Putorti
Map by David Lindroth Inc.

Manufactured in the United States of America

1   3   5   7   9   10   8   6   4   2

Library of Congress Cataloging-in-Publication Data has been applied for.

ISBN 978-1-5011-9145-9
ISBN 978-1-5011-9147-3 (ebook)

The bitter wind pierces my body.
My feet are sore, my cheeks are pale . . .
I have endured so much suffering
my body has grown feathers.

—"Buile Suibhne" ("The Frenzy of Suibhne")

The Crook
P

Isle of Lismore

Isle of Rousay

Einhallow Sound

Cendalaeth's
Broch

Priestesses
of the North

Woodwick Bay

THE
ORCADES

THE
ORCADES

Firth of Clyde

Bullfort of
Bridei

PICTLAND

MANNAU

GODODDIN

STRATH-
CLYDE

SELGOVAE

BERNICIA

DALRIADA

RHEGED

SCOTIA
(THE
WESTLANDS)

EBRAUC

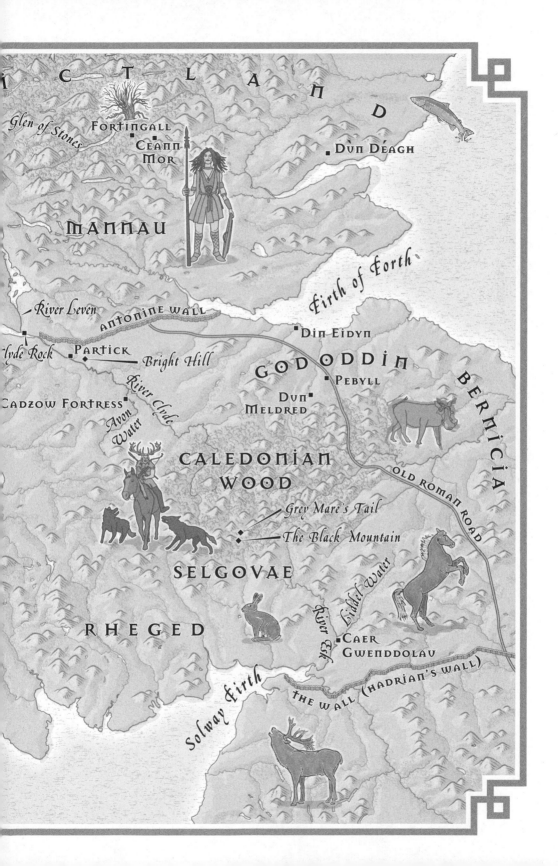

ICTLAND

Glen of Stones

FORTINGALL

CEANN
MOR

DUN DÉAGH

MANNAU

Firth of Forth

River Leven

ANTONINE WALL

Din Eidyn

Clyde Rock

PARTICK

Bright Hill

GODODDIN

PEBYLL

BERNICIA

CADZOW FORTRESS

River Clyde

DUN
MELDRED

Avon
Water

CALEDONIAN
WOOD

OLD ROMAN ROAD

Grey Mare's Tail

The Black Mountain

SELGOVAE

RHEGED

River Esk

Liddel Water

CAER
GWENDDOLAU

Solway Firth

THE WALL (HADRIAN'S WALL)

THE PEOPLE

Kingdom of Strathclyde
House of Morken
Aela: Languoreth's servant
Brant: Dragon Warrior, Lailoken's cousin
Brodyn: Languoreth's chief of guard, Lailoken's cousin
Lailoken: Languoreth's twin brother, Gwenddolau's counsel
Languoreth: Lailoken's twin sister, Rhydderch's wife

House of Tutgual
Angharad: youngest daughter of Rhydderch and Languoreth
Cyan: second son of Rhydderch and Languoreth
Elufed: queen of Strathclyde, a Pict
Gladys: firstborn daughter of Rhydderch and Languoreth
Morcant: eldest son of Tutgual
Rhian: Morcant's wife
Rhydderch: second son of Tutgual, Languoreth's husband
Rhys: eldest son of Rhydderch and Languoreth
Torin: guard
Tutgual: king of Strathclyde

Kingdom of Pendragon
The Dragon Warriors
Diarmid: Wisdom Keeper

Eira: servant

Emrys: the first Pendragon

Fendwin: warrior

Gwenddolau: Uther Pendragon, Emrys's successor, Lailoken and Languoreth's foster brother

Maelgwn: warrior, Pendragon's general

Kingdom of Ebrauc

Euerdil: Gwrgi and Peredur's mother, Urien of Rheged's sister

Gwrgi: king of Southern Ebrauc, Peredur's brother

Peredur: king of Northern Ebrauc

Kingdom of Gododdin

Cwyllog: wife of Meldred

Meldred: chieftain of Southern Gododdin

Kingdom of Rheged

Gwendolen: Urien's daughter

Taliesin: Song Keeper

Urien: king of Rheged

The Christians

Brother Thomas: culdee

Father Natan: Tutgual's advisor, tutor to Languoreth's children

Mungo: former bishop of Strathclyde

The Scots

Aedan mac Gabrahn: king of Mannau and Dalriada

Artùr: Aedan's son

Cai: warrior, Artùr's foster brother

The Picts

Ariane: priestess, the Orcades

Bridei: high king of the Picts

Briochan: Wisdom Keeper

Eachna: high priestess at Fortingall

Fetla: Eachna's daughter, Elufed's elder sister

Muirenn: chieftain of Dùn Déagh

Talorcan: Muirenn's lover

PHONETIC PRONUNCIATIONS

House of Morken
Brodyn: "BRO-din"
Lailoken: "LIE-lo-kin"
Languoreth: "Lang-GOR-eth"

House of Tutgual
Angharad: "An-HA-rad"
Cyan: "KY-ann"
Elufed: "El-LEAF-ed"
Gladys: "GLA-diss"
Rhian: "REE-AHn"
Rhydderch: "RU-therk"
Rhys: "REEse"
Tutgual: "TOOT-gee-al"

Kingdom of Pendragon
Eira: "EYE-ra"
Emrys: "EM-riss"
Gwenddolau: "GWEN-tho-lye"
Maelgwn: "MILE-gwinn"

Kingdom of Ebrauc
Gwrgi: "Ga-WHERE-gi"
Peredur: "PEAR-REE-dur"

The Christians
Moluag: "Ma-LEW-ig"

The Picts
Ariane: "Ah-REE-AH-nee"
Bridei: "BRI-dee"
Briochan: "BREE-o-can"
Eachna: "AUCK-na"
Muirenn: "MEER-in"

In the 1830s, a group of quarrymen discovered a body buried on a hilltop two miles east of Dunipace, Scotland. The skeleton had been laid to rest in an ancient coffin of unhewn stone. No weapons, jewelry, mirrors, or combs were found in the grave. The only accompanying artifact was a large earthenware vase; inside it were the decayed remains of parchment. A report was published in the *Second Statistical Account of Scotland*, and the skeleton was removed so quarrying could continue.

The body, the coffin, and the earthenware vase have all since been lost.

Along with the parchment and whatever was written upon it.

I.

The battle of Arderydd
between the sons of Eliffer
and Gwenddolau, son of Ceidio.
In which battle Gwenddolau fell:
Myrddin went mad.

–Annales Cambriae,
entry for the year AD 573

PROLOGUE

Lailoken

Hart Fell, the Black Mountain
Kingdom of the Selgovae
Late December, AD 573

The snows have come.

The cold seeps into my bones. Winter cuts into the mouth of this steep and dead-grassed valley, and the men huddle closer to the hearth, but no fire can warm us—winter in its bleakness leaves us shut for too many hours within these squat, wattled huts. We cannot escape the ghosts that followed as we fled, friends and fellow warriors. Cousins. Nephews. Brothers.

I wake in the night to the haunting blast of a battle horn. To the sound of a thousand feet rushing toward the fortress through the river below. In sleep, I see bodies piled in heaps, bloodied. Sightless eyes. In sleep, my heels are slipping once more in mud, sliding backward into the muck, spears thrusting at my legs and swords battering my shield as I brace myself in the shield wall. "Hold," I cry. "Hold!"

I wake to find only hollow-eyed survivors, their eyes understanding in the dark.

When the cavalry charged, the thundering of horses swallowed our battle cry. Never had I seen an army so vast—an angry horde of Britons, my own countrymen. We shared ancestors with even the most despicable among them; cowards who would not join us to fight the Angles came now, to finish us.

We watched from high atop the fortress walls as they crept across our fields like so many fleas. We lit the brush fires. Let the smoke sting their eyes and clog their throats—let them taste our bitter battle fog.

And as we stood, grim-faced in our armor, spear shafts in hand, a moment before the nightmare began, a single red deer fled from the forest below.

A doe.

A shaft of sun caught the glory of autumn leaves and her sleek, tawny pelt, and for a moment I was a boy again, standing with my twin sister, Languoreth, on the banks of the Avon Water as we watched a stag drink in the shallows of the river.

A moment of grace before the horror of destruction.

Now it is Yule, the day of the longest night.

There are twelve days in winter when the sun stands still, and we warriors with our night terrors and our ill-knitting wounds and our bloody-faced ghosts need to conquer the darkness or we will be consumed by it. And so, at sunset, the men stood or propped themselves up as I spoke the old words and lit the Yule log.

The woman who minds the goats had come the day before to take the stale mats from the floor, laying down clean woven rushes that smelled soft and sweet, a distant memory of summer. She brought with her the charred remains of a new year's fire, an offering to bless our hearth. "For luck," she'd said, "so far from your homes."

Her gaze lingered upon the mottled scar upon my cheek that runs from temple to chin, the welt I'd borne now for eighteen winters, half-hidden by my beard.

"Christians," I'd said.

She'd nodded as if I needn't say more. Here in the lands of the Selgovae, Christ had not yet taken hold. Perhaps his priests were too frightened by the shades and sharp-toothed creatures that frequent the vast Caledonian Wood.

Now my beard grows long.

I think of my wife and her thick, honey-smooth hair, the way she tilted her head to gather it, sweeping her fingers across the back of her neck. She is yet alive, I can feel her across the distance.

I can feel she is breathing.

She tethers me to my body when my spirit wants to flee, for as the days pass, my mind turns dark. When I sit in contemplation, my mind begins to slip. There is a beast that stalks in the pit of night.

I fear it will take me.

On the bleakest mornings, I climb the icy path up the valley to seek solace at the spring. The trickle of mountain waters is speaking.

Iron in blood, iron in water.

My sister's husband hunts us with dogs.

Old Man Archer says, "Rhydderch may have dogs, but we Selgovae are wolves. He will never catch you out, not whilst we conceal you here."

It is true—no one steps foot in the Caledonian Deep without being seen. The Selgovae have watchers who appear and disappear as if made from mist. And we warriors of Pendragon can climb quickly, those of us who are sound. We can slip into the deep chasm of these hills while Rhydderch and his hunters are still specks far below.

And yet one ear is ever pricked for the crow sound of our watchmen.

I do not know whether I fear him or am calling him as I stand upon the boulder, high above the iron salt waters, looking out over the winter hills.

I stand upon the boulder and wait for Rhydderch and his men.

I wait.

I watch.

And I remember.

CHAPTER 1

Lailoken

Strathclyde to the Borderlands
Kingdom of Strathclyde
Late Summer, AD 572

I t was the time of year when daylight stretched long. Travelers were often spied long into the lingering hours of dusk, yet on this day, the moors still blazed hot beneath sun when we stopped to make camp for the night.

We were bound for the Borderlands, two days' ride from my boyhood home, the fortress of Cadzow. We'd followed the wide and glittering twists of the river Clyde south and east, through lofty patches of oak and ash, past merchants rowing upstream in their currachs and men fishing from little coracles. We passed timber-built grain mills and neatly thatched tenant crofts as we traveled through the villages of my distant kin: men and women yet loyal to me and my sister, the children of Morken. Our father had been a fierce and honorable king. But as the people gathered to greet our caravan along the road, it was not me alone they cheered. They rushed from their huts to catch sight of the man who rode by my side—Uther Pendragon. Though he was not their ruler, he and his warriors had fought for many a winter to keep the Angles of Bernicia at bay.

Gradually, the terrain shifted, and we left the villages behind. Soon hills rose turtle-backed in the distance, where pastures gave way to the wild, boggy expanse of moor. It was this land that spoke to me, for it led into the heart of the new kingdom that had become my home. The kingdom ruled by my foster brother, Uther.

But Uther had not always been my foster brother's name.

He was a boy of fifteen winters called Gwenddolau when he first joined Emrys Pendragon. Emrys was a leader who'd inspired a brotherhood to rise up against the Angles, invaders from across the North Sea. The Angles had gained footing on our soil as hired mercenaries, but before long, through violence, they'd carved out a kingdom from stolen land and named it Bernicia. In resisting them, Emrys and his men became known throughout our land as the Dragon Warriors. There were battles, and then there was peace for a time. But when Emrys was murdered, war stirred once more. We chose the man best suited to defend Emrys's lands. In becoming Pendragon's successor, Gwenddolau became something more than a man. He became hero, protector, king.

He became *Uther Pendragon*.

The Other Pendragon.

And I . . .

I'd become more than a warrior, or son of Morken. I was a Wisdom Keeper, trained from a boy to be a king's counsellor, his most trusted advisor. We defended our stretch of the Borderlands through the vigilance of our scouts and the brunt of our swords. Our tenant farmers were grateful. The Gods protected us. The land produced. All we required, we possessed in bounty.

We traveled fast on fleet-footed horses. We traveled light, with thick cloaks and thin bedrolls, with little more than the sack full of oats each man strapped to his horse to be fried with water or blood from wild game. Thirteen leagues in a day we passed with ease.

And yet on this day, we'd scarcely traveled through Hawksland

and the Blackwood when my young niece bolted upright in the saddle before me and cried out, "Stop!"

My horse tossed his head as I yanked back on the reins, gripping Angharad to keep her astride as the caravan came to a halt. "Angharad. What is it?" I asked.

The Dragon Warriors drew up their mounts, restless and questioning. They'd never traveled with a child. Who among us had? Now we traveled in the company of a freckled girl of eight winters whose gray eyes were yet swollen with tears. At sunrise, Angharad had left all she had known to train with me as a Wisdom Keeper. That I was her uncle was little consolation.

"The feathers," she said now, pointing to the ground.

"Feathers." I followed the line of her finger to the place where, indeed, a cluster of crow feathers lay, their ink glinting rainbows in the sun. "And so they are."

It was this child's curiosity about the natural world that had first endeared her to me, and now I was to foster her. Yet despite my reassurances to my sister, I was still learning the way.

"Angharad. Surely you've seen crow feathers before." I leaned forward only to see her brow furrow.

"But I want to pick them up."

"Well, of course you may. But you must take more care when alerting me to feathers on your next sighting. You nearly tumbled from Gwydion's back."

Angharad's face flushed scarlet, her voice a whisper. "I'm sorry, Uncle."

There'd been little admonishment in my tone, yet my words alone were enough to flatten her. She pursed her lips in an effort to hold back tears, and guilt struck, pointed as a spear. "Oh, no, Angharad. Please. You mustn't cry."

The warriors looked baffled as I glanced round in search of aid. Gwenddolau sat mounted at a distance beside my cousin Brant, expressions vigilant yet uncertain.

"She's your kin as well," I grumbled, then motioned to Maelgwn, who already trotted toward us on his horse, green eyes alert.

"What's happened?" he demanded.

"She's weeping," I said.

"Aye, I can see." He dismounted and went to her, taking her small hands in his. "Angharad, what is it?"

"I didn't intend for all the men to stop. I only wanted the feathers," she said.

"Tell me why."

She took a breath, searching the sky. "My mother told me our hearts are like birds, pricked full of feathers, and that each time we say good-bye, a feather will fall. One for a friend, two for a sweetheart. Three for a child."

At the mention of Languoreth, Maelgwn's gaze softened. "And here you spied three feathers, just as your mother said."

Angharad nodded. "She promised if I found a feather, it had fallen from her heart. She promised if I picked it up and held it close, it would keep me safe."

"Then you must have them," Maelgwn said.

I watched as he handed Angharad the cluster of crow feathers. Long had Maelgwn loved my sister, Languoreth.

As Angharad drew them to her chest, I searched for the right words.

"I know your sadness, little one," I began. "Languoreth and I, we lost our own mother when we were no more than ten winters—"

Angharad's eyes widened at the very thought. "But my mother is not *dead*."

Fool, Lailoken.

"Aye. I mean, nay! Of course she isn't." I reached for her. "I only hope to say I know how your own heart must feel. We may collect each feather you see. But you need no such talismans to keep you safe. I swore to your mother—and I swear the same to you—you are safe with me, Angharad. I'm your uncle, your own blood, and . . . I love you." The last came too gruffly, and I cursed myself again. Maelgwn frowned.

But Angharad only wiped at her eyes, casting a weary look over her shoulder. "You're not terribly good with children, are you?"

I smiled in spite of myself. "You're right, then," I decided. "We've traveled far enough. We shall stop here for the night."

Gwenddolau approached, swinging down from his horse. "A rest is fine, but we cannot yet make camp. We haven't passed more than five leagues, Lailoken."

"Well enough," I said. "But 'tis only the first day of our journey, and Angharad is unaccustomed to long days upon horseback, brother. You cannot expect her to last from dawn 'til dusk in the saddle."

Gwenddolau's clear blue eyes swept the broad expanse of moor, resting on the grassy mound that rose in the distance. "Surely it is ill luck to make our camp so close to a hill of the dead. I have seen enough shades in my day."

"Aye, we all spied the mound, and many a time have we passed it," I said. "But the hill lies upstream, and the ashes within it are sleeping. Besides, we are not far from the old ring of stones. I'm certain Angharad would wish to see it. If you'll not brave the shades for me, brave them for your niece, eh?"

The look I received was one of predictable gravity—Gwenddolau's humor had gone with seasons past. "I feel no more ease bedding beside a stone ring than I do a mound of the dead."

Brant drew up his horse, his brown eyes touching on Angharad with concern. "The ring will make a good enough boundary for the horses," my cousin said. "They'll not stray beyond it."

"Aye," Gwenddolau agreed at last, signaling for the men to dismount. "They're ill at ease, as I am, round places of the dead."

In truth, I knew rest would suit Gwenddolau as well, whether he cared for it or not. His old battle wound was on the mend, with thanks to Languoreth's remedy, but he needed to recover his strength. Thirteen leagues in a day or half that, what did it matter? Angharad was ours now—all of ours—and I meant to tend to her as best as I could.

The thought seemed to weigh upon Gwenddolau, too, for as I watched, he placed his sunbrowned hands round Angharad's waist, lifting her from my horse with a smile at last. "Well enough, Angharad. Come, then. Let's find a suitable place to make camp."

I dismounted, following behind. "It's bound to be boggy. I'll fashion a bed so Angharad might sleep in the cart."

Next to me, the old warrior Dreon chuckled.

"Oh, go on, then, Dreon. Let's have it," I said.

"Well. I have naught to say but this: a handsome lord, in his prime at thirty-two winters—a Wisdom Keeper to boot—already become staid and matronly as an old mother hen."

"An old mother hen?" I said. "You should mind you don't choke on a chicken bone."

Dreon lifted his hands. "Eh, now! There's no need for bandying curses about."

"When I curse you, you shall know it."

"I believe you." The warrior clapped me upon the shoulder. "Whatever you may do, you mustn't fret, Lailoken. I have bairns of my own, and I'll lend you some wisdom—children are like wolves. They can smell your fear."

I'd met Dreon's offspring. A wild pack of stoats, more like.

"Well," I said, "seeing as you're such a master of your own fine progeny, perhaps you'd like to try a hand at fostering mine."

"Nay." He frowned. "And rob you of the joy?"

I waved him off and found Gwenddolau and Angharad crouched at the water's edge, looking upstream.

"We call this water Wildburn," Gwenddolau said, bending to splash his face. Droplets clung to his golden beard, and when he stood, he shook the water from his head like a dog, smiling at his niece.

"Wildburn." Angharad looked about. She'd drawn the black feathers from her cloak and clutched them like a doll. "Uncle." She turned to me. "Is it true there's a ring of stones nearby?"

"Aye. Just beyond that rise."

Her face brightened, a joy to see. "May we go there? May we go now?"

"Indeed," I said. "I'm to train you as a Keeper, am I not? Here you are, eight winters, and you haven't yet stepped foot in your first ring of stones. Come now, and we shall see them."

"The midges will be upon us," Gwenddolau called after us. "Mind that Angharad has some salve."

"Seems I'm not the only mother hen," I said beneath my breath. Stopping at my horse to take the ointment from my saddlebag, I smiled at Angharad and dropped it into my satchel.

The Dragon Warriors were moving through the rhythm of setting up camp: laying out bedrolls, watering the horses, and rinsing in the burn, while the youngest men gathered fuel for the fire and unpacked the cook pots. My twin sister had sent us away with great flats of dried beef and a bounty of summer crops, perfect for a stew of wild game, but her face had been ashen as we said farewell that morning. And as we'd ridden off through Cadzow's gates—I with her youngest child before me in the saddle—I'd looked over my shoulder to see Languoreth standing on the platform of the rampart, watching us depart. It was enough to wound her that I was taking Angharad away. But her lover, too, traveled in my company.

"No ale before supper," Malegwn called to the men. His jaw was

tight as he joined Gwenddolau beside the stream. Each of us had left
Cadzow carrying our burdens, it seemed.

Yet Angharad was no burden. Languoreth and I had been so very
close when we were children, before our fates had compelled us to
live kingdoms apart. Now, with her daughter at my side, I felt the
rift somehow mended. Angharad threaded her fingers in mine as she
so often had upon my visits, when she and I would walk the woods
together, naming things. She had my sister's tawny-red hair and the
winter-gray eyes of her father, Rhydderch.

It felt right, in that moment, that she should be with me. That I
should be training her in the way of Wisdom Keeping, raising her as
my own. I felt my confidence return, pointing as we drew close. "See
it there? The ring of stones lies just beyond that rise."

But Angharad had already spotted them. "Oh," she breathed. I
wondered if the ring was quite what she'd expected.

Far to the north, I'd visited the ancient, imposing stones of
Pictland—towering behemoths that brooded against molten silver skies. I'd sat within vast circles of sixty stones or more that rose
amid thick sprays of heather. I'd walked, enthralled and nearly se-
duced within intimate stones, places where the rocks had been weath-
ered so round that their curves resembled the finest bits of a woman's
body.

Each circle felt different, and rightly so. For buried deep at the root
of the stones were the ashes of men and women who had come before, awake and then sleeping with the shifting of stars and the rise of
the moon. Though flesh had failed them, rock had become their new
earthly body. Now their spirits were ever present. I could feel them
regarding us now, as if the stones themselves were breathing.

These stones were not set in a circle. They formed instead the
shape of an egg, sunk into the moor in perpetual slumber, rimmed
protectively by a gently sloping dyke. The tallest among them was

scarcely the height of a man, while the others stooped, irregular and hobbled. Still, they beckoned with their own particular enchantment, and Angharad made to enter swiftly before I caught her hand.

"It is ill luck to enter without seeking permission," I said. "These stones are guardians—men and women of old. They do not take kindly to trespassers and can cause all sort of maladies if they wish."

Surely your mother has taught you as much, I nearly said. But Languoreth was no Wisdom Keeper. There was a time when she'd wished more than anything to train, as our own mother had. As I was Chosen to do. But Languoreth was not Chosen. The gift had fallen instead to her youngest daughter. Languoreth had known Angharad was marked. That the child possessed gifts was evident—a thought that stirred excitement in me even as it raised protectiveness in my sister.

But I, too, had seen things as a child. Things that frightened me. Things I could not understand. It was enough to make old spirits out of young ones. Perhaps this was the reason I felt so compelled to teach Angharad how to wield her gifts—so they would not become a burden. So they could not break her.

"Some Wisdom Keepers are showmen," I told her now. "They would have our people believe that spirit speaks in great booms, like thunder. But spirit speaks in whispers. The best Keepers understand this and keep quiet so they might hear. Close your eyes and be still."

Through the joining of our hands I could sense her, alert as a rabbit. A little fearful. And beneath the surface, sorrow issuing in a foul and muddy water. I could take it from her if I wished. Draw it into myself, and she might experience some relief. But the source of such wellsprings ran deep. Water will find its way—it would only rise up again. Better to let her come to it in her own time. Her own way.

"Be still," I repeated. Angharad's eyes flared with frustration, but she closed them, her cinnamon-colored lashes settling against her freckled cheeks.

I waited until her face began to soften. She had found her way to the quiet, the place where deeper meaning could reside.

"I will teach you the blessing Cathan once gave me," I said. "Commit it to memory. The words will serve you well." I moved through the old chant twice, then once more for good measure. "Tomorrow we will return, and those words will be yours to speak. Yes?" Angharad nodded and I released her hands. "You may enter now. Touch the stones if you like."

"Sunwise?" she asked.

"Aye. Isn't that the way of it all?"

A summer wind played, flapping at the corner of Angharad's gray cloak as she stepped into the stones—a gentle sort of greeting. As she began to explore the circle, I told her what I knew of their story.

"This ring was built by your ancestors, those who came to this great island and first dwelled in the north. I speak of a time long ago—time out of memory. What you see are not only stones. They are your people, your clann. Their alignments track the course of moon and sun. The sunrise at Midwinter, the movements that mark the quarter year, too. In this way they are Time Keepers. Cathan brought me here—to this very circle—when I was but a boy. I saw for myself how this stone pairs with yonder hill." I pointed to the slope that rose in the distance. "If you stand just here on Midwinter sunset, there is a cairn upon the summit that marks the grave of an ancient king. You can watch the evening sun slip down its curve like the yolk of an egg, until it disappears into the earth."

I turned back to find that Angharad was not listening and fought the compulsion to throw up my hands. Such inattention from a novice was inexcusable. But Angharad was my kin, and the girl had never before visited a circle. I held my tongue and watched her explore, fingers tracing the pale lichen that bloomed from the speckled skin of a stone.

But then.

It was as if the air around us had gone cold. I looked up, expecting to see a swift-moving storm, but the sky was cerulean, dotted with fat, friendly clouds. Strange. Yet there could be no question—the atmosphere had shifted. I could scarcely focus on Angharad's form, my sight gone blurry.

Stones had a particular fondness for the attention of children. But with Angharad in the stones, this was something more. Ill at ease, I closed my eyes and turned inward, searching for the cause of such a shift, and felt suddenly as if I were being observed.

Nay, not observed.

Stalked.

My blood beat against my temples. These stones were born of my own kin. Never before had I felt such malevolence. What dared stalk me now? What dared stalk my niece?

Angharad stood with her palms pressed flat against a stone. I strode into the ring, but she did not notice my presence. The wind shifted again, but now the smell that met my nose was rank, like flesh gone rotten. I did not wish to speak, fearful of lending more power to this unnamable thing, yet I could sense it, a shadow approaching, traveling across the ages. Ancient. Such power stirred I nearly reeled.

A strange look had come over Angharad's face.

"Angharad, step back." I spoke evenly, not wishing to cause her alarm. But the child did not hear me. It was as if she were entranced. "Angharad. Step back, I said."

Pulling her from the rock was a danger, too abrupt. She had clearly joined some part of herself with the stone. There was risk in tearing her away that all of her might not return. But I could not wait. Reaching out, I yanked Angharad's hands from the granite and drew back, startled, as she rounded on me, crying out as if wounded.

"It is coming for you! It comes for my mother!" she cried, then slumped against me, boneless. I caught her limp body in my arms. She weighed little more than a sack of feathers. Her freckled skin had gone waxen.

"Angharad. Speak to me. Are you all right?"

Even as I held her, even as I questioned, I knew what had taken place. Angharad had experienced a Knowing.

My tutor Cathan was wont to have them, but he'd held such mastery over himself, his utterances were more akin to a common suggestion than a vision arrived from beyond the veil. Few Keepers I'd known had possessed sight equal to his. For me, divinity spoke through nature. Augury and rhetoric were my skills. Book learnings and king lists. Strategic maneuverings. I was a counsellor—an advisor—not a priest as such. Yet I knew some Seers suffered exertion from their visions, and I imagined the effect could be more taxing on someone young, one who did not yet know how to wield it.

The girl was far too open. Angharad had opened herself and something had come, something unbidden. And I had unwittingly placed her in danger.

I should not have brought her here, I thought. Not without yet understanding her. Then she stirred in my arms and my shoulders dropped with relief. Angharad looked up at me, blinking.

"I'm all right, Uncle. Truly."

I studied her. "Nay, not quite. But do you think you might stand?"

Angharad nodded and I placed her down gently, searching her eyes. Her gray eyes were stormy, but thank the Gods, wherever her vision had taken her, it seemed all of her had returned.

"Angharad. You must tell me what happened," I said.

"What happened . . ." She spoke slowly, as if only just remembering the use of her mouth.

"Aye," I encouraged, and her gaze turned distant.

"The stone felt soft. Soft as a sea sponge. And empty. Hollow. As if I might push it. As if I might push it and fall right through."

"And did you? Did you . . . fall through?" I watched her intently.

"No, for there was something else then. Something coming as if through a tunnel deep in the earth. It rushed toward me like a wind, fast as a thousand galloping horses."

"And then? Angharad, I do not wish to press you, but I must know the entirety of what happened so I know you are now truly safe. This spirit. Did it feel an evil thing? A . . . beast of some kind? What did you see?"

She frowned, frustration mounting. "I saw nothing, Uncle! It was a feeling, that's all." She struggled to find the words to explain it. "It was . . . a Thing."

"A Thing." I drew her to me. "I should not have brought you here. Not so soon. There are things I must teach you. I made an error, one I shall not make again. I am sorry you were frightened."

"But I was not frightened."

I could not hold back my surprise. "Were you not?"

"Nay. The Thing did not come for me," she said simply. "It came for you."

A shiver traced my arms, and I pressed her more tightly. Then quite suddenly Angharad's face shifted and she drew away, laughing. "What is it, Uncle? Why do you embrace me so?"

"I—I wish to comfort you." I blinked.

"Comfort me? Whatever for?" She smiled. "I am sorry, Uncle, for I must not have been listening. I cannot recall what you did say! Tell me again what such stone rings were built for. I do so wish to explore."

The child had no memory of the events that had taken place only moments ago.

"Nay, Angharad." I reached for her. "Perhaps tomorrow. But the stones are before you. Now you have seen them! You will be hungry. Come, let us return to camp. The air grows chill. It will soon be time for supper."

She furrowed her brow but followed nonetheless. As we picked our way back over the grassy tufts of moor, I puzzled over what had taken place. I had spent time in shadow. In caves and underground pathways. In ancient stone chambers built for the dead. I'd faced my own darkness and my share of shades—in this world and the other. Yet never had I encountered such a . . . Thing.

At our camp beside Wildburn, the night fire was crackling. We slathered on ointment to fend off the midges that swarmed with a vengeance. Dreon whittled a shaft of ash with his blade, shaping a new spear. We filled our stomachs with hot stew, and the men took turns recounting tales of the woods until Angharad's lids dropped and she slept where she sat. I picked her up and laid her gently on her bedding in the cart, tucking the sheepskin round her face, so peaceful now in sleep.

But I did not close my eyes that night for fear that the Thing, whatever it might be, should return, that Angharad would somehow be lost to me. I sat awake the long night, spine slumped against the wheel of the wagon, watching the shadows cast from the fire as they flickered and shifted, growing in the dark.

CHAPTER 2

Lailoken

"Uncle, why is it you have no wife?"

Angharad twisted in the saddle before me, searching my face in earnest.

We'd broken camp at sunrise, determined to reach the fort before evening. It was our third day on horseback and overcast—the air threatened rain. We had traveled scarcely a league, and it occurred to me now that the day would be interminable if this were to be Angharad's line of questioning.

"Ask me another question. Something clever. That's poor use of our time."

Angharad only waited.

"Perhaps you should like to hear the tale once more about the birth of our great island?"

"You are quite handsome, even with your scar," she said.

"I thank you," I said. "You are not the first lady to tell me so."

Angharad looked skyward with a laugh, but despite my jest, I did not suffer from vanity. I'd studied my own countenance reflected in bronze. I had a fine nose. Two rather widely spaced blue eyes, graceful brows, and sandy hair I wore long, shaved in the front from ear to ear in the manner of a Keeper. My beard was full, but I kept it neatly trimmed. If I turned my face to one side, the puckering scar dealt me at fifteen winters became a trick of the mind, a vanishing act. That I was handsome I knew, and women agreed. There had been a time when I found ease in the bounty of their affection. But with time I'd learned the body was only a shell built to house the spirit.

"Go on, then, Lailoken," my cousin Brant said. "Tell wee Angharad why you've not wed."

"I suppose I've not yet encountered the right lady."

Brant scoffed, for this was not exactly true. I'd encountered many ladies and had found them all exceedingly pleasing. It was precisely my joy of encountering women that left me with little interest in tethering myself to any one in particular.

"Nay, Angharad, don't be led astray," Gwenddolau said from his saddle. "The truth is your uncle may well have encountered the right lady, but she wanted nothing to do with the likes of him. Is that not right, Lailoken?"

"Ah, I see your humor has returned at last," I said. "You must be feeling better, brother. You were growing quite dull, you know."

Brant smiled, but Gwenddolau only lifted a brow.

"Never fear, Angharad," Brant reassured her. "When Lailoken chooses to wed, he will have his pick of gentle ladies."

Angharad had turned to Gwenddolau now, her attention blessedly diverted. "And why have *you* not taken a wife, Uncle? After all, you are a rich and powerful king."

"So I am rich and powerful, while your uncle Lailoken is handsome. Is this what you say?" Gwenddolau frowned.

"Oh, you are quite handsome, too," she answered. "But never so much as when you smile."

"And am I to be only handsome, not rich and powerful as well?" I asked.

Angharad looked between us. "You tease me."

"Right you are. For there isn't a citizen of Strathclyde who doesn't know I possess a great many more gifts than my incredibly fine looks," I said.

"Humility, for one," Maelgwn said as he drew his mount up beside us. Angharad laughed. But with talk of marriage, Gwenddolau fell silent.

Strong-featured with pale hair, Gwenddolau suffered no lack of women. But when it came to finding a wife, I'd searched the length of the isle, and no king or chieftain would wed his daughter to Uther Pendragon. Despite Gwenddolau's wealth and the reputation of his retinue, our kingdom was small and pressed by the Angles of Bernicia in the east. What land he possessed the Dragons had carved out. The risk, these fathers feared, was too great. My own sister, at least, did not doubt our strength. Had she worried over our survival, she'd never have allowed me to foster her youngest child.

As Gwenddolau's counsel, I'd strengthened our alliances as best as I could. We'd visited the powerful King Urien of Rheged by arrangement of his Song Keeper named Taliesin, a man I called a friend. We'd made a treaty for trade with Aedan mac Gabhran, a powerful Scot, now king of Mannau in the north. And on Gwenddolau's behalf, I traveled often to my sister and her husband, Rhydderch, at Cadzow and Clyde Rock.

Still, our enemies only mounted. The power of the Angles in Bernicia had quickened, and they sought to test the boundaries of their new kingdom in sudden and violent raids. Raids came, too, from the kingdom of Ebrauc, ruled by Gwenddolau's cousins Gwrgi and Peredur. Their father had routed Gwenddolau's father from his throne when I was but a boy. Now the sons carried the feud their fathers begot; they attacked and we countered. Blood flowed on both sides.

It was time for the Dragons to find a safe haven. And if I could not secure a marital alliance for Gwenddolau, I must craft a political one. Thus, our visit to my twin sister at Cadzow had been at my urging. Strathclyde was a great power, and Rhydderch its likeliest successor. I had appealed to Rhydderch for support, but the visit had not been a success. Gwenddolau refused to swear fealty, and Rhydderch would not take up Gwenddolau's cause without it—to do so was to risk losing the favor of his father, Tutgual. Tutgual had not yet named a tanist, his chosen successor. In the end, the Council of Strathclyde must agree to Tutgual's choice, but to be named Tutgual's tanist was a mighty thing.

Now we returned to our kingdom to see to our defenses. Let the kings of the north have their doubts. The warriors Pendragon were among the most feared in our land. We would fortify our ramparts and triple our scouts. We had survived before and would do so again.

Thinking of it, I turned to Gwenddolau. "All has been quiet in our absence. The men have seen to the rampart, yes? They have deepened the dyke and dug the new pits?"

"Aye," Gwenddolau said. "And tomorrow we will ride out to bring the southern settlements some ease. What happened at Sweetmeadow shall not happen again."

With talk of adult things above her station, Angharad perked. "Sweetmeadow? Is there a story? I do love a story."

Gwenddolau and I exchanged a look.

"It was a raid," he said. "A raid by our enemies. That is all."

The memory of what I'd seen—what Lord Gwrgi had done—surged back unbidden. The dark-haired woman hanging from the stables. Bodies strewn like dolls. Girls. Little more than children. Rage pulsed at my temples, working its poison, but I could not turn from the visions. Let the girls be remembered for their suffering. After what Gwrgi of Ebrauc had done, it was better they had not lived.

"Uncle, you hold me too tight!"

I looked down to see I'd been clutching Angharad as if she might slip from my grasp.

"Sorry, I am sorry," I murmured, releasing her.

It was nearly sunset by the time our caravan reached the fortress. Along the river, the sun lit the parchment of birch trunks like melted gold. In the shallows, a waterbird stood, one foot lifted, scouring shadows under rock for its evening catch.

There had been a cliffside fortress at the meeting of the Liddel Water and the river Esk since twilight times. It was a seat of power when I was but a boy, though it had since been burned and rebuilt. The fort commanded tribute on goods traveling north into Strathclyde as well as south into Rheged. We earned a portion of wealth, too, from any wares arriving or departing from the salt waters of the Solway Firth. Caer Gwenddolau might be small, but the reach of Pendragon's influence was mighty.

As we neared the edge of the forest, the warriors' wives and lovers came rushing from their huts to greet them, children close behind, and Angharad shrank into the saddle as if she wished to disappear. But I saw her smile as Dreon's daughters threw themselves at their father like a pack of wild dogs. His youngest shared a birth year with Angharad. They'd make suitable friends.

The warriors who dwelled in the huts below the fortress dropped from their horses and waved us off, taking their loved ones under their arms. Only those who sought escape would join us for supper in the hall this night.

I urged Gwydion into the lead as we mounted the narrow trail carved into the eastern slope of the hill, but as we rounded the bend, there came a brown flash of feathers and the muted thundering of wings.

"Quail!" Angharad said with delight as the flock scattered. They fluttered to and fro in a such a panic it made me wonder at their survival. An omen, perhaps.

I looked up at the timber guard tower as we neared the outer rampart, lifting my arm in greeting. "Ho, Fendwin!"

The ruddy-haired warrior raised a hand in welcome from the lookout. "Well met," he called out. "And just in time. Einion killed a stag. We've been waiting all day now."

"Fendwin. All right?" Gwenddolau called from behind me.

"Aye, Pendragon. All's well." Fendwin peered from the tower with a broad smile for Angharad. "Is this the niece, then, I've heard so much of?"

"The same. Angharad, meet Fendwin," I said.

"Are you the gateman?" she asked, craning her neck.

"Nay, little lass, not exactly," he said. "We're all gatemen here. It's the Pendragon way."

"The Pendragon way?"

"Our warriors share in all stations of service," I explained as we passed through the gates. "Dragon Warriors are not like other soldiers, suited only for one task, kept in only one position. Today Fendwin mans the tower. Tomorrow he may ride out to scout. The day after that, he may lead a raid. We are not only an arm or a leg. We are every part of the creature. Even myself. You'll soon see, for while you may study as a Keeper, you'll be given your tasks as well."

"I should like to mind the gate," she said.

"Well. First you must learn to wield your mother's blade. Then we shall see."

We left our horses to graze and climbed to the summit on foot. The hounds heard us coming. Their bays echoed over the summer pastures as we passed through the gate of the inner rampart. Inside, the evening breeze was milder. There were trees here—hazel and ash, crab apple and rowan. But the hilltop was large enough for only the necessities: granary, smithy, kitchen house, guard lodgings, temple, and tanning shed. At the highest point, our timber hall stood, thatch-roofed with a pair of fierce-toothed wooden dragons keeping watch above the heavy oaken door.

"There you can see the hall. And beyond it, the well." I pointed. "Beside the well is the temple, home to Diarmid, a friend and fellow Keeper. He is a diviner. Uther's birds are kept within."

At the mention of Diarmid and the birds, Angharad's eyes lit. She lived in a land of priests. Seers of the Old Way were banned from Tutgual's court. Aside from myself, Diarmid may be the first of her own kind the girl would encounter.

"You'll soon meet him," I assured her. In fact, I planned to visit Diarmid as soon as I was able. I was anxious to speak with him about Angharad and what had taken place in the stones.

I watched as she took in the tidy buildings tucked within the fortress's inner rampart, wondering how it appeared to a child so accustomed to Partick, with its bustling market and fine trappings, its scores of monks and richly plumed ladies of Tutgual's court. But Angharad was a child of Cadzow, I reminded myself. A child of the forest, like her mother. Like me.

"It's a mite smaller than you're accustomed to," I ventured.

"It's just as I imagined it," she answered. "I was only thinking of Rhys. He talks of nothing but you and Uther and the Dragon Warriors—I've seen him in his chamber. He spends ages hunched over his little pine table, staring at this very place on his map."

The mention of my nephew brought a smile. "Rhys will come. Would that he'd come long before now, but he cannot go overlong without seeing his favorite sister—not to mention his favorite uncle. You shall see. Rhys is a man of seventeen. He will soon make his excuses and visit us here."

Even as I said it, I did not believe it. Rhydderch kept his eldest son close. Perhaps he sensed how brightly his son's passion for the Dragon Warriors burned and hoped to keep the boy's affection from catching alight.

The door to the hall opened and our shaggy gray hounds rushed out to greet us, thumping their tails and shoving their wet noses into the folds of Angharad's cloak until she burst into laughter.

"Back, you beasts!" I bent to wrestle my favorite, who stood taller than Angharad with his paws upon my chest. Across the yard of the fortress, the servants moved about their duties, their eyes lingering upon the little tawny-haired girl.

"Come, Angharad," I said. "All are eager to meet you. But first we shall get you settled in your quarters. You'll want to rest before supper."

I led Angharad past the great room and into her little chamber as the servants began to unpack her belongings. As I closed the door to my own small room, the silence felt a blessing after three nights spent beside snoring men on a bedroll. My chamber—as well as Angharad's—lay off the great room, and it dawned upon me there would be a ruckus in the evenings. What if the child could not sleep?

Sweet gods! Dreon was right. I was becoming staid as a mother hen. I recalled the sight of the ale waiting in the great room on the tables beside the central hearth. Perhaps I did require a servant woman to mind Angharad. Languoreth had wanted to send her woman, but I'd refused; it wasn't the way. "A Keeper must not travel with servants when they undertake their training," I'd said. But for all my adherence to custom, I had not anticipated the difficulty. I loved the child, but it would be impossible for me to see to her every need. And tomorrow we would ride out to answer Sweetmeadow. I craved the blurry sort of heat lent by a horn of liquor and the comfort of a beauty in my bed.

Leaning over my washbasin, I rinsed my face and dried it with a cloth, pulling loose my sandy hair from its binding. My white robe was brown with muck from the road, and I tugged it off. Within the walls of this fortress, all knew my station, so I preferred to wear a warrior's tunic. I pulled one of red linen over my head and stepped into a soft pair of trousers, belting them at my waist.

"A mother hen," I mumbled. The smooth skin of my stomach stretched taut over ridges of muscle. I was a man at my zenith—face unlined, body strong and able. How long had it been since I'd lain with a woman? I felt the need stir. At Cadzow I had been too preoccupied with matters at hand. But now we were returned to ride out in search of Gwrgi. My blood drummed at the thought of it. It was a dangerous thing to ride out after the head of a king. I would need to stoke my battle madness, to summon my frenzy. Nay, I would not sleep alone this night.

But first I must secure Angharad a nursemaid.

In the great room, I swiped a mug of ale from the table and swallowed it down as I headed across the courtyard, calling for our housewoman. "Hedwenn!"

It was a warm summer evening, and the door to the kitchen house was propped open. I stooped beneath the entryway, but not low enough to avoid slamming my skull against the lintel.

"Ow. Hedwenn!" I rubbed my head with a frown. "Where's Hedwenn?"

It took a moment for my eyes to adjust to the dim. Bushels of marjoram and stringy roots of lovage hung from a length of twine stretched between the roof beams. The hind Einion had killed smoked over the hearth on a spit, and I caught the pungent scent of wild garlic mingling with the earthy char of mushrooms. Suspended from a hook above the fire, an iron pot of broth was simmering.

Hedwenn stood with her strong back to the door, bent over a wicker basket of whortleberries. "Ah! Here you are, back home!" She straightened with a grin. "Come here and I'll feed you."

"Nay, Hedwenn. I've come on another errand." I paused. "Well. Perhaps just a bannock."

"A bannock, then." She beamed and plundered a warm bannock from a cloth-lined basket beside the hearth. It gave off little crumbles as she pulled it apart, dunking it into the pot of broth before offering it to me.

"Hedwenn," I moaned as I stuffed it in my mouth. The juices trickled down my chin. "Why must I ever leave you?"

She flushed with pleasure and handed me a linen to wipe my beard. "Ever the flatterer."

I glanced round at the bustle of servants, and an unfamiliar woman caught my eye. She sat at the table near the wall, half-hidden by the dim light of the kitchen house. Her long brown hair was tied back but had slipped from its plait, further obscuring her face. Her fingers were short and slim, her collarbone fine. How curious. A new servant. Quite possibly a pretty one.

I nudged Hedwenn, squinting into the poor light. "Who is that?"

Hedwenn lowered her voice. "She's just come from the quay. Been here a for'night. Rhiwallon brought her."

"Brought her from where?"

"Don't know. Won't say. She doesn't talk much. But she's a good worker and fine enough help, aren't you, love?"

The woman straightened, pushing the hair from her eyes with the back of her hand. Her eyes were blue as a dunnock's egg, rimmed with dark lashes. Hedwenn must have seen the look upon my face because she planted herself firmly between me and the servant, crossing her arms over her bosom.

"I need more help than Pendragon's allowed me, Lailoken. And you can tell him I've said as much! My back's been painin' me. And my eyes—"

"Hedwenn. You're a treasure, and you shall have all the help you deserve," I said, craning my neck to get a better look at the woman. "But I've come on an errand of particular import, and I've a feeling about this one."

"Eira."

I was taken by surprise when the woman spoke—her voice was soft but firm, and there was a richness in her tone that belied her age, for she didn't appear to be older than twenty winters.

"Pardon?" I said.

"Eira is my name."

Snow, it meant, in the tongue of the Britons. And it was fitting, for her skin was smooth and pale. But the look upon her face made it clear she did not appreciate the flippant way I'd referred to her.

"Eira. Very well." I offered my most disarming smile. "I have need of a nursemaid for my niece. She is eight winters. You have been here only a fortnight, but I am certain you've heard of her arrival. She has left behind her family, and though I am her uncle, it seems she could use a companion. I fear she is most lonely."

At the mention of Angharad, Hedwenn flapped her arms, birdlike. "Aye, goodness me, Angharad! Don't think I've forgotten. I've put aside some sweets for her—I baked them off just this morning." She took my elbow firmly in hand and drew me toward a little parcel set aside on the table.

"You're trying to distract me, Hedwenn. It won't work. It's Angharad I'm thinking of. You must see my reason."

Hedwenn put a pudgy hand to her hips. "M'lord. Surely you can't mean to have a servant girl as your niece's companion."

"Why ever not?"

She cast about for a reason. "Well, for one thing, they're not always trusty. Letting her into the hall when she's been here not one moon?"

Across the room, Eira stiffened.

I studied her. "She seems trusty enough. After all, you've got her preparing Pendragon's dinner."

"We'll seek out someone more fitting on the morrow," Hedwenn assured me. "I shall find you the perfect lady, one far better suited to keep company of a wee princess from Strathclyde."

"Perhaps I've already found her."

Hedwenn glanced at Eira, dropping her voice to a whisper. "M'lord."

"Yes."

"Well, it's only I don't think it's fitting to bring a woman from the kitchens into the main hall. And this one . . . I won't say she's trouble, but she has a tale, I can promise you that."

"Servitude is no easy life. All servants have a tale."

"What I mean to say is, I'd be lyin' if I didn't tell you I feel motherly is all." Hedwenn clutched her apron between her hands. "'Bring me a sturdy young boy with a strong back,' I tell Rhiwallon. And he come back with this one! I muddied her up best I could, but the men have been sniffing round her like a pack o' wolves. You're a fool to think you're the first."

I bristled and nearly asked Hedwenn which men had been sniffing round, but we'd all had girls from the kitchens, hadn't we? "Best not to task Rhiwallon with picking the servants next time, I'd say."

But I couldn't rightly blame Rhiwallon. There was something striking about this woman. Had I seen her, perhaps I would've bought her, too.

"Look, Hedwenn, don't fret. I've heard your words. I only wish to speak with her."

Across the kitchen house, the woman—Eira—was chopping root vegetables with renewed vigor, but I could tell she was listening.

"I won't trouble you," I said. "I only mean to speak to you is all."

"Then speak." She returned her eyes to her task.

"I . . . er . . ." Damn it all, she flustered me. I frowned, mastering myself. "I wonder, do you . . . enjoy your work in the kitchens?"

She did not stop her slicing, only glanced up as if I'd gone completely mad. As if any servant truly enjoyed his or her position. It was protection. Labor. Survival.

"Forgive me," I began again. "What I mean to inquire is, have you any knowledge of children?"

At this she ceased her work, setting aside her knife. "Aye. I suppose I do."

"What sort?"

She swept the vegetables into a waiting basket. "I was eldest of five."

"And do you *like* them? Children."

"I do." Her answer was swift. Earnest.

I considered her a moment. "Very good, then. You'll come with me. We shall get you cleaned up, and I'm certain Angharad will be eager to meet you."

Eira frowned but stood all the same, brushing peels of parsnip from the coarse brown fabric of her dress. By now all the servants in the kitchen were watching. They'd envy her now, if they hadn't already. They'd be spiteful. Hedwenn was not wrong—there was a reason we left servants in their places. Perhaps I was being selfish to want this woman to serve a purpose of my own. But I thought of the men. If what Hedwenn said was true, Eira would be safer as Angharad's nursemaid than here in the kitchens. Under my protection, the men would not take such liberties in pursuing her. Besides, if she was not a match, I'd simply return her to the kitchens. No harm done.

"This way." I motioned for Eira to take her leave. She inclined her head to Hedwenn in passing, and I reached to take Hedwenn's hand, brushing my lips over her dry knuckles. "Thank you for the sweets. Angharad will be grateful."

"She's got a tale, Lailoken." Hedwenn frowned. "Be kind to her is all."

"I am always kind," I said.

Taking the packet from the table, I left Hedwenn to get on with supper.

CHAPTER 3

Lailoken

I stopped at the soft sound of weeping from beyond Angharad's door. As I reached to knock, her breath hitched, and she called out, "Who's there?"

"It's your uncle Lailoken."

"Does she not know who her uncle is?" Eira murmured behind me. Truly, this woman was far too petulant for a servant.

"Uther Pendragon is an uncle as well," I informed her.

"I see," she said.

I turned, half considering sending this Eira back to the kitchens. But I needed her aid and could not help but marvel at her transformation, one that had been achieved in little time. Her brown hair had been washed and drawn back from her face at the temples, secured by a pair of painted wooden combs. A thick wave of curls, still damp and smelling of sweet oils, tumbled down her back. Hedwenn had found a robe in one of our spare trunks, and though it hung a bit loose, it was dark blue and made Eira's skin look pure as fresh skimmed cream. I'd leave it to Angharad, I decided. Eira was to be her serving woman, after all. The girl had a right to choose.

I opened the door to find Angharad perched at the edge of her bed, wiping the tears from her face.

"Are you feeling quite rested?" I asked. "Is the chamber to your liking?"

Angharad nodded, then looked at me pointedly. "You've brought someone."

I thought she might be pleased, but the look upon her face had me uncertain. "Yes, I've brought someone. A companion. Her name is Eira."

"I thought *you* were to be my companion."

"Well, of course I am. But I must ride out before too long, and you'll need to stay here. Eira will keep you company."

"The raid," she gathered.

"Yes, the raid. And Eira was the eldest of five. She will make a fine companion, I think. She told me she quite likes children." I stepped back, and Eira gave a graceful bow.

"Lady Angharad."

"Hello," Angharad said, taking her in. She kicked her feet as she did when she was nervous—a habit my horse, Gwydion, was none too fond of. "So . . . you're to be my serving woman?" she asked.

"If you would like," Eira said.

"I'm not sure. Is that all right?"

"Yes. That's all right."

Angharad looked at Eira, her delicate face shifting. "Have you come from the kitchens?"

"Yes." Eira looked surprised. "How did you know?"

Angharad smiled. "You have a binding on your finger."

The linen knotted upon Eira's finger had escaped my notice, but I knew the truth of it. Raised among priests, Angharad had been brought up concealing her gift, especially among those she did not know. She had become quite clever about it. Quite clever, and it pleased her, so now she shrugged. "Also, you do not color your face."

"Angharad," I said. "Don't be rude."

"She is not rude. She is observant," Eira said. "I cut my finger just this morning, chopping wild garlic. And I do not paint my face because I have no use for such things."

"Not even lily root powder?"

"Not even lily root powder."

"But lily root looks quite pretty," Angharad said. "My older sister Gladys uses stain on her lips and upon her cheeks. She's even allowed to kohl her eyes now. But not me. I'm too little."

"Beauty is not always a virtue," Eira said.

"I do not think you could ever appear plain, even should you wish it," Angharad said. But where any other woman might smile from the flattery of a child, something else flashed behind Eira's eyes. Something like a secret. Angharad noticed, too.

I knew if she willed it, the girl could likely pry into Eira and perhaps be rewarded with a piece of her story. I nearly wished she would, for then Angharad might learn that prying could unearth things one did not wish to see. But I remembered the moment at the stones and cleared my throat. "Angharad."

Chastened, she looked down, folding her hands in her lap. "Have you lived here very long?" she asked, changing her course.

"No. Not very long at all." Eira looked about the room, then motioned to the little stool beside Angharad's table. "May I sit?"

Angharad seemed uncertain how to respond. Servants should stand. But Angharad was unaccustomed to adults asking her if they might sit or stand—this was the realm of her mother.

"You may sit," Angharad said. "I've only arrived here today. I'm to live with my uncle now. Did he tell you? I'm to become a Wisdom Keeper."

"That is a very noble thing," Eira said.

I watched the two of them as Eira settled upon the stool. Hedwenn had claimed Eira didn't often speak, but it seemed to me she had a fair plenty to say.

"Well," I said after a moment. "Perhaps I should leave you."

"Yes, you may leave us." Angharad looked at me.

"And, Eira, you will help ready Angharad for supper."

She looked up. "Yes, of course. Good-bye, my lord."

"Good-bye, then." I looked to my niece but could not escape the feeling I had been rather unceremoniously dismissed. "Until supper."

Well enough. It was good they should come to know each other, and I wanted to visit the temple. I had time enough before supper to speak with Diarmid.

I found the Wisdom Keeper bent over a small table he'd set in the grass behind the structure, disemboweling rats.

"And where are your robes?" he addressed me without turning.

"Sullied." I leaned over his shoulder. "You should make the birds work for their supper."

Diarmid only grunted. "They like the slimy bits."

The sleeves of his white robes were rolled up past his elbows, his forearms covered in coarse hair and sunspots. He kept his graying hair cropped close, and his brown eyes were hooded, sharp as those of the eagles he tended.

"Where's the little lass?" he asked.

"Resting just now, but she's eager to meet you."

"She's a Seer," he said. Not a question. "And likely more."

"Aye, I've discovered as much. You might've told me."

"You've trained enough young ones. It was only a matter of time before you discovered it yourself. Who does it come from, then?"

"Not my own mother; she was a healer. Angharad's mother did not have the gift. I can only think it comes from her father's side. Rhydderch's mother is a Pict. The girl has a way with animals, too."

"Ah. Perhaps then Angharad will be an augur, like her uncle."

"The truth is I think she could be a great many things."

"Special, eh?" Diarmid pushed the entrails into a shallow bowl with a sweep of his knife. Setting his blade aside, he wiped his hands on a broad strip of fabric, then tossed the cloth to me. "Give the hounds a good sniff and set them loose in the granary. That's where I trapped these two." He nodded at the carcasses, tipping some water from a nearby bucket to clean the gore from his hands. "Bad luck, rats in the granary. But it's not yet autumn. There's still time."

Something in the Keeper's tone told me he was speaking of more than rats.

"I took Angharad to the stones at Wildburn," I told him. "Something troubling happened there."

Diarmid looked up. "Come in, then. We should not speak of it here."

I set the bloody cloth on the table and followed Diarmid to the front of the temple. Inside, the stone floor kept the air cool and blocked the sounds of domestic bustle from the courtyard. I breathed in the soothing char of burned resin and heard Gwenddolau's golden eagles chattering to one another, ruffling their feathers. At the center of the room, a wooden effigy of Herne loomed, cluttered with offerings. Blossoms, gold and silver from our plunder, antler, bone, fresh mead, and a small but skillfully rendered wooden figure with an enlarged phallus, carved by Dreon from the look of it, though I could not imagine, given the number in his brood, he lacked the gift of virility.

Diarmid tossed the entrails to the birds as I removed my leather shoes, nodding to the effigy. It was a representation only. A god of wild places did not favor the confines of any man-made temple, even one hewn of stone. All Britons knew this, not only the Keepers. But it suited to have a place where the people could come during snow and wet weather to sit with their gods, where favors could be asked and offerings could remain unscattered by wind.

"Well?" Diarmid called. "Tell me of the stones."

I followed him behind the wicker wall that cordoned off his sleeping quarters. In the space, he kept a thin cot, a small bedside table, and a candle in a rude wooden holder. He eased himself onto the cot, and I sank onto the floor across from him, drawing my knees into my chest.

Diarmid listened as I told him of the shift in the air, the smell of it. Of what Angharad had told me, the beast that was threatening. At last Diarmid spoke. "Lailoken. Do you truly believe that men are the wagers of war?"

I considered Diarmid's question. "Aye. It is men who draw their weapons, who plan their attack. We may beseech the blessings of our chosen gods, but it is we who fight for land, for power, for freedom."

"Nay." Diarmid wagged his finger. "The force that drives war is far more terrible than any single man. It is a power—animate and complete. It has a hunger that cannot be sated by the corpses of one hundred thousand men. Always it hungers for more." He met my eyes. "The beast that comes is war."

"War," I echoed. I had felt it, had I not? The immensity. The hunger. "So Angharad warns us of a battle to come. We have fought battles before. Long have Gwrgi and Peredur fixed their eyes upon our land. We will prepare. Angharad's Knowing is fortuitous."

"I do not speak of battle. I speak of *war*," Diarmid said, and his ferocity startled me.

"Go on, then. I am listening."

The diviner stared off into the distance a moment, as he did when playing *fidchell*. "Raids. Battles. Thievery. Lies. All such things only serve to stir the beast. I fear this is larger than revenge sought or justice reclaimed. I fear a greater threat comes for our people, the Britons."

"We Britons have made our home on this island for time out of memory," I said. "We will not be undone by this, whatever it may be. With Angharad's warning, with my counsel and your sight . . . surely we can find a way to stop this beast in its tracks."

Diarmid threw up his hands. "Perhaps. Perhaps not! Lailoken, you are a learned man. You know as well as I, vision alone cannot prevent catastrophe."

I rubbed my forehead wearily. "If only there were fewer kingdoms from which danger may come. That is our first trouble."

There could be a mass of sea raiders from Pictland, or a scourge of Angles sweeping the country from east to west, as they had done when I and my sister were but little. We could see an attack from Gwrgi and Peredur from the kingdom of Ebrauc, but what strength had they, without a confederation of kingdoms at their backs?

Surely the kings of the Britons were too preoccupied in raiding their neighbors and the rising threat of the Angles of Bernicia to take up arms against the Dragon Warriors, our island's own protectors. And Rhydderch of Strathclyde was a brother by marriage. He may not have agreed to an alliance, but he would never be my enemy. Take up arms against us? What cause had we given him?

No. Gwrgi and Peredur were our greatest living threat, and on the morrow we would ride out to crush them. "Do not tell me we should not claim our revenge," I said.

Diarmid's face shifted. "I crave justice as much as you, Lailoken, but I worry this is not the way."

"But this very eve I saw success for our campaign. A bevy of quail— the way they flushed underfoot. Herne knows my mind. He knows I seek after it."

"Aye?" Diarmid's eyes flicked to the effigy. "And a quick wit has Herne, sending birds."

I nodded at the memory. I'd been ten winters when my sister and her servant had chanced upon Gwrgi in the market. He'd tormented them by tearing the throat from a chicken with his bare teeth. My cousins and I had seen his deed repaid and tenfold. We'd stolen into his chamber at the inn and filled his bed with chicken heads enough to satiate his hunger. It seemed so long ago now, but the memory summoned some pride. To protect my sister, to answer for a wrong. To do so in a way that was clever yet did not incite a blood feud. That day was the first I understood what it was to be a true warrior.

Diarmid stood, and together we walked to the threshold of the temple.

"Are you prepared, then, to ride out?"

"Nearly," I said. "We finalize the attack tonight. Truth be told, I hunger for it."

"Hunger?" Diarmid lifted his brows. "Beware the beast, eh, Lailoken?"

Laughter carried across the courtyard. The door to the hall stood open, and overhead, the sky was awash in purple evening light. In the great room, no fire was lit. With the golden glow of oil lamps, there was no need of it. My eyes fell upon our standard tethered between the posts at the back wall of the great room. The twisting body of the dragon seemed to breathe as the breeze from the open door fluttered the rich blue cloth.

Our Song Keeper, Yarin, was perched on a stool beneath our wall of round painted shields, head tilted to his *cruit* as he tested its strings. Around the hall, warriors relaxed on pine benches or fleece-lined couches, hunched over gaming boards or cradling cups of ale.

"Escaped so soon?" I chided Dreon, then clapped the muscled shoulder of Fendwin, who sat beside him. Women had come up from the settlement below and arranged themselves on benches beside the warriors, if not upon their laps. Their eyes touched upon the Dragon, but Gwenddolau sat alone, his blue eyes distant.

"I've come from Diarmid," I said, joining him at his table.

"Tell me," he said, but his voice was weary.

"Later."

"Well enough. How does Angharad fare?"

"She's settled in her chamber, as can be expected." I paused. "I found her a companion."

"Aye. I've heard as much. Hedwenn is not pleased." He looked at me. "A servant from the kitchens?"

"Aye, but she suits Angharad well; isn't that what matters? And besides, there was something about her."

"Something about her, eh?" His eyes fixed on me as if he would say more, but then our littlest charge appeared in the doorway, Eira by her side.

The men stirred to life as Angharad entered, smiling and hoisting their ale aloft. They might have shared only three days with her on the road, but from the warmth in their eyes I could tell my niece had already won their affection. She stopped and looked about the room, cheeks flushed, hesitant to be the focus of so much attention.

Gwenddolau stood, and the room fell quiet as he gestured for Angharad to come close. Eira ushered her forward.

"To any who have not yet met my young niece," he began, "this is Angharad of Strathclyde, daughter of Rhydderch. She has come among us to train with Lailoken—she is to be a Wisdom Keeper! But she does not brighten our fortress with her countenance alone. Her presence is a reminder that the bond between the Dragon Warriors and Strathclyde endures. She has been entrusted to our care. We, now, are her family." He lifted his own cup and turned to gaze down at her. "Welcome to Caer Gwenddolau, Angharad. Welcome home."

CHAPTER 4

Lailoken

When the last of the platters had been cleared, Yarin called up
his bards with the bodhran and flute, and the music began in
earnest. The women took to dancing, tugging the warriors to stand,
and even as the sturdy planks of the floor began to shake, Angharad
yawned, nestling herself into the crook of my shoulder. Soon she was
dreaming.

Why had I worried? This child could sleep through a siege. As soon
as I thought it, I prayed she would not have to. Eira sat across from
me, eyes bright from merriment and possibly from drink, for I would
admit some guilt in refilling her cup. I harbored no dishonorable
intentions—rather, I'd been curious. As she ate and drank, I'd seen
the tightness in which she enveloped herself begin to unfurl. Now I
watched as she reached across the narrow table to smooth a strand of
hair behind Angharad's ear.

"My littlest brother had red hair. So very much like hers," Eira said.

I had not looked overlong at her features while we ate. When I
heard the delicate and surprising sound of her laugh, I'd acknowledged
it was a fine laugh, but no finer than any other. And I certainly had
not glanced down her bodice as she leaned to brush the crumbs from
Angharad's dress. A breath of wind drifted in through the open door

and carried her scent to me. She smelled fresh, like meadowsweet. I grimaced at the baseness of my own desire.

My blood was hot, my need stirring. But I'd given my word to Hedwenn, and that was no light thing. Across the room, young women lounged on the couches with lily-white breasts beneath their dresses and invitations in their eyes. I'd lain with a few of them, and the memories were pleasant. Surely there was a far more suitable companion to ease what urged me. I would not make advances upon Angharad's new companion. Eira would sleep on a pallet beside Angharad this night and, if Angharad so chose, for countless nights after.

I looked down at my niece, fast asleep upon my shoulder. "Angharad has her red hair from her mother," I said.

"Languoreth," Eira said. "I've heard much of her."

"Have you, then? I should not be surprised. My sister's fame far exceeds my own."

"I'll not flatter you, if that's what you seek. You know the Song Keepers tell stories of you."

"And what tales have you heard? I am curious to know."

"Well, I myself recall only one story. I heard it when I was but a girl. It was long ago now."

"I think I know the story of which you speak."

Her eyes met mine. "It was a sad tale."

"What makes you say so?"

"It was the story of a young lord who rode out to protect his father's grain. There had been too much rain. Winter had come early and tarried too long. Many in Strathclyde were hungry. That was when they came to raid. The boy thought to make himself a hero. But he arrived to find his father's men overwhelmed by a mob. Starving and desperate. Fueled by rage. They captured the boy and held him down. They marked him with the same mark his father bore."

Her gaze shifted to my scar, and I felt heat creep up my neck at her scrutiny. But her story was not quite right. I set down my cup. "I hear nothing sad about that tale. The acts that mark us lead us to our fate."

"And what is your fate, my lord?"

I did not like the course of this—it ran too close to my core. And so I said, "Hedwenn tells me that Fendwin purchased you at the quay."

"Yes." She shifted in her seat.

"How was it you came there?"

"I came there as any servant does. In bonds."

"Aye." I nodded. "But what I do not know is how you came to be there. Who was your master? Where do you hail from?"

"I cannot see why it should matter."

"Is it so unusual a question?"

"Well, I do not wish to say."

"Yet I wish to know."

The look she gave me was cutting. "Are you ordering me, then, to tell you?"

"Nay, I will not order you. I am curious about you, that is all."

"I come from nowhere of consequence. Keep your curiosity. Or if you cannot, send me back to the kitchens."

I looked at her, taken aback. "You've been drawn from the kitchen with a chance now to serve. Any kitchen girl would be thankful. And yet you are not."

"I had no desire to be pulled from the kitchens."

"Do you desire, then, to return?"

Uncertainty flickered behind her eyes, but then she lifted her chin. "Perhaps I do." Silence fell a moment, then she spoke again. "Angharad tells me on the morrow you will ride out to punish Gwrgi of Ebrauc."

"Aye."

"I pray you will find success."

"Thank you for your wishes, but success will be nearer if I am not preoccupied with the well-being of my niece," I answered.

"Then you must not be preoccupied, for I hear Gwrgi of Ebrauc is a dangerous man."

"Aye. But we are dangerous as well." I looked at her. "Will you stay with Angharad until I return? If by then you are still eager to return to the kitchens, I will tell Angharad myself, and we shall find another nursemaid. But I must know in my absence she will be kept safe and in good comfort. I cannot fight shouldering that worry, and I should most like to return home alive."

Eira considered it, then inclined her head. "Very well. I will stay," she said.

"Good. And perhaps when I return, you will reward me with your story."

"My story. Is that your price for my service, then, or will you demand more?"

"You mean to address me as 'my lord.'"

"My lord," she said, but her face flushed in anger.

"I'll exact no such payment, none the likes of your mind," I answered. "But I will advise you thus: if you wish to play servant, you might learn to speak like one."

Her face blanched. "I play at nothing! You may live a life of sport, but this is no game for me." She glanced round the hall and smoothed her dress, but I could see her fingers trembled.

I lowered my voice. "You speak like a noble," I said. "You have only to open your mouth, and you've given yourself away. Where have you come from, then? And why will you not tell me the reason you have left?"

"I cannot say." She straightened her spine, blue eyes pinning mine. "And if you are a man of any honor, you must swear to tell no one what you suspect."

I did not like the course of this, but I considered her nonetheless. "Very well. I will tell no one. But in exchange, upon my return,
whether you stay with Angharad or wish to return to the kitchens,
you will tell me your secret."

Eira bristled. "And if I will not?"

"Then I will return you to the quay, where you may try your luck
with new overlords. I cannot imagine they will be so kind."

It felt almost cruel to exact such a bargain, but I had a responsibil-
ity to our men and, most of all, to Gwenddolau. If a woman of noble
blood was concealing herself in our fortress, somewhere there were
noblemen in search of her.

"You must understand," I said. "We are Dragon Warriors. We cannot harbor secrets. We cannot afford them."

From across the room, I felt Gwenddolau's eyes upon us. Eira followed my gaze, then stood. "I must take Angharad to bed."

"Let me carry her." I made to stand, but she stopped me.

"Nay, I can manage. Come, Angharad." Her voice was gentle as
she stirred my niece. "Cling to me just here."

Angharad blinked drowsily but did as she was bidden, wrapping
her gangly legs around Eira's waist and securing her hands about her
neck.

"There, now. Off to bed with you." Eira strained at the weight of
her, and I rose from my seat.

"Angharad, you're certain you've everything you need?"

"Uncle, you sound an old biddy," Angharad mumbled as Eira carried her away. I watched them go, ill at ease over Eira and her secret.
Perhaps I should not have prevented Angharad from prying after
all—I might have learned what caused this woman to seek escape
behind our walls.

Then my cousin Brant's low voice came at my shoulder, drawing me back from my thoughts. "You've found Angharad a serving woman."

"Eira," I said.

"Eira." He watched as they crossed the hall, slipping from sight into Angharad's chamber. "She looks quite suited for Pendragon, does she not?"

"Pendragon?" I turned to him. "Nay. She is far too . . . tall. And her back. Look at the way it curves. It's a wonder she can stand at all."

Brant raised a brow.

"I only mean to say—perhaps she's not horrible to look upon, but it's rather unfortunate about . . . well." I gestured below my belt as if to indicate some bedding disease. "The men would do well to keep some distance."

Brant shook his head with a smile. "And that's your best effort? I've known you far too long, Lailoken."

I was quite fond of my elder cousin, but I felt suddenly quite certain I might thrash him. Yet as darkness closed in round the fort, the mood in the great room had shifted. Our minds had begun to turn to the raid. When you wake and eat and slumber with the same men as long as we had, you become like one great aspen—many quivering shoots of the same tree.

Gwenddolau gestured from his table nearest the hearth, where Maelgwn had joined him already. They sat with their heads bent over a stretch of ale-stained vellum as Maelgwn made a rough sketch of the neighboring lands with a pointed reed and ink. Brant and I took our seats beside them.

We knew every old tree, each tenant farm, river, and streamlet. But maps moved our minds to these places. Sometimes a map could anticipate something we might not see. I let my eyes roam it unfocused as I told them of Diarmid's words and Angharad's warning.

"You saw success should we ride out tomorrow," Gwenddolau said. "Have you changed your mind, brother?"

"Nay, not exactly."

Gwenddolau looked at me. "Your lips say one thing, but your eyes say another."

"It is only I now wonder what series of events this might beget. It is evident Gwrgi and Peredur mean to provoke us. We cannot refuse to answer the wrongs that have been wrought. Yet in doing so, we give Gwrgi and Peredur reason to come against us again."

"Rhiwallon has just returned from his scouting ride," Maelgwn said. "He tells me Gwrgi collects his rents from the harvest even now. There may not be a better moment to strike."

"Fairhaven is closest to our border, so we cannot strike from there," Gwenddolau said. "It must be a point Gwrgi will not expect. A place he believes is farther from our reach."

"What of Featherstone?" Brant asked. "It lies deep in the hills. Their food rents will be scarce, but they have mining goods. Tin and lead. If we strike there, we would have Gwrgi's head as well as a bounty in metal."

Gwenddolau looked to me. "What say you?"

Brant was a seasoned warrior and I trusted his instincts, yet something felt unsettling. "There is risk in traveling so deep into Gwrgi's lands," I said. "I worry for our men. Let us strike somewhere closer to our own border."

The Dragon Warriors were among the best men-at-arms. But more and more of late, Gwenddolau relied upon our prowess. Now the horror of Sweetmeadow had muddied his judgment.

Gwenddolau scanned our men as they sipped their drinks. They would raid if he asked it, no matter the risk. They thrived on it. But Featherstone was not a risk he needed to take.

"Think on it, Pendragon," I advised him. "Perhaps now is not the time to strike."

"I want Gwrgi to fear that nowhere in his kingdom is safe from our grip," Gwenddolau decided. "Featherstone it is."

I pinned him with a look. What good was my counsel if he would not follow it? "As you say. Long have I admired your leadership, Gwenddolau."

My use of his birth name was purposeful. It caused him to blink as if stirring from sleep. But just as quickly his pale eyes turned stony. "Long has it been since I sacrificed the boy called Gwenddolau to become Uther Pendragon," he said. He looked down upon the map, his deep voice rising. "It was Uther, not Gwenddolau, who was chosen to protect our kingdom when Emrys was murdered. It was Uther, not Gwenddolau, who wed himself to the goddess of the land. Uther took a spear to the lungs. Uther wets his sword with Angle blood. Uther keeps their kingdom at bay. *Uther!* I am not yet forty winters, yet my yellow hair turns white. I carry the weight of this island upon my back. You jest and say I no longer smile, eh, Lailoken? Look at me. Look at me and see the cost of your freedom."

Around us, the warriors in the great room had gone silent. Gwenddolau looked up and searched the men's faces, his eyes questioning the allegiance of each and every man.

How readily they gave it.

Satisfied, he stood.

"Tomorrow we ride for the head of Gwrgi of Ebrauc. We ride to avenge the horrors he has brought upon the people of Sweetmeadow. We will act with what honor we possess, but we will show no mercy, for none has been granted those who lie dead," Gwenddolau said, then fixed his eyes upon me. "Such is the cost of war."

CHAPTER 5

Anharad

Caer Gwenddolau
Kingdom of the Pendragons
Late Summer, AD 572

Angharad's uncles rode off at dawn. She watched from the small timber tower perched above the gate a long while after, until the birdsong became a cacophony and the summer heat made her linen dress cling to her back. The warrior called Rhiwallon kept watch beside her, eyes fixed patiently on the lush green pastures below. Angharad adjusted the belt at her waist; the gold-handled knife sheathed there had once belonged to her mother, and its presence made her feel less lonesome. For although Eira had followed her dutifully up the ladder, Angharad could feel Eira's thoughts traveling leagues away.

Men were forever riding off. To dangerous things, mostly, like the time her elder brother, Rhys, reached his fifteenth winter, disappearing with her father and her uncle Morcant. Days later he returned driving a stream of stolen cattle. Thereafter, Rhys had been full of shadows.

"A dull occupation, keeping watch, until it is not," Rhiwallon said, startling Angharad from her thoughts.

"My uncle hoped it would divert me," she answered. "Yesterday I told him I would quite like to mind the gate."

"Oh, I don't know," he replied. "Perhaps he wished you to learn our ways so you might carry your weight in earnest, as all of us do."

A voice came from down below. "Or perhaps he wished to demonstrate that diversions are impossible without training the mind." Angharad leaned over the opening to see Diarmid the Diviner squinting up into the sun.

"You must have terribly good hearing," Angharad said.

"Children's voices carry," the Wisdom Keeper replied. "You would do well to remember that."

Next to her, Eira smiled, amused.

"Come down, then," Diarmid said. "Keeping to towers is a waste of your time."

Angharad turned to Eira. "May I?"

"I don't see why not."

Angharad climbed down carefully and looked at the diviner. His expression was frank, but his brown eyes were kind and full of stories.

"Would you like to see Pendragon's birds?" he asked.

"The eagles? Oh, yes. Very much," she replied.

"Excellent." He looked to Eira. "I will return her to you."

"Of course," she said.

Sun through summer leaves dappled the grass as Angharad followed the Wisdom Keeper into the courtyard. "Is it true you can divine the future?" she asked.

"Aye. What the Gods allow."

"Have you done the Bull's Sleep, then?"

"Aye. I've done many a Bull's Sleep."

"Is it true you must chew the bull's flesh without even roasting?"

"Aye."

"And does it taste very awful?"

"I find it quite mild. 'Tis better, though, if you take no issue with gristle and fat."

The thought made Angharad want to retch, but there was so much more she wanted to know. "Is it true you can cloak yourself from sight?"

At this, Diarmid turned to her. "In a way," he said. "Would you like to know how?"

"Oh, very much," she answered.

"Then look." Diarmid pointed. Angharad followed his finger in confusion before spotting a little streak of brown disappearing behind the kitchen house.

She screwed up her face. "A mouse?"

"Precisely."

"I don't understand."

Diarmid looked at her. "Imagine you are brown as dirt. Imagine you are little more than a mouse. Think on it. Who knows? Perhaps then you shall see."

They stepped through the door of the temple, and Angharad bent quickly to remove her leather shoes. A tingle rose as the cold flagstone met her bare feet. Before her a wooden statue stood, the figure of a man with a great pair of antlers branching from his head. Herne, she knew. Beyond the effigy, Angharad heard the rustle of two powerful golden eagles. They sat perched in a tall wicker enclosure, eyes blinking as they regarded her.

"Magnificent creatures, aren't they?" Diarmid said. And at the sound of his voice, one of the eagles tilted its head. "Go on, go and greet them. But don't get too near. They do not much care for strangers."

Angharad moved nearer. The birds seemed nearly as large as she. The ends of their beaks were curved and looked sharp as needles.

She could feel the Wisdom Keeper watching her. "Lailoken told me of your encounter in the stones," he said.

"Had he not told me, I would not have remembered what took place at all."

"Yes, that is the way at first." Diarmid nodded. "But in time you will gain mastery over it. Seers live in two worlds, Angharad. The outer and the deep. I admit I sometimes forget which is where. It is only natural that, in the beginning, memories are lost between the two. Better that the memory is lost rather than you.

"From the tower where you sat, one can scarcely see beyond the farthest pasture," he continued. "There are much more efficient ways to see. Your uncle may instruct you on augury and the study of omens in nature. But, child, I can teach you how to become an instrument of the Gods, if you will it. Are you ready, then, to learn?"

"Yes," Angharad answered eagerly.

"Good. First we shall quiet your mind. Then we shall see."

Angharad went to the temple each morning as soon as she'd swallowed down her breakfast. There she and Diarmid sat on reed mats in the cool quiet, and he taught her the way of slowing her breath. Of waiting without waiting.

It was not seeing. Not truly. It was more akin to listening. Sensing. Angharad began to understand it in the way one catches a scent on the breeze for a moment, before it is gone. But now, on the eighth day since her uncles' absence, she sat trying to listen, to no avail. Everything had become so loud. The feathery rustles from the eagles' enclosure. The thudding of her own heart. As she sat in Diarmid's stillness, the tiny red lumps on her arms from the midges at sunset itched with renewed vigor until Angharad felt she'd go mad. She squeezed her eyes shut, screaming inside her own head.

"Enough for today," Diarmid announced, as if she had spoken aloud.

"A few moments more," Angharad begged.

"Nay, we must cease, Angharad. We shall try again tomorrow. Besides, your uncles will soon return."

"How do you know?" Angharad asked in wonderment. "Did you divine it?"

Diarmid gave a small smile. "Your frustration, child, is a mirror of their own."

"Whatever do you mean? Please, Diarmid. Tell me plain."

"The warriors have failed in their raid. They could not catch Gwrgi out. You felt their rage as I did. Only I intended to, whereas you did not."

Angharad frowned. Diarmid could not be right. Her inability to sit still had always enraged her. Or had it indeed? For she'd sat quite happily the day before, and the day before that.

"Come now, no frowns," Diarmid said. "Your uncles will be in need of a welcoming face."

Relieved as she was at the thought of their safe return, Angharad found it difficult to believe the Dragon Warriors could set out with such fervor and fail at their task. She knew Gwrgi of Ebrauc was a horrible man. She had seen him in Strathclyde, for he never missed their summer games. She had seen the way her mother stiffened at the sight of him. Heard the way her mother spoke his name, as if it were a curse.

"If they have not slain Gwrgi, will he not seek revenge?" Angharad asked worriedly.

Diarmid's dark eyes were solemn. "Yes, Angharad. He will seek revenge."

"And what will happen then?"

"When that day comes, you must do as we say. But a child like you needn't worry." The Seer patted her hand reassuringly. "There is a great plan for you, Angharad, for you are Chosen. The Gods call their children to them, and shelter none so much as those who do their work. Your course was charted long ago, so whatever may come to pass, you must not fret. You will be safe from harm, Angharad of Strathclyde. I, Diarmid the Diviner, do promise you that."

II.

Myrddin . . . was a white hawk
when the fierce battle would be fought,
when there would be a joyous death,
when there would be a broken shoulder,
when there would be heart's blood
before he would be put to flight.

—"Peiryan Vaban" ("Commanding Youth"),
translated by John K. Bollard,
The Romance of Merlin

CHAPTER 6

Languoreth

Tutgual's Hall
Partick
Kingdom of Strathclyde
October, AD 573

Imprisoned in the dark of my chamber, I could not see the sky, but I knew rain was coming, for my body ached in places I was overworn. My hips, from bearing four children. My wrist, from bracing my fall the time I'd been struck by a man. And then I was thinking of my eldest boy, Rhys. Of Angharad. Of Maelgwn and Lailoken and my foster brother, Gwenddolau, and the beast descended to devour me once more.

At first there had been no words.

All I could do was retreat in my memory to the time we began—my twin brother, Lailoken, and I.

In those days, our father yet lived. I danced beside the blaze of a Midsummer fire and loved a black-haired warrior named Maelgwn under a temple of trees. My youngest daughter Angharad had not yet been taken from me. My firstborn, Rhys, had not yet ridden off to war.

These were the days I chose to inhabit. I left my body like a shell and buried myself there.

Time passed. They had given me, at least, parchment and ink.

Scarcely pausing to eat or sleep, I wrote of all that had taken place, sometimes through laughter but more often through tears, until my story had unraveled and I arrived back at the place I now dwelled—a prisoner in my own chamber, armed guard at my door.

My husband and eldest son had ridden off to make war upon my brothers.

It had all happened so quickly.

Gwrgi and Peredur of Ebrauc had arrived at Tutgual's gate demanding an end of Uther Pendragon. I'd been barred from their War Council, but their claims, I knew, would be threefold: that Pendragon's violent raids against Ebrauc were evidence of his dangerous thirst for power. That Pendragon was weakening, and should his lands be seized by the Angles, all of our kingdoms would be vulnerable to attack. Last, they would cite Pendragon's refusal to pledge fealty to any overking. If it came to war with the Angles, Uther Pendragon could not be trusted to join a Brythonic confederation.

And so Tutgual agreed, and together their armies left to crush Gwenddolau once and for all.

And yet there was a darker, more insidious reason this battle had been waged, one not spoken aloud.

The people of our island were divided by belief. Gwenddolau and his kingdom kept the old gods, while kings such as Tutgual, Gwrgi, and Peredur claimed devotion to Christ.

The battle against the beliefs of our ancestors had begun when I was a child. I came of age in a time when a Wisdom Keeper still possessed the power to speak first, even before a king. Now Wisdom Keepers were replaced by bishops who worked with a willing nobility to create a new order, one that subsumed the power of our Keepers. Still, for as many Christian families as there might now be, there were just as many who kept the ways of those who'd come before. Slaying

Uther Pendragon would be a devastating strike against the people of the Old Way.

Knowing my devotion to both my brothers and the Gods, my husband shut me away so I would not send warning. But I had already sent my groom by the time I heard the ominous slide of the bolt against my door. I only prayed my warning had reached Caer Gwenddolau in time.

Now, when I slept, I dreamt of my daughter.

I'm all right, Mama, I'm all right, Angharad called out. But she was not all right. She was treading chest-deep in an ocean of blood, her tawny hair soaked with it, eyes wide as she struggled to keep to the surface. I plunged into the viscous depths, felt it seep into my dress as I struggled to reach her. My nose filled with the smell of rust, and I woke.

Angharad. In the tongue of the Britons, her name meant "most beloved."

I had railed and pleaded and screamed and wept until the guards became deaf to it. Time passed, and I began to understand there was no escape from the prison save death itself. I understood that this chamber was not the prison. The prison was of my husband's making—the war he was waging even now against those I loved most.

Then I remembered that while Angharad and Rhys were away and in such terrible danger, I had two children yet here. Two children yet with me, and they needed their mother.

And so this time I did not beat at my door but tapped softly upon it. The guard must have recognized I'd returned to myself, for at last, after too long, he opened the door.

"Please," I said. "Bring me my children."

He looked me over, then turned away. Moments stretched. I smoothed my hair and pinched my cheeks to summon life I did not feel. And then my serving woman Aela came. With her were Gladys and Cyan.

"Mother!" Gladys ran to me, but Cyan stood at the door, regarding me as if I were a stranger. I clutched Gladys as she shook with her tears, her slender shoulders somehow more womanly though it had been only days. How many? Truthfully, I did not know.

Gladys drew back, eyes wild with fear and with anger. "Why have they not let us come until now? Why are they keeping you here? Did they discover your groom?"

"Gladys!" I gripped her, glancing hurriedly at the door. "You must not mention it. Do you understand? Not ever again. That I would send warning . . . the king would have my head for that."

"I'm sorry, Mother!" She burst into tears anew, and I cursed Rhydderch's family again and again, pulling her close.

"Never mind it. Tutgual only means to keep us safe," I lied. "Strange things happen in times of war. Men's minds are bent. We will be out of harm's way here in the capital, in the hall of the king. We are together now—that's all that matters." I looked up in search of my youngest son. "Cyan, will you not come? Please. I would hold you."

He gave in at last and let me embrace him, but his gaze remained fixed upon the floor. He would not forgive me so readily for abandoning him. His fair hair smelled of candle wax, and when I took his hands in mine, I saw his fingers were stained with pigment.

"You've been drawing. What have you made? Will you bring it to me? I should like to keep it in my chamber."

It was this that summoned his tears, and his gray eyes filled. "Will they not release you, then?"

"My boy. My love." I drew him back into the circle of my arms and hugged them both so fiercely I wondered they did not break. "It will all be over soon. Your father and Rhys will return, and with them will be Angharad. We must believe it to be true. We will survive it no other way."

Rhydderch would have traded for Angharad before they attacked. And even had that somehow gone awry, Maelgwn had sworn to me, the day she had left with the Dragon Warriors, that he'd keep Angharad safe.

"And what of our uncles?" Gladys asked. "What of Lailoken and Uther?"

I looked to Aela, questioning, but she gave a slight shake of her head. No news, then. They would keep me here, keep me in the dark.

Yet what right had I to complain of darkness when I was surrounded by all my belongings, when I slept dry and warm in my own chamber each night? Even now, those I loved could be dead or wounded, fleeing through the frigid autumn woods. Even now, Tutgual held my cousin Brodyn in the prison pits beyond the hall. If I could not be trusted, Brodyn of Cadzow was something worse in the eyes of Strathclyde. He had taught Lailoken and Gwenddolau in weaponry. And his brother Brant was a Dragon Warrior. So now my own blood, captain of my guard, languished in a hole in the earth.

"How many days has it been?" I asked. "How many days since they rode out?"

"More than a fortnight," Aela answered.

"Dear Gods." Had it been a fortnight since Elufed had slipped into my chamber and pressed the mushroom into my palm, the one that had brought me such visions? It had wracked my body with sickness and sweat—I realized now how close I'd truly come to death.

But I had seen men escaping through fire. A broad-shouldered mountain covered in snow. There was a vision of Angharad, grown to a woman. My brother, his body stooped with age. Why had I not been granted such visions of my son?

"It is over now," I said, even as sickness crept into my belly. "It must be. And until they arrive, we must keep ourselves occupied, and we must pray to the Gods to bring them safely home."

"I pray to Christ every morning and night that he might bring Father home," Cyan said.

"To Christ?" I said it more sharply than I intended, and Cyan drew away. "I'm sorry, Cyan. To each his god. You are praying; that is what matters."

I smoothed back his hair. *Each to his god*, Cathan would say. But Cathan had been speaking of the gods of this great island with its mountains and lochs, its glades and bog lands and forests. The gods of the Britons. *Who would we become*, he might ask, *if we banished the choosing of one's own devotion?* Freedom in thought and devotion had always been our way. And as we chose our gods, surely the gods chose us, too. Lailoken was a son of Herne. For my love of healing, I belonged to Brigid. I was a daughter of Clota, our river. And so it seemed Christ had beckoned my Cyan. Perhaps it was only Christ who could deliver him to his greatest purpose.

"Has Elufed been minding you, then?" I asked.

Now, as if the mere mention of her name had summoned her, the guard opened the door and the queen appeared, her golden hair exquisitely coiled and her slate-colored eyes impassive.

"I heard you were at last among the living," Rhydderch's mother said. But Elufed's voice betrayed what her eyes did not—I knew her well enough to hear her relief and her fondness.

"Thank you for minding the children," I said.

Elufed inclined her head but then frowned. "It smells like a souring wound in this room. Aela, open the shutters."

"I'm afraid I cannot, my queen." Aela bowed.

"Why ever not?"

"They've been hammered shut."

Elufed strode to the door. "Gavin!" she called out. The guard appeared without the good grace to look shameful. "Did you truly believe Lady Languoreth would attempt to steal from that utterly insignificant window? And from an upper chamber? She would surely break her bones."

"I was only keeping to the king's word, my queen."

"You will pull the nails immediately. She is Rhydderch's wife, after all."

"Aye, my queen."

Rage rose at the mention of Rhydderch's name. My own husband had locked me in my chamber, too much of a coward to even bid me good-bye.

Elufed seemed to sense my anger and turned to look at me. "Languoreth. Are you quite well?"

The look I gave her was incredulous.

"Never mind it," she said. "There will be plenty of time to speak. You must wash. Aela will help you dress, and then you may join me. I shall meet you in the great room when you are ready. Come, children. Your mother must bathe and recover from her ordeal."

She gestured for my children to precede her, then paused beneath the lintel. The thunk of a ladder sounded from the other side of the window. I heard the efficient groan of iron wrenching from wood as the nails were yanked from their moorings, and the shutters clattered open, fresh air rushing in through the open window.

I was a prisoner no more.

With the children and guards beyond hearing, Elufed spoke. "I could not help you. I am sorry."

"I understand."

"The gift I brought. Did it help you see?"

I gave a slight nod.

"Will you tell me of it?"

Elufed was not only Rhydderch's mother; she had become an ally, a friend. But something gave me pause. My vision had been a gift, had it not? Despite the pain it had brought, I did not wish to share it. At least not yet. "I do not know. Perhaps."

Her pretty face darkened, but she accepted my answer. "As you like. It is done now, in any case."

"Please. I must have news," I begged.

"Of course you must. I have been waiting. But we cannot speak of it here. Come to me in the great room. I will tell you all I know."

"And Brodyn?"

Guilt flickered, but beneath it I sensed her anguish. Brodyn was, after all, the queen's lover. "I could not go to him, but you might. They bring him food—I saw to that much. But until the king and his men return, there is nothing more we can do."

"We cannot leave him until Tutgual's return. You know what will become of him."

Tutgual would not risk an enemy within his own walls, whether or not his united army had crushed that of Brodyn's brother. Either my cousin would be left to die in the pits, or he'd be efficiently dispatched by sword. Elufed did not answer, though I knew she'd thought of it. Instead she reached to press my hand. "Take heart. You are no longer a captive. Soon you shall forget all about this terrible business."

She released my hand and I caught sight of my own fingers, nails broken and bloody from days of prying at the shutters, beating at the door.

I said nothing. Then she was gone.

With the shutters cast wide, I saw it was late afternoon. Storm clouds towered like giants, limbs plump with coming rain. Aela returned with warm water for washing. I stood before my dressing table, eyes fixed on the reflection in my little bronze mirror as Aela helped me strip off my soiled clothes. My blue eyes were murky, my skin sallow, my light snuffed out.

I took the emerald ring from the pocket I had sewn into every dress and placed it upon my dressing table. Aela had asked after it once. I told her it had come from a loved one. One who was gone. And gone he was, living in the Kingdom of Pendragon, for Maelgwn had given it to me. When I touched it, I could still feel him near.

Maelgwn was Gwenddolau's war leader, and so they would make a prize of his head. I swayed a little on my feet, and Aela reached to steady me.

"There now, m'lady. A wash will do you good," she said.

"No. No washing. Just help me dress, please, and quickly."

"As you say."

Elufed had received word from the battlefield. I was ravenous for it. When Aela was too gentle, I tugged my dress over my breasts, waving her away as she made to help with my shoes.

"I'll manage," I said, bending to fasten them. I straightened and took up my ring from the dressing table, slipping it back into my pocket. Our eyes met then, and all that had transpired since the dawn the war party rode out passed between us. For a moment it seemed Aela might weep. I covered her hand in mine. "It's as Elufed said. Perhaps it is best if we can put these dark days behind us."

"Are you able, m'lady?" Her eyes searched mine, but I could not tell Aela a lie.

I pressed her knuckles.

"Whilst I'm gone, have the servants clean my chamber," I said. "I would have it seem a different place when I return."

"Of course, m'lady." Aela bowed.

I could not bear one more moment in that putrid room, the air thick from a fortnight of agony and grief.

Three warriors waited beyond the door to follow me down the corridor. After so many days of isolation, the activity of the high king's hall assailed me—the heavy thud of goods being unloaded from a cart outside, the harsh rush of voices, the servants and their scurrying glances. I took a deep breath to steady myself as I descended the narrow stair of Tutgual's hall, concealing my disdain out of habit.

How many years had I loathed Rhydderch's father? How many winters had I prayed for his end? I'd become accustomed to swallowing my anger and consuming my pain. Soon the men would return and I would dine upon it again.

Elufed was not in the great room. I found her in the chamber left for our weaving instead, seated at her loom. As I entered, she fixed her wintry gaze over my shoulder to address her husband's men. "Gavin. What brings you? Are you so keen to try your hand at a woman's art?"

"We only do what we must," the warrior said. "Lady Languoreth must be kept under watch."

"Well. It seems to me you have become little more than a shadow, and you are far too handsome for that. Lady Languoreth is quite secure, I assure you. Wait just there if you must, but let us work our looms in peace. We find it ever so soothing." She turned to me expectantly.

"Indeed," I said. "I've been kept so long from my weaving. If I might only pick up my pattern once more, I might soon forget my unpleasant confinement."

I took my seat at the loom beside her and lifted my fingers to the threads.

"What is it, then?" Elufed asked.

"I've left my work unfinished. Such ill luck with our men still from home."

"Ill luck, indeed!" she said. "Carry on, then. We'll soon set it right." She called out to a serving girl, "Bring wine and food from the kitchens. That lovely cheese I like."

Tutgual's men drew back watchfully, and as the servant went to fetch our sustenance, she closed the door behind her, leaving us at last in solitude.

"Fools." Elufed's eyes bored through the wood to where Tutgual's men yet stood. "They take their best to war, and to guard us, they leave only the donkeys. I've two bards about to begin making music in the great room. They'll wander off soon enough."

I dropped my hands from the loom, unable to bear a moment more delay. "Please," I said. "I must know."

Elufed leaned close, speaking in a rush. "It was a terrible battle. Caer Gwenddolau has been set aflame, the villages round it ransacked and burned. Rhydderch and the lords of Ebrauc won the day. But your brother, Lailoken, was not found among the dead. Neither was Pendragon, though I hear he was badly wounded. Rhydderch is now tasked with hunting down any who fled. Those they slaughtered were buried in the orchard beyond the fort. At least, in this, they have afforded them some honor."

I closed my hand upon the little green ring in my pocket. Elufed did not know of Maelgwn. She could not. But even as her words sank me, I pleaded for more, for that which was most important. "And my children? Tell me of my children."

"They have not yet found Angharad."

The stabbing in my chest nearly doubled me. "And Rhys? What of Rhys?"

Elufed's face fell. For a moment she said nothing. I shook my head to prevent what I knew she would say, denying the words even as she spoke them.

"Rhys fell in battle. Languoreth . . . he is dead."

Rhys, my firstborn child. Dead. I closed my eyes.

"I am sorry," Elufed said.

The moment before the war horn blasted its summoning through Partick, my son and I had stood together in my chamber, our foreheads pressed close. I had felt his tears slip between my fingers as I pressed my palms to his cheeks, felt the hitch of his breath as he sobbed in silence, trying to be a man. Trying to be a warrior. Rhys had known what this battle would demand: that he face his uncles and fight. I had made him swear he would do what he must to survive. My son. Such a skilled young warrior, yet too full-hearted. He had not been able to stir the rage needed to kill the family he yet loved.

And Angharad. Shivering and alone. Crying out for me. She was but a child! I thought of the wolves in the Caledonian Wood, the vast forest that lay just beyond Gwenddolau's kingdom, and lurched forward, certain I was going to be sick.

Dead, dead. My babies were dead.

I opened my mouth, but there was no air, no air, and I gasped, open-mouthed like a fish, sinking to the floor in search of an anchor. From somewhere distant, I felt Elufed kneeling beside me and I clutched at her, I pushed her away, I wanted her away, to unsay the words, even as the walls beyond me ceased to exist. How had Rhys been slain? One thousand death blows assailed in an instant, each one more horrific than the last, beating at me in a madness. I saw my son slashed open and bleeding, in agony. I saw his skull split wide. Limbs hacked and hemorrhaging. Arrows, spears, axes. A sob rose, hoarse as a donkey's bray, and I doubled over, my forehead pressed against the planking, heaving as if I could retch it from me, this intolerable pain, this violent ripping of my entrails.

"Hush, hush," Elufed's voice came. "I know what you suffer."

I gathered my dress in folds and buried it against my face to muffle the sound of my weeping.

I sobbed until there was no water left within me, until I was a husk lying upon the floor. Elufed was beside me, holding me too close. My eyes were swollen. "I cannot breathe," I said. She smoothed the hair plastered to my cheek with persistent hands. Then I whispered, "I want to die."

At this, she gripped my face, forcing me to meet her eyes. "Languoreth, you cannot die. Think of Gladys and Cyan. And what of Angharad? Rhys may be gone, but Angharad may yet live. She will be terrified, in hiding. But she is such a clever girl. She will know what to do. We will send men for her. Men of our own."

"You mean to say you have not sent them already?" I looked at her, bewildered.

"Grief has stolen your reason. Do you imagine I have not wanted to? Just because I am not imprisoned in a chamber does not mean that I am free. I cannot send scouts without the sanction of the king. Besides, my most trusted man rides with Tutgual and has not yet returned. It is possible he is dead."

"Surely we need no permission to go in search of my child! She is Rhydderch's own daughter! Even now she could be starving or perishing in the cold. Surely the king would—"

"You are not yourself." Elufed pinned me with her gaze. "You are the daughter of a king. You know the king's law during battle as well as I. We can do nothing until Tutgual returns. Your friend Cathan foretold this, did he not? And I, too, dreamt it, years ago. Rhys was not yours to keep. In your heart, you have always known it was so."

I stared at my hands. I could not imagine how to go on. "Why was he given to me only to be taken away?"

"This only the Gods can know."

"If only Rhys had been more like his father," I said bitterly. "To sup with kin on one occasion and slit their throats on the next."

Elufed stiffened. "You test our friendship when you speak so of my son."

I blinked at her, uncaring, for only I knew the truth. Rhys was not

Rhydderch's son. And this was the trouble of it. Rhys was too much like the noble warrior who had fathered him. Rhys—like his father, Maelgwn—possessed a heart.

I watched as Elufed stood, smoothing her skirts as she did when she wished to gather herself.

"You have only just learned your firstborn son is no longer," she said. "But you cannot allow grief to be your master. It will be your undoing. Noblewomen are given many luxuries, but grief is not one."

I sat mute. My father had said as much when my mother died. I'd seen how he suffered. Yet still, he had answered Tutgual's summons. Always we were doing Tutgual's bidding.

"You must continue," Elufed said. "That your husband has routed the enemy will be some advantage. But all will be watching you; the enemy were your people. And because I am often in your company, they also watch me. Do you understand?"

Her words cut even as I saw their necessity. "I understand. Of course. I am not the child I once was."

"You say as much. Yet you are still not the master of your emotions."

I looked up, keeping my voice low. "My son has been killed. My daughter is dead or in unimaginable danger. Do not speak to me of mastering my emotions!"

"Good. Yes," Elufed encouraged. "Grief is expected. But even now I can see your fury etched into the lines of your face. No one must see you in this state."

I bit back the poison simmering in my throat. I wanted to spit this venom, to make her suffer as I did. Elufed did not realize what mastery I truly had.

"Leave me, please" was all I said.

Elufed paused a moment, then bowed her head, slipping quietly out the door.

Time passed. No one disturbed me. And then a knock sounded, startling me as I rushed back to myself.

"Mother?"

It was Gladys and Cyan.

"Come," I called. I scrambled to my feet, smoothing my dress out of habit. They stopped when they saw me—eyes swollen, shoulders hunched.

"It is supper now, Mother. Will you not eat?" Gladys asked.

"No," I said gently. "I'm afraid I cannot eat. I must speak with you. With the both of you. Come." They moved closer on heavy feet, and I took their hands.

"You have word from the battle?" Gladys asked. Cyan's eyes were cast down, but Gladys's met mine with hesitance. I could feel her teetering within, as if she stood upon the edge of a cliff. She, too, had been waiting.

"Yes."

I pressed their fingers in mine, and we stepped from the precipice together.

I bathed that evening for the sake of my children, sitting numbly in the wooden basin as Aela lifted the heft of my hair from my neck. Tipping my head back, I closed my eyes while she poured warm water over my scalp.

Submerged in water, I could feel each part of my body. The thick muscle of my heart hemorrhaging, fury boiling in the vat of my stomach. My ears still echoed with the sobs of my children as I told them of their brother's death. That we did not know the whereabouts of their sister.

Aela dunked a linen and rubbed it with soap. "Perhaps it'll be as the queen said," she said, beginning to clean me. "Soon you shall feel more yourself."

The visions playing behind my eyes were only of murder. But in the wake of my grieving, my mind had gone clear. "No, Aela. I do not believe I shall ever be who I once was."

Her hands stopped their work. "Pray be careful, m'lady. Everyone will be watching." She leaned over to look at me, biting her lip. "My mother once said, 'Deadly are the seeds sown from anger.'"

"If your mother once said that, then she was wise."

It was true. No good ever came from impetuous acts of vengeance or spite. Wise women were patient.

I took the soapy linen from Aela and moved it beneath my arms where the scent was musky. No matter how much I might trust Aela, I could not say more.

When I was a little girl, Brant and Brodyn had taught me how to wield a knife. The blade had been a gift from my father, and I'd wanted nothing more than to be a warrior like Boudicca, the queen of old who'd commanded an army of Britons, uniting tribes that had been warring for generations to answer the tyrannous might of Rome.

I was taught to wield a knife even as I was told that women were no longer warriors.

Now I had survived nearly twenty winters at Tutgual's court, and I'd learned that women and warriors were more alike than one might suspect. I'd watched women eat their pain, watched them sicken and suffer from it until their skin went dull and they wasted away from the inside out. Even Rhydderch, who swore that he loved me, meted out such suppers time and time again.

When my family had feuded with the bishop Mungo, Rhydderch had done nothing. Mungo's battle against my family had ended with an attack upon my father's granaries and a scar upon my brother's face.

Since then, my husband was often absent, treating with the many petty kings and chieftains across Strathclyde who paid tribute to his father, the high king. But even upon his return, I still felt unseen. Then I discovered Rhydderch had known of Sweetmeadow. What Gwrgi had done. He had known, yet told me nothing.

Now he hunted my twin brother even as our son lay lifeless upon the ground. Even as our daughter of eight winters—

I shut my eyes.

"What is that, my lady? Are you all right?" Aela's voice was full of worry.

"I'm all right, Aela. I'm thinking, that's all." I would not cave to it. Could not. I sat back instead, pulling my knees to my chest in the water.

Yes, women and warriors were more alike than one might expect. After all, the entirety of a woman's life was made of blood. Our wombs seized and shed each month. Our babies were born of such agony and gore men could not comprehend.

Both women and warriors were students of pain.

On the day my cousins had taught me the way of a knife, they'd said to my brother, *It seems you are not the only one gifted with the warrior's way.* My brother's words returned to me now: *I would be proud to have my sister battle at my side. I think someday she shall.*

Now my battle had come.

I stood as Aela dried my body, wrapped a covering around me. Gathering it to ward off the chill, I stepped from the basin. "You needn't worry, Aela," I assured her.

For I was a warrior now. I had learned such lessons of pain. And in the days to come, I would begin to build an army of my own design. One only a woman could muster.

Tutgual had brought his war. Now I—in time—would bring mine.

Yes. Wise women were patient.

And I had become far more dangerous than any could know.

CHAPTER 7

Anagharad

Caer Gwenddolau
Kingdom of the Pendragons
14th of October, AD 573

There were blackberries in her fist. Plump little jewels, blacker than whelks. Then the blast of the horn came and Angharad startled, berries scattering across the table. Two more blasts and her uncle was on his feet, yanking his padded leather vest over his tunic and taking up his weapons. "Go. We must go!"

Three blasts of the horn meant danger. Grave danger. Something was coming—something terrible. Eira stood, glancing round the room. "What should we gather?"

"Leave it all; it does not matter. Quickly, now. We must get inside the gates." There was a sluicing as her uncle yanked his sword from its baldric and threw open the door. Eyes trained on the forest, Lailoken hurried them toward the safety of the fortress gates.

They had been laughing, the three of them.

Today had not been a day for lessons; it was the last day for eating blackberries. Light was streaming through the unfettered window of the hut the three of them shared in the forest. Angharad thought it was wonderful living beneath the fortress with Eira and her uncle.

The two of them had been handfasted at Midsummer. But Angharad had known they were in love because when the two of them stood in the same room, the air around them grew bright. She liked very much to be around them when the two of them were together like that, Eira making bread and Lailoken watching her, his eyes lit with warmth and something else Angharad could not quite understand. The way Lailoken looked at Eira seemed to make her nearly glow.

That morning they'd gathered clippings of blackberry bramble, ivy, and rowan for Samhain wreaths with berry-stained fingers.

"My mother and I made wreaths with Gladys each year," Angharad said, watching Eira as she began to intertwine the greens strewn about the table.

"I fashioned these with my mother as well," Eira said, but did not smile at the memory. Angharad picked at a rowan sprig, peering at Eira from beneath her lashes. "Your mother . . . but she was not truly your mother. Only more of a mother than the first had been."

Eira paused in her work.

"Eira has asked you not to pry," her uncle said.

Shame heated Angharad's cheeks. "I didn't seek it. It isn't my fault if it came to me."

"Of course it isn't your fault," Eira said gently. "But, Angharad, you must understand, there are reasons I've asked that you not rummage through my past."

"If you told me your reasons, I would not feel so inclined to rummage," Angharad answered.

"I've promised you, when you are older. And I shall keep to my word. Now, never mind it. I'm not angry, and I don't wish you to feel shamed or sad." She looked up with a reassuring smile. "I am ready for the ivy. Pass it here."

Angharad had done as she'd asked, contenting herself with her fistful of berries. Best to gorge upon them now, for it was ill luck to harvest them after the frost. She'd reached for a second handful when the clatter of hooves sounded on the forest path and her uncle looked up.

"Rhiwallon and the scouts," Eira had said.

"Too soon," he'd answered.

A moment passed. All was quiet. Angharad had a strange feeling. Then the horn had blasted from the guard tower. And everything had changed.

Women and children streamed through the forest toward the safety of the fort as Angharad caught the hand of Dreon's daughter.

"Angharad, what do you see?" she whispered as they hurried along together.

"All will be well," Angharad lied, for everything was red. When she closed her eyes, all she saw was blood.

They rushed into the great room, where Diarmid and the Dragon Warriors had gathered, their faces grim.

"What's happened?" her uncle demanded.

Angharad went to her cousin Brant, and he tucked her beneath his arm.

"A messenger has come from Partick," Maelgwn said. "Languoreth's groom. Gwrgi and Peredur march this way at the head of a great army."

Beside them, Eira went rigid.

"And there is something else." Maelgwn's green eyes shifted to Angharad.

"Say it. Speak it all. She, too, must know what comes," her uncle said.

"The army is led by Rhydderch," Maelgwn said. "Strathclyde has come against us, too."

Angharad fell against Brant as if she'd been struck. Her father? Her father was bringing war upon her uncles? "I don't understand," she said. She looked to Lailoken, but he only blinked, for a moment appearing almost childlike.

Wounded, Angharad realized. Her uncle could believe it no more than she.

"How many?" Lailoken asked.

"Thousands."

"And how much time have we?"

"Half a day, less or more," Maelgwn said. "Pendragon is with Fendwin, gathering what men they can before nightfall."

The warriors stood in silence, but beneath their hard exteriors, Angharad felt their churning. An army of thousands marched toward them even now. Angharad felt as small as a raindrop in a lake. *They will swallow me,* she thought. *They will swallow us all.*

Her uncle must have seen her face, for he came to crouch before her.

"You will have nothing to fear, Angharad. Your father loves you above all. He will send a messenger, someone to trade for you. You will be safe from harm long before any battle begins."

"And what of you?" Angharad said. "What of all of you?"

"You mustn't fret over us, little cousin," Brant reassured her. "We have fought many a battle in our day."

"But until then, we must keep you safe," Maelgwn said. "The others must leave for the Caledonian Deep. Will the Selgovae have them?" He looked to Lailoken.

"Aye, the Selgovae may be fierce, but they will abide by the law of hospitality. They will not turn our people away."

"Good. Come, then," Maelgwn said. "Let us gather the weapons and ready the men. There is no time to waste."

The warriors strode from the hall with an urgency that only made Angharad more afraid. Beside the hearth, her uncle hurried to Eira, clasping her hands.

"You must go from here quickly. Take the women and children to the huts to gather their things. It'll be no more than two days by foot to the cover of the Caledonian Wood, even with the little ones. The Selgovae will shelter you there. If you leave now, you'll make good distance before night closes in."

A wave of panic struck Angharad, and she rushed to Eira, clutching. "No! You mustn't leave!"

Eira reached to smooth Angharad's hair, looking at her uncle. "I will not leave. I will stay here with you and your uncle. Lailoken, you are consumed with preparations," she went on. "Angharad is frightened, and you cannot care for her with an army marching near. I will stay until she is delivered to her father. She cannot be left alone!"

"I will stay with the child," Diarmid offered.

Her uncle leaned in, beseeching. "A great army comes, Eira, and Gwrgi and Perdur along with it. You have suffered enough. I would see you safe. How can I be your husband if I cannot be your protector?"

A look passed between them, and Eira's eyes filled with tears. "Promise me you will do nothing foolish, Lailoken. I do not care for justice. Only that you should live."

"I swear to you I'll do nothing foolish. Please. Think of the children." Lailoken pressed her hands, and Eira looked to the ground.

"Very well. The Caledonian Wood. I will wait for you there."

"That is where I shall find you." Lailoken leaned to brush Eira's lips with a kiss, then Eira bent, gathering Angharad in her arms.

"I will see them off, but I will not leave you," Eira whispered. "If anything should go amiss—anything at all—you must come to me in the hut."

"But you promised—"

"I will show the others the path, then return. If time passes and you do not come, I will know you are safe, and I promise I will flee. Do you understand?"

Angharad nodded, and Eira kissed her upon the forehead before straightening. "You must promise to be brave," she said. "And you mustn't worry for us, Angharad. Only think: soon you will be back with your mother. Just think of that, my love. Think of her happiness when at last she sees you."

Angharad's blood beat in her ears. Death marched in the minds of the men, and she could feel it seeping through the cracks beneath the doors.

Diarmid came, taking her hand, his brown eyes steady. "Come. Sit with me, then, and close your eyes. We will practice our breathing."

Angharad's stomach soured, but she sat, folding her legs beneath her. Squeezing her eyes shut, she took a breath through her nose.

"Good," Diarmid said. "Again. Then tell me the words, and let us pray you shall not need them."

Angharad blew the air from her mouth, her voice dutiful and small amid the chaos of the room.

"Imagine you are brown as dirt. Imagine you are green as bracken. Imagine you are little more than a mouse . . ."

CHAPTER 8

Lailoken

Battle of Arderydd
Kingdom of the Pendragons
15th of October, AD 573

The pasture was at our backs. Above it, two ramparts protected the fort.

There had been no grand speeches before we descended. Only our war chant and the feeling of brotherhood as we stood upon the hilltop, each of us knowing the horror to come.

There would be no victory for the Dragon Warriors this day. It was only a matter of how we wished to die.

With great difficulty, we decided.

How many wounds could our bodies sustain until they split open and ceased to obey us? How many of the enemy could we drag kicking and wailing to the land of the dead?

My nephew was with Rhydderch. I did not want Rhys to witness my end. The vein at my neck thrummed. Had I even known this man I once called a brother? Rhydderch had not even seen fit to trade for his own daughter. He knew my weakness for his child, knew I would send her, and so he conceded nothing. Each warrior coming against us would be under the clearest order to find Angharad and bring her to safety.

My fury strained, threatening to unleash. Still, I could not be the one to kill Rhydderch. There was another deserving of death even more.

Bring Gwrgi before me in your chaos, I prayed to the Morrigu, goddess of war. *Bring Gwrgi before me so he might pay for all he has done.*

I would gladly die to drag Gwrgi into the afterlife, where he belonged. I only hoped to live long enough to find him.

Gwenddolau ran his horse along the front line of our army as their footmen neared, his jaw tight in defiance. Pressing through our wall of warriors, I stood before the thundering host and screamed my rage. The cry of all my brothers was deafening at my back.

Aye. We would die together.

But first we would make them pay.

Their spearmen charged.

The Dragon Warriors rushed into the fray.

Time on a battlefield is slippery, uncatchable. It is a punishing, bloody fog in which moments become shape-shifters, inhabiting an instant or a lifetime. I was hunting for the colors of Ebrauc. I cannot say how long we had been fighting. But whether it was the bond of our hearts or the bond of our blood that connected us, our eyes locked across the heaving masses.

Mine eyes and my nephew's.

Rhys's sword was brandished. He'd cast his javelins. At seventeen winters, he stood tall, deadly as any man, golden torque at his neck, black hair hidden beneath his helmet. His green eyes were fierce with battle, but when they fell upon me, they faltered.

How many days had we sat idly, watching our fish traps in the river?

How many nights had I passed in telling him tales as he grew to be a man?

How many times had I guided his feet in sparring or helped him train with his spear? *Slide your hand back a palm's width. Now draw the shaft back, level with your ear . . .*

Beneath his helmet, his battle mask fell away. And in the heat of the slaughter, I saw Rhys's fury turn to anguish.

To fear.

The sight of me had chased away the beast he'd conjured, leaving in its place only a man.

"No!" I shouted. "Fight!"

Rhys blinked as if waking from a trance and gripped his blade just as one of the Dragon Warriors charged him, battle-axe in hand.

Rhys was here. We had plowed through enough of their forces so that we had come to the heart of the army—Strathclyde and its men. My eyes scarcely leaving my nephew's, I ducked a blow and dispatched the warrior before me, turning back only to see Rhys cutting down one of my brothers in a single stroke. He glanced up, tracking me like a fledgling falcon; now that he had seen me, he would not let me from his sight.

"Rhys!" I shouted. "Mind your back!"

He rounded, shield raised, just in time to ward off a killing blow. Catching his attacker off balance, he hacked his sword across our warrior's armored stomach.

I'd never felt such relief to see my friends die.

"Fight!" I shouted again, praying Rhys could read the volumes behind my eyes. I would not watch him die on this day. I would offer up my own arteries if only to save him.

Yet now that he'd spotted me in the tumult, Rhys could not fight as he had before. I took stock of the battle, frantic, for I could see Rhys had strayed too far into the fray. *Fool of a boy.* What was he imagining, breaking past his own warriors? He was too deep beyond the line held by his father's men. He should have been fighting within reach of his guard, within reach of his father.

Movement flickered to my right, and I raised my shield instinctively, nearly too late, for the force of my opponent's blow sent me tumbling back into the embankment. A brute, then. I scrambled to my feet to see Rhydderch's brother Morcant standing before me, his sword running with blood, his boarish eyes feral with the rush of gore and battle.

He mistook my surprise for fear. "Don't fret, Lailoken," he said. "It's a good day to die. Your cousin thought as much."

Brant, dead?

He's bluffing, I told myself. *He means to throw you off.* But then I looked over his shoulder. There, beyond the dyke, Brant's horse had fallen. My cousin lay motionless beside it.

Gripping my shield, I charged.

I am a tall man—there were some who said my father was descended from giants—but Morcant was equal in height and denser with muscle. I lost sight of Rhys as I braced and blocked, waiting for an opening.

Then, somewhere in the midst of our parries, I saw it dawn upon Morcant that while he was more powerful, I was quicker and more skilled with my blade. Blocking my strike, he ducked just out of reach. I grunted and sprang, striking again, but he reached behind him, grabbing a footman by the breastplate and thrusting him before me.

"Coward!" I shouted, slamming my shield into the face of the approaching man. The blow drove his nose bone into his brain, and as he fell back, I rushed into the crush of bodies.

Brant was gone, and soon so would I be. I had to find Rhys and get him back behind his father's line. Victor's side or no, my nephew would not survive here in the brunt of it.

Someday I will fight with the Dragon Warriors, he'd said as a boy. *Someday, Uncle, I will fight beside you.*

Sweet gods. That was when I understood.

Rhys intended to fight his way to me. He wanted no part in his father's war. He imagined he might be the bargaining piece in the trading of men. My nephew meant for me to take him as a hostage. Perhaps he even imagined the kings would be content to slay Gwenddolau and grant his warriors quarter.

Until that moment, I had not known real fear.

How could Rhys fail to understand? This was a ridding. An annihilation. We were fighting with the grim honor of warriors who meant to be their own masters, even in death. I was in no position to take hostages.

I swore and wished for my spear as a soldier caught sight of me and took aim with his own. My arm trembled from the force as I blocked the barbed point. My shield arm was growing weak. With a roar of impatience, I ran at him and finished him with my blade.

It was then I saw Rhydderch.

Aye, I spotted my sister's husband amid the flail and crash of metal upon metal, weapon on skin. Rhydderch, my friend, whom I had called a brother for eighteen winters. He looked up, and suddenly my eyes were locked with those of a stranger.

Nay. In this battle, there would be no hostages. In this battle, there would be no quarter.

I caught sight of Rhys and changed my course. The wave of combat had carried him across the field. Nearly one hundred men stood between us now. But that was not what made my guts plummet. Rhys had engaged Fendwin, of all men, seasoned by threescore more battles than my nephew had ever seen.

"Fendwin!" I shouted, but my voice was swallowed by the din.

Rhys's jaw was locked, though his helmet was gone—had been knocked clean off. He blinked blood from his eyes as it streamed down his forehead. Fendwin readied himself. The two collided.

Rhys dug his heels into the mud and, leveraging his shield against

Fendwin's chest to shove off, gained enough space to reset his stance, slashing at the warrior's throat. Fendwin's block sent him stumbling back onto his heels. I raced toward them, blindly hacking with my blade, dealing and ducking blows, my eyes trained on the two warriors.

Rhys yanked his shield tight, protecting his torso from Fendwin's sword. But even as Fendwin struck with his blade, I saw him dip low, his free hand skimming the cuff of his boot.

Rhys did not know Fendwin favored a dirk.

"Fendwin! No!" I cried. Fendwin rose in a flash, thrusting his dirk home.

It would feel, at first, like a blow to the stomach. But then the cleaving. The searing hot pain as the blade ripped through the soft and slippery entrails.

Fendwin spun on his heel as I closed the distance between us. Only then did he see who approached. Only then did he see my expression.

He looked down at Rhys, and it dawned upon him who his opponent had been. We both could see the boy would not live. Fendwin bowed his head. An apology. An understanding. I fell to my knees.

Rhys lay on his back, eyes wide with pain, choking on his own blood. His hand clutched at the grass, at his stomach.

"I'm here. You're all right. You're all right, I'm here." My words were a chant as I bent over him, taking his bloody hands and gripping them to me. But how could he know me? My face was contorted, my voice broken with tears.

His eyes sought the source of my voice but could not find me. Though my fingers pressed him, I did not know if he felt me near. I held on to him as his body convulsed and his green eyes searched the blue sky overhead.

Give him peace, give him peace, I pleaded. *Mother, Father. Come take him home.*

I pressed his wound as if I could somehow push his entrails back into the cavity of his stomach, but the damage had been too great. Too final.

Rhys's breath hitched. His eyes fixed on a distant point, and I watched as they went vacant, translucent as glass. Then his chest rose no more.

I clutched him as if I could force him to return to his flesh, but his spirit sifted like sand through my fingers. I clutched him until I felt the moment he had gone, the moment his body became a shell.

From somewhere overhead came the clatter of blade and shield. Fendwin meant to protect me until I regained my wits. Fendwin was a brother. Fendwin was a friend.

I sobbed into the chaos. "That was my nephew. That was my boy."

But the beast heard nothing.

The beast was consumed in its feeding, tossing back its head as it feasted upon the bodies of the dying and the dead.

Christians speak of a place called hell.

They claim it is a world made for the wicked and that those who are doomed travel there when they die. But the Christians are wrong. Hell does not exist in some distant realm.

Hell is watching a man you once trained with in weapons take a spear through his chest.

Hell is slashing your sword into the neck of a warrior you feasted with at your sister's table.

Hell is the look upon your foster brother's blood-spattered face as he commands you.

Run.

CHAPTER 9

Angharad

Caer Gwenddolau
Kingdom of the Pendragons
15th of October, AD 573

I magine you are brown, brown as dirt.
  Imagine you are little more than a mouse.

Angharad repeated Diarmid's words over and over, fingers trembling as she clung to the embankment, pressing herself into the earth. Men were shouting down below. They stood knee-deep in the river with spears, eyes scouring the cliff for any who might flee. Her breath came shallow and quick as a bird's. She was supposed to call out to them. Her uncle had made her swear to do so, and round her neck she wore her slender gold torque. They would know her for Rhydderch's daughter. But now the din of battle drowned any sound she might make. Each clang sped her heart faster and faster until she wanted to fling herself from the hilltop if only to make it all cease.

I want Mama, I want Papa! She closed her eyes and saw her mother's chamber. She could smell the flower water her mother dabbed at the hollow of her throat, imagined folding herself into her mother's arms, feeling the shush of her lips against her hair.

Mama.

The men roaring as they thrust their spears, the clatter and blood. It was all a horrible dream.

I want Mama, I want Papa! But there was only the cliff, the battle raging above and the soldiers shouting below.

Her father was supposed to have traded for her. Something had gone terribly wrong, and Lailoken's blue eyes had been nearly wild. He had gripped her shoulders so hard his fingers had bruised her. It was then Angharad knew things were very bad.

You must go to the warriors at the river and tell them you are Angharad of Strathclyde. Tell them you are Rhydderch's daughter. They will bring you to safety.

Yet Angharad clung to the cliff between one side and another, unable to make herself cry out. These were not her father's men. These men were not safe. They were hard-faced and hulking. They jeered and howled like foul creatures, their eyes fixed on the fortress above, their faces painted dark with streaks that looked like blood.

Brown as dirt, nothing more than a mouse.

Angharad had heard tales of Wisdom Keepers who could walk unseen among men. But she had only just begun her lessons. It had been only the turning of one year.

When Angharad had lost her way in the woods of Cadzow, she would kneel in the brambles or lay her hand on the trunk of a hazel tree. Then the whispers would come. She would know which way to go. She tried to curl inside herself now, to find a place that was safe, a place where she might still be able hear the whispers, but she could not block the nightmare from above: the thud of bodies falling from the ramparts. The cries of the Dragon Warriors, the wet yielding of flesh from metal. The gurgling and choking, as if on blood.

Angharad thought of Maelgwn and Brant, of Gwenddolau and Lailoken. Diarmid had been standing high above the fray, chanting curses into the sky like an angry god. Gwenddolau's birds had been set loose from the temple. She could not bear to think what might become of them.

The cliff was thick with nettle, spiny with thorn and gorse. The Dragon Warriors once said they sorrowed for any who attempted to scale it. Now reaching the bottom was Angharad's only hope.

She rubbed the tears from her eyes. She would not fall. Could not—it was too far to the water below. If she could only get down to the river's edge, she could race to the little hut where Eira would be waiting. Eira had promised. She would know what to do.

Together, they would be safe.

Thorns snagged and tore Angharad's wool stockings, catching the flesh of her legs as she took a shaky step down. Clutching hurriedly to steady herself, she turned too late to see she was grasping for a fat stalk of nettle. Angharad wrenched her fist away from the sting, hot as a hornet's barb. An instant was all it took. Her balance teetered, and the earth beneath her feet gave way.

Nettle, thorn, and sticks pierced and battered her as she tumbled down the cliffside, her body tossing like a doll's. Earth and rock burned past as she clawed, flailing and slipping, picking up speed. One branch after another was wrenched from her hands until her fingers gripped determinedly at something. She cried out as her arm jerked, feeling as if it might rip from her shoulder, but it held—a tree root.

She was not dead. She was only still. Angharad looked about to discover she'd fallen nearly the length of the cliff, tumbling just out of sight beneath a low copse of prickly gorse. A place too thorny for men, where only hares or red foxes might hide.

Her legs were scraped and bleeding, her palms torn, embedded with thorns. She stiffened her fingers to keep them from moving, for she knew if she looked and saw the dozens of prickers poking from deep within her flesh, it might be her undoing.

The gorse was spiked, thick-trunked, and dense. Sliding on her belly to keep herself hidden, Angharad made her way bit by bit toward the water until a boggy wetness soaked her dress and she stood half crouched, her feet sinking into the welcome muck of the river. Here, tall autumn reeds hid her from the eyes of men. Stretching into the woods on the opposite bank of the water, she saw the forest path beckoning her to safety in the woods. Once in the trees, it would not be far to their hut. But to reach the forest, she would have to ford the water.

From her place in the reeds, Angharad looked up at the hill. Smoke billowed from the ramparts, but whether it was from the Dragon Warriors' brush piles or the fortress itself, she could not tell. From somewhere in the fray, the startling blare of a battle horn sounded.

A man standing downriver shouted, his voice eager. "We've breached the dyke! Close in tight now. Any come down, finish them here!"

Gods protect them, Angharad pleaded. *I will obey your whispers forever and ever if you will only protect them.*

The men in the river beat their spears against their shields with a roar. No. She would not go to those men. And if she was to find Eira, it must be now. The warriors had begun to close in upon the fortress, wading through the water. Angharad dashed from the cover of the reeds.

Brown as a field mouse, brown as dirt.

She gasped as the icy water soaked in, burning her wounds like fire while she sought purchase along the river's slippery pebbled bottom. Her body caved as the current rushed against her, threatening to sweep her downstream. But she was nearly there. She struggled across the final stretch, nearing the opposite bank, and closed her eyes, imagining she was nothing more than a drift of fog. But she was no Wisdom Keeper. Not yet. She was only a girl.

And so as she pulled herself from the river's grip, exposed on the stark bank and plastered down by wet wool, she heard a man shout, "Stop!"

Angharad looked up as a warrior in a leather helmet plunged into the water after her. Yanking up the hem of her waterlogged dress, she bolted from the riverbank, stumbling toward the waiting shelter of the wood.

"Catch her!" one of the men commanded.

"Come here, you river rat!" The warrior splashed, erupting from the water, but Angharad was on the forest path now, and she was fast, faster than her sister or any of her brothers, faster than any of these stupid soldier men.

"Leave her," she heard the commander call out. "We have the forest. She won't get far."

Angharad's boots slipped on the blanket of decaying leaves as she left the trail and cut a new path through the underbrush. A secret way, deeper into the wood. Was it only yesterday they'd walked with baskets on the crooks of their arms, humming and laughing as they picked blackberries? When the horn had sounded, they'd left the hearth fire burning. But when she reached their dwelling beneath the cluster of ash trees, no smoke breathed from the thatch.

Angharad stopped. The sturdy wooden door of their hut lolled open, half-splintered on its hinges. The sight sent a shiver through her, and she bit back her rising panic of tears.

Be brave, Eira had told her. She could see no men in the forest. Quickly, Angharad dashed through the door.

Inside, the hut was dim. The pine table had been overturned. Berry pulp stained the floor beneath the unlatched window, where Eira's wreath lay limp upon the ground.

"Eira?" she whispered.

An autumn wind gusted through the open door. Eira's weaving waved in strings from her broken loom.

"Eira?"

Angharad stepped toward the overturned table, and broken pottery crunched beneath her feet. Then a strong hand gripped her and yanked her to the wall, nearly knocking her from her feet. "Angharad, sweet gods, I nearly struck you!"

Eira had pulled her into the shadow of the broken door. One hand clung to Angharad and the other, white-knuckled, gripped an axe. Eira's dark hair was disheveled, and one eye had swollen nearly shut. Blood ran in a rivulet from her nose. Eira dropped the axe as Angharad collapsed into her arms. "You waited!" Angharad's voice shook with her tears.

"Oh, Angharad! My sweet girl. Hush now, hush. You're here now. You're safe." She pressed her lips to Angharad's hair and held her tight with trembling fingers. She drew back, raking the little girl with her eyes. "You're soaked to the bone. What happened? You were meant to go to your father!"

"He did not come. He did not trade for me!" Angharad cried.

"I cannot understand it." Eira cupped her face, kissing her again in relief. But when she reached down to take the child's hands, Angharad cried out. Eira's eyes widened as she saw the mass of embedded thorns. "Oh, Angharad. You've endured too much. We must find your father."

"No, no!" Angharad panicked. "I don't want to go back to the war!"

Eira glanced worriedly over Angharad's shoulder. "Angharad, I know you are frightened, but we cannot stay in this hut. The soldiers who come—they set fire to everything. They are slaying any in their path. It is not safe here. Can you walk?"

"I . . . I can walk," Angharad said. "But you are bleeding."

"Never mind it." Eira swiped her face with her sleeve. "Come, we must hurry. Until we can find Rhydderch, we must keep ourselves from sight."

Eira drew the girl under the shelter of her arm to hurry her from the cottage, but something slick covered the floor. Reaching too late to catch herself, Angharad's feet slipped from under her, and she landed on all fours in the dim.

Eira cursed and bent to help her up—tried to keep her from seeing—but it was too late. Angharad was staring into the vacant eyes of a dead man, his head attached only by sinew to his neck. She screamed, scrambling back like a crab.

"Shh! Shhhhhh!" Eira squatted, clamping a hand over Angharad's mouth. "He was a bad man, Angharad. That is all." She leaned her forehead to Angharad's, forcing the child to look into her eyes. "But if they find us with this dead warrior, they will kill us. They will kill us, do you understand?"

Angharad nodded, and Eira stood, hurrying to the wardrobe. She yanked out a dry shift, thick socks, and one of Lailoken's spare woolen tunics. "You must have warm clothes. Here, quickly. Put these on."

Angharad struggled out of her soggy boots and torn stockings, pulling on the dry garments. She swam in her uncle's tunic, but upon her the short sleeves were long, and it had a hood like a cloak.

"Good girl. Let me help with your boots." Eira bent to shove the waterlogged leather back onto Angharad's feet. As they rushed through the door, Eira's gaze lingered on the axe.

"Take it," Angharad said.

"We cannot risk it. If Gwrgi's men should find us first . . ." The look on Eira's face frightened Angharad. It was as if she could not speak. Eira cleared her throat. "If Gwrgi's men should find us, it will be better if we are not armed."

"But then we cannot fight."

Eira bent to draw up Angharad's hood. "You will fight no one, do you hear me? We must hide from the men we cannot trust, and seek out those who wear your father's standard instead. Do you understand? Angharad. Tell me you understand."

"I understand," Angharad said. But her fingers moved in secret to the gold-handled knife Eira hadn't noticed was still belted at Angharad's waist, hidden now beneath her uncle's tunic. The knife her mother had given her.

They ran through the forest, dropping into thickets at the slightest snap of a stick. Soon Angharad no longer knew which direction they'd traveled. And as the day wore on, she did not know how much time had passed, only that they were alive. The sky had gone dull, and now Angharad's feet in her wet boots tormented her with each step as if poked by knives. At last she cried out and could go no farther. Eira sank down beside her, half her face swollen into a woman unrecognizable, her upper lip crusted with dried blood. "We must rest," she said. "You have done so well, my love. So very well."

Night had fallen, and with it the cold. Angharad could feel it in the tightness of her cheeks and the clamminess of her blistered feet.

"Sit just here and drink." Eira nestled her in the hollow of a log and handed her a skin of water. As Angharad drank, Eira looked about, shaking her head. "I thought I had some idea of where we might be. But the sun is gone. For a time we were following the water, but now even the burn has disappeared."

"If we are lost, perhaps we are safe," Angharad said.

Eira threw up her hands. "No, Angharad, we are not safe! We are alone in the wild, among warriors and wolves and all manner of terrible creatures! We have been traveling all day, and I no longer know whether we are running from battle or toward it. I must get you to your father! That is the only way you will be safe from danger."

Eira turned her back to Angharad and her breath caught, shoulders shaking with silent tears. Angharad stood with some effort and went to her. She wrapped her arms round her waist and buried her head against Eira's stomach. They wept until they were wrung out, the black wood heavy with names they would not say. Those of their loved ones. Those of the dead.

Angharad loved those on both sides of this battle. Even now her father could be lying in the field high above the river. Or her uncle Lailoken. She swallowed. Her brother Rhys.

Had there been any food in her stomach, Angharad would have been sick.

"It will be very cold, Angharad. It may even frost," Eira said at last, straightening. "We must build a fire. We may be seen, but there's nothing for it. Besides, it will keep the animals at bay." She sniffed gently and bent to her satchel. "I could not carry much, but I have a flint. Stay here and gather the driest kindling you can find. I'll fetch some fallen wood. Then we will remove your thorns, yes? You cannot sleep with them digging like that."

Angharad nodded. Once she'd gathered a pile of kindling, she returned to the log to wait, pulling her knees to her chest.

Soon a fire was burning. They set Angharad's boots and socks to dry beside it. Her bare feet were swollen, fluid weeping from her blisters. Eira divided a loaf of bread, and they fell upon it, too hungry to speak. Eira had given her the larger portion, and Angharad could tell she still hungered by the way she glanced away as Angharad ate.

"Here, take mine," Angharad offered.

"Nay, little one. I've had enough to fill me up. Here. Come nearer to the light. I'll have a look at your hands."

"It will hurt." Angharad heard the fear in her own voice. Already her hands pulsed with pain. At the thought of Eira digging the skelfs from her palms, Angharad began to sweat despite the cold. Eira searched her satchel and came out with a different skin to drink from, one that smelled sharp. Angharad knew it held whiskey.

"Sip this. It will help with the pain."

Even to sniff it burned. Angharad had only ever drunk watered wine. But she closed her eyes and swallowed it down, coughing as its fire blazed into her belly.

"More," Eira urged. Angharad tipped the flask again as Eira reached to unfold her palm. "I will have to use my fingers. I have no pincers. Would that we had a knife."

"I have a knife."

Eira looked up. "Angharad, I said no arms! What should happen should one of Gwrgi's men find a blade on you?"

Angharad reached beneath her layers and drew out the knife. "But Lailoken bade me wear it."

At the mention of Angharad's uncle, Eira expelled a shaky breath. "Your mother's blade." She took it gently. "We must not give up hope. We must believe we will all be reunited soon."

Angharad could find no comfort in her words. The well of Eira's sorrow felt bottomless and swirled with shadows of doubt. She dared not look too deeply lest she fall in.

Eira flexed her hand gently toward the firelight. "You mustn't watch," she said. "Speak to me. Or I shall speak to you."

Angharad tensed, fixing her eyes on the night forest as Eira applied the blade's tip to the first thorn.

"Ah!" Angharad tried to jerk away, but Eira held fast. Tears sprang, hot and unrelenting.

"Drink, love. Drink," Eira said. Angharad could not speak. She could only weep. With her free hand, she raised the flask and sipped, then sipped again.

"Good girl. I will give you something else to think on. This battle. Do you understand what has happened?" Eira asked.

Angharad squeezed her eyes tight, trying to play along. "My father has waged war upon my uncles."

"Yes. Though it is not only your father who has waged this war. I saw many standards I have seen before."

"Which standards did you see?"

"The otter of Dunawd the Stout. The serpent of his cousin Cynfelyn the Leprous, petty kings whose lands lie south of Ebrauc. And I saw the lion of Urien, king of Rheged. No doubt you have learned of these men in your lessons."

Angharad sucked in her breath as Eira began work on another thorn. "A mighty confederation has united to end the reign of Uther Pendragon," Eira said, then fell quiet.

A mighty confederation. Angharad felt at once bleary and crystal sharp, her insides all thorns and spiked edges.

Her father had not sent for her.

Perhaps she, too, was considered the enemy. The thought was a barb in her chest, and Eira looked up, understanding.

"Your father will have commanded the entire army to find you and keep you safe, Angharad. Even now you must believe he is doing everything in his power to find you."

"But why did he not make me safe before the attack? He did not trade for me or offer terms. They attacked knowing I was within!"

"Nay, he could not have thought so, or he would never have let a single spear fly. No doubt he knows how much your uncle loves you. I am sure he imagined you'd be offered up safe."

Angharad could not understand. She had watched her father and uncle play *fidchell*. Seen how they laughed. Now her father had brought war on her uncles and left Angharad to die. Eira mistook her tears for pain from the digging.

"Enough for tonight." She wiped the knife clean and slid it back into Angharad's belt. "If your father did not trade for you, it was with good reason. Dreadful things happen in times of war. Men are not themselves. We must try to get some rest. Everything will seem clearer in the morning."

They dabbed Angharad's wounds with the last of the whiskey. Then Eira banked the fire, gathering Angharad close. "You have been so very brave." She stretched an arm beneath Angharad's head for a pillow, covering them both in the warmth of her heavy fur-lined cloak. "Sleep now," she said.

But Angharad could not sleep, though her body was wrung out and hollow as a shell. Instead she settled in Eira's arms and tried to go still. It was easier now, without the clanging of weapons.

Or perhaps it was due to sheer exhaustion, for when Angharad closed her eyes, she could clearly envision her home. It was dim in her mother's chamber. Embers were dying in the hearth. Her mother lay in bed, chest rising in sleep, dreaming. Angharad felt her feet upon her mother's floor. The cold seeping up from the slate.

"I'm all right, Mama. I'm all right," she whispered, but her mother did not wake. "Mama, I'm all right," she said, reaching to stir her, and now her mother bolted upright with a gasp.

"Mama!"

Her mother blinked into the darkness, eyes searching. But she could not see Angharad. Could not hear her. And as the Knowing struck, her mother's chamber was ripped away.

Angharad opened her eyes, feeling utterly alone. In the shadows thrown from the firelight, she saw faces of the warriors she had come to know, men who'd been strangers only one winter ago, now so warm and familiar.

Lailoken and Gwenddolau. Brant. Diarmid with his graying hair and dark, sparkling eyes. Fendwin. Rhiwallon. Maelgwn. Even more than Angharad's uncles, it was he who'd told her silly tales when she was sad, who'd swiped at her most persistently with bug salve at evenfall. Something in Maelgwn had always felt safe. Perhaps it was his kind green eyes—they brought to mind her brother's.

She tried to summon her brother's face. But at the thought of Rhys, Angharad felt her throat fill with tears. Yes, surely this liquid was tears, for she was lying on her back, choking on it, drowning, unable to breathe. Then, suddenly, it was no longer nighttime in the forest. Angharad smelled mud and felt its wetness beneath her soak into her clothing. The sky overhead was blue, racing with thin white clouds. In her ears there was a burgeoning deafness, a dull and aching thud. But if she strained, if she gave way to it, someone was speaking. It was the voice of her uncle. Deep and reassuring. Heavy with grief. Angharad struggled to sit, to clear her throat of the choking sea, but her body was not hers to command.

Sleep took her instead.

Angharad sank deep into the mercy of her dreaming, to a place where she struggled no more.

CHAPTER 10

Languoreth

Tutgual's Hall
Partick
Kingdom of Strathclyde
29th of October, AD 573

A guard followed at my heel as I fastened my cloak and stepped onto the covered porch of the hall.

Night had fallen, but I could not visit Brodyn until Gladys and Cyan were asleep. I balanced the heavy wicker basket readied by the kitchens over my arm, a thick woolen blanket tucked within it, and turned to the guard who had followed me, nodding at the bundle of unlit torches on the porch. "We need light."

The guard reached for a torch with a resigned look. Across the courtyard, twin torches lit the wooden gate, casting shadows on the timber palisade that encircled Tutgual's hall. The watchmen nodded as we neared, lighting our torch from their flames.

Somewhere in the distance, hounds bayed. The sky was black and moonless, air biting with the threat of winter. The only other sound was the heavy shush and rustle of the guard's boots as he followed me through the dying grass of the courtyard, past the stable, toward the back field where the prison pits lay.

The pits were dug narrow and deep, marring a field once planted with barley, lined with stones that grew slick in the damp. There would be creatures down there, all manner of insects that ate human dung. There would be a stench like soiled chamber pots.

The pits were open to the weather, topped only by grids of bound sticks weighed down at their edges by flat, heavy stones. A ladder was kept nearby, but the guards had little reason to tend prisoners sent here. Men were thrown in, left to suffer the consequences of falling. Some pits held ten men, pressed so tightly they took turns to sit and to stand, but I could not imagine which could be worse—to be nearly suffocated by others in their prison rot, or to be tossed into the muddy earth alone, no bodies to warm you, silence beating upon your ears until it drove you slowly mad.

Brodyn had been at the mercy of the elements for a fortnight, knowing an army marched upon Gwenddolau and Lailoken, boys he'd trained in weapons. Knowing he could not ride out to fight alongside his brother, Brant.

The torch flickered in the wind. There was a snap to the air that made me shiver, but the cluster of guards had a fire—close enough to keep watch on the pits but not near enough to warm the men below. They looked up as I neared, and I saw their disdain. Sister of Strathclyde's enemies—Pendragon and his druid counsellor.

My blood heated, but I lowered my eyes in a semblance of respect, adjusting the basket on my arm. "I've come to see my cousin," I said.

They glanced at one another, and a fair-haired soldier stood. "Apologies, m'lady, but you cannot trespass here."

"Of course. I see." I paused. "'Tis only . . . Well. The battle's been won. Surely there can be no harm in it. Brodyn of Cadzow has been captain of my guard for many a winter, as well you know. Some bread and meat, a skin of wine. That is all. Please. I've brought the same for you."

I took their offerings from the basket and handed them to the fair-haired guard who approached. He tossed the packet to the man by the fire and leaned forward to prod the remaining goods. "What is this?" he asked.

"A blanket only, to ward off the chill." I shifted aside the foodstuffs to reveal it, growing short on patience. "Tell me. What is your name?" I asked him.

"Torin."

"Torin." I met his eyes. "My cousin is a warrior and a noble, nephew of Morken king. If he was suspected of any trouble or flight, he should have been treated as a hostage of war, kept by our laws in the warmth of the hall with all its comforts, not tossed like a common thief into the pits."

He studied me, then gestured to a pit a short distance away. "Well enough. A few moments only." I went to it and knelt, the smell assailing me.

I turned to the soldier who'd followed me. "Lower the torch, please. Or give it here. I will hold it myself."

He frowned but did as I asked, squatting down. "Brodyn," I called out. At first the flickering light illuminated little but the dank stone walls. Then I heard a soft dragging sound and felt a sudden, sharp awareness come from the dark. At last the eerie glow of Brodyn's face came, looking up from below.

"Languoreth." His brown eyes were black in the torchlight.

"I can scarcely see you," I said. "Are you injured? Are you chilled?"

"Nay. I'm hale."

I heard the gentle scuffle once more as he shifted farther into the light, bracing himself against the slick stone wall.

"Your leg. Is it the bone?" I asked.

"Twisted, I think," he said, giving a quick smile. "Never a healer round when you need one."

"This is no time for wit," I said.

His shoulder-length hair was loose and tangled. I could see how much gray was now threaded amid the brown. I supposed we lived so closely I hadn't noticed before that my cousin was a man approaching fifty winters. His beard had grown, his mustache drooping low over his mouth, but he did not look bloodied. They might have thrown him in the pit, but at least they had not beat him. My shoulders sank with relief.

"Have you news, then?" he urged. Brodyn's face was steeled with a warrior's practice. Expectant. But the guards' ears were pricked. I had to speak carefully.

"Strathclyde and the kings of the south were victorious," I said.

Brodyn sank back against the wall. He knew I could not say more. But we were kin. Our eyes met, and I knew he understood: Gwenddolau was most likely dead.

"Then the king will soon return," he said.

"Yes. I am certain he returns to Partick even now. And when he does, I will speak to him. We will see to your release."

Brodyn nodded, his dark eyes fixed on the wet stone of the pit. Tutgual set prisoners against each other for amusement. Now that the captain of my guard was the kin of Tutgual's enemies, I did not like to think what the high king might do.

The weight of it settled between us. This murdering of our family under the pretense of war.

"I've brought food and a blanket," I said, hoping to cheer him. I wrapped the packet in the blanket and pushed it through a wooden square of the pit cover. He caught them and hastily dug through, tearing into the food.

"Thank you, Cousin. It does me much good to see you," he said.

"And I shall come again," I said. "Samhain draws near."

Brodyn glanced up and I caught his eye. He tilted his head. "How many days 'til Samhain?" he asked.

"Three days' time. I will return and bring blessings then."

He nodded. "Thank you, then, Cousin. Until Samhain."

"Until Samhain." I stood and gathered the empty basket. Was that enough? I prayed Brodyn would somehow glean my intent. Tutgual had brought war upon our family, and Brodyn would be honor-bound to answer his violence. But Tutgual had not grown old by letting men who threatened revenge live, and I would not stand by while he made a spectacle of my cousin's death.

Nodding to the warriors, I left them to drink by their fire in the dark. There had been something about Torin, the fair-haired warrior guarding the pits. He was young, admittedly. But I could smell it on him. Ambition. He was better than the others he stood guard with, or at the very least he thought so. He dreamt of a ranking that would take him from prison guard to warrior of the court. And no matter my feelings, I would soon be in need of a new captain of my guard.

Back in the warmth of the hall, Aela unfastened my father's brooch from my cloak, and I closed my fist around it, my fingers tracing the sleek silver hounds set within their protective thicket of interlacing. A gift from my mother to protect him from harm. I wore it often, but it was especially fitting to call upon its strength as Samhain drew near.

Of all the high holidays, none was more powerful than the eve of our new year. It was a night for honoring the dead. On the eve of Samhain, when the veils of the Summerlands parted, our loved ones traveled the mists to sit once more at our table for the night, leaving blessings of good fortune when they departed our homes. On Samhain, things often happened no one could explain. People saw visions reflected in water or heard voices in the forest that belonged to no earthly man. Elders told tales of cats shifting shape into peat-black steeds, of wild hosts of spirits storming through crossroads in search of warmth and food. Things once lost at last reappeared. Things kept close somehow went missing.

On the eve of Samhain, with Torin's help, I would work my own mystery.

On the eve of Samhain, I would make Brodyn of Cadzow disappear.

CHAPTER 11

Lailoken

Battle of Arderydd
Kingdom of the Pendragons
15th of October, AD 573

"Run," Gwenddolau commanded.

But I shook my head. "Hold the wall!" I shouted, dropping down beside him. Too many wounds to identify the worst. His skin had gone waxy.

"Hold!" Dreon echoed, thrusting his body to his shield.

"Stand, brother, you must stand!" I tried to ease Gwenddolau to his feet, but blood spouted from his mouth. I pressed my hand to his abdomen, the worst of it, but could not stanch the flow.

The clatter of weapons was deafening. The cries. I'd felt my shoulder shatter in the shield wall, heard the unearthly crunch. The pain was blinding, and in the moment my grip had loosened on my spear, Rhydderch's men had broken through. Gwenddolau had been wounded.

Now we'd rushed before him, holding our line, holding the dyke. But we could not hold for long. Dreon's shield arm trembled with the strain as he turned to me.

I shook my head. The old warrior's face stiffened. "Then you must go," he said. "They must not have his body."

"Dreon—"

"Go!" he shouted. I glanced at our men in the shield wall, faces strained, determined. They were of one mind; they had chosen their sacrifice. They would hold back Rhydderch's war band as long as they could so the rest of us might retreat.

I held Dreon's eyes. "We will draw the fight to the wood," I promised. For all of us would die. But those who remained could cluster and attack—we'd kill more of the enemy there.

Dreon nodded. They would hold the dyke.

I roared as I stood and hefted Gwenddolau over my shoulders, gripping an arm and a leg.

"Retreat!" I shouted.

Maelgwn glanced up, saw Gwenddolau upon my back. Saw our men's tenuous hold of the dyke. I saw it flash in his eyes—he would not abandon them. "You waste your life here!" I shouted. "We will avenge them. Retreat!"

With one last strike, Maelgwn turned to see our warriors in the shield wall giving their last, as I would soon do. As we all would do.

The men who had made their choice remained. Here, at the dyke, this was their end.

Only then did we run.

CHAPTER 12

Angharad

Battle of Arderydd
Kingdom of the Pendragons
16th of October, AD 573

Angharad woke to a stirring of dead leaves in the early-morning chill. The fire was ash and embers, smoldering in wisps, but Angharad was warm stretched against the length of Eira's body, tucked under the safety of her heavy fur cloak. She nearly drifted back to sleep, her body still wracked with exhaustion. But there it came again—the soft rustle and crunch of leaves underfoot. They were no longer alone. Angharad opened her eyes, senses alert.

Mist banked in wraithlike billows through the forest, and the air was wet and dewy, smelling of earth and of rain. Too frightened to move, Angharad lay motionless, peering into the trees from her place upon the ground. And then she saw it. A flicker of movement, the flash of a stormy cloak.

Just beyond the dying fire, a woman stood.

Her hair was black as a crow feather and her skin pale as the moon. She strode past the fire with purpose, a simple wicker basket over her arm. *She hasn't seen us*, Angharad thought. Then the woman stopped.

Her head swiveled as she fixed Angharad with a stare. Her eyes were pale blue, the color of a morning sky. Angharad tried to search the woman, even as the woman was searching her. She opened her mouth to speak, but the woman raised a hand, a finger to her lips. *Shhhh.*

Was that her voice or a whisper of wind?

Angharad tried to move, but her limbs were weighted. Her tongue felt thick, as if her mouth were full of honey. *Help us, please help me,* she tried to say.

And though she could not utter the words, she heard her own voice. The woman lifted her arm, her cloak slipping up her forearm as she pointed to a nearby stand of poplars. *That way.*

Angharad scrambled to put her feet beneath her. Somehow she knew this woman would help them. Somehow she knew this woman would not lead them astray. But the woman had turned and was already traveling briskly into the forest. Angharad watched, helpless, as she disappeared into the mist. *Wait, please! You must help us. Please, wait!*

"Angharad!"

She opened her eyes to find Eira crouched over her, worry etching her face.

"You were crying out," Eira said. "You were having a foul dream."

Angharad propped herself up on one elbow, rubbing her eyes. The morning was clear and fine—Angharad could no longer see mist. In the trees overhead, birds chirped. There was no woman. No track of rustled leaves. Where had she gone?

She wanted to tell Eira, and yet she did not. It felt like a secret.

It felt like a Knowing.

"Foul dreams are dreadful, but they're only dreams," Eira said. "They haunt warriors far rougher than you after a battle. Once we see you safe, they shall fade." Eira's swelling had worsened in the night, making her look like a stranger. She must have noticed Angharad's shock at her appearance, for her smile faltered.

"Are you hungry? Of course you are. Come and eat. I've caught us some breakfast," she said.

Angharad glanced at the fire to find it had not died down; rather, it burned hot, a rodent roasting over the flames on a hastily made spit.

"Is that . . . a squirrel?" she asked.

"Yes."

"But however did you catch it?"

"You wish to know?"

Angharad nodded.

"I lured it with hazelnuts, then wrung its neck. Come now. We must eat. We will need all our strength."

Angharad remembered the friendly red squirrels she'd trained to eat from her hand on summer days at Cadzow, then ate the meat anyway, all the while thinking of the woman. It had been a dream. Or could the woman have been a spirit? Perhaps she had even been a god. Gooseflesh traced her limbs.

Samhain was approaching, Angharad remembered, and she had always felt its sway. It was a time of year when the whispers became voices, when gods and goddesses of the Summerlands could slip between the worlds that lay beneath and within. Diarmid had told her of innumerable gods she had not known of: the god of the hazel wood and the roe deer, the goddess of the Esk, the goddess of bees. In the year she'd trained with Diarmid and her uncle, the forest and burns had come more alive than ever before. But she was only a novice, just beginning to understand the language of mystery.

Angharad searched the poplar trees. She thought she could make out the slender arc of a herd trail emerging from the other side.

"We must find water," Eira said, smothering the fire with earth. One red squirrel, split between two. Angharad's stomach still kicked with hunger.

"Perhaps we should travel that way." Angharad pointed to the trees. "There's a trail. Mightn't it lead to water?" She was thirsty, too. So very thirsty. She stood slowly, testing her feet. Her blisters jabbed like needles. She felt Eira's watchful gaze. Eira had become accustomed to Angharad's visions, but they did not often speak of them. That was the realm of her uncle.

"Very well, then. We shall follow the herd trail." Eira stuffed the rest of their belongings into her satchel and slipped it over her shoulder.

The forest was an autumn splendor. Leaves crunched underfoot as they followed the meandering track through the trees, listening for the shouts or rustle of soldiers, but the only sound was the low whistle of wind in their ears as it plucked gold and vermilion leaves from the branches overhead, sending them spiraling gracefully from the canopy. They drifted into Angharad's hair, touching upon her shoulders like momentary blessings. They passed the morning that way until, just beyond the tree line, the acrid smell of charred timber stung their noses. Soon smoke was clogging the forest, gusting in billows from the fields. Their eyes began to water and weep.

"Your tunic." Eira gestured. Angharad covered her nose and mouth, taking shallow breaths through the cloth. "Angharad, keep low," Eira warned her. "We must keep from sight."

Creeping through the brush, they lowered themselves onto their bellies, peering into the cultivated field beyond. There were no sheep or goats, no cattle or horses. Where there had been a village, only smoldering frames now stood, some still licking with flame. Others had collapsed in upon themselves, leaving little more than soot stains. Blackened forms lay in the grass, and as Angharad watched, a scattering of crows settled, feasting on the bodies of the dead.

A Song Keeper once sang of kingdoms far across the sea made entirely of sand, of leagues upon leagues where neither tree nor creature nor rivulet could be found.

How empty and lonesome, Angharad had thought.

This was what her father had done. He had taken a kingdom and turned it to sand.

"Why have they done this?" she whispered.

"Because this is the way people extinguish one another." Eira's voice was hard. "Come, Angharad. You have already seen too much."

They carried on a long while in silence through the wood. Then, suddenly, Eira stopped. "Listen. Do you hear that?"

It was the trickle of water.

"The burn," Eira said. "Angharad, you've found it!"

They rushed to the bank where crisp, clear water rushed beneath moss-covered boulders. There was a flat little island of pebbles just below the bank, and Angharad scrambled onto her belly at the water's edge to cup her hands and drink and drink. Never had water tasted so sweet.

"It will be running toward the river." Eira knelt, filling their skins. "We will follow it that way. At the river, there are bound to be boats."

Hope fluttered in Angharad's chest. A birdcall sounded, and for a moment she wondered if it might be some sort of omen. Angharad had taken quickly to birdcalls and their meanings, but this one she did not know.

She did not see the spear until it was pointed at her chest.

She gasped, and Eira turned, scrambling to her feet. A warrior stood on the streambed above in a dark leather helmet.

"Be still," he warned.

"Please," Eira said. "Lower your spear. She's only a child!"

But as Eira glanced at the warrior's shield, her face shifted. Red and black, the colors of Ebrauc. Never before had Eira looked so afraid.

"Someone's already found you," the warrior said with a smirk, eyeing Eira's swollen face. He thrust out his chin to make a bird call, and a moment later a dozen men on horseback came crashing through the wood, a cluster of footmen following behind.

"Get up." The warrior jabbed his spear at Angharad and she groped her way to her feet, but Eira pushed her away, planting herself between Angharad and the soldier.

"Lower your weapon!" she said. "The girl is a noble! Can you not see her torque?"

"Mind your tongue, slave girl." He poked his spear at the curve of Eira's breast, and her face reddened with anger.

"What have you found?" The voice was commanding but soft, almost curious.

Angharad turned as a dark-haired man wearing rusted battle armor and a heavy golden torque pushed through the crowd of warriors. His hair was cropped close to his head, darker than it should have been, for he looked to be the age of Angharad's father, but the subtle stain of plant dye yet lingered at his temples.

Gwrgi of Ebrauc.

"Leave off," he said, and the warrior obliged, leveraging his weapon off Eira so that it nicked the skin. She winced as blood sprang to the cut.

Gwrgi stopped and tilted his head, gazing at Eira as if transfixed. She averted her eyes, her tangled brown hair coming over her face.

"You," he said. "What is your name?"

"Eira."

"Eira. You remind me of someone. Someone I once knew." Gwrgi stepped lightly onto the pebbled bank and leaned in, taking a breath as if to gather the scent of her. "And where have you come from, Eira?" he asked.

"Pendragon's lands. You've come upon Angharad of Strathclyde, a noble," she said roughly. "I'm her nursemaid. We're searching for Lord Rhydderch."

Gwrgi seemed to have scarcely taken notice of Angharad, but now he gave a short laugh, peering down at her face. "'It'll be war,' my brother said. But what good is war without its spoils? And you are a speckled little chick. Lord Rhydderch is keen to find you, you know. Though who can say where he might be. We are all of us a-hunting now." He lifted his brows in delight. "We are out hunting Dragons."

Angharad's eyes dropped to his breastplate. No, it wasn't rust. The burgundy stain of his armor was that of dried blood. Blood of the Dragon Warriors. She glared at him with the loathing he deserved.

"Oh, aye. I know that look," Gwrgi said. "So like your mother."

He stood so near that Angharad could make out the sunspots marking his pale skin. His breath smelled of fennel, as if he had sweetened it, for beneath it was foul.

"You have found me," Angharad said. "Now take me to my father!"

"Is this how they raise a daughter of Strathclyde? To shout? I've just told you I've no idea where he is."

"Take me to my brother Rhys, then! Or summon him. He will come for me."

Gwrgi inclined his head. "Would that I could. But your brother is dead." Angharad stumbled back. "You did not know. Of course. How would you? It is a sorrow, truly. He showed such promise with a blade."

"Rhys?" Angharad's vision was coming in flashes. She sank back and Eira clutched her, pulling her into her arms.

"Oh, Angharad. Oh, my sweet," she whispered.

Gwrgi studied Angharad as if deciding what to do before turning to his men. "Lord Rhydderch. Where's he gone, then?"

"Can't say, my lord," the spearman answered.

"Surely someone has seen him."

"He was last seen following a band of men fleeing west," another of his men called out.

"Well enough. Send word that we've got her. She will stay at camp until Rhydderch can fetch her. I am a king, not a courier."

"And the nursemaid?" the spearman asked.

Gwrgi searched above the trees for the sun's height, face tight with impatience. "Take them both. I mean to resume the hunt while we still have light."

Angharad clung to Eira as the spearman ushered them toward the horses. She looked at the men and recognized faces she had seen at the river.

The bad men.

"We mustn't go with them," she whispered.

"Hush now, all will be well," Eira said. "They cannot harm you. You are a noble. They would never risk angering your father." Her voice was reassuring, but her blue eyes fixed upon Gwrgi as he pulled himself astride his mount.

"If that is so, then why are you afraid?" Angharad asked.

"Because Gwrgi is mad," Eira answered. "You must do nothing to anger him, Angharad. We will bide our time until you are delivered safely to your father."

"Up you get." The spearman came and pulled them apart, passing Angharad off to a warrior on horseback. The warrior gripped her too tightly, and Angharad stretched out her hand to Eira.

"Stay close," she begged.

"I am here," Eira said, but there was confusion in her eyes, for no man had taken Eira upon his horse.

"Bind her," the spearman commanded. A warrior produced a length of rope from his saddlebag, and Angharad looked at the men in horror.

"Whatever can you mean? No!"

It was as if he did not hear her. Yanking Eira roughly, he knotted the rope about her wrists, handing its end to the spearman mounted upon his horse.

"She is my nursemaid," Angharad shouted. "You cannot treat her so!"

The spearman kicked his horse into a walk, jerking the rope with a look of satisfaction. Eira stumbled, hurrying to keep her feet beneath her.

"You might be a noble," the spearman said, "but she's none such."

Something had shifted. Angharad had imagined they were Gwrgi's guests. But now that they were in hand, she felt more like a prisoner.

"She is my chamber woman!" Angharad said, staring at him until at last he turned round.

"Nay. Perhaps once, but no longer," he said. "Now she is something better. Now she has become our Pendragon whore."

CHAPTER 13

Lailoken

The Caledonian Wood
26th of November, AD 573

We never intended to survive. We only wanted to kill.

We slaughtered men in the forest for a fortnight and a month, and we were slaughtered in return.

Gwrgi and his warriors of Ebrauc hunted us, even as I hunted them.

One hundred and forty men carried the fight to the Caledonian Wood.

Now only nine of us yet lived.

Maelgwn and me. Fendwin, Rhiwallon, and five others.

I'd carried Gwenddolau upon my back until my legs gave out, his blood running down my neck.

I buried my brother in the heart of an oak grove.

We ate roots and small game, but our enemies were many, and soon animals were scarce. For weeks we scoured the wood for any sign of our women or children who'd fled from the fort. When I asked the wind, it only rattled the trees.

Eira.

We spoke little, then not at all. Stomachs sunken, we counted our ribs.

We killed in a stupor. Light as bone, emaciated shades of death. We fashioned gifts of the warriors we snared, draped them upon branches, carving curses upon tree trunks. Five men of Ebrauc we burned alive, only to trap others who rode after the sounds of their screams.

Then, one day, our enemies were no more.

For two days we hunted woods bare with coming winter. We stalked with a fervor that soon became a madness.

Dead men stood in my path as I walked the woods in search of food.

Not only dead men. My nephew. Rhys.

My eyes had been trained upon my boots. I felt him before I saw him.

Uncle, he called.

I looked up to see him standing before me in such detail I noticed a thread had pulled loose from the fine weave of his tunic. His skin was browned from a summer spent in sun. His gaze was expectant, as if he'd been awaiting my arrival overlong.

Rhys was yet living? I fell to my knees.

Uncle, he said. But his lips did not move.

Only then did I realize I was seeing a shade. I folded over myself, sobbing, beating at my head.

I did not wish to remember. We had not intended to survive. We had wanted only to kill.

But when you wish away your memory, you cannot choose what you keep. Soon I began to forget—even those I once loved.

With no more enemies to hunt, we began to turn upon one another. Our eyes became small and unyielding. We layered our bitterness about us as if it brought warmth. Days grew dark and short, blending with night. We'd discovered a small cave where we slept and sat by day, blinking by a fire.

The beast had consumed us.

And then, one night, she came in a dream.

We were moving in the twilight of morning, our lips interlocked, my breath was her breath. The smell of her was intoxication. Her skin was velvety as a fig, and the perk of her nipple stirred the animal in me. I raised myself over her, bracing so I could see her, watch her, as I entered. Her eyes were pale and deep as the sea. The world fell away. The only world I cared for lay beneath me, her fingers kneading the straining muscles of my arms, roaming my back, until I felt the sharp dig of her nails claim me as she lifted her hips, begging, demanding.

Lailoken.

I came awake. I remembered.

I am a Wisdom Keeper and a counsellor. My name is Lailoken. I am loved by such a woman.

I'd said good-bye to Eira knowing I would not live to see her again. And yet somehow I still was not dead.

I kept my eyes closed a moment, as if I could keep her near, but water pressed painfully at my bladder. I shifted and cursed. Pieces inside my shoulder were loose and aching. I stood, making my way out into the cold to relieve myself.

Outside the cave, the first snow had fallen. My urine burned a yellow stream into the white eiderdown, and I felt aged as an old man.

I was tucking away my member when I heard a familiar creak that warned of death—the draw of an archer's bow.

Before waking from my dream, I had not cared if I lived or if I should die. But now I had remembered. And I would not die before finding Angharad and Eira. I turned, slowly.

The archer stood not ten paces from me, arm drawn back and arrow pointed between my eyes. "Move once more and I'll let it fly," he warned.

His silver hair was long and straight, tied back from his face. He wore a thick brown bratt, clasped at his shoulder by a simple silver brooch. I squinted, making out the figure of a dog upon it. No. A wolf.

Selgovae. Any other would've killed me by now.

I lifted my hands slowly, wincing at the pain.

"Who are you?" he demanded.

It had been days, if not weeks, since I'd spoken aloud. Now that words were demanded, I could not find them. But the Dragon Warriors had heard the man's voice and scrambled from their pallets. They appeared at the mouth of the cave now, weapons drawn, ready to strike.

"I'd stay as you are," the archer addressed them. There was a sifting of snow, and I blinked as three dozen Selgovae armed with bows and spears stepped from trees where no men had stood only a moment before. We were outnumbered.

"Your name," the man said.

My voice was a husk. "Lailoken, son of Morken."

He studied me, his brown eyes keen. "You are counsellor to Uther Pendragon."

I looked down at the snow. "Uther Pendragon is dead."

"So they say," he answered. "Are these your men?"

I nodded. Maelgwn was Pendragon now, but I'd not endanger him by putting him forth.

"Dragon Warriors." The man stood back with his bow yet drawn, raking us over. "Battle-sick, the lot of you. Suppose you didn't think you were frightening our children, leaving the dead as you have, all scattered round our wood?"

We glanced at one another with a bewildered sort of shame, and Maelgwn took half a step forward. "I am sorry if we frightened your children. That was not our intent," he said.

"And who might you be?" the old man asked.

"Maelgwn. Pendragon's general." Maelgwn nodded at our men to lower their weapons, and at last I found my tongue.

"We sent our women and children into the wood. Have you seen them? Have you come across any others?"

"Could be so," the archer said gruffly.

"Sweet Gods." I took a breath to keep from weeping. "Please. Can you take us to them?"

The old man looked at me. "I suppose you're in want of shelter, too."

Shelter. We'd not thought to live long enough to need it. But to hear that Eira may have reached them, that she and the others might yet be safe? I looked at the nine of us. Half-starved, covered in filth and blood.

"We would be grateful for shelter if you might grant it," Maelgwn said.

"Call me Archer." The man lowered his bow, slinging it over his shoulder. "Come, then. I'll get you into the warm."

Snow creaked beneath our boots as we followed Archer and his men deeper into the forest. Shady dark towers of emerald pine. Oaks so vast we became little more than a wandering chain of beetles. There were fortresses buried in the Caledonian Deep for those who knew how to find them. I quickened my step to obey the drumming of my heart as Archer turned, cutting a path uphill into the snow. She would be there among the others, safe and warm by the hearth. She would turn as we opened the door, and I would see everything that had come to pass mirrored on her face.

The forest was silent in its drifting snow, silent and without wind. There were watchers in these woods; we should have known they had seen us. Now, as we moved farther into the Selgovian land, warriors draped in brown fur dropped from trees to follow us, faces impassive, impervious to cold. This old man Archer was a lord or I was mistaken. The Selgovae kept close to their gods and the beings of the old forest they tended. Those I'd met had little care for finery, though they possessed wealth in plenty, for they traded in furs—wolf, bear, rabbit, hind. Their huts were warm and dark, tight against the weather. Their halls were modest and made entirely from wood, devoid of the rich outer carvings beloved by our people.

Soon we reached the foot of another small hill, and their huts appeared, hunched beneath the snow-covered branches of the forest. People peered from opened doors, then disappeared quickly. I could not blame them, given the sight of us. At last we climbed an ice-slicked footpath through rusty spines of bracken, and my face was met with a gust of woodsmoke. The hall was long and narrow, with tidy thatching, a heavy set of oaken doors waiting beneath unadorned beams.

I followed the men inside, stepping into the dim of their feast room. Archer gestured to the far wall, where a cluster of figures sat by a pair of looms, nearer to the hearth light for weaving. I heard a sharp cry as they saw us, and my breath caught as a woman stood. Rhiwallon's lover rushed from the shadows, throwing herself into his arms.

Nine Dragon Warriors remained, and less than a score of women and children. The Selgovae waited in silence as we sought the faces of our loved ones in a room in which absence meant death. Seren, Dreon's wife, searched the men's faces eagerly, her arms wrapped round their children. There was a woman without her daughter. Three little boys, brothers, blinking in the dark. I swallowed the dryness in my mouth, my mind racing. Perhaps Eira was in another hut. Perhaps I had not yet seen her. But as my eyes grew accustomed to the low light, I could not deny it. Eira was not among them.

I ran a hand over my face. She was not here. How could that be? Across the room, Seren stood, Dreon's children clinging to her skirts. I went to her and reached for her hand. "He held the dyke," I said softly. "Dreon chose a hero's death."

Seren shook her head, her face reddening as she looked at me. "And what death did you choose?"

I bowed my head. "One that has not found me yet."

She did not release my hand. I waited until I could wait no longer. "Seren, please. Tell me what happened. Where is Eira? Where are the others?"

She drew back her hand to wipe her face, glancing at her children. "The others are gone," she said. "Warriors came upon us, and we ran. I found an overhang or we would've been taken. Taken or worse . . ."

My chest tightened. "And Eira—was she among them? Did you see where she went?"

Seren frowned. "Nay. Eira was not with us at all. She took us as far as the hill path, then turned back for the huts."

I shook my head. "No, she was with you. She swore it."

"I am sorry, Lailoken." She straightened, wiping her face. "You are not the only one who has lost their lover."

"Of course. I am sorry," I said, while fear crept into the pit of me.

"Here, you must drink. We have had nothing for days." Maelgwn's face was somber as he handed me a cup.

"She is not here," I said.

"No," he said gently.

I turned to him. "I cannot stay. I must go and find her."

"If you do, then you are a fool. Winter is upon us, and we are hunted men. Eira knows the Selgovian lands. I am sorry, brother, but you have taken leave of your senses. You must stay here, where Eira might find you. It may not be until spring, when the weather clears. But if she lives, she will come. You must believe it."

"Nay, Maelgwn. You do not understand."

Red and black banners swam in my vision, but I could not tell him what I knew. Yes, I'd hunted Gwrgi of Ebrauc even as he hunted me.

And on every encounter, he had slipped away. Why would the fates not deliver him to me?

I'd sworn Eira's secret was safe in my keeping. That she had once been known by another name. Her story had left me roiling with fury with no place to spend it. It had left me holding her in my arms as if she were a bird's egg that at any moment might break.

And by which name, then, shall I call you? I'd asked, drawing back gently to brush the tears from her face.

Eira, she'd said. *For it was the name I chose when I began again. And now I have found another beginning with you.*

No, I could not tell Maelgwn. I could only speak my fear—the fate that, for Eira, would be worse than any death.

"What if she was taken by Gwrgi?" I said.

Malegwn bowed his head. "If she was taken, Lailoken, then there is nothing we can do."

CHAPTER 14

Languoreth

Tutgual's Hall
Partick
Kingdom of Strathclyde
Samhain
31st of October, AD 573

The eve of our new year dawned misty, the air rich with the loam of wet autumn leaves. Beyond the gate came the steady clomp of cattle as the cowkeeps returned with their lords' herds from their high-summer steadings. A shiver traced my neck.

Word had come that Tutgual and his army would soon return, and we were to prepare a hero's welcome. This eve of shades and lost loved ones, when things happened beyond our understanding—this night was my only hope to salvage what family I had left. Once I'd seen Brodyn safe, then could I sit beside the fire and wait for Rhys to come. I would not curse Angharad by believing she was gone. But I would light the Samhain fire this night so that my firstborn child could find his way home.

The weaving room was empty of women.

"The queen must be yet in her chamber," Aela said, looking round as we entered. "Shall I let her know you are here?"

"Nay, but thank you, Aela," I said, adjusting my shawl to sit at my loom. "But there is another errand I'd have you attend to. There is a warrior who keeps guard by the pits by the name of Torin. Go to him and tell him the queen wishes to speak with him. You may deliver him here."

She hesitated, but bowed nonetheless. "Aye, m'lady."

Before long, I heard the efficient shuffle of Aela's leather slippers followed by a heavier bootstep, and Torin entered, shoulders tall and squared off, blue eyes confident. He was handsome, so perhaps he'd expected this—that he might someday catch the eye of Elufed. When he did not see her, he faltered.

"Come in," I said. "Sit down."

"I will stand," he said stiffly.

"Well enough."

"Shall I go, m'lady?" Aela asked, uncertain.

"Stay, Aela. Your presence is most welcome." I would not have talk of an affair with a soldier.

She sat in the corner of the room, and Torin cleared his throat. "I take it the queen does not seek me," he said.

"I fear not. At least not the queen you are thinking of. But there is another queen who seeks you—one who has yet to be anointed. My husband led a successful campaign. Rhydderch is favored by the council as well as his father. It is the queen of days to come who wishes to speak with you now."

I could see him taking my measure. His gaze flicked to Aela.

"You may speak freely," I said, beginning to work at my weaving.

"You wish me to free your cousin."

Across the room, Aela's eyes widened almost imperceptibly, but I knew how fond she was of Brodyn. She would not betray me. It was Torin I must be sure of.

"You interest me," I said. "I should like to learn more about your aspirations, Torin. Where do you come from? Who is your kin?"

"My father's lands lie on the Isle of Man."

"Your father is Turloch, then?" I brightened. "My father spoke of him. He thought him a strong and honorable chieftain. Why, then, do you seek your fortune elsewhere?"

"I have many brothers."

"I see. But why not serve in your father's guard? Or perhaps an elder brother's if you stand no chance to inherit?"

"I have proven my skill here."

I sat back from the loom to look at him. "Tell me why you left."

It was a request, not a command. I watched him battle himself. He did not wish to warm to me but found that he was. Charm was a proven skill of my own.

"I fell out with my brother."

"There was a young woman," I said gently. "I can see love's mark on you. You carry it like a boulder upon your back."

Torin did not answer, but I knew I had struck it.

"I have not seen your skill with weaponry," I continued, "but I am in need of a new captain of my guard. As you know, my cousin Brodyn is currently imprisoned. I needn't tell you it's likely he'll be killed."

I was not gifted with Angharad's sight, but I had learned much of people. Torin was a damaged fledgling of a warrior, bumped from the nest by his brothers. Perhaps someday he might earn Tutgual's notice. But Rhydderch had his own men—far beyond Torin's standing both in weapons and in blood—and it was these men who would rise with Rhydderch when he came to the throne.

It was a woman's right to choose her own guard. I could offer Torin a home. And even should he outgrow my nest, he'd stand a far better chance of catching Rhydderch's eye in safeguarding his wife than standing guard at the prison pits.

"And you will keep your word?" he asked.

"I will keep my word so long as you are proficient with a sword. Will you keep me safe?"

"Aye," he said. "I will."

"Good," I said. "But first you must see my elder cousin safely off to exile. I should like to know, though I may never again see him, that somewhere Brodyn of Cadzow will grow to be an old man. Do that, and the station is yours."

Torin's blue eyes went keen. I knew he was suited.

"Go on, then," I said with a smile. "Tell me your plan. Then I shall tell you mine."

A few hours before sunset, the children and I dressed in our dark clothes and winter-lined cloaks, and I took my seat beside them in the horse-drawn cart. A shock of golden elm leaves clung stubbornly to their branches against a dreary late-afternoon sky. Aela had kohled my eyes and polished my torque. Beside me, Gladys wore her chest-nut hair plaited and coiled, the bone comb that once belonged to my mother tucked gracefully at the back.

"It looks so well on you," I said, touching it. "And, Cyan, what a proper young lord you look."

Cyan brightened a little beneath my praise, and I gazed out the back of the cart as we left Tutgual's hall behind. We were meant to be decorations in Partick on days such as this.

At Cadzow, I kept holidays with our warriors and tenants as I pleased, seeing to the food and readying for the festivals. But here in Strathclyde's capital, I'd been warned that a balance must be struck. Tutgual permitted me and my children to attend the townspeople's festivities so long as I kept a measure of distance—that my influence not grow too great was left unspoken.

Strathclyde is a kingdom of two faiths now, he'd said. The king had made clear which faith he intended to win out. He had already banned female Keepers from his court by the time I wed Rhydderch, but many winters had passed since then, and the king did not yet have the power to also bar the men, for they held too much sway. More than half of Strathclyde's chieftains kept the old gods. And White Isle lay only a stone's throw upriver, where young male initiates yet went to train.

The tip of my nose was chill to the touch. Outside the cart, the road was lined with festivalgoers hurrying to the Samhain hill on foot, their children's faces disguised with woad and soot. They did not yet know of Tutgual's victory or the kingdom he had crushed. They knew nothing of Strathclyde's dead prince and lost princess. Uther was a hero and Emrys Pendragon before him. Tomorrow the crowds might hail their king, but for many, tears would fall in the silence of their huts. Gladys and I leaned out of the cart to wave, but Cyan sat still, watching.

"Cyan, it was not long ago I colored your face on such a night," I reminded him.

He looked at the children almost wistfully, then frowned. "Father Natan says Samhain is a foul night, filled with wicked and wandering spirits."

"Is that so? Just this night I saw Father Natan place an empty bowl at his table as I passed by his open door." I offered what I hoped was a smile. "Samhain is a night to honor our loved ones who have left us, Cyan. Even Tutgual's Christian counsellor seeks the blessing of his ancestors who have come before."

I spoke, yet all I could think of was Brodyn. Eight armed men had traveled with our cart—*For safety*, I'd said, hoping to draw as many men from Tutgual's hall as I could.

Elufed traveled in her own cart ahead. She would not keep the Samhain feast, but would attend to give the townspeople her blessing. She was a woman of Christ—or so Strathclyde believed. She bore witness to the baptisms or sent servants on her behalf; she joined the monks in prayer. Only I had seen her tuck aside a portion of food on Samhain night. Only I had seen her steal from the hall under the heavy cloak of darkness to stand barefoot in the courtyard, eyes fixed on the Hunter's Moon. Though her lineage as a Pict was broadly known, her allegiance was to Strathclyde, to her husband, to his god. Few knew the depth of her Pictish roots. And though her king professed to be Christian, still, each Samhain, all the fires of Tutgual's hall were duly snuffed out, to be relit with the flame kindled from the Samhain need-fire.

The crowds thickened as we drew nearer to the festival site. They peered into the cart as we passed; a dark-haired boy chewing an apple for good fortune, an old woman shaking her fist. "There rides Strathclyde's princess on this holy night as we travel by foot!" she cried out.

"Stop the cart!" Cyan shouted. "Mother, you cannot be disrespected! Have the soldiers give her a thrashing."

"Cyan!" Gladys exclaimed.

I looked at him. "Yes. Stop the cart," I called out.

"You shall see, Gladys. The poor cannot speak to us thusly," he said.

I accepted a soldier's hand and stepped down from the cart. The old woman and her boy had stopped, her face indignant, his uncertain. I strode toward her, my eyes upon hers. Then, placing my hand gently upon her arm, bowed my head and gave the Samhain blessing. "*Bendithio Samhain.*"

She considered me a moment in the way only an old women can, then nodded. "*Bendithio Samhain,*" she answered.

I smiled and gestured for her to lead on. Gladys, Cyan, and I followed behind on foot now. The look Cyan cast me was stormy. I turned to him, praying my lesson would not be lost. "Listen to your people, Cyan. Deaf tyrants are toppled. You would do well to remember that."

As we neared the top of the hill, I felt at last I could breathe. Meat dripped its juices from spits, soon ready for carving, and music carried on the air along with the sumptuous smell of roasted hazelnuts in honey. Angharad's favorite. Children raced round the hilltop and into the nearby wood, gathering ferns and thin stalks of *gàinisg*, tinder for the ritual fire.

Angharad would be one of them, I thought, and my longing was crippling.

But as I looked round the hilltop, I realized I was not alone in my suffering. For something was different. Hundreds had gathered. Yet before me stood only women and children. All of our men had been summoned to fight.

Even in my grief, I understood my good fortune. These women did not have the privilege of messengers. Only tomorrow—upon the presence or absence of a loved one's face—would they discover whether he lived or had died.

"Look, Mother!" Gladys pointed. "They've raised the tent."

The Keepers of White Isle walked the hilltop in their pearl-white robes, greeting the people and bestowing their blessings. But within the tent the priestesses were at work, readying for the rites.

"Go and help gather the tinder," I urged Cyan and Gladys. "It'll soon be dark."

To my surprise, Cyan followed his sister, and soon they, too, were galloping round the top of the hill, aiding the little ones who dropped sticks and nodding respectfully to the Keepers by the pyre. As the women stood, watching our children, we found solace, I think, in one another's eyes. We were the women, the life givers. The battle belonged to none of us here.

I was gazing rather absently into the wood when I felt the sudden touch of a hand clasping mine.

"*Bendithio Samhain.*"

I turned, startled to see an older man had come to stand beside me, joining his hand in mine as if he were my *taid*, a grandfather. His gray hair curled round his ears, and his beard was neatly kept. He wore brown trousers beneath a simple checked tunic, and his cloak was made of coarse wool that was equally unremarkable. My guards, of course, had failed to take notice. That or they simply did not care if a stranger should accost me.

"*Bendithio Samhain,*" I replied, bewildered. Truly, this man was far too familiar. Yet I did not wish to be rude. I'd just made a point of tutoring Cyan in how to be kind.

The man patted my hand, and as he did, I felt a soothing warmth surge through me. I'd heard about such people—those who could heal by a laying on of hands. There were Keepers who professed to do so, and Christians said Jesus of the Desert had been such a man.

"What sort of Keeper are you? Or are you a priest?" I asked, for it occurred to me that despite the fact he wore neither the robes of a Keeper nor the hood of a monk, he must indeed be one of the two.

"I am one who wishes to keep peace," he said.

I smiled. "Then you are a peace keeper," I said.

"Aye. Rather like you," he said, then turned to look at me. "I am so very sorry about the loss of your children."

I wanted to demand *How did you know?* But his blue eyes were brimming with compassion, with the love of a father. And my own father had been gone such a very long time. "I do not know if I shall ever recover," I whispered. I shared too much, yet could not stop myself.

"Time is not a masterful healer, but at least it is persistent," he said.

"Take comfort in those who are yet living. And take comfort from yonder hill."

I followed his gaze to the slope of Bright Hill. "Take comfort?" I asked in confusion. "What can you mean? That hill was taken in violence. Our sacred oaks cut down. There is a monastery now at the foot of Bright Hill. It was taken, and it is forever changed."

"Nay. For as long as there is memory, Bright Hill will remain just as it was. Memory, when preserved, can never be taken. You might tell them to remember."

"Tell whom?" I asked.

My children were brought up on the story of Bright Hill, I'd made certain of that. They knew well the tale of the pale-haired monk called Mungo who'd arrived in Partick and, soon after, buried a dead Christian on a hill sacred to the druids. In so doing, Mungo had nearly torn apart the kingdom of Strathclyde. I did not disguise my hatred for the man who was responsible for disfiguring my brother. He may have been exiled, but beasts must be remembered so they cannot be made again.

"Tell whom?" I asked again, turning, but the man was no longer beside me. I craned my neck only to catch sight of him retreating downhill. He did not look back, yet must have felt my eyes upon him, for he raised one hand in a gesture of farewell.

"Aela?" I called, seeking her out. "Did you see that man? That man just there!" I pointed, and she stood on the tips of her toes to peer above the crowd.

"Only now, m'lady. Who is he?"

"I don't know. He wouldn't say. But there was something about him. Something rather strange."

"Shall I call the guard?"

"Oh, no. No need for that; he isn't harmful. I'm sure of it."

"If you're certain?"

"Yes. It's all right. Never mind it."

Across the hill, the pyre towered in height. Suddenly the drums kicked up, sounding like a heartbeat from within the burlap tent. When the last light faded, the veil would lift, and the dark half of the year would be upon us.

Gladys and Cyan came running, cheeks bright from the chill. "Mother, we must take our seats!"

"Yes, Elufed will be waiting," I said, and Cyan came around to slip his hand in mine, a gesture not often extended. I offered my other arm to Gladys as we made our way into the thick of the crowd.

Elufed looked up as we joined her on the benches set aside for the *bonheddigion*, those of noble blood. "Where have you been? Never mind it. You look very well. Elegant."

"As do you."

She did look every bit Strathclyde's high queen this night, with her fair hair plaited and piled to reveal her slender neck, and her garnet brooch fastened at her breast. Snow-white ermine lined the hood of her cloak, setting off the winter gray of her eyes.

"Tell me again of the priestesses from Isle Cailleach," Gladys said, taking my hand.

"Well." I bowed my head. "Long ago, it was said they were weather workers. That, through fasting and suffering and prayer, they could move fog with their hands and draw rain in dry weather. On their isle in the loch, they live in utter seclusion. Neither man nor woman may trespass without invitation from the priestesses themselves. They leave their island only once, at Samhain, the turning of the year, to light the need-fire from the torches they kindle on the Cailleach's own isle."

"More likely, they kindle it from the inn down the lane," Cyan said.

"Nay, Cyan, it isn't so," I said. "They keep it close in oil lamps as they travel over the rough gray waters, bringing it in their caravan to this very site."

On the eve of Samhain, Britons snuffed out their hearths. Once the Cailleach lit the pyre, the people of Partick would touch their own tapers to it, carrying it home to relight their fires so their hearth might blaze through winter with the Cailleach's blessing.

"And is it true the priestesses must take turns playing the part of the Cailleach so they mightn't go mad?" Gladys asked.

I'd thought Elufed was not listening, but now she turned to Gladys with a frown. "They play at nothing," she said. "The Cailleach is winter and storm, death and blight. She destroys to create. She is not readily held in any woman's body, no matter how holy she may be."

"I understand," Gladys said, inclining her head.

I wondered, not for the first time, what long-buried memories these rites evoked for the queen. I wondered, but had learned better than to trespass.

The beat of the bodhrans thundered to crescendo, then stopped.

We stood, waiting for the processional of the Cailleach to begin.

The ancestors appeared at the crest of the hill, young initiates in tunics and bratts, their eerie white faces mirroring those of our ancestral dead. Their song was low and full of heartbreak. Haunting.

"They are recalling their time among us," I said.

Upon their heels came the harbingers of the dark time, of death. They lurched along the processional, naked chests painted black and hungry eyes scouring the crowd. Cyan edged closer on the bench as they stuck out their tongues and pulled frightening faces, making children cling to their mothers' skirts.

"Never fear," I whispered. "Now the Keepers shall come."

Their robes were the white of a swan's wing and glowed in the dim as they strode, banging their drums with purpose, sending death into the shadows to wait for its mistress. The crowd held its breath. And then they appeared.

The priestesses of Isle Cailleach.

Their robes were not the white of other Wisdom Keepers but a shade of dark blue. Their hair was hidden beneath the hoods of their cloaks, and their kohled eyes looked feral, the way a wildcat's appear just before it strikes. Two torchbearers guarded the need-fire in their covered lamps.

The horns sounded, discordant.

The priestesses parted to reveal the Cailleach.

She did not walk. Rather, she seemed to float, like wind over water. Her face was painted the hue of a storm cloud, her hair plastered in a snow-white paste so that it clumped and tangled over her shoulders, a wild woman of the highest peaks. The Cailleach did not wear a cloak. Hers was a heavy dress of gray wool with a bratt overtop. The last sheath of the grain crop decked her headdress, a thin linen veil coming down, concealing her face. One could feel the might of her with blinded eyes. But unlike her consorts of winter, the Cailleach did not pay the crowd any notice. She was to be gazed upon. She did not gaze back.

As the Cailleach neared the place where we stood, she stopped. The singing ceased. The faces of the priestesses flickered with surprise. And then the Cailleach turned her head.

I could not make out her face beneath the veil, but the power of her gaze struck like an adder. Was she looking at me?

I stood, unable to move, so heavy was the weight of her stare. Then she lifted her hand to beckon, and my throat tightened. There could be no question.

Me.

The priestess nearest the Cailleach spoke. "You. Come. The Cailleach wishes to see you."

The revelers parted in awe as I moved to do her bidding.

I'd only ever seen the Cailleach on procession. Now I stood before her.

In her veil, she was faceless. *Woman or god?* I could not quite say. Her storm-painted skin smelled of holy oils. When the Cailleach tilted her head to whisper in the ear of the priestess beside her, her voice was the hiss of ice on a fire.

"You will light the need-fire," the priestess said.

A gasp came from the crowd.

Me, light the need-fire? The blaze was lit by the Cailleach—it had always been so. What if the winter should bring bitter snows and starvation? I would be to blame. I could only imagine this was some sort of trick, a test of my devotion.

"I am no Wisdom Keeper. Nor am I a priestess. It is not my place. It is not my right," I said.

But the Cailleach only waited with an air of expectation. The priestess came forward, offering her lamp. There was nothing to do but accept the flame.

I stepped into the processional, following the Cailleach with the flame. As we reached the unlit pyre, the priestess turned. "You must speak," she said.

I was not trained to give the need-fire blessing. Searching, I looked out over the field of faces. Beyond the crowd was the rise of a distant hill, a sleeping blue shadow in the coming night.

You might tell them to remember, the old man had said. Now I understood. But was memory enough? I lifted my voice, hoping it would carry through the dark.

"There was a time when our need-fire was lit on the mount of Bright Hill," I began. "Where the old grove of oaks was tended by our Keepers, the memories of our people nestled in their roots. Our hearths extinguished, our kingdom waiting in darkness, the fire lit on Bright Hill was a beacon of light, of hope and blessings, of protection for our herds and our fields, our families and our flocks. Keepers from Strathclyde and beyond would wait for this signal to light their own blazes. Briton, Pict, or Scot—on Samhain, it matters not which kingdom we claim. On Samhain, the need-fire unites us all in one purpose. Honoring our ancestors and our gods." I searched the faces in the crowd. "Now Bright Hill is a tomb for those of a new way. Now we mourn loved ones sent off to war. And yet here we gather. Here we remain. This night we shall see that the fire of our ancestors cannot be so readily extinguished. Let our fire blaze on, let it carry our message to the hilltops of every land. The people of Strathclyde stand firm in our age-old tradition. The gods and goddesses of our land will yet reign."

I saw the light on their faces, yet the air was full of waiting.

The priestess brought me before the Cailleach, and I bowed my head to receive her blessing.

I felt the graze of her fingers on my temples. And then, as they met my skin, a pulsing like the clench of a heartbeat or the kick of an infant muffled by the depth of a mother's womb. It filled my ears with a rush as the crowd beyond fell away.

For a moment it seemed I stood on the top of a mountain, looking out far beyond the gray-green waters of the loch. I felt the thrum and churn of soil far beneath me and the gathering wet clouds as wind raced over the water. My body was stone. Wind and weather gathered at my head. My feet stretched their roots down through the mountain, connecting my tendrils across great distances, until I became every mountain that rose in our land.

Every cave and hollow was known to me then. I felt the curl of a bear as it bedded in a pile of winter leaves, the scratching of goat hooves upon salt-sprayed cliffs. I felt the whole of our vast island, thrumming from its core at the bottom of the sea.

And then she released me.

I stood, head spinning and senses overcome. Somehow I bent, uncovering the lamp, and touched the flame of the need-fire to the pyre.

The Cailleach lifted her arms, and for a moment it seemed as if she held all the great world between her two hands. The fire caught in a roar of orange flame.

It was done.

Drums struck up, and voices rang out in celebration. The Cailleach turned, her priestesses following as she retreated into the tent. Onlookers made way as I moved, light-headed, back to my seat.

Elufed reached out a hand to steady me. "The Cailleach has given you her blessing," she said.

"Yes."

She lowered her voice. "And before all the people. Soon the news will carry through the capital into Strathclyde and beyond. If Rhydderch has not proved his place, you have now secured it. But what you said to the people, Languoreth—you must not say such things."

"Nay, Elufed," I said, "I will keep silent no more. Bright Hill, and all we have lost, deserve the honor of our memory."

"You shall be little more than a memory should you speak like that again."

She might say as much, but the crowd had shifted. The people stood straighter. The fire burned in earnest now, and as I looked into the darkness, I saw jewels of distant fires lighting up the night. The skin of my temples yet buzzed where I'd felt the Cailleach's touch.

Later, as we rode home by cart, Gladys leaned in from the shadows. "Mother?"

"Yes, my love."

"When the Cailleach summoned you, were you not afraid?"

"I was not so much afraid. Awe was what I felt."

"Did you see her face?"

"Nay, I could not see beneath the veil. It did not seem . . . respectful to look."

She dropped her voice to a whisper. "What did it feel like when she blessed you?"

I thought a moment. "Like a thousand winters and a thousand summers all passed in one moment."

Gladys sat back. "I wonder if Angharad has ever felt such a thing."

At the mention of her name, we fell silent. It was a bottomless, wicked pain, the loss of a child. And it was such a very thin night. For a moment, across the distance, it was almost as if I could feel her, lost and alone.

I closed my eyes. *Keep her safe*, I begged the Cailleach, queen of death.

Rhydderch would be searching. I had to believe Angharad would yet be found.

The cart jolted to a stop in the courtyard. As we climbed down I heard the men bolt the gate behind us. It felt as if I were being sealed in a tomb.

But this night was not yet finished. Across the courtyard, Torin met my eyes, then turned from the gate to stride back toward his post at the pits.

Samhain would work its mysteries yet.

CHAPTER 15

Angharad

Battle of Arderydd
Kingdom of the Pendragons
October, AD 573

The dark-haired woman had led her astray.

The dark-haired woman had led them into a terrible trap.

Why, oh why, had she trusted her vision? The spearman had called Eira a horrible thing. Lord Gwrgi now rode at the head of the scouting party. Angharad looked over her shoulder, but Eira did not look back. The soldier gripping Eira's rope was giving no slack, she had to nearly run to keep from dragging behind his horse, and her breath was coming fast, her face red with exertion. Tears welled in Angharad's eyes. She wanted to beat at their captors with her fists. This was all her fault, she thought. She could stay silent no longer.

"Unbind her at once!" Angharad shouted. "You cannot treat her so. I swear to you, you shall pay when I tell my father!"

The spearman did not look at her, only yanked the line, and Eira fell hard upon her knees, plummeting forward as he kicked his horse into a trot. She cried out as her arms jerked at the shoulders, her body dragging along the forest floor.

"Stop, stop!" Angharad screamed. Pulling his mount unhurriedly to a halt, the spearman turned at last.

"Go on, then," he said. "Give me another order."

Eira scrambled to her feet, reaching gingerly to explore her face. Pebbles and sticks had left her already swollen features scraped and bleeding. "Angharad, please. Say nothing more, I beg you," she said.

Angharad swallowed, forcing herself to look away. Satisfied, the soldier urged his mount into a walk.

Lailoken had taught Angharad to be faithful to the urgings that rose within her, but since the battle, everything Angharad heeded had been wrong. She could not trust her own senses. Now, as they moved through the forest, Angharad struggled to gain her bearings, but the woods felt like a stranger. By day's end, they'd begun to climb. The track took them into the hills and through a lofty pass. She heard Gwrgi's camp before they reached it—the clumsy plucking of a *cruit* came through the trees along with men's voices and the fatty smell of roasted meat. Gwrgi had said he meant to summon her father, and she believed that to be true. She and Eira must only bide their time. Her father would set things right. He would make that spearman pay.

A score of tents was pitched on the high ground beyond the forest. Warriors milled the grounds, some sharpening their blades, some sitting round gaming boards, while watchmen strode the perimeter with a satisfaction only victors wore. Up ahead, Gwrgi dismounted, and the warrior bearing Angharad drew up on his horse.

"My lord. Where do you want the girl?"

"Put her in my tent."

"And the other?"

"See that she minds the girl twice daily. Otherwise, take her. I have no taste for mutton."

Angharad looked to Eira in panic as the spearman dropped from his horse and began to pull Eira away. All Angharad could think to do was scream. She opened her mouth and let out an ear-splitting cry. The horse that held her reared up as Angharad let out another scream and another. The warrior wrenched the reins to settle his mount as Gwrgi reached for Angharad and grabbed the length of her hair, yanking her from the horse. Her neck twisted, and her cry was of a different sort as she slammed to the ground.

"Silence!" Gwrgi shouted, smothering her mouth with his fist, but Angharad's fury burned hotter than her fear, and she bit down on the fleshy part of his fist and spat, tasting blood. He wrenched his hand away in pain and surprise, and she kicked and thrashed away from him, screaming and screaming even as she stood. The lord of Ebrauc's face contorted with rage and his arm flew back. Angharad winced, but no blow came. Angharad opened her eyes and stilled her mouth. Gwrgi stood within a hair's breadth of her, a strange look on his face.

His hand wept blood as he lifted his palms to cup her face. Beyond them, the camp was silent, the eyes of Gwrgi's men upon them. Gwrgi only sighed and traced his thumb along her cheekbone, smearing his own blood like battle paint. "Look what you have done." He pressed closer.

Angharad did not understand. "I want my nursemaid!" she said.

"And you shall shriek until you have her, is that it? I should almost like to hear it. The sound of your cries as you scream yourself raw. Rhydderch's daughter or no, you mistake yourself if you imagine I do not thrill to a little girl's cries. But you irritate my men, and you startle our horses."

Gwrgi's breath was hot on Angharad's cheek. She did not move. Then he blinked, looking round as if recovering himself. He stood, smoothing the lower portion of his tunic. "Take them both. We are wasting good light. I would see if we can catch more Dragons before nightfall."

Eira clutched Angharad as the two were escorted to Lord Gwrgi's tent. Inside, it was dim, more cramped than the sorts of tents Angharad had bedded in before, the spacious chambered tents at Lughnasa.

There was a rude sheepskin pallet laid upon the ground. A trunk that likely contained Gwrgi's clothes. A tincture that wafted fennel sat beside a wooden comb on a rickety pine table. It was the same scent that clung to the wretched man, and to distract herself, Angharad searched her memory for its purpose. The seeds came from across the sea at some expense; the plant did not favor the clime of the Britons. Yes, that was right. Mother had prepared it to aid stomach pains.

"He's ill," Angharad said. "There is a rot in his stomach. Perhaps his wickedness shall eat him from the inside out."

But Eira was not listening. Eira was not well. Her swollen face was drawn with the fear of a child as she paced the confines of the tent, her breathing shallow. "I cannot be here, I mustn't be here . . ." Her voice was a panicked whisper as she looked about as if in search of escape. It was as if she were going mad. "I cannot be here, I cannot—"

"Eira!" Angharad grabbed her, beseeching, and Eira startled as if struck, wrenching away from her.

"Oh, Angharad," she said, her voice a whisper. "You do not understand." Eira sank down, bound hands cradling her own head.

Angharad could feel Eira's fear as if it were a creature and it beckoned—it wanted to show Angharad its secret. Eira's secret. But Angharad did not like the feel of it—there was a clever sort of wickedness, like that of a water spirit that lured fishermen to their death. And she had sworn she would not seek after it. She sat down instead beside Eira and did as Lailoken had taught her. She was a flower, drawing her petals closed against night. Nothing came when Angharad was enfolded like this. From outside the tent came the sound of horses galloping away.

Eira lifted her head slowly, speaking softly so the guards beyond the tent could not hear. "We cannot stay here, Angharad. You are not safe. I imagined Gwrgi could abide by his vows, but I fear he is not his own master. It is not only his stomach that harbors a sickness. You are young. You cannot understand. But you must trust me. We must leave this night."

Angharad leaned her head to Eira's. For a moment, even though it had been Gwrgi who'd discovered them, it had seemed so close—that Angharad might go home. "But my father?" she asked, her voice small.

"We must find our own way."

They startled as the tent opening slapped and a warrior came bearing a platter of food. He set it down upon the trunk along with a jug of drink. "Eat," he said, and left.

Eira reached shakily for the jug before Angharad remembered her bound hands and reached quickly to pour ale into the waiting cup.

"Thank you," Eira said. They took turns, drinking it down thirstily.

"Give me your hands. I shall cut the bindings." Angharad reached for the knife belted at her waist, and Eira's good eye widened in surprise.

"Your mother's blade!" she whispered. "Oh, thank the blessed gods, I'd nearly forgot. Cut it just here, Angharad, we must be able to retie it so they mightn't notice." Angharad did as she was told, and they ate in silence, for Eira seemed deep in thought.

Soon as they had eaten their fill, Eira leaned in. "Would that we could leave now, but there is too much light. I fear we will be caught. We must wait until dark. Tonight, when I tell you, you must run. Fast as you can! No matter what. You must run to the woods, and take cover in the nearest thicket you should find, and bury yourself amongst the leaves. Can you do that?"

"Yes," Angharad said.

"It will be dark, and they will not expect you to stay so close."

"And you will be right behind me. You will bury yourself, too."

"Yes, I shall be right behind you, and I shall do the same. You must lie still for a long while, 'til they've come back from their search, 'til they've given up looking. Then I will call to you. When you hear my voice, you may come out. But you must promise me one thing."

Eira paused.

"You must swear to me that no matter what, you will not look back." Eira's gaze was fixed to the ground.

"But you will be right behind me."

"Yes. I will be right behind you. But you must swear now."

"I swear."

"What do you swear?" Eira lifted her eyes, locking them on Angharad's. "Angharad, you must say it."

The hardness in Eira's voice brought a tremble to her lip, but Angharad repeated the words. "I swear I will not look back."

The weight of what they must do felt overwhelming. Fat, silent tears rolled down Angharad's face, and Eira reached tenderly to draw her near, cradling Angharad to her chest. "Oh, my love," she murmured.

"I am so afraid."

"Do not be afraid. You will be gone in a blink, and they shall never find you. Think of your mother. Think of your father. You are such a very brave girl. Braver than any I have ever met."

Eira bent to kiss her brow, then straightened, a newfound determination in her voice.

"Now, then," she said. "Give me your knife."

The camp was quiet. Moments stretched, and Angharad's body began to betray her, remembering a comfort nearly forgotten: a full stomach. As darkness fell beyond the tent, her limbs grew heavy, her eyes dropping in sleep. Music drifted. Laughter. But it was the jeering of men that rattled her awake. She sat upright, blinking.

A candle burned in an iron holder on the pine table, and on Gwrgi's trunk, a clay oil lamp had been brought in for light.

"That's right, little one. Keep awake if you can. You must be ready when the moment comes." Eira's face was etched with pity in the dim.

Soon the scouting party returned. They waited in the silence of the tent as the men whooped and hollered, their ears straining for the sound of prisoners, but there did not seem to be any. The mood in Gwrgi's camp was celebratory that eve, and the men drank long into the night. Angharad lay, stomach churning with nerves, her head resting on Eira's lap. A few times she must have drifted into sleep, for she woke to Eira's gentle shake and the feeling her nursemaid had allowed more rest than she knew. And then, just as it seemed the night would never end, voices sounded, nearing the tent.

Angharad did not need waking then. Her blood raced already at the thought of what she must do, and it took all of her might not to burst from the tent like a flushed quail when Gwrgi's voice came.

"Take the nursemaid. Keep her away."

"Aye, my lord." The man's voice sounded hesitant. "But what of the girl's father?"

"She's only a speckled little chick . . ."

Angharad did not hear what he said next, for Eira's whisper was a rush in her ear. "When I strike them, you must run."

She nodded as Eira stood and snatched up the oil lamp, pressing flat against the wall of the tent, just beyond the opening.

Escape seemed impossible.

But Angharad could not think of that.

She must only run.

Cold air gusted in as Gwrgi and his warrior pushed through the tent flaps, their faces lit ghoulish in the low light. Then, in the moment before their eyes adjusted, Eira struck, shattering the clay lamp over the warrior's head. Oil and shards scattered over the bedding as Angharad scrambled to her feet, and the warrior dropped, senseless and bleeding, to the floor. But Gwrgi was not senseless. He looked at

Eira, hunched, ready, holding Angharad's knife, and raised his dark brows as if this were all a wonderful game. "Your hair is darker," he said. "And your face fouled from beating, but I do say you remind me of a girl I once knew."

Eira's face hardened and she lunged at him. "Angharad! Go!" she cried. But Gwrgi dodged the stab of her knife and turned to face her, arms barring the opening, eyes lit like a demon in the dark.

"Nay, little chicky, don't go," he said. "It'll be worse for you if you do."

Angharad looked between them, heart hammering. Eira's eyes strayed to the little pine table where the single candle yet burned. They both moved at the same moment, Eira kicking the table over as Gwrgi lunged for her, knocking her from her feet. Shouts rang out from the camp as the candle toppled onto the sheepskin bedding, fire catching the oil from the shattered lamp.

"Run!" Eira shouted. Gwrgi was on top of her, wrestling for the knife as she slashed, cutting his face. He struck her and she turned to Angharad, eyes wide with terror. "Angharad, run!"

Angharad ran.

Men were rushing toward the tent now, spears lifted and swords drawn, but their limbs were sluggish from drink, and Angharad was a flash in the dark. She did not feel the pain from her blisters. Rhys had taught her to duck and to dive. To feign. And so when a warrior closed in, she threw a feint, and as he lunged, she slipped by him like a river eel, streaking into the woods.

She raced on, arms pumping, trying not to crash into tree limbs and boulders in the blackness. She knew the thicket when she saw it.

Here. It gave her its promise.

The warriors were thundering into the forest behind her, leaves scattering in a storm as Angharad dropped into the thicket, scurrying on her belly into its heart. Rolling hurriedly onto her back, she swept loose leaves over her prone body with outstretched arms, then yanked two of the nearest branches to cover her, fighting to silence her breath.

Brown as dirt, she thought.

"Where's she gone?" someone called out.

"She can't have got far."

She was certain they would hear her pounding heart. The thicket was scarcely large enough to shelter a deer. Surely they would see her. Surely they would discover her and drag her back to the tent.

But just then, something sounded in the forest beyond. The sound of a cry that might have belonged to a child.

"This way," the warrior barked as they crashed away through the forest.

Angharad dared not move.

One summer, not long ago, she and her mother had stumbled upon a fawn curled beneath a shrub in Cadzow's wood.

"Mother, look!" she'd exclaimed. The creature looked up at Angharad, long lashes blinking, seemingly unafraid. Its pelt was speckled, its nose smooth as a river stone. Kneeling down, she reached to stroke it.

"No! Do not touch it," her mother said quickly. "Your scent will frighten off its mother."

"But its mother has left it," Angharad said, saddened.

Her mother moved to stand beside her. "A mother never leaves her young. She's gone foraging so she can provide milk, but she will not be far. A mother always returns."

The memory was too much. Rolling onto her side, Angharad curled tight, hugging her knees to her chest. Her mother would never return, for her mother had not left her. Her mother had given her away.

And now Angharad had abandoned Eira, the woman who'd become her own family.

The look of terror on Eira's face was etched in Angharad's mind. She heard the sound of Gwrgi's blow, bone against flesh.

You're a coward, Angharad admonished herself.

But Eira had made her swear. And if she could find her father, she could save her friend.

The silence of the forest was unnerving. But Angharad should have welcomed it. She knew that now. For the silence did not last.

She had been listening all the while, praying to the gods that somehow Eira had escaped, that she would come calling as they had planned, but Angharad was some distance from the camp now, or so she thought. It was not until the men returned that she realized how near to the tent she must be.

The sound of Eira's screams echoed through the night.

Angharad could not see the blows, only hear the sounds that issued from Eira as she felt them. The sound of Eira's suffering stabbed, and Angharad flinched with every cry, beating at her ears as if she could block them from hearing.

It continued for eternity.

Then, sometime before dawn, Eira's cries faded away.

Angharad did not feel cold, though her body shook. She knew she should make her way through the woods while darkness yet clung, but she could only lie there, eyes swollen, blinking.

The sun rose. The men whistled, and she smelled a cook fire lit. She heard the early-morning clamor that came with packing up camp.

She needed to relieve her bladder but dared not stand. It seemed wrong to make water, to be whole and unharmed, when Eira lay in suffering on the very same earth only a short distance away. But Angharad's body would not be denied. She spread her legs, peeing where she lay. Wetness soaked her thighs, and she felt like a baby.

By midmorning, Gwrgi's men were gone.

CHAPTER 16

Angharad

Angharad crawled out from beneath the underbrush and moved her feet—one, then the other. Again.

Soon she was walking.

Angharad had no idea where she might be, only that they had traveled some distance. She was nearing the farthest reaches of Gwenddolau's land, that much was certain. Angharad looked up into the bare-branched trees. She was alone in the wood, but she did not fear wolves or bears or wild boar. Angharad feared only men.

Birds called. Her feet thudded against leaves. Her stomach grumbled. She did not know which way to go, only that she must go in the direction opposite Gwrgi and his men.

Up ahead stood a copse of mossy-footed beech trees, their thick silver fingers stretching gracefully toward the sky. The forest floor was covered in mound moss and dead leaves, and Angharad's footsteps spoke as she shuffled uncertainly into the grove. *Shush shush shush.*

The air within it felt peaceful. Welcoming and safe. It lacked scrub for shelter, but there was an abiding stillness here that urged her to rest.

In the center of the copse she spotted a magnificent old beech with a depression at its base, as if a deer might have bedded there. She would sit, if only for a moment. Perhaps then she might know which way to go. The moss sprouting from the trunk was dry from too little rain, and as she leaned against it, Angharad knew the tree was quite thirsty.

I have no water, either, she thought.

She was so accustomed to being held by her mother and father. By Eira or Lailoken. Being held by a tree was different. Its body was unforgiving, where her mother's was smooth and soft in all the right places, a happy dream. But beneath the bark, the tenderness Angharad felt was a mother's touch without fingers. It traveled in gentle waves against her back, filling her body with a remedy she could not quite comprehend.

I am lost, Angharad told the tree, tears rising in her throat.

Not lost, the tree replied. *Just where you need to be.*

"How can you say such a thing?" Her voice was loud in the quiet of the grove.

It was clear the tree did not understand what had happened. Angharad closed her eyes to share the flashes of violence and gore now trapped within her skull. The death her father and Tutgual had brought with their war. A chill breeze kicked up, rustling the branches of the grove like a sigh.

Not lost, it repeated. *Just where you need to be.*

The old beech was not bothered. It only held her, in its way. The woods always spoke in whispers. Still Angharad did not understand. Should she wait precisely where she was, or continue in the direction she'd been walking?

Does this way lead to my father? she asked. But the tree had nothing more to say.

After a while Angharad realized it was early afternoon. Night would soon come, and she needed warmth and shelter. Her body ached, wracked with exhaustion from her night in the cold, and she longed for a draught of her mother's elderberry and honey drink. No. Safe as she felt, she could not linger any longer. Angharad pressed her cheek against the old beech tree's trunk. *Thank you,* she said.

The dark-haired woman might have tricked her, but trees never lied. Somehow, she was just where she was meant to be.

There was always a river. Eira had taught her that. She mightn't know which river she searched for, but if she could find any river at all, surely there would be travelers upon it. Surely there would be someone who'd help send word to her father. The thought was enough to rouse her to her feet.

Please, she begged. *Which way to the river?*

She waited, fearful at first that no sign would come. Then she decided to wait with expectance. After all, the old beech had told her she was just where she needed to be, so why would the woods not show her the way? Then she saw it. A bird alighting on an ash tree beyond the grove. Angharad whispered her thanks and followed.

There. In the distance, a rusty spray of fern caught her eye. Beyond it, the faint outline of a herd trail. Each time Angharad was in doubt, something came to show the way. A roe deer, as if waiting. Sometimes it was only the encouragement of a gentle wind, or a rustle in a thicket.

Twilight threatened, yet still no river came in sight. Then, at an oak, the path she had been following suddenly branched. Just as Angharad began to despair, she saw it, half buried in leaves, a few paces from her feet.

A feather. Angharad burst into tears. "Mama!" she cried. She crouched to grab it before it could blow away, pressing it to her chest as if it could save her, as if it could seal the leaking wound of her heart. Her voice was a whisper in the woods. "Mama."

Even though the sight of it pained her, for the first time since striking out that morning, Angharad did not feel so alone. She stood slowly, tucking the feather into her tunic for safekeeping. There must be something up ahead, something that would help her find her way home. And yet she dared not fully believe.

She followed the path as it twisted through a stand of papery birch. Then she blinked.

A roundhouse stood at the far side of a clearing. It was reed-roofed, with walls made of wattle and daub. No smoke breathed from the thatching, and the little wooden door seemed to keep watch like a sentinel. Angharad remembered the dead man with staring eyes in their hut. But she was tired and hungry, and the feather was tucked close to her heart. Quickly, she took her torque from her neck, securing it beneath her tunic with her belt. Better to keep it safe. She could always reveal it if need be. Then she hobbled toward the hut, stopping at the door.

A symbol was marked in charcoal on the wood, a circle sprouting a cross beneath it. Angharad knew the symbol well—her brother Cyan often traced it on slate. It was meant to be the Christ God, pierced upon the cross.

The hut lay within the confines of her uncle's kingdom, yet a Christian mark had been made upon the door, and the hut was not in cinders.

This hut had been spared whilst the others had been burned.

No sound came from within as Angharad reached for the latch. Swinging open the door, she squinted into the gloom.

Empty, it seemed. As her eyes grew accustomed to the dim, she made out a hearth pit in the center with an iron cookpot suspended above. A wooden bed covered with a sheepskin blanket sat opposite a table set with one stool, one wooden bowl, an eating knife, and one spoon. Angharad stepped inside.

The earthen floor was neatly swept, and before the bed lay a simple reed mat.

All was spare, save one detail. Hung round the room, high and low, secured by tiny iron nails, were dozens upon dozens of carved wooden crosses.

This was the house of a monk.

Father Natan at Partick spoke of men who sought Christ in solitude, traveling deep into forests, glens, and mountains to dwell and worship their god. He'd given a name for such men: culdees. Perhaps this hut belonged to such a monk.

Beside the hearth, she spied a flint and birch shavings for tinder. The pit was stacked with peat, and on the table, a little clay pot of reeds sat to light tapers from the hearth fire.

Wherever the monk had gone, he'd soon return. Surely he would not turn away a child. She crouched and set to work showering the birch shavings with sparks until they caught. Soon flame licked, catching the peat.

With the turf burning, the hut seemed warm and almost friendly. Angharad's stomach kicked with hunger, and she looked round, wondering about food. Everything was ordered; only the reed mat before the bed lay slightly askew. Pushing it aside, she found two short planks set over a hole dug into the ground. Foodstuffs had been squirrelled away: a loaf of barley bread. Flour, oats, and a jar full of honey.

"Oh," Angharad breathed, fingers nearly trembling. Food, food! She snatched up the loaf and the sack of oats, carrying them to the table. She had just begun to slice a thick hunk of bread when a voice came from above.

"Hello."

With a shriek, Angharad turned and looked up. A face hovered in the beams over the doorway, glowing orange in the turf light. She spun round to face it, the knife in her hand sending oats from the sack scattering like snow. If the thing fell upon her, she would stab it, then run, she decided.

"Nay, nay," the face said. "Please. Don't be frightened. Here. Let me come down."

Her eyes widened as the face drew into the light, attached to a neck and a lean set of shoulders. It was not a monstrous beast after all, but a man dressed in brown clothing. To his rough brown tunic, he'd affixed panels of reeds, and his face was smeared with something viscous and brown. Angharad blinked in astonishment. He had disguised himself! He'd been watching from the rafters all the while.

"Please. There's nothing to fear, it's only mud," the man explained.

Still, Angharad gripped the knife as he dropped to the floor with the grace of a stable cat. His eyebrows were sandy, like her uncle's, but thick and drawn in what looked like concern. His light eyes appeared kind. But Angharad did not trust men, even ones who might claim to be holy.

The man stepped closer, and Angharad stabbed at the place between them with the knife. "Get away!" she shrieked.

"I am Brother Thomas," he said evenly. "And who might you be?" When Angharad did not answer, he lifted his hands. "I will not harm you. I only wish to help."

Angharad searched his eyes, trying to take his measure, but came up wanting and frowned. *How curious*, she thought. She tried once more but felt as though she'd run headlong into a drystone wall.

"Are you a monk?" she asked tightly.

"Of a sort," Brother Thomas said.

"Are you a culdee, then?"

"Yes." He smiled. "The same. So you have heard of my kind."

Angharad gave a slight nod.

"Good! Then you know I will not harm you. Come. Set down that knife and tell me your name."

She did not set down the knife. "I'm called Angharad," she said.

"Angharad," he repeated. "I know the name well, but she is the young daughter of Rhydderch. Rhydderch of Strathclyde." The way he spoke, Angharad understood that somehow, he already knew it was she. "Whatever are you doing here, so far from home?" he asked. "You find yourself in the middle of a war."

Angharad had been fleeing the battle for two days in a waking nightmare. Now, as she heard her father's name and the tenderness with which Brother Thomas asked what had befallen her, the dam keeping back her tears splintered and gave way. Dropping the knife to the table, she began to cry.

Brother Thomas moved carefully to sit beside her. He did not try to embrace her, only sat. "Whatever has happened, you are safe here," he said. "You are safe."

Safe. The word only made Angharad's breath turn shallow, for Eira's screams had come again, resounding in her head. She pressed her hands over her ears, shaking her head with a wail.

The monk drew her to him so efficiently, so assuredly, Angharad did not even think to resist. She curled into him as if his arms were a cave, and as he embraced her, a wave of calm came over her. She drank and drank from it, until gradually, her breathing slowed, and her eyes dried out, wrung of all their water.

After a while Brother Thomas stood and went to the cookpot, pouring some liquid from a jug into its belly and setting it over the fire to boil. "You will be hungry, I imagine," he said. "Take off those soggy boots, if you will."

Angharad bent and gingerly removed them, watching hungrily as he took up the sack of oats from the floor and sifted a portion into the pot.

"Why were you concealing yourself?" Angharad asked carefully.

Brother Thomas cut a thick slice of bread, slathering it with a dollop of honey before placing it before her. She stuffed it into her mouth without shame.

"You are not the first to stumble upon my hut. Some days ago, a soldier came to my door. He knew me for a man of god. He told me I must mark my door with the sign of the cross and no harm would befall me. Since then, not only men of Ebrauc have come, but many who are in need. They rifle my belongings, take my food, my warmth, and my hut, all of which are given freely. Sometimes I am here, sometimes I conceal myself in the rafters or the trees. They soon depart. I do not play at sides. A need is a need."

"And what of the Dragon Warriors?" Angharad asked eagerly. "Have you seen any of Pendragon's men?"

"Nay. An elderly tenant who did not muster to fight. A mother and two boys. No Dragon Warriors," he answered.

Angharad's shoulders sank. Still, it could be that her uncle survived. He'd promised to find her and Eira with the Selgovae should they make it to the Caledonian Wood.

Brother Thomas stood as if waiting for an explanation, but when she gave none, only shrugged. "You've spilled my oats, Angharad of Strathclyde. Go, then, and pick them up. As you know, food is quite hard to come by."

His face was stern, but his voice was gentle. Angharad eased to her feet and accepted the oat sack from him, bending to collect them flake by flake. An impossible task.

"There will soon be more food," she said quietly. "The battle is over now. My father has won."

Brother Thomas checked the cookpot, then moved to the table and began to untie his reed wrappings from about his middle. "The battle is not over. It has only just begun. You and I are speaking of different battles, I think."

Angharad looked up. This culdee was full of riddles. "Which battle do you speak of?"

"If you do not know already, I fear you will soon discover it."

It felt like a warning, but the stab of Angharad's hunger left little space for talk of such things. The oats were ready. Brother Thomas drew out the stool from the table and gestured for her to sit. Saliva pooled as she watched him serve two steaming ladles of porridge into a wooden bowl and top it with a scattering of hazelnuts. Fixing himself a helping, he crouched beside the fire and murmured a blessing. The culdee had removed his reed dressings, but his face was yet darkened with mud.

"You conceal yourself in the rafters, even whilst men and women are sleeping below?" Angharad asked. Brother Thomas gave a slight nod. "And they do not see you?"

"They do not see me until I wish to be seen. As it was with you."

"But that is a gift of a Wisdom Keeper."

"If you believe such things are only for Wisdom Keepers, you know very little of God," he said.

They ate awhile in silence, porridge warming her from the inside out, soothing places that were raw—her throat from screaming and tears, her stomach from its near-continual twisting in fear and grief, hunger and revulsion. Somehow, she'd forgotten the blisters on her feet and the prickers embedded in her hands. But now that Angharad sat in the warmth, the skelfs that Eira had been unable to remove ached and pulsed, biting little things.

Brother Thomas must have been observing the way Angharad hobbled and cradled her spoon, for he glanced at her bowl with a nod. "If you are finished, we must dress your wounds."

He moved to the wooden shelf on the wall, squinting at a tidy row of earthen jars before selecting one, then prepared some soft linen wrappings.

"Dry your feet by the hearth whilst I tend to your hands," he said, waiting. Angharad offered her palms hesitantly. He took them gently, tilting them to the light. "Thorns," he observed.

"No digging."

"Very well. I will not dig," he said. "But the holes are going sour."

"No digging," she insisted.

"As you say." Brother Thomas lowered his head and began to clean away the dirt. "I imagine you are looking for your father."

Angharad nodded, averting her eyes as he worked.

"It is chaos beyond this door. Something that once might have been so simple is not so simple now."

"But he is searching for me," she said.

"Then he has had very ill luck. And where did you think to encounter him?"

"I was looking for the river when I came upon your hut."

"I see." His eyes were so kind, Angharad wanted to tell Brother Thomas of all that had transpired. But he was a stranger, and a man, and the well of her sorrow was too deep. He sat back a moment, then began carefully applying the salve.

"There was a time long ago when I found myself full of thorns," he said. "They had pierced the skin, embedded."

"How did it happen?" Angharad looked at him, curious.

"A thorn is a thorn. How it came to be does not matter so much. It was what I learned that is perhaps more important. Pluck the thorn, and it is gone from you. The hole will heal, and your skin soon forgets. Let it linger, and in time, your body may eat the thorn away, bit by bit. But it will never be gone from you. The thorns will be in your blood, going round and round within you, forever."

He glanced up as if to make sure she understood. Angharad looked down at her palms, and suddenly, it was as if she stood once more upon the heights of Caer Gwenddolau, the battle raging all around her, the cries of men making her cringe, the shouts as the warriors hacked, splitting each other's bodies as she struggled to descend the cliff. She had lived there little more than one year, but Caer Gwenddolau was her home. She did not want to forget.

"Leave them," she said.

"As you say." Brother Thomas wrapped her hands, securing the linens with a knot. "The salve will draw out the heat. We will wrap them along with your feet and change the dressings in the morning."

"Thank you," she said. "And in the morning, if I am well enough, will you help me find my father?" She tried to sound brave but could not keep her voice from wavering.

Brother Thomas paused a moment, searching her. Angharad tried to hide from his scrutiny but knew it was too late. He'd seen within her, seen the girl yet trapped in the dark of a forest, belly pressed to the earth beneath an autumn thicket.

Brother Thomas bowed his head, his face somber. "Yes. If you feel well enough on the morrow, I will do my best to help you find your father."

His gaze was distant as he finished dressing the blisters on her feet and stood to put away the salve. He fluffed the straw-stuffed pallet of the bed, lifting the sheepskins to shake them out. "You may sleep here," he said, gesturing.

Angharad moved gratefully to the bed, slipping beneath the fleece. Brother Thomas checked the bolt on the door before adding more turf to the fire, then drew the reed mat beside the hearth. Lying down upon it, he folded his arms beneath his head to make a pillow. A culdee. And one who could mask his presence, just like Diarmid and her uncle.

"You asked how I came to be here," Angharad said. "I was training with my uncle to become a Wisdom Keeper."

Brother Thomas did not turn. "Your uncle is Lailoken."

"Do you know him?"

"I know only that he is Uther Pendragon's counsel. He and Uther were good enough to grant me peace here in the forest, at the edge of their lands."

"Diarmid the Seer was teaching me how to cloak myself," Angharad said.

"Ah."

"Do you know how to cloak yourself?"

Brother Thomas seemed ill at ease with her question. "Culdees are not like other monks" was all he said.

"Then I am glad to have found a culdee."

Brother Thomas was quiet.

"My father did not trade for me," Angharad said. "He knew I was within the fortress. He attacked us all the same."

"Perhaps he meant to rescue you. Perhaps he meant to find you," he offered.

"But he did not."

"No. He did not." That the culdee acknowledged it did not heal, but it granted Angharad comfort.

"Rest now, Angharad, and sleep well," Brother Thomas said.

Angharad shifted upon the bedding, and her torque scraped against her back, but its presence was reassuring. *Remember who you are*, it said. Angharad looked up at the reed roof, willing sleep to find her. All was silent, the only sounds the soft burn of turf and the gentle draw of Brother Thomas's breathing. But in the silence, she still heard Eira weeping.

Beneath her dressings, thorns pulsed into Angharad's blood the things she would never forget.

CHAPTER 17

Languoreth

Tutgual's Hall
Partick
Kingdom of Strathclyde
Samhain
October 31st, AD 573

The children were asleep when Elufed caught my elbow, just inside the door.

"Whatever are you doing?" she whispered. "You must not be seen
by the pits this night!"

I steadied the oil lamp between my hands, the door still open at my
back. "The pits? I've only left an offering for the *aos sí*."

Elufed peered beyond me to the basket I'd left for the old ones by
the rowan tree. "Do not play me for a fool, Languoreth, I do not speak
of offerings left for the dead. I speak about the living. You risk too
much."

"And you do not risk enough."

Elufed lifted her chin. "Well, then. It seems neither you nor I shall
be able to say farewell."

"No," I said.

Her wintry eyes gave nothing away, but her voice—in that moment, she sounded almost a child. I knew Elufed and Brodyn had lain together. Perhaps she even loved him. I thought of my cousin, slipping away into the dark.

"And your new man. You trust him?" she asked.

"His task will bear it out. But nothing shall come back upon me. I was at the Samhain pyre, well within sight of Tutgual's men."

"I suppose we shall have to see what tomorrow brings." Her smile did not reach her eyes. "In any case, it is done now, and for the best." She glanced down at the oil lamp in my hands. "Are you going to his chamber, then?"

Rhys, she meant. I nodded.

"I will come with you and sit awhile."

"No," I said. "But thank you. I should rather wait alone."

"I understand," she said.

I did not know if I could bear the sight of my eldest son's chamber. I had not entered it since hearing of his death. But if Rhys did return this night, he'd be in want of his mother. He'd be in want of his bed. His soul would be so very weary.

I entered to find the shutter closed and rushed to thrust it wide, nearly sending the oil lamp clattering. Sweet gods. The window must be open. What if my boy had come already and could not get in?

"I am sorry! I am sorry!" I cried. Beyond the narrow window, the stars were snuffed by cloud. Nothing stirred. The air was still and thick, expectant.

There now. There, Rhys.

I closed my eyes to night, letting the cold soothe my cheeks.

Come to me, I called to him. *Come home.*

I am here. I am waiting.

* * *

"Taken! Can you believe?"

Two servants were speaking by the door to the kitchens, heads bent as if conspiring. I stopped just beyond the door, listening.

"Taken by the *aos sí*," the other said. "There at sundown, gone by morning. I heard voices in the wood. I knew it was they."

I stepped from the doorway, offering a smile. "Who is it you speak of? Who is gone?"

They exchanged a somber look. "Why, didn't you hear, m'lady? Brodyn of Cadzow, your own cousin. Gone from the pits! Quick as you like!"

"They took 'im," the other said. "But it weren't voices in the wood. It were chantin'—his, no mistake. Heard him myself. Chanting and wailing all the night long. He called, and *they* came. Simple as that."

My fingers fluttered to my throat in feigned alarm. "My cousin is gone?"

"Aye! The alarm was called at first light!"

"I heard voices. I thought I'd been dreaming."

Nearly all in Tutgual's hall had taken up the Christian mantle—in name if not in faith. Maidens still crept out before dawn on Beltaine to wet their faces with morning dew, and there wasn't a milker who dared forget a portion for Brigid each time they squeezed the goat or sheep's utters.

Which gods we prayed to did not matter in this case—we were a people who believed in the power of spirits and their world of mist.

Elufed swept into the kitchens with two servants at her heels, catching the last of our conversation.

"You believe Brodyn was taken, then, and did not somehow escape?" She stopped, blinking at the servants in expectation. What was she playing at?

"Well, surely Brodyn of Cadzow had no friend among the guard," the elder woman said.

"You are right," I said. "And they were quite unkind when I went to see him."

I saw it then: Elufed was leading the servants to strengthen their own conclusions. It was Samhain, and if a crack should open between the worlds, a person could be snatched, never to be seen again.

"And there were three men guarding the pits!" the other pointed out. "They'd n'er let him out."

"Were that the case, the king would certainly put his guards to the sword," Elufed said, meeting my eyes. "He may yet, upon his return."

I never intended to cost any man his life. If it was Torin, I would sorrow. But I would not regret it. Such were the lessons I had learned.

"I must excuse myself to get ready," I said. "The men will soon be here."

Elufed waved me away, turning to matters at hand. "Let me taste the stewed apple," she said, reaching delicately into a pot before wrinkling her nose. "Still too sour. We must fix it, or make it again."

The marketplace was teeming with women and children despite the chill in the air. The women's eyes were fixed on the road that led into Partick, while their children perched like squirrels in the trees to catch the first glimpse of the war band's return. Tutgual's men milled among the gathering crowd. They'd quartered off a place for the noblewomen. Our benches from the Samhain rite sat along the road, where Elufed waited already, attendants by her side and wine in hand. I had no attendant, as Aela was needed at the hall to aid in preparations, but I was not the queen. Beside Elufed sat Rhian, Morcant's flaxen-haired wife, draped in gold jewelry, but her kohled eyes and berry-stained cheeks were unable to mask her dread. Morcant and

Rhydderch might have been brothers, but one was a boar, the other a stag. At least I'd thought as much, before my husband had ridden off to murder my brothers.

Rhian leaped to her feet as we climbed out from the cart, jostling Elufed's cup. "Your seat, Languoreth! Come sit beside me."

"Thank you, Rhian." I greeted her with a kiss. Elufed looked at her.

"Oh goodness, your cloak! I am so dreadfully sorry, my queen."

"Never mind it," Elufed said, and leaned back so her servant might brush away the spill.

"Auntie!" Gladys and Cyan rushed to embrace her, and Rhian beamed at them as they took their places. Morcant had many children, none who'd been born of his own wife.

"The marketplace buzzes like a hive," I said.

"Yes." Rhian glanced down the road. "Any moment now. Here. Take some wine." Rhian passed me a cup, but as I reached to accept it, she noticed my fingers, still scabbed and bloody from clawing at my door. "Oh, Languoreth," she whispered.

"It is nothing. These marks, at least, are my own." I met her eyes.

That Rhian should pity me, when the bruises she so often wore were left by her husband, was just one mark of her kindness. But Rhian only shook her head. "Nay, Languoreth, make no mistake. These wounds you bear are no more your own doing than mine."

The last I had seen of Rhydderch was the back of his dark head disappearing into a sea of men in the great room, that day the lords of Ebrauc had arrived, and Tutgual had summoned the war counsel. In all the hours I'd spent imprisoned, in all the anguish I'd felt wondering who was dead and who was yet living, the thought of my own husband had been little more than a shadow. Perhaps that made me a monster.

But if that were so, was Rhydderch not more a monster than I? I drank deeply from my cup, and Rhian watched, eyes all-knowing.

"Have you thought of what you might say upon his return?"

I lowered my voice. "It has been preying on me, all the things I might say, since the moment I heard the bolt slide against my door. But now that I am faced with his return, in truth, I do not know."

"Morcant lives for battle," Rhian said. "I cannot sleep for imagining all the terrible things he has done."

To your brothers and the Dragon Warriors, she would not say.

Searching for distraction, I cast about the crowd. A group of women I knew to be Christian stood by the well, wives of warriors who'd been summoned to fight. I met their gaze and lifted my hand in greeting, but the smiles they returned did not reach their eyes.

"They seem displeased we are conversing," I said.

"Then they are not truly Christian," she said. "Goodness. Love. Kindness. Let them observe us. Perhaps they shall learn a thing or two about both the Old Religion and the new."

"You bring to mind an old man I met."

"Oh?"

"Yes, at the Samhain rites. He was a holy man. He spoke like a Scot. But he did not declare himself a Wisdom Keeper."

Rhian considered it. "A hermit of some kind. From the West and holy, you say?"

"Quite. His touch . . . his hands . . ." I could not rightly explain it.

"And did he travel alone?"

"Yes."

"Well." Rhian laughed. "Then he was not Columba of Iona. For he travels nowhere without his armed guard. Moluag, however . . ."

"Moluag," I said. "The holy man of Lismore?"

He was a Christian, I knew, and a much hallowed teacher. Cathan had spoken of Moluag. He had considered him a friend.

"But Lismore is days away by boat," I said. "Whatever would bring him to a Samhain rite in Partick?"

"I could not say. Never mind it! I suppose it could have been any old hermit." She smiled.

"Nay, thank you, Rhian. I shall tuck it away." I had the strangest feeling this was not the last time I might see the man, whoever he might be.

Children raced around their elders' knees, playing at games of war. The people's anticipation was building like a coming storm; at any moment, the sky would crack.

And then, from a distance, voices carried. Hundreds of voices lifted in song. At first I could not make out the words. But as they drew nearer, their singing rang clear.

All along the Eskside hills
The battle fog was blowing . . .

They'd crafted their battle song on their victorious march, a song of blood and spite. Visions flashed unbidden—warriors creeping through the wood—making me feel as if my skin crawled with mites. I smoothed my hair, and then the river of men was upon us.

The spearmen strode first, their backs straight as rods. The cheering was deafening as the people of Partick stretched out their hands, welcoming the men back into our fold.

Nothing could have prepared me for the roiling wave of poison that rose. I wanted to spit my own blood. Which of these men had taken aim at my lover? Who among them had sought the prize of my brother's head?

I took a steadying breath as the warriors on horseback appeared. Some of the footmen were poulticed and wrapped. Either I was mistaken, or there were fewer men, fewer horses.

The Dragon Warriors had given them a fight.

On the bench beside me, Cyan's face was plain with his longing for his father. The working of a child's heart was so simple. But as I searched, I could not find my husband among them.

"Where is Rhydderch?" I wondered, trying not to sound alarmed. But Elufed, too, had noticed her son's absence and stood, craning her neck.

"Why is Father not here?" Gladys said, her voice rising. "You told me he lived!"

"He does not ride with them," Elufed said. "There must be good reason."

"Yes," I assured them. "We will soon find out. We had word he was hale."

"There is Morcant." Rhian pointed. "And the king."

We watched as they drew closer. Tutgual's snowy head was held high, torque at his neck and piercing eyes fixed ahead. His eldest son rode close behind, but Morcant did not stare nobly into the distance. Nor did he seek his wife. His gaze sought me instead, his heavy brows lifting slightly as he neared.

Upon his javelin, a man's head was pierced.

My face did not alter. From somewhere within, a voice directed me. *Breathe. Blink. Do not weep.*

"Gladys and Cyan, cover your eyes," I said quickly.

Morcant must have imagined this moment all the long leagues between here and the Borderlands—my horrific panic, the way my heart would be drumming in my chest.

To whom did the head belong? Uther? Lail? Oh, sweet gods. Maelgwn?

I searched for breath as if I'd been knocked from a tree. The man's neck was a ring of gore, face drained of blood, now white and distorted. The only thing known to my eye was the tumble of dark, untethered hair.

Maelgwn. No, no, no, my love . . .

I could not bear it. I could not fathom it. I plunged my trembling hand deep into my pocket to clutch the emerald ring.

Breathe. Do not weep, I thought, reasoning at the sight of it. It could not be. No one save Lailoken knew of our love.

I kept utterly still. The man's hair was not black but brown. Brown as an acorn and threaded with silver.

Brant.

Brant, who'd taught me to wield my knife. Brant, who'd loved and protected us the whole of our lives. The head on Morcant's spike belonged to my cousin.

Vomit rose, and I swallowed it.

But Cyan only stared in fascination as Morcant passed by. "Was that not our cousin?" he asked.

"Sweet Gods, Cyan, do not look!" I exclaimed.

Gladys's eyes flew open and she gasped. "Oh, no, no!"

I drew her to me, staring at Morcant with a hate that could burn a man to cinders. "Do not let him see you weep. Do not feed his wickedness," I said into her hair.

But Morcant was not the only man bearing a trophy of gore, for each warrior in his retinue rode with a head pierced upon a pike.

I pressed my lips to keep from weeping.

Dragon Warriors all, greatest of our land. Bulls of our island, protectors from the Angles. Their souls would have no peace now. They had been given no honor. I knew these men. They had supped at my table at Partick and at Cadzow. They deserved to be named, if only in silence.

Dreon.

Einion.

Brant.

They had stood against an impossible confederation. They had stood upon that hill and seen the war bands creeping over their fields and had known they were going to die.

Who would sing of their heroism? Who yet lived to remember them?

There is you, I told myself. But when I was gone?

Theirs would become a forgotten kingdom.

I stood stone-faced, holding Gladys, as the procession carried on. The ladies of Strathclyde would stay, as was custom, until every last warrior had been welcomed back home.

Heads on pikes, jostled and lofted for cheers from the crowd.

But not all the citizens of Partick were battle-mad. As I looked, I saw I was not alone in my grief. Here. And there. A woman. An old man. Another and there, another. More and more as I looked, standing as if stunned, tears streaming their cheeks.

They remembered the day the Angles had first risen in a rage of fire and sword, and how one man called Emrys—a warrior from the Wall—had fashioned a banner from the bloodied tunics of his men to become the first Pendragon. They remembered twenty and more winters of Dragons on the Wall, heroes on horseback who had battled and slaughtered generations of Angle kings.

I searched out their eyes, and as they looked up and saw me, I sent them my strength. One by one, they ceased their weeping. I bent down to Gladys, squeezing her gently. "Look, Gladys. We are yet among our people," I whispered. "Show them you are here. Show them you are unbroken."

I clasped her hand. Gladys wiped her face and looked up, her eyes slowly brightening as she gazed over the crowd.

"Do you see? This sorrow is not ours alone. The sharing of our pain has forged us new kin."

Gladys tilted her chin as she looked at them in return. In the midst of all my sorrow, I did not know if I had ever been so proud. "Good girl," I told her.

We remember.

I prayed my eyes spoke the words I could not say.

I could not explain it, save to say it was a healing. Something had shifted. I had felt it when the Cailleach placed her hands upon my head. I could not yet name it, but it pulsed, steady and strong as the beat of my heart.

The Old Gods were summoning. We would answer their call.

CHAPTER 18

Languoreth

Partick
Kingdom of Strathclyde
1st of November, AD 573

Last came the prisoners. Gwenddolau's people.

They traveled in a caravan of three wooden carts drawn by tired horses, bodies packed against the high-sided slats, faces bleak as the dead.

I had waited for the captives despite not knowing how I might aid them. They would be tenants and former servants, tradesmen. Perhaps a Wisdom Keeper, if any remained. Women and children who could be traded or sold. Farmers who'd seen the signal fire and rallied to the banner of the Dragon. Torin and the men from the pits stood at the road, ready to escort the carts back to Tutgual's hall. I stood helpless, willing a discovery that eluded me. And then, from within one of the carts, someone cried out my name. "Languoreth!"

I searched the press of bodies for the source.

"Languoreth!"

It was a woman, body thrust against the slats of the first cart—a woman with wild eyes and brown hair. Her dress drooped from her shoulders as if it had been torn. Her face was swollen with blood and bruises.

"Stop!" I called out. "Stop the cart!" I broke through the line of noblewomen and dashed into the procession before any of our guard could stop me.

"Languoreth!" The woman stretched her hand through the planks, but Torin reached her first, sending the blunt wooden end of his spear into her stomach.

"Do not strike her!" I cried, reaching for her hand.

She gripped my fingers. "Please help me, please," she said. Her voice was a rasp.

Torin spun round on me. "Get back! Are you mad?"

Perhaps I was mad, for the captives now saw a chance for salvation. I cried out in pain as a dozen hands clawed, gripping my arm in a frenzy. They yanked and tugged, dashing my cheek against the wall of the cart.

"Languoreth, Languoreth!" they cried as they crushed and piled, thrusting their hands through the slats. The warriors beat at their hands until they released me, and I stumbled back onto the grass. But now the carts were rocking as the captives shook their wooden prisons, desperate for release. "Languoreth! Languoreth!"

"Go, go!" Torin shouted, and onlookers scattered as Tutgual's men surrounded me, forcing me down, their shields coming over my head.

"Stop this!" I shouted.

"You've done this," Torin shot back.

"Let me go, they will not harm me," I said, even as the prisoners shrieked beyond the shield wall, struggling to break free.

"Get her back to the hall," Torin commanded, "and get the carts gone!"

The driver snapped the reins, urging the horses forward at a clip as prisoners tumbled and collided. The other two carts followed, disappearing from sight.

The warriors stood, lowering their shields, fuming. Torin looked at me, shaking his head. "What were you on about? You nearly caused a riot!"

"That woman, she knew me. She called for me!" I said. Even as I said it, I knew I sounded a fool. Who among the imprisoned did not know me? I was Uther Pendragon's foster sister, twin to his counsellor, Lailoken. My dress and hair were disheveled. I felt a sting and reached to my cheek. My fingers felt the wet of blood.

"You are bleeding!" Rhian said, hurrying to my side. "Come, come. Elufed and the children are already in the cart."

I took Rhian's hand and she helped me in. Elufed's eyes were calm, but her chest was rising rapidly. I felt her stare and looked away. "'Tis only a scratch, Rhian. I am hale, truly."

We rocked as the cart drew away from the marketplace, my children watching me in stunned silence.

"Mother, are you all right?" Cyan asked.

"She's been through a shock," Elufed said, but I scarcely heard her.

"Three carts," I murmured, casting back to the laws Cathan had taught us so well.

"Three carts! Why, they are war prizes, aren't they? One for the king, one for each of his sons, Morcant and Rhydderch."

Elufed looked as if she might shake me. "You mean to claim a slave cart? Your cousin disappeared and your brothers—our enemies—dead or in exile, and you would make demands of the king?"

"It is not a demand. It is my right. My husband is not returned. Who else should claim his booty?"

"I will claim it!" Cyan piped up.

"Be quiet, Cyan." I reached for his hand.

"Cyan, your mother has struck her head and gone silly." Elufed frowned. "I will not aid you in this, Languoreth."

"I would not ask it of you. I would only ask your help in securing a new captain of my guard. I must keep my word."

She knew I meant Torin, but she only crossed her arms beneath her fur cloak, saying, "We shall see. And what will you do with a cart of prisoners, in any case? Sell them? You don't know the first thing about it."

"They are my property by law. I shall do with them as I please."

But I must attempt it without angering the king. I thought about the woman in the first cart, the look upon her face. I would have her cart, I would see to it. For the moment, I could do no more.

We drew to a stop, and Elufed gathered the deep purple skirt of her dress, stepping down from the cart. I bent to speak softly to Gladys and Cyan. "No matter how we may feel, we must be certain to welcome your *taid*. We must welcome the king home."

They nodded, and we descended into a mass of revelers milling in the courtyard. The music thrummed too brightly as warriors held their children close. Sons and daughters looked up with stars in their eyes at their hero come home, and Cyan watched them, feeling Rhydderch's absence with no way to reconcile it. Why had my husband not returned?

I put my arms round my children. "Come, then. Let us go in."

The hall was a crush of dank leather and sweat, but the warriors parted as we trailed behind the queen, her face shining as she strode toward her husband. "Tutgual King."

"My lady queen. All is well?" Tutgual stood readily from his oaken chair to embrace her, but my healer's eye noticed the frailness that accompanied a man of sixty-five winters.

"All is well now you're returned," Elufed said. Her body did not stiffen, though I knew she did not love him, and her wintry eyes were warm as she turned to look upon her eldest son. Did she not feel betrayed that her body had borne such a vile and hateful man?

Rhian brushed Morcant's cheek with a kiss as I stepped forward to greet the king. "Tutgual King. We are so happy to see you come home."

Tutgual studied me with his birdlike gaze, then nodded. "You have lost a son. I am sorry for it." The king had been fond of Rhys, a gifted fighter. He did not mention my daughter.

"Thank you, my king. I had hoped at least to see my husband."

"He hunts the men who fled," he said.

My brother. I closed my eyes a moment, forcing myself onward. "When might we expect Rhydderch's return?"

"When his errand is complete. He is tanist now. He must see the task done."

"Then I shall await his return," I said lightly. "Tonight we raise our cups to you. Our king is hale." I bowed and shifted away, then stopped. "My king, I beg your favor. There is one item I wish to discuss."

"Speak." The king blinked, impatient.

"You are an exceedingly generous king, but I would never presume . . . I noted there were three slave carts. Do you intend one share to go to Rhydderch for his spoils?"

"Aye. And what of it?"

"In his absence, I would claim it if I may. I need servants at Cadzow, we are down to bare bones."

"Nay. Rhydderch must trade them. They will fetch a good value."

Tread carefully, Elufed's gaze warned me. Morcant was a shadow at Tutgual's shoulder, and one of the king's men had come now to speak low in Morcant's ear.

"Of course," I said. "It is only I worry over our provisions at Partick. Winter will soon come, and three carts of slaves will surely be a strain on your food stores. We had a strong harvest at Cadzow. Allow me to take Rhydderch's cart there. We are most eager to welcome Lord Rhydderch home, and Cadzow is nearer his return, if only by a day—"

Tutgual's look silenced me. "I have only just returned, yet you come seeking spoils before the feast has yet begun?"

"Her heart bleeds for their rescue," Morcant cut in. "I hear from my men she nearly caused a riot."

"If my heart bleeds, it is for the fact that you carry home war trophies on pikes while you neglect to bring home the body of my son. I think only of our sacrifice," I shot back.

"Enough of this bickering." Tutgual looked between us.

I bowed, not daring to meet his eyes. "I mean only to mind the cart for my husband's homecoming. As I say, I have provisions enough. And readying Cadzow for Rhydderch's return would be a welcome diversion."

"Which cart would you have?" the king asked.

"The middle, if it please you."

"No, my king," Morcant said quickly. "I would have the middle."

"The first cart, then, if I must." I tipped my chin as if I'd been defeated.

The king considered it. "Take it, then, and depart at your leisure," he said at last. "But remain obedient to my summons, should I desire your return."

"Of course, my king. Thank you. I am grateful."

Tutgual waved two fingers dismissively, but his eyes did not leave me until I reached my seat. I sank down, worn through. But in a far chamber of my heart, I felt a flutter of hope. I'd done it—I had bested Morcant, the fool. And I was to take the survivors to Cadzow, away from the hawkish watch of Morcant and the king. I dared not believe it until I stepped over the threshold of my hall.

Aela came to stand beside me as the bards ceased their playing and the king's *sencha* called for silence, for he had witnessed the battle and now must prove himself worthy of his keep in the recitation of his tale: the warriors lost and their battle-hardened prowess. The virtues and generosity of Tutgual, the king.

"Take the children to the courtyard so they might join others their age," I bade Aela, and she whisked them away.

I sat motionless, imagining myself submerged in an icy burn as if it could numb my senses, for I could not yet leave. I must stay to honor my son. It seemed an eternity before, at last, it came.

"None was strong as Rhys, son of Rhydderch, defender of the faith. He made the ground red with Dragon blood before he found his end at the ramparts . . ."

I swallowed sickness as I saw Rhys on his back in battle mud, crying out my name. Suffering.

Mother.

He'd wanted me beside him, and I could not save him from his pain. I pressed back my tears, struggling to quiet my breathing.

Defender of the Faith.

Was this how my son was to be remembered? Rhys, who kept the Old Gods? Rhys, who had never chosen Christ? Rhys was a boy of the burn and the forest and beloved of Herne, just like his uncles. I looked to the doors, sickened by tales twisted by victors. If I did not leave soon, I would take a spear from the wall and ram it through Tutgual's throat.

I stood. Across the room, Elufed's profile was regal, but when her eyes caught the lamplight, I saw that they shone with unfallen tears.

Grief is a weakness and emotion a danger. Such is the burden of a woman with power, Elufed had said, tutoring me in how to survive. I crossed the room, my face smooth as a winter pasture, to bow before Elufed and the king. "I am quite tired. If you will permit me?"

Tutgual gave a nod but did not turn my way. I hurried from the great room, meeting Aela at my chamber door. "There is a woman in the prison carts who's been badly beaten," I told her. "She has dark hair—Torin will know her. The cart is now mine. Take one of your hooded cloaks and fetch her, please. Bring her the back way and draw up the cloak's hood. I should like to avoid any trouble."

"A prisoner from the Borderlands?" Aela asked.

"Yes."

"But m'lady, do you know her? How can you be certain she is safe?"

"Please, Aela. Just do as I say."

I paced in the stillness of my chamber, readying my healing supplies while the muffled sound of music echoed from the courtyard. Aela was right, I did not know this woman. I was pulling her from the prison carts and did not know what she might say or if I might trust it. But I could not turn from the desperation in her voice. And in return, I hoped she would tell me what she had seen the day of the battle.

At last the iron latch lifted with a clank, and Aela guided the woman into my room. She walked stiffly, leaning slightly on Aela's arm, and was tall, I noticed. Nearly tall as I.

"Hello," I said. "Please. Come sit."

She bowed her head, face hidden in shadow. Now that we were in close quarters, she seemed hesitant to remove the cloak's hood. I did not press her. "Aela, you may leave us."

Aela glanced at my healing supplies. "I could stay, m'lady. We will need to clip her hair," she said softly. The woman had nits, she meant.

"I will tend to her, thank you. But please bring water for washing and something to eat."

Aela nodded, hurrying away as the woman sank gingerly into a chair. I took the chair opposite. "You may remove your cloak if you wish."

She reached slowly to push back the hood, and her face came into the light. Her brown hair was oily and matted in tangles, but as she smoothed it back, I saw the telltale angry bites—lice—at the base of her neck. Her face was the work of boots and of fists, but her blue eyes were steady. She did not seek my pity.

"We will need to shear off your hair," I said gently.

She touched it hesitantly, then nodded.

"I am Languoreth," I said.

"Yes, I know." She had a low-toned voice, like a woman of gentle blood.

"Here, you will be thirsty." I passed her a cup from the table beside me, and the slim hands that accepted it shook, though from fear or exhaustion I could not tell. "I can see you have been treated abominably. I am sorry. You must know you are safe here. No more harm shall come to you."

She nodded, but I saw from her eyes she could not believe me.

"You must believe I only wish to help. But I hoped you may be able to help me in return." I swallowed the emotion clogging my throat and looked at her, beseeching. "It is only that I have loved ones who are missing, you see. And I wondered if you might know what has become of them."

The woman closed her eyes. A tear slipped from beneath her lashes onto the swollen slope of her cheek.

"I am sorry, I do not mean to press you," I said gently. "Perhaps you could begin by telling me your name."

The woman took a breath, then opened her eyes. They were pale blue and deep as an ocean. "My name is Eira, but it was not always so," she began. "I was once known as Gwendolen, daughter of Urien. And I am handfasted to your brother."

CHAPTER 19

Lailoken

Hart Fell, the Black Mountain
Kingdom of the Selgovae
January, 574 AD

Lungs burning from the climb, I reached the trickle of the spring.

The water came from the heart of Black Mountain, bubbling from the hillside where the valley narrowed into a cleft. Black scree piled high above the burn here, trapping and exacerbating winter's icy grip, and I stopped in the snow.

Outside the stifling closeness of the huts Archer had granted us at the foot of the mountain, winter had come in earnest, burying us in silence.

Come to me, Rhys. I am listening, I am here.

The air was heavy and smelled of metal, of blood.

Gwenddolau, my brother. Come to me, I am listening. Come and I will follow you . . .

I opened my eyes to a stark and barren world. Rock, snow, and the half-frozen burn. No dead men stirred today.

In the beginning, I'd taken sustenance from this holy place. Its iron waters felt like silver, brightening my body as I bent down to drink. But the days wore on. At my request, Archer sent scouts to

Strathclyde, but they discovered no news of Angharad's return. She was lost, and they had no better fortune discovering anything of Eira.

I dreamt of a man with dark, piercing eyes who wore a cloak of feathers.

I dreamt of battle and gore, of Angharad and Eira.

Across the leagues, a wound lay open between me and my twin sister. There was a time, when we were young, when we felt each other's pain. Now it happened once more, in waves upon waves. My broken shoulder, my wrist, the muscle of my heart. Hers or my own? Perhaps this was the drowning; each of us carrying the suffering of the other until we both sank. I felt my blood going bitter.

Tutgual and Rhydderch will answer for what they have done, only show me the way. The thought of revenge consumed me.

The spring no longer spoke. Still I climbed the icy path each day, regardless of weather, shouldering a fool's hope that refuge dwelled here.

High above the valley, the crows were flocking; they would not cease. They glided on silent wings, black as ink, their caws rasping through the deep winter valley in rain and in snow. Death birds.

I gathered my mucus and spat upon the ground, loathing the gods who had spared me. "Come and finish me," I shouted. "For I have turned my back on you. Lailoken is no longer your son. Lailoken is no longer your slave!"

But it was not I who had turned my back upon the gods. It was the gods who'd turned their backs upon me. Upon all of us.

I heard a murmur, a voice, and whipped round to scour the hillside, heart racing. Was that Gwenddolau who called out? I could have sworn I saw the flash of his yellow hair. Had I not just heard him laughing?

Come! Come and follow me, brother . . . The crunch of footsteps sounded in snow, and I straightened. But it was a visitor from the land of the living. I brushed the snow from a boulder to sit as Maelgwn appeared in his heavy fur-lined cloak.

"Rhiwallon told me you'd come here," he said.

"Aye."

He took out the empty bladder he'd brought, and I heard the gentle creak of his knees as he bent to fill it with spring water.

Maelgwn did not know the truth of it: that he'd lost a son he'd never come to know.

I'd seen his face the day he'd set eyes upon Rhys, scarcely two summers ago. They shared the same dark hair and green eyes. Yet where Maelgwn's skin was olive, Rhys possessed my sister's fairness—skin white as fleece. Seventeen winters had passed since Maelgwn had first lain with my sister. He must have known.

And yet.

Languoreth had not told him, and the knowledge was not mine to give. Now, here in the mountains, I sat beside Rhys's own father, yet I carried the weight of his death alone.

Maelgwn broke the silence. "I have been watching you these past weeks, my brother. You do not seem yourself."

I glanced at him. "Is that so? And who among us is unaltered now? I hear you cry out in your sleep."

"Aye, I am scarred, Lailoken. Each man on the battlefield is merely a boy trying to silence the loud rage of war. But there are empty stomachs in the huts down below, and today we must hunt."

I'd worn the mantle of leadership for so long it felt burdensome now, dragging about my neck, but I stood, following him down the icy path, for the men needed meat. We'd parceled out the oats Archer had given us for porridge and bread so we might stretch them until spring, but we could not survive on oats and barley alone. Game was ours to catch.

Outside the huts Rhiwallon stood waiting beside Old Man Archer, and the chieftain glanced up as we neared, giving a wave of his bow.

I nodded. "Lord Archer. You would join us?"

"Aye, for a portion of meat," he answered. In truth, he had no need of it, he had his own provisions. But Archer was kind. The deer would be skittish and thin this deep into winter. It'd been weeks since any had been spotted. Only he knew the places they'd likely be foraging in search of tender bark. He knew we were proud, and he did not wish us to go hungry.

I ducked into the hut to gather my bedroll and take up a spear, but as I passed through the fence of sharpened stakes into the forest, Archer caught my arm, raising a brow. "No prayer from our Keeper? Ill luck, Lailoken."

Archer was devout in his worship. I and the gods may have been quarrelling, but he need not know.

"A prayer for the hunt," I answered. The men bowed their heads, and I called out to Herne, though my heart was not in it. "Who leads a man to his quarry? Herne, Cernunnos. He is the pulsing of blood through the veins of all beasts. Without him, no gift of death can be given. Grant us meat this day, that we might thrive through the winter. Bless the pierce of our weapons and guide our aim strong. Keep these men safe from the dangers of your wood."

Archer nodded and we took up our weapons, venturing into the bleak.

Snow muted all sound save the creak of pines in the wind. The winter woods felt watchful, and a shiver traced my neck. The Romans who built the Wall lived in fear of this forest. They knew of the wildcats and brown bears, the wolves and wild boar. But what frightened them most were the tales brought back by the scouts they sent into the Deep. Most never returned. Those who did spoke of skull fences and night shades, of groves strewn with human limbs. You never knew what might happen in the Caledonian Wood. My mother often said the very trees were home to the dead. Not those who dwelled in the Summerlands. The lost ones, the Forgotten, who lingered unseen.

"Tell us a tale, Lord Archer?" Rhiwallon asked, for he must have been feeling much the same.

The old man glanced at him. "Well enough. A quick tale, so as not to scare off our prey." He shifted the bow on his back, gazing up at the trees. "A temple once stood, long ago, at the foot of a waterfall," he began. "The temple lay within the walls of a fortress, ringed by a ditch and a rampart of stone. The waterfall was holy, and high as a mountain. It coursed snowy and white, spilling over the cleft of the hills like the hair of the Goddess herself. Great rites were worked there. Rites of power. And the Keepers of that temple were revered among the most learned in our land.

"Then one day, a Keeper of the temple slept and dreamt. He woke in a madness, believing he could fly. His people tried to warn him, but their words fell upon deaf ears. He fell into a frenzy, toiling night and day to craft a cloak made of feathers. On the day it was finished, he climbed to the height of the falls and leapt to the air. But he did not soar. The Wisdom Keeper fell to his death. After that, his spirit would not rest. The temple was cursed. The Selgovae abandoned the fort. A settlement was built on a crannog instead, in the waters of the twin lochs. They say the Mad Keeper's shade still dwells in the glen."

A cloak made of feathers. A memory stirred from a dream.

"Cursed, you say?" I asked Archer.

"Aye." He nodded. "No one has dared to inhabit the old temple since."

"Curious," I said. "I might wish to travel there."

"Surely we needn't awaken any foul curses," Fendwin spoke up. But I did not answer.

The cold air tightened our faces as we made our way deeper into the wood. Bears would be slumbering in their dens. It was the wolves I worried over—five men to a pack of fifteen. Then Rhiwallon's stomach grumbled, and Archer frowned.

"If your gut startles a hind, it'll be your bollocks we'll bring home to roast," he scolded, and the men broke out laughing. The first true medicine we'd had all winter.

We stopped to take some dried beef. The day wore on, and still we hunted. I missed the help of our dogs, but our dogs were dead. Soon the light would grow weak. The men's faces turned grim as we began to consider a night shivering in our bedrolls rather than sitting beside a blazing hearth with meat over the fire. But then we heard the garble and croak of a bird. Stopping midstride, I looked to the naked trees overhead, where a pair of ravens were perched, their figures huddled against the darkening hibernal sky.

"Wolf birds," I said. The raven closest to me bent its inky head as I observed him, scrubbing his beak against the branch as if sharpening a sword. The birds, too, hungered. They were no strangers to hunters in the Caledonian Deep, and they meant to get their raven's share. They meant to lead us to game.

"Move on," Archer said. "Let us see if they'll fly."

The birds flapped eagerly from their roost and began to beat their way west. They'd seen something, then, perhaps a wounded animal. The trees were taller here, their thick branches casting the snowpack in dim light as we picked up our pace, trying to keep our scent downwind as we tracked the ravens' silhouettes through the sky. Leagues passed beneath our feet and the light began to wane. And then, suddenly, the ravens vanished.

Fendwin cursed. We stood upon a rocky outcropping. Down below, a shallow burn rushed, and beyond its banks were hollows and fissures in rock, offering safe haven for any manner of creatures.

"We'll be near enough now. This way," Archer said.

We scaled the rocks and waited, sensing the forest. Then a flap of wings sounded, and the ravens reappeared, settling on the ground a short distance away. A carcass, it seemed, but it was hidden by brush. Signaling the men to wait, I crossed the stream, gripping my spear. The ravens took wing with a throaty rattle of discontent as I neared the spot where blood had congealed on the pebbled streambed. Peering into the foliage, I caught a glimpse of reddish hair and stumbled. *Oh, gods, no. No, no. It could not be.*

And then I had to see her, had to go to her. "Angharad . . ."

I crashed into the bushes only to find myself standing before the carcass of a wolf. I blinked. Male. Gray and white. Not a child's hair; it was the tawny flash of fur lining the underbelly that I had seen. Sadness eddied in the stream of my relief as I knelt beside the fallen creature to study his wounds. Mauled? Gored, more like it. Two piercing wounds had slashed deep across his ribs. A beautiful creature and not to be wasted. We'd take the pelt for warmth. But it seemed strange the ravens would lead us here. What need had they of us? They'd feast fine enough on the carcass themselves.

"Who ended you?" I asked. Casting about, I spotted an indication: a dark smear on the nearby trunk of a birch. I bent to touch it, lifting my fingers to my nose. The sharp stink made my eyes water.

Boar.

And a beast of one, to finish a wolf. I turned to the men and held up my fingers, showing them the scat. Their shoulders tensed in the fading light. We Britons were famed for our skill in boar hunting, and even we did not venture it without the help of our dogs. Boar could grow to the size of a small pony and spill a man's guts with one toss of their head. I'd seen men thrown into tree trunks. Always it was a bloodletting.

My feet were midstream when Maelgwn gave the soft call that served as a warning. I looked up to see his gaze fixed over my shoulder.

I turned slowly, weapon at the ready. Forty paces downstream stood a bristled black boar, his hind leg stained dark with blood.

I had seen wild boar before. Something of this beast was different, almost otherworldly. Evil. There were gouges on his chest and foreshoulder from the wolf's fangs. Breath fogged from his nostrils as he caught my scent on the breeze. In his eyes I saw the blackness of never-ending night.

So this is my end. Let him come for me.

He tossed his head, eyes piercing mine. And then he charged.

Maelgwn and the men splashed into the stream, shouting, "*Yahhhh! Yahhhhhhh!*" But I stood motionless, preferring to be speared in the front than in the back, fleeing without honor. And then something within me shifted. Broke open. Rage boiled up from deep within me, rage that had been seething untouched, rage that bellowed from my throat with a scream at the thundering black pig as I drew back my spear and, aiming between his eyes, thrust it with all of my might at the hurtling beast.

It was scarcely enough to knock him off course. The boar gave a snort as the spear glanced off the thick armor of his hide and I dove into the thick stand of brush. Thorns tore at my cloak as I scrambled to my feet to recover my fallen spear, flicking it back into my grip with the tip of my boot. The boar was already circling, rounding for another attack. Five men were as nothing to a beast enraged by the frenzy of survival.

"Stand apart!" Archer shouted, and we heeded him, becoming multiple targets as the boar plowed again, riverstone scattering in a spray beneath his hooves.

He charged Rhiwallon this time, tossing him like a child's doll into the water, where he lay as if stunned.

"Get up, man, get up," I shouted, and at the sound of my voice, the beast turned once more and bent his head like a shovel.

Enough. This would be the creature's last charge. I could not witness any more death.

The collision felt as if a giant had flung me into the face of a boulder. My spear snapped in half, dropping from my grip, and a liquid-hot pain sliced across my legs as I was thrown to the side. I fell, grasping, my palm splitting open as I caught the hoof of his hind leg. Not enough to hold him, but enough to make him stumble. Fendwin shouted, and I saw the flash of his sword as the great boar twisted and swung back round to finish me, prone as I was upon the ground. We were a blur of movement, tumbling, scraping. A stab in my chest like a dagger and the crushing weight of the creature on top of me. With a roar I reached, clawing at the creature's eyes, rolling and kicking as I clutched at him, striking and mauling with my fists. Then a streak of light exploded like the spark of a flint as my temple was struck, my head knocked to the side. The tip of my broken spear lay upon the streambed and I grasped for it. No sooner had I gripped it than I turned back to see tusks coming at my throat. Razor-sharp tips tore my arm as I sent my hand up, thrusting the spear deep into the tender joint where neck meets chin. Blood erupted in a fountain, blinding me beneath him.

The sound was rage, then agony. A piglet's squeal.

I sank into the ground as the boar dropped lifeless on top of me, the weight of him sending the breath from my lungs in a gust of exhaustion. Of relief.

"Lailoken." Fendwin's voice came.

"Aye." I blinked and smeared the blood from my eyes as he and the men hoisted the beast from on top of me and the carcass thudded onto the ground. Battle fury yet pulsed through my veins, dulling the worst of any pain, but as my heart worked to recapture its rhythm, I glanced over my wounds, gauging the destruction. My legs were most worrisome. Fendwin bent, and I offered up my tunic, which he gripped, ripping between two fists to fashion a binding to stanch the blood.

Nodding gratefully, I sat back on the rocks. A rank smell came from the boar. I looked at the beast, then at Fendwin. "You pierced his bladder."

His eyes widened in disbelief. "Is this how you thank me for saving your life?"

"'Tis only he won't be much good to us now. The meat'll be spoilt."

"Then you'd better do a swift job of cleaning it." He yanked the binding around my wounds a bit too tightly. We warriors wore our wit like armor, but it still lay between us, that Rhys had died by his hand.

I looked at him. "You had no debt, Fendwin. And still it has been paid."

I did not know if I could forget the sight of his dirk slitting my nephew open, but I could see how he suffered for it. "In any case, you needn't have risked yourself. Mine was clearly the death-dealing blow."

Fendwin stood. "Is this not my sword embedded in his brain?" He reached to reclaim it but stopped, his eyes on the water. I turned.

Rhiwallon lay half submerged, fair hair streaming in the water like a merrow's, eyes open to the rushing burn.

No one spoke. I dropped my head into my hands. We were twilight men, then, and I know we all thought it: to survive the battle only to be felled by a pig. Death dined with a ferocity we thought we had known but did not truly comprehend.

Slowly, painfully, I stood with Fendwin's aid as Archer and Maelgwn pulled Rhiwallon from the stream. I bent over him, reaching to touch his face, waxy from the icy water, easing his eyelids shut.

"Sleep, brother. And wake to claim your place at our ancestors' table."

Placing my hands over his heart, I spoke the death blessing. We could not build a blaze hot enough to make ashes of his body. The earth was too frozen to dig a grave, even had we the proper tools. In the end, two men carried his body deeper into the wood and laid him out. The wolves and the ravens would have their share after all.

"We must make camp," Archer said. I could scarcely walk. Others had been injured, though less gravely. We would need to build a fire and tend our wounds.

In the end, the boar could have been salvaged, but the thought turned our stomachs. "He is a foul and wicked creature," Archer said. "We dare not eat such meat."

Yet I took the wolf's pelt, then set aside a small cutting from the boar's flesh. I had a mind how to use it.

Archer felled a doe just before dark and we cleaned her, eating round the fire in silence. Maelgwn and Fendwin had fashioned a shelter and we sat beneath it now, dry enough as night pressed in. Snow came. I watched the flakes fall, spitting into nothingness in the flames, and thought of Angharad and the stones. Of the beast and her warning.

It had come for me twice now. Each time I had set my mind to die, yet clawed like a wild man simply to live. Loathing turned my stomach, and I set down my meat. Arderydd might have been finished and the black pig dead, but something in me warned this beast would not be so easily vanquished. It would come again, though I did not know when.

We tended to each other's wounds using what salves and ointments we'd brought in our healer's pouch, then took turns sitting watch, staring into the darkness and banking up the fire to keep those who were slumbering warm. My watch came just before dawn. Beyond the flames, the burn rushed ever on. In the trickling of its water, I heard Rhys's choking gurgle and the wild boar coughing its own blood. I thought of the Mad Keeper and his feathered cloak.

Light returned to the sky, and we fashioned a stretcher using Rhiwallon's discarded cloak and tunic. The men carried me home as I clutched the deer meat to my chest.

Back at the huts, we lit a fire to heat rocks for the *fulacht fian* on the streambed, dropping them into the rectangular stone pit until the water hissed and sang. I bundled herbs for healing, and we crawled beneath the skin-covered wicker frame to bathe and steam our wounds clean. But the ritual only served to awaken something unsettled, turning me restless and irritable.

Days passed. My body began to heal well enough that I could walk, though painfully. My wounds had not soured, yet my emptiness remained.

The next morning I gathered my things, fetching the wolf pelt and the strip of dried boar, and went to see Archer. Archer had said the Wisdom Keeper had gone mad. But there was a madness in me also. It stirred like an animal. If I did not leave, it would swallow me whole. I did not know what awaited me there. But the Keeper in his cloak of feathers had come in a dream. I knew I must meet him. I could no longer ignore my summons from the dead.

"I would go to the temple at the waterfall," I said.

Archer looked at me as if I'd gone mad already. "It is forbidden."

"Forbidden for the Selgovae, perhaps. But not so for me."

He shook his head. "As I told you, it is cursed."

"And what if I, too, am cursed?"

"If you truly think it, then why go to such a place, Lailoken?"

I hesitated, uncertain whether I should tell him. But I was a guest in his lands. "I would travel there to undergo the Bull's Sleep," I said. Archer studied me a long moment from his antler-backed chair.

There are times a Wisdom Keeper must seek solace, Cathan once told me. When nightmares will not leave. When anger or violence become master. When he can no longer tell the living from the dead.

The Bull's Sleep was a ritual kept for diviners. Men such as Diarmid would use it to See. A bull was slaughtered, its hide and a morsel of meat kept aside. The Keeper was wrapped in the skin of the beast, meat in his mouth, blindfolded and bound, left to pursue the animal as it raced into the Otherworld.

"I suppose you have considered the obvious," Old Man Archer said.

"Which is?"

"You wish to undergo the Bull's Sleep, and yet you have no bull," Archer said.

"I wasn't aware you might spare one," I said, and Archer gave a small smile of amusement. "I have the skin of the wolf and the meat of the boar. You saw the beast, Archer. There was something more to it. I am an augur, not a diviner, but I cannot silence this urging."

Archer's point was sound. I did not know if the rite could even be worked with animals such as these, nor so long after death. But somehow I knew Archer would understand.

"So be it," he said. And nodding to his men, Archer readied to take me into the wild.

My legs made for slow moving. Archer moved ahead, kicking footholds in the snow. The wind whipped, biting.

We walked a good ways, then crested a hill. Dropping down the far side, we disappeared once more into the Caledonian Deep.

CHAPTER 20

Languoreth

I sheared away Eira's brown locks. When it was done, I stood behind her with cedar oil and a comb, pulling the nits from her hair as Eira told me her story.

"I was born to Urien of Rheged," she began, "raised beside the salt waters of the Solway Firth. But my mother went on to bear four other children to my father. And though I tried to make myself useful, when I was but a girl, I was sent to be fostered under the care of my aunt, Urien's sister. Euerdil is her name."

"The mother of Gwrgi and Peredur," I said. At the mention of their names, Eira startled beneath my hands. Something dreadful had befallen her. "I am sorry," I said. "You needn't tell me anything that pains you."

"No, no. I must," Eira said. "It is important you know all." She took a breath. "I was bright, you see, and my aunt prone to melancholy. My father sought to soothe his sister in sending her some light. Or so he said. I soon learned the truth of it—a powerful king does nothing out of kindness alone. When my aunt's husband, Eliffer, had died, Gwrgi and Peredur were chosen to rule—Gwrgi in the north, Peredur in the south. Now the Angles of Bernicia were testing their hold on the land. Ebrauc is all that stands between Bernicia and Rheged. Euerdil was no longer queen. But if I were wedded to a lord of Ebrauc, and if I should bear him a son, my father and brothers would hold influence over Ebrauc again.

"I believe they meant to take the land. And so away I was sent. My brothers wept the day I left. However, my aunt made me most welcome, and my seasons in Ebrauc seemed as if charmed. Of course, I missed my family. But my aunt was kind and glad for company. I thought myself fortunate it was only my aunt and me, along with her servants. She gifted me beautiful dresses and all manner of things. But then autumn came, and the raiding season was over. Her sons came home."

I paused in my work. Already I felt sickened.

"My aunt knew of her son's wickedness. Perhaps she thought me too old. But my aunt was a fool," she said quietly. "Gwrgi left me for dead. 'Throw her in the river,' he told his man, for he could not be bothered to do it himself. And his man would have done, had I not woken up. I woke as my body hit the cold water, and I screamed. I begged. I suppose he could have drowned me. Perhaps he thought I did not stand much chance of surviving in any case. He brought me instead to a woman who lived at the edge of the forest. It was the place the people of Ebrauc brought their dying and their dead—an unlucky place, one Gwrgi did not care to visit.

"And I did not die. I decided to live."

I set down the cedar oil and sat, for I could not continue.

"The woman treated my wounds and concealed me whilst I healed. She taught me to darken my golden hair so I mightn't be found. I soon discovered my aunt had sent word to my family that I had died from fever. Winter came. The woman told me I must find a new name—that I must never speak of Gwendolen again. I chose Eira, after the snow."

"But could you not have returned to your father?" I asked. "Surely he would have made things right. Surely he would have punished Gwrgi for what he had done."

"Return to the man who had sent me to hell?"

"I am sorry," I said. "'Tis only I have heard Urien of Rheged is an honorable man . . ."

"Yes, my father would have brought war upon Ebrauc and slit Gwrgi's throat. But I was at least my own master. Daughters must be wed for their father's gain." She looked up, meeting my gaze. "Perhaps this is something you understand."

Her words struck. Eira would rather live in poverty and obscurity than be another man's property. I'd had a similar choice—there was a time I could have fled with Maelgwn, but what was a life lived in exile, in hiding? I'd told myself I was wedding Rhydderch to protect the way of life for my people, yet all this time had passed. And what had I done? My cheeks reddened.

"You inspire me," I said. "Yours was not an easy choice."

"The woman, Hila, she loved me." Eira smiled. "Love makes all things easier. She decided to raise me as her own. But we could not stay in Ebrauc. We traveled south, to her sister in Elmet. There we built a small hut with the help of her sister's family. Hila was a woods witch who traded her remedies for food. I learned to hunt and do many things a gentle daughter of Rheged would not so that we might survive. But Hila was aging, and her sister—whom I then called an aunt—had too many mouths to feed. I could not earn my barters as Hila once did; I did not have the healer's touch. My uncle knew a warrior at Gwenddolau's fort. They had been boys together. Rhiwallon passed me off as a servant, bringing me to serve in the kitchens at Caer Gwenddolau. That is how I came to meet your brother."

"And Lailoken, he knew the truth?"

"Yes. After a while. Lailoken and Rhiwallon alone." Then she stopped and looked up, reaching for my hands. "You must know how very much I love your daughter, Languoreth."

My breath caught. It was this I had been starving for, but Eira had been so mistreated, how could I have pressed her? Now I took her hands in mine. "Please," I said. "Tell me all that you know."

And so Eira told me the story of the battle and Angharad's escape from the cliffs, how my brave little girl had found Eira at their hut in the wood. How they fled, together, until they were discovered by Gwrgi and his men.

Rage seethed inside me. For a moment I felt my body could not contain it, that it would drive me raving. "Tell me he did not harm her."

Eira fell quiet, looking down at her hands. "I told her to run. She never would have gone had she known I intended to stay behind. I promised I would follow, though I knew there was little hope of my own escape. They did not find her."

Eira's eyes filled with the nightmare of all that had come after. I expelled a shaky breath. No words could speak to her sacrifice. I sat, feeling helpless.

"How can I ever repay what you have done?" I asked.

Eira looked up. "You took me from the carts."

"Oh, sweet gods." I dropped my head into my hands. It sat between us, the horror she'd been through. We said nothing for a while. Then I risked the question I knew was most important to her. "Did Gwrgi . . . know you?"

She closed her eyes a moment. "He said he had no taste for mutton."

His warriors, then. I felt sickened all over again. "They traded you off when they met with Tutgual and his men. Is that how you came to be in our prison carts?"

Eira nodded. I stood, pacing out my anger, my helplessness, my resentment of men.

We still had no news of my brother or Maelgwn. Angharad was lost and utterly alone in a wasteland of her father's making. But now I had some idea of where to send scouts. And at Cadzow I'd be nearer to Gwenddolau's lands, if only by a day.

I turned back to Eira. "I am leaving for Cadzow tomorrow. I should very much like for you to come. However, if you do not wish to reveal your noble blood, I fear you would have to join my service as a servant. You would assist in my chamber, of course, or wherever you so wish. You have sacrificed many times over for your freedom, and at such great cost. I would never deign to take it from you. But I cannot explain your presence in any other way." I sought her eyes. "Sister."

She nodded, wordless, and I sighed in relief.

"I am so very happy we shall come to know each other," I said.

The shuffle of Aela's shoes let me know she had been standing there for some time. "I've brought food and the washing water, m'lady," she said.

"Thank you. Aela, this is Eira. She will be joining you in my chamber service."

"You are most welcome, Eira," she said with a bow of her head. It was then I knew just how much she'd overheard.

"Will you help Eira to bathe?" I asked. She nodded.

"We must be very careful, Aela. Before all other eyes, we must treat Eira as a servant."

"I understand," she said, helping Eira to stand. "Come, m'lady. I will tend to you now. We will wash away your ills."

*   *   *

Torin appeared the next morning, standing taller. He'd been gifted a new tunic and cloak by Elufed, signaling the release of him and two others into my service. The men who'd aided in Brodyn's escape. "The carts are ready, m'lady," he said. But as I pinned my cousin's old brooch upon his chest, Torin's blue eyes were troubled.

"What is it?" I asked. "I should think you'd be happy."

"I am pleased, m'lady. It isn't that. It's . . ." He stopped.

"Tell me."

"Morcant has done a foul thing. It will disturb you."

Instantly, I knew. "Brant."

Torin nodded. "By the carts."

I clenched my fists to keep them from shaking.

"What would you have me do?" he asked.

I shook my head. I was finished with this man. I refused to be Morcant's toy any longer.

"Load the children and my serving women into the cart, and bring me a burlap sack from the kitchens. I shall be out shortly."

I closed my eyes and thought of my cousin until my breathing steadied. Then, shoulders back, I strode into the light.

Elufed and Rhian stood waiting to see me off. I could tell by their stiffness they had already seen the sight that awaited me.

Brant's impaled head, the pike thrust into the ground just beside the carts. His face was distorted, dark eyes glassy.

Curse you, Morcant, curse you to die.

He imagined it would shock me, that I would scream. He'd meant to stir horror, yet he'd left me an offering.

Torin came forward with the sack, now gleaning my intent. "Let me," he said.

"Nay, Torin. I will do it myself." I stood a moment, looking into Brant's eyes. *You are with me, now, cousin. I am going to bring you home.*

Brant's brown hair stirred in the wind.

"My cousin's head is no trophy." I spoke loudly, so that wherever the coward Morcant was, he might hear. "Torin, please. Hold the bottom. Hold the pike."

He gripped the weapon shaft as I hoisted the sack up, bringing it down over Brant's head. I could not see his face now, ruined in death. In my mind, I could see him as he'd once been. I swallowed. Beneath the burlap, I felt the shape of his ears as I placed my palms upon either side of the sack, pressing, then pulled up.

The weight of it fell into my hands as I drew the sack closed. I looked round the courtyard.

"I pray the gods will forgive Morcant for what he has done," I said. I nodded in farewell to Rhian and Elufed, cradling the sack to my chest as I climbed into the cart.

My heart recovered its pacing only when Partick had faded in the distance.

An icy rain fell as we traveled along the road leading back to the forests of Cadzow. I thought of the priestess at Samhain. Of my little girl, alone in the woods. I thought of my lover.

A wise woman once told me, *We may not always have the choice we would like, but we always have a choice.*

Eira and I.

Elufed and Rhian.

We each made our choices in how to be free.

CHAPTER 21

Angharad

The Forest
Battle of Arderydd
17th of October, AD 573

Angharad woke in the hut of Brother Thomas to the smell of simmering oats. Porridge again, but she welcomed it. It was difficult to tell the time of day in the windowless hut. Angharad felt as if she'd slept through winter. No dreams. Brother Thomas looked up from the cookpot.

"Is it morning?" she asked.

"It is," he said.

Her sleep fog evaporated at the thought of Eira, and Angharad swung her feet over the edge of the bed. The sooner she found her father, the sooner she might save Eira.

"Is it early morning? Or have I slept overlate? We must set out. Please, we must go."

She looked about to gather her belongings but remembered she had none, save her torque and the belt that once holstered her mother's knife.

"Those who are wise know better than to travel on an empty stomach," Brother Thomas said. "Straight after we eat, we will set out for the river Tyne."

Angharad sat dutifully at the table, studying a freshly carved cross resting there. Intricate interlacing patterned the wood. In the center was a star, its points radiating outward, beyond.

"It's only just finished," he said. "It is meant to bring protection."

"It's lovely. You are quite good at carving."

"Woodworking was my craft at the monastery before I came here to the woods. I learned it from my father, and he, his father before him." Brother Thomas placed her bowl of porridge on the table. "Eat, then. We will change your wrappings before we depart."

It was a cool, clear morning as they stepped outside the hut, and Angharad took a deep breath, blinking in the light. The forest was a pulsating world of color and sound after her deep hours of sleep, and though her worries had not left her, at least she was rested. Brother Thomas tilted his face to the sun filtering through the trees. Looking at his sandy hair and blue eyes, Angharad could not help but be reminded of her uncle Lailoken, though Brother Thomas seemed older and possessed poorer teeth. Yesterday she'd set out to find the river but come upon Brother Thomas instead. Now she had someone to bring her to the river in safety. The trees had been right. She'd been just where she needed to be.

"Is it very far?" Angharad asked as she followed him on the forest trail.

"Far enough that until recent days, my hut received few visitors," Brother Thomas replied. "But we shall reach it by midday."

They walked in silence a stretch before Angharad turned to him. "Brother Thomas?"

"Yes."

"Why did the man come and demand that you mark your door?"

He looked at her. "Why do you think?"

"Because the armies would spare Christians."

"It would seem so," he said.

Angharad thought on this. "Do you not feel terrible that your hut was spared while the homes of women and children of the Old Way were burnt?"

"I do not like the burning of any huts, nor the harming of any people, no matter which god they might choose. But if my hut had not been spared, I could not offer those same women and children food and shelter."

"The armies—my father's men and the other kings—they sought to punish people of the Old Way. But I am of the Old Way. And so is my mother."

"Belief among kings is nearly always about power," he said. "Perhaps there was more than one reason the kings wished to topple Uther Pendragon."

"But he was a hero. He and my uncle Lailoken and all of their men!"

"Yes. And as such, they had great influence. Uther's lands also levied much tribute from merchants taking their goods both north and south. And his kingdom stands between other Brythonic kings and Bernicia. Men fear what they cannot control. And they could not control Uther Pendragon."

"But why are there lords and chieftains who despise the old religion so?"

"I do not believe they despise the Old Way, not truly. It is more so they recognize Christianity can lend them more power."

"But how?"

"Let me pose you a question." Brother Thomas bowed his head. "Two men of power enter a room before a great audience. Who may speak first? The Wisdom Keeper or the king?"

"The Wisdom Keeper," Angharad replied. "It has always been so."

"That is right."

Angharad considered this, stopping midstride. "The kings wish to be beholden to none other but themselves."

"You are quite clever for a girl of nine winters."

"But that has nothing to do with gods! It is only about power! And why must it come to a war between this way or that?"

"Because men are fools."

"But you chose a life among men, at a monastery," Angharad pointed out.

Brother Thomas did not smile. "And now I am a hermit, living in the woods."

"A culdee," she corrected him. "Why did you leave?"

"I fell out with the priest there, and I wished to be closer to God. That is all you need know."

"Your god or mine?" Angharad asked.

Brother Thomas looked amused. "Are they not one and the same?" He quickened his pace. "Come on, then. We're getting close now. With any luck, a vessel will pass before too long."

Brother Thomas was kind, Angharad knew, but also powerful. She'd tried to see into him, and it was as if she'd run headlong into a rampart. She fell quiet. At last they emerged from the trees to find themselves standing before the river. Waist-high brown river grass led to a place where the bank sloped into dark flowing water. Blue sky and clouds drifted in its reflection, as if one could step foot on the river's surface and stride across the sky. But there was no sign of any boat.

Brother Thomas drew out some bread and cheese from his satchel, and they ate. A curlew called from the shallows. Still no boats. Angharad picked dirt from beneath her fingernails. Time stretched. Then at last Brother Thomas stiffened, narrowing his eyes as he looked upriver. "A vessel, I think! It comes this way."

It was a flat-bottomed currach with four men at oar, a fifth sitting at the stern watching. Brother Thomas stood, waving, but Angharad's stomach was full of moths. The boatmen wore Brythonic-style caps and woven checked tunics, but something about the men made Angharad ill at ease.

"I do not think these men are good," Angharad said.

"I am here. No ill shall befall you," Brother Thomas reassured her. "Let us speak to them, in the least. We shall see what they know."

The currach drew up, the boatmen stretching their oars to pull the boat ashore. Only as they drew closer did Angharad realize they weren't men, not all. Two of the oarsmen were women. They wore tunics and woolen trousers, their shoulders muscled beneath their shirts, but both had the unmistakable rise of breasts. Wives? Sisters, perhaps? Either way, Angharad felt a sway of relief. There was safety in women.

The man at the stern leapt lightly from the boat and scaled the bank, offering a smile. His hair was light brown and the beard beneath his chin trained to a point. He wore a belted tunic with an embroidered hem and a padded leather vest. His eyes were pale, more gray than blue. "Good day," he said, and Angharad heard an accent.

Brother Thomas drew Angharad behind him. "Greetings. You're the first vessel we've seen all morning. Where do you travel from?"

The man smiled but appeared confused. "Traders." He tapped his chest, nodding toward the boat.

"Ah," Thomas said. "They do not possess a good grip on Brythonic. Have you seen any warriors?" He lifted his arm as if gripping a spear, and the man's eyes sparked with understanding.

"No, no," he said. He pointed upriver, shaking his head again.

"And where is it you've come from?" Thomas asked again, but Angharad could tell he was growing frustrated.

"Bernicia."

Brother Thomas's face brightened. "Ah!" He spoke something to the man that sounded like Anglian, and the trader smiled broadly in return, exposing a row of clean white teeth. "Stay here a moment. I'll see what we might learn," Brother Thomas said.

"But he's an Angle." Angharad tugged Brother Thomas's cloak.

The trader stiffened. "We must all be born some place, Angharad. Not all Angles are evil, and as you well know, not all Britons are kind," Brother Thomas said.

"But—"

"A moment, only." He stepped away and Angharad slunk back.

What did she know, in any case? At every turn she'd been wrong. She'd abandoned the fortress and gotten separated from her family. She'd followed the dark-haired woman and led Eira into danger. How could she be Chosen? How could her uncle, her mother, and even Diarmid believe her to be? Angharad's chest tightened, and she forced her eyes from Brother Thomas and the trader, looking instead at the women in the boat. They spoke in low voices with the men as the currach bobbed in the river's eddy, their eyes wary and their skin a pale leather of weather and wind. They were more muscled than other freewomen. Then again, Angharad had never seen an Angle before. Perhaps they all rowed boats and dressed like men. One looked up, feeling Angharad's eyes upon her, and offered a smile that did not reach her eyes.

Angharad startled when Brother Thomas touched her arm.

"It's all right, it's only me," he said gently. "They're traders from Bernicia, here to make what profit they can from the strife. Word of Gwenddolau's fall has traveled. People are desperate for sheepskin and food and all else imaginable. For a price, they've agreed to take us to Rheged."

"To Rheged?" she asked.

"Yes. Urien is a fair and generous king. If we do not meet your father's men along the way, he will certainly receive us. You will be safe there until your people can fetch you home. But we must buy passage. Have you anything to trade? Anything at all?"

Her mother's knife was with Gwrgi and his men now, but her slender golden torque was still fastened by the belt at her waist, hidden beneath her tunic. It was all she had left of home, and she could not part with it. Angharad shook her head.

"You needn't fret. Perhaps he'll accept a carving. Come, Angharad. We must not tarry."

They followed the trader to the riverbank, where the oarsmen waited, steadying the boat.

"I can offer this." Brother Thomas drew the cross he'd finished only that morning from his satchel. The trader squinted at it, then laughed.

"Doesn't like my handiwork, it seems," Brother Thomas said. Clearly, the trader was not a Christian.

"I have nothing else." Brother Thomas held up his hands. The humor fell from the trader's face. He looked at them a moment, then gestured impatiently, taking the cross and thrusting it into his vest. The woman who'd been eyeing Angharad from the boat stood to help them aboard, offering Brother Thomas her hand. He stepped in, but as she reached to hoist Angharad in beside him, the torque pinched between her hand and Angharad's back. They settled into the currach beside the cargo, and the trader hopped in.

As the woman took up the oar nearest their backs, she said something that sounded like an admonishment. The trader glanced at Angharad, and they pushed off from the bank, easing the currach into the river's swift current. They'd found a boat. They were under way. But the trader did not take his place at the stern. He moved instead to crouch before Angharad, looking at her expectantly.

"We've paid you. The girl has nothing," Brother Thomas said. The trader raised a brow and spoke in Anglian, holding out his hand.

"He claims you have jewels," Brother Thomas said.

"Jewels? I haven't!" Angharad lied. Her torque had belonged to her mother before her, and it was worth the price of a thousand currachs, besides. She heard an impatient *tsk* from behind her, and the woman reached roughly beneath Angharad's tunic, yanking the torque from her belt and slapping it into the trader's waiting hand. He looked at it, then at Angharad, his pale eyes keen.

"Where did you find that?" Brother Thomas admonished her. "Thievery is a sin!"

Angharad's face heated with anger and confusion—the trader had taken her torque, and Brother Thomas knew she was a noble! Then he looked at her with meaning, and she realized. He did not wish the trader to know that Angharad was of gentle blood. She needn't know why, but she trusted him.

"I am sorry." She bowed her head, watching with a sinking heart as the man tucked the treasure into his vest.

"It is better he should have it, for you must learn the way of things." The culdee spoke so the man might hear. "Steal from another, and another shall steal from you. What is ill begotten, ill begets."

The trader clapped Brother Thomas on the back and moved away. Angharad swiveled in her seat to look at the woman rowing behind her. The woman only returned her stare.

Horrid! Angharad turned back to the water, brows drawn in fury. "That was all I had of my mother and my father. I *curse* you! I curse you! I curse you to die," she whispered.

Brother Thomas heard her and straightened. "Angharad! You mustn't curse people! Take it away," he said.

Angharad shook her head. Brother Thomas pushed aside a sack of sheepskins to sit nearer. "I am very sorry for the loss of your torque," he said. "But you mustn't wish ill upon people, Angharad. It can be very dangerous indeed. Enough evil finds its way. Do you truly wish to aid it?"

Angharad's vision blurred as she looked downriver, and Brother Thomas sighed, taking her hand. "Nothing can take your mother and father away. They cannot be found in a trinket. You are made of them, always, and they of you."

The words brought her some comfort, but her anger remained. Stealing from a child. Let the woman and man reap what they sowed. At the far end of the currach, the trader stood, lifting his arms to take in a deep breath of river air. Then, reaching into his vest, he drew out Brother Thomas's cross and, with a careless flick of his wrist, tossed it into the water. Angharad watched as it sank beneath the surface, disappearing from sight.

"Your carving," she said.

Brother Thomas regarded him in silence. "It does not matter. I will make another."

"But you labored so long over it."

"It was a possession, nothing more. I am made of God, and God is within me, always. That is something no river can drown in its current."

They carried on in silence. The Bernicians spoke little, but when they did, Angharad thought their tongue sounded lisping and thin, wanting of meat. Clouds gathered, obscuring the sun, and a fine mist settled. She watched as the trees drifted by, their bare fingers eerie in the billowing mist, her body so worn she could no longer tell if the currach was gliding or idling in an eddy while the trees drew up their roots and moved on instead. Her eyelids grew heavy, and she slumped against the hull, the sound of sloshing water lulling her to sleep.

She was startled awake sometime later by a *clank*, heavy and certain, like metal on wood. She opened her eyes to find it was twilight. What had been mist had become a dense and impenetrable fog while she slept.

Clank.

Angharad spun round, then saw it. A grappling hook, gripping the currach's edge only an arm's length away. She blinked. The river was silent. But then a sharp jerk rocked the boat, icy river water rushing onto Angharad's lap. She gasped as the currach lurched, tipping perilously, and Brother Thomas threw his arms out to shield her.

"What's happening?" she cried.

"Keep down, Angharad, we are under attack!" he said. The Bernicians scrambled as the trader shouted what sounded like orders.

Clank.

Behind them, an oarsman cried out, and Angharad twisted in Brother Thomas's arms to see the barb of a grappling hook piercing the man's thigh, pinning his body to the currach. He flailed against the siding, leg pulsing blood, and still more hooks were sailing.

Clank.

Clank.

Two more sank home through the fog, slamming Angharad and Brother Thomas to the boat bottom as the currach was yanked from its course. The traders dropped their useless oars, provisions scattering as they snatched up weapons hidden amidst the cargo. A sword, a dirk, and a bow and quiver—this, one of the women took up, drawing it tight as she peered into the gloom. Water slapped into the currach as they were hauled helplessly against the current, closer and closer to the banks of the river. It was not until the trees were nearly upon them that any of them could see. But then Brother Thomas looked up, his eyes going wide. "God save us," he said.

Half hidden by mist, men with spears were hunched like vultures in the trees, their grappling ropes wrapped round boughs as they yanked the boat through the water.

"Raiders!" Brother Thomas said. "Keep your head down! Keep your head down and pray."

Angharad's stomach dropped as a raider perched overhead drew back his arm. The spear struck before she even saw it fly, a scream echoing as the Bernician woman at their back lurched forward, clutching wildly at the space in between, the wooden shaft of the spear protruding from her eye. Angharad screeched. Blood soaked the boat. The woman she had cursed was choking, flailing. Angharad saw the panic on her face before she dropped to the vessel bottom like a boulder.

The trader glanced back, surveying the craft as his archer loosed arrows into the tops of the trees, sending a raider tumbling from the branches into the water with a splash. One woman dead and a man pinned to the gunwale, howling with each yank of the hook as the raiders took hold.

The trader shouted something to the archer, then hurried to the injured man, crouching before him, cradling his face between his hands. They looked at each other. The oarsman stopped struggling and nodded. With one violent jerk, the trader snapped the oarsman's neck. The man's head dropped, lolling against his chest. Without a backward glance, the trader leapt onto the gunwale and launched himself into the river, the archer and last remaining oarsman splashing in behind him. Spears shot in a storm from the trees as the raiders sought to impale the Bernicians in the water, and Brother Thomas pushed Angharad flat into the sloshing cold, shielding her with his body. She was blinded beneath the bulk of him but closed her eyes all the same, sobbing at the *thwack* and *thunk* as spears plummeted from above, knowing the next would pierce their bodies like salmon in a pool.

"Please!" Brother Thomas shouted. "Please, there's a child! She is only a child!" He needn't have shouted, for it had gone quiet now. His voice echoed through the dim.

Angharad listened, still robbed of her sight.

A shower of feet dropping onto grass from some height. The tipping and sift of water on earth as their currach was hauled up onto the shore. A man barking orders in another unfamiliar tongue. Angharad might have placed it, but she was terrified and shivering, soaking in blood and damp. Brother Thomas drew back and she clutched at him, mute and blinking. Only now could Angharad see the raiders clearly. They were clad in short gray cloaks and tunics, belted at the waist, with tight woolen breeches and stout leather boots oiled against water. It was their bare places that made Angharad stare—their faces and arms were covered in secrets branded in ink: wolves and sea eagles, horses and serpents, or markings like stick figures with limbs blazing fire.

"Picts," Thomas whispered. "They have a reverence for women, and you are a child. If they wished to kill us, they would have done so already. Look. He must be their commander."

Angharad leaned against Brother Thomas as a broad-shouldered man with black hair and a drooping mustache strode toward them. His blue eyes were piercing, and two blue-black fish were tattooed upon his forehead, arcing to meet in the middle of his brow.

"This child is a noble," Brother Thomas said. Yet the man carried on as if he'd heard nothing, nodding at his men to take Angharad and Brother Thomas in hand as they claimed their stolen cargo. But as the commander's eyes swept the lifeless bodies of the traders, they caught upon the woman. He took in her cheekbones, the curves of her womanhood beneath her tunic, and his expression darkened with something that looked like regret. Bending, he touched his hands to her hair and murmured words that felt like a prayer. Then, bracing her head, the commander retrieved his spear with a sickening *squelch*.

Within moments the currach was emptied, save for the bodies of the dead. Angharad watched as the raiders strode to the underbrush, tossing aside branches to reveal a vessel hidden upon the forest floor. A raiding ship, bigger than the Bernician currach and built to move in deeper waters. With some effort, they got behind it, pushing it toward the water's edge, where it slapped with a great splash into the river's draft.

The raiders nudged the two of them toward the waiting vessel with the tips of their spears.

Brother Thomas hoisted her into his arms, and she clung like a limpet as he stepped toward the boat, but the raider nearest them frowned, reaching to yank her from Brother Thomas's grip.

"Stop, please! She's frightened," he insisted. Angharad kicked at the raider, and the commander's face hardened. In two strides, he was before them.

"Please, allow me to carry her," Brother Thomas said. The commander answered with his fist. The blow knocked Brother Thomas to his knees, sending Angharad spilling from his arms, and she clambered to her feet as the commander drew his fist back again.

"No, no," she cried. He stopped short, eyes fixed on Brother Thomas. The monk's skin had split just above his brow, but he did not flinch, only blinked, as blood trickled down. Satisfied, the commander stepped back and Brother Thomas stood. They waited, soaked and shaking in the river's dank as the raiders bound their hands.

"This girl is a noble," Thomas said again, wincing as they yanked the coarse rope too tight. "She is Angharad of Strathclyde, daughter of Rhydderch."

At this the commander stopped. He turned, scrutinizing Angharad as if to ascertain her worth.

"He speaks our tongue, he understands! Please, take me to my father!" Angharad cried. "Please! I want to go home!"

The man only turned, stepping lightly aboard the boat. Angharad's eyes stung with tears as the raider she'd kicked took up their ropes to pull them roughly on board. He sat down heavily on the nearest oar bench, watching them with interest. There was blood beneath his fingernails, and his hands were soiled with dirt. As he shifted to adjust his belt, his cloak slipped up his arm, revealing an ox charging in a whorling sinew of dark blues and blacks from forearm to wrist.

Angharad had never met a Pict, save her own *nain*, Elufed. She searched for the words Elufed had whispered at her bedside at night. The language was lilting, filled with earth and light. But her *nain* did not speak it often, if she spoke it at all.

Noticing Angharad's stare, the raider frowned, pulling his cloak to cover his markings. Still, the smallest spark of hope lit, and she turned to Brother Thomas. "My *nain* is a Pict," she said. "Surely that must count for something. She's the queen of Strathclyde. We need only explain, if only he'd listen!"

"Your grandmother," Thomas said. "But what of your mother? She's a Briton, is she not?"

"Yes."

"Angharad, surely you remember. The Picts trace their blood from the mother's side. Your father, Rhydderch, would be counted a Pict to this day, should he so choose to claim it. But you come from the belly of a Briton."

"But surely—"

"Nay, Angharad. In their eyes, you are foreign as any other." He sighed, rubbing his face with bound hands. "I am sorry, Angharad. But your grandmother's blood is no help to us here."

The Picts offered them no sheepskins for warmth. As the wind picked up and night fell in earnest, Brother Thomas gave the commander a stormy look, lifting his bound arms round Angharad to warm her, but his own robes were damp, his skin wet and clammy. "You mustn't fall sick," he said. Angharad's body shook. She willed herself to become a snail, seeking a new shell, but the cold had sharp teeth, and try as she might, she could not slip from her body.

The Picts knew the river's course like the track of their veins. The night was moonless and still choked with fog, yet their vessel raced on. As the craft cut through the water, they passed the eerie orange glow of a lantern marking a ferryman's dock, and Angharad saw the murky forms of huts. Here, the huts had not been burned to cinders. But the raider's eyes darted nonetheless as they stroked at their oars, letting Angharad know the land they traveled was not that of a friend.

"Where are we?" she whispered.

Brother Thomas looked round. "*Lloegr*," he answered. "We must be, by now."

"The Lost Lands."

"The same," Thomas said. "Not long ago, these lands belonged to the Britons. Now they are claimed by the Angles of Bernicia."

So this was the reason the Picts rowed in silence, using fog as their cloak. Angharad stared at the rope sawing her skin as she shifted her bottom. Her *nain* was so beautiful and mysterious. Angharad had once longed to meet the First People. Now she was their captive, wrists chafing in their bonds.

She took a breath and tasted salt on her tongue. Angharad might not be able to see in the dark, but at least she could feel. She spoke to the water. *Tell me*, she said.

The river had no worries. She felt its narrow body rushing toward the freedom of a broad saltwater bay. But beyond the river, Angharad sensed a watery world of terrifying new gods, ancient and algae-covered. Deadly in their deep.

Then through the fog came a soft, blinking light. The Picts changed their course, heading toward the beacon. A voice called out from a distance, and the raiders pushed against the oars, slowing their boat. Angharad clutched Thomas's hand as a small Pictish fleet emerged from the mist, proud sails tethered as the vessels bobbed ominously in the dark. They stood thrice as tall as the boat that now carried them. Seafaring longships, awaiting the raiders' return. Angharad heard the efficient sound of sheeting as the sails were loosed. Together the vessels traveled onward, carried by the wind, and they slipped into the mist, disappearing into another world.

III.

From a secluded place
rise up and declare
books of inspiration without fear,
and a tale of a maiden
and a dream in sleep.

—"The Prophecy of Myrddin and Gwenddydd,
His Sister," *The Red Book of Hergest*,
translated by John K. Bollard

CHAPTER 22

Lailoken

Caledonian Wood
Kingdom of the Selgovae
January, 574 AD

Archer and I forded the river. I'd whittled a walking stick from a fallen oak and beat its rhythm steadily upon the ground.

"I can only take you as far as the burn," he said.

"Then that is where you'll leave me. It was kind enough for you to leave your hearth."

"It's no bother, Lailoken. Winter is a friend."

To undergo the Bull's Sleep alone was a danger. With no one to stir me, I might never return. So I was going to the temple of the fallen keeper to descend into madness. I was going to the cursed pile of stones to die. For either would I die or, in dying, I would somehow be reborn.

Archer stopped as the burn came into sight, bowing his head. "Gods keep you, Lailoken. If you do go mad, I should hate to end you with an arrow upon your return."

I clasped the chieftain's arm. "I should hate to be ended. Thank you, Archer. Truly."

I stood on the stream bank with no small sense of foreboding as Archer turned, heading back into the hills. But then, only a short distance away, I saw it. I scarcely noticed the pain in my wounds as I quickened my pace.

The waterfall seemed to tumble from a break in the sky. Cloud-white water cascaded in sprays from a craggy split between the forbidding hills. It looked like the magnificent tail of a white horse, or the silvery flow of a maiden's hair. Here some goddess had lain down her head, spilling her locks over the edge of the earth. I stopped and stood before it, unmoving. Its beauty was entrancing. It cracked something within me. I wanted to laugh.

I wanted to weep.

Beyond the bank of the burn, the old settlement stood silent, its stony rampart covered in snow. Ice groaned beneath my feet as I navigated the rocks that yet forded the burn. The Selgovae had robbed no rocks from the fortress, so concerned were they with inviting ill luck. The outer wall stood four men high. There would have been watchmen once, posted on platforms raised inside the stone, or perhaps, as elsewhere in the Caledonian Wood, they relied upon more hidden eyes.

Leaning on my stick, I descended the snow-filled ditch and climbed the slope toward the gap in the stone that once would have held the gate.

Reaching out, I pressed my palms to the weatherworn stone of the entrance, making myself known. Doorways persist long after wood rots away.

After a moment, I felt an easing, a giving way. A wet, pelting snow began to fall. I stepped through the threshold of the cursed fortress.

Inside the ring of stone, my ears burned with silence, but a feeling of peace prevailed. Remnants of roundhouses lay like discarded cocoons where wattle and daub had fallen away. I looked across the enclosure and saw only one structure intact. It was a small building the shape of a bee's hive. There was good reason this structure had stood up to the elements—unlike the others, it was built entirely of stone. The pieces had been dry-stacked, increasingly inward and up, until a single smoke stone could cap the top, to be shifted aside for hearth smoke. Such structures were kept only by holy men. I'd sleep this night in the Mad Keeper's home.

I crouched to duck through the child-size doorway. The dead winter grasses were free of snow and bedded in pebble. It brought to mind the hollow hills of the north, where bones were kept to speak with the dead—grandmothers and chieftains. Infants, birdlike, their spirits flown too soon. Yet such places were grand. This was little more than a cell.

A cell built for dreaming. The thought came unbidden.

There was room enough to sleep if I tucked my long legs. I unbound my bedroll and set out my cook pot and single cup. Not far from the door lay the charred remains of a fire. So the Selgovae had not forsaken this place, not altogether. For herders in need, shelter was shelter.

Satisfied, I left my belongings and struck out in search of fuel.

Night closed in, and soon I found myself in darkness, hurrying back to the cell where my stiff fingers fumbled with the flint. When the spark came, instead of casting the dim cell in a welcome glow, it made me feel ill at ease.

I am Lailoken. I, too, am a Keeper of the Robe.

But my words did not shift the air that surrounded me. I'd spent days upon end in chambers and caves far closer than this, but suddenly the cell felt confined, as though someone were behind me, standing too close. One who did not wish me there.

A voice came. Or had the words indeed been spoken?

Mine.

The fire cracked, then sputtered. My hackles raised. I would not be put off. This was my land, that of the living. It was the lingering shades who trespassed, not I.

What happened, brother? Did you indeed go mad?

No answer came. Beyond the cell's doorway, snow fell in earnest. By morning I might find myself half buried within. A sudden wind gusted, scattering sparks, and I stamped out an ember that sank with a burned smell into my fleece.

"I'll thank you not to burn my bedding," I said.

Perhaps I should not have spoken, for the next moment, another gust whipped through the cell and the fire snuffed out.

I cursed. Hovering over the wood, I rebuilt my tinder and struck at the flint 'til my fingers cramped, but no fire would catch. I stood, straightening to my full height in the hive. I was a warrior of Pendragon. This icy cell was a luxury. With the heft of my sheepskin and the nearness of the cell, I'd have warmth enough to last through the night.

"Go on, then," I said. "Extinguish my fire. It has been many long years since I have been fearful of the dark."

The night cell felt watchful. My mind roamed, tireless, my face burning with cold. I tucked my head beneath the fleece where my breath clouded warm, but the air soon went stale. It was many hours before sleep found me. When it did, at last, I dreamed of a stranger. A girl who was searching. It seemed she dwelled in some distant time. Her longing was vast as the mountains. I cannot explain it, but I knew what she sought. She sought to remember.

There were temples once, I told her. They dotted the land like pinpricks into veins, tapping in to power that thrummed beneath the land of the living: the land of the dead. There, would you sleep in a cell, dreaming in darkness, and when you woke, the Keeper would ponder and tell you its meaning.

There were star trackers once, who lifted their eyes to skies within circles of stone that thrummed into veins. They sang songs of summoning, and through the long, hollow halls, the ancestors came to be honored and held close. They came to be remembered.

The girl sat beside me, but it was as if I were not there.

She walked a land vacant as a desert, a land of shades and blowing grasses. She walked and sought the places where temples once stood, but for too long they had lain altered, neglected. For too long the ancestors of the girl had been sleeping.

I was weeping for them, then. All the lost children. Rocking beneath the wave of their sorrow. And then I woke.

I lay blinking, my face wet with tears. It was the blue hour before morning, and I had been weeping in my sleep. But there was a sensation, too, that had brought me awake. A nudge in the ribs, as if by a boot.

I searched the cell, eyes straining in the semi-dark.

A man stood looking down upon me, half hunched beneath the tapered stone roof. His hair was shorn in a crescent above his forehead, his eyes kohled in the manner of a diviner, of a priest. He shifted ever so slightly, and the cloak about his shoulders trembled. The cloak was made from cloth, or so it seemed, yet there was an unusual texture, something mounded high upon his shoulders that made him appear hunched, like a wood troll. The cloak was sewn with feathers. Layers upon layers.

He cocked his head, studying me with the black-eyed intelligence of a crow.

"What is it you want? Why have you drawn me here?" I asked.

The man did not speak. But as I watched, his eyes shifted to the scar upon my cheek.

I must have blinked, for then he was gone.

Was I truly awake? Or had I been dreaming? I stood and went to the place where the man had loomed only a moment ago, searching the ground.

Fool, Lailoken. What are you hoping to find?

And then I saw it. Perhaps it was the purple light playing tricks, but I thought I discerned the slightest imprint, the shape of two boots denting the brown winter grass.

I sat back upon my bedroll, dragging a hand over my face. This was why I had come, on the eve of the Wolf Moon, the moon before Imbolc. At the far edge of the cell, the wolf pelt sat in a heap. *Follow me*, it said.

Aye, I would follow. But could I return?

That I could drop myself into the world below ground was a matter of fact. I had done so before. The traveling was deep, the pathways frequented only by those who could find their way home. That was what I'd feared when I'd dragged Angharad from the stones. The body rouses, but the spirit is yet roaming, lost in between.

Perhaps that was the fate that had befallen the Keeper. The Keeper of the Falls had summoned me here. The cursed Keeper of the Falls had stirred me from a dream. Soon I hoped to discover why. But the Sleep must be done in darkness, under the strength of the moon.

So I stepped out into the morning, eerie with white. A good measure of snow had fallen in the night, transforming the falls into a craggy magnificence of towering ice. The burn beside the fort was frozen solid. I headed out in search of more fuel.

An uphill climb was nothing, but I was weak from fasting and my wounds were yet mending. There would be scant wood on the desolate slopes, yet I still found myself climbing the steep path that led up past the fort. Soon I stood where the water spilled over the cliff. It was barren here—dark rock and dead grasses jutting up from the snow. As I picked my way higher up the burn's course, the grasses gave way to dead moss and thick brown tufts of heather. The blood in my legs pulsed and pounded, threatening to seep, and I stopped where I stood, breathing. In the place in between breaths, memories of my loved ones came rushing back to claim me.

Memory is a danger. It unlocks the door to madness.

A shiver traced my arms beneath my furs, and then something skittered on the steep slope above, sending a scattering of rocks below. I looked up the hill and spied a lone goat standing, white as the snow. Its winter coat was shagged with fur, its horns were black as night. Its bright eyes were yellow, piercing with a strangeness that belonged to no mortal creature.

The names of my god came unbidden. *Herne. Horned One. Cernunnos.*

But Herne had forsaken me. He'd given no warning of the men who had marched to kill us. I'd asked him for sustenance on our hunt, and he'd sent a living demon instead.

I looked at the goat. "Now you come. What is it you would tell me?" I demanded. "Show me. Show me! What must I do?"

The only sound was the barking of a raven as an icy rain began to fall. The wind rushed up the valley, tugging at my hair. The raven sounded with the sharpness of a pin being driven into my head. The goat looked down at me, watching.

Perhaps I could not blame my god for the beast. Perhaps he could not keep it away. But I could no longer sense the origins of my own thoughts. Such things happened from hunger. Frustration mounted, and I suddenly wanted to beat at my own head.

I stared up at the goat as if my eyes alone could spear it. *Nothing, nothing, again and again!* I threw back my head with a scream—long and half-human, a cry born of rage. It startled my own ears, sending the animal bounding, disappearing from sight.

I cursed and balled my fists. My beard was soaked, the hairs bristling to ice upon my cheek. Down in the valley, any fuel would soon be wet.

There were no messages for me here.

I fasted through the day, gathering what dry wood I could from the strip of forest that followed the frozen burn down below, bundling it to carry back to the cell upon my shoulders. My nose ran from cold by the time I returned, stacking the kindling to dry beside the fire.

It lit, at least, and did not go out. Night neared. I unrolled my bedding and fed the flames. It would die while I lay sleeping. When I woke, I'd be near frozen, if I woke from the Sleep at all. I felt the same pit in my stomach that churned before battle, but I took the packet from my satchel, setting my cook pot over the fire to heat the old brew. Roots, mushrooms, and plants, elements for dreaming. I bent my head over the pot, inhaling the steam, earthy and sharp. It smelled like revelation. I sat and waited as it steeped, watching the fire.

Who would aid me now? I closed my eyes, summoning the bloodline of those who had come before. *Morken, Morydd, Mor. Cathan, my teacher.*

"Idell, Mother," I said. "Bless my dreaming. Keep your son safe."

I struck a small split of wood against the pot in a slow, steady rhythm.

The drink was a bitter, welcome heat. I drank it down and pulled out my rope, binding my feet. I knotted my blindfold, fumbling in blackness to bind my own hands. Stretching out, I pulled the wolf pelt to cover me, then took the dried boar skin, biting between my teeth. There was a repellent bristling—as if the elements of the two animals yet carried the memory of their feud—but I required both for the rite, and I hoped the wolf might aid me where the black boar would not. I caught sight of them, standing, and then they both began to run.

My body was hollow, insides scraped clean. Beneath the blindfold, I closed my eyes, following the creatures into the dark. Soon the blackness was swirling, spinning swiftly into what felt like a pool. I felt the rise of vomit and turned to my side, but the medicine was quick. The cell dropped away. I fell out of my body and into the earth.

There were passages there, down in the deep. Tunnels that cut through earth and through stone. I traveled them, one moment as if winged and the next moment inching through suffocating gaps, over and between boulders. Before me, the tunnel narrowed into a chute. Here I could not pass unless pressed upon my stomach. I dragged myself forward using the strength of my fingers. Beneath me, the rock went for leagues, down into the earth. Above me pressed the weight of passing eons.

Others had traveled here. I could see the scrape of their fingers in sediment, hear their tormented cries echoing in the stone. Men and women, trapped since time out of memory.

Help me. Help. I can no longer breathe.

The air had grown heavy. The tunnel had gone stale. And then I began to realize it was not rock that pressed up from leagues down below but a pile of bodies. Bone upon bone. I sensed them beneath me, not only Keepers but line upon line of wanderers, those who'd attempted to travel this hidden world since man had first been born from the Gods.

They are not real. They are not here, I told myself. *This is the path of my journey alone.*

From somewhere in the distance came the warning that my chest was scarcely rising. The only way up was to discover a way through.

I blinked in the darkness, searching for light. And then I saw it. A flicker, a crack. It was so simple—see it. And then I was through.

I stumbled from the suffocation of the cave into the light. The hollow into the deep yawned at my back, its entrance unassuming, a craggy overhang where an animal might shelter from the cold. The forest before me was oak and ash, and beyond it was a loch. A gentle sweep of wind made ripples in the water. Birds called. The air smelled of leaf mold. The sky was gray, warning of rain.

Your body lies bound, dreaming in snow.

It was a trick, a quality of light, but this was not the world owned by men. This was a twin place, one far beneath. I could not linger here, I knew. I must keep alert. For this place was not like the world of men.

In this place, things were not always as they seemed.

CHAPTER 23

Languoreth

Cadzow Fortress
Kingdom of Strathclyde
November, AD 573

Through the pasture where I once threw my blade at targets. Though the sturdy gates of the outer rampart where I stood to watch so many leave. Past the dormant wych elm that scattered the earth in snowy petals in spring, and into a nestled world of trees high above the Avon water. Here oak and pine remembered those I most loved. My children. My father and mother. Gwenddolau and Lailoken. Ariane and Cathan, Wisdom Keepers. Crowan, my old nursewoman.

Maelgwn.

My power was here. And now I had returned.

The white cattle were home from their summer steading for winter's keep, and they lifted their heads as the carts rolled by. Their warm coats had come in, their shaggy underbellies black with mud. As I nodded to the warriors minding the innermost gate, a tear escaped, and Cyan turned to me.

"Mother, why do you cry?"

"It is only I am so happy to be home," I said.

The old timber hall stood unchanged. I had last visited near summer's end, at Lughnasa, when Rhys and I had overseen the harvest.

Since that day, so much had been taken from me. I suppose I had feared nothing of Cadzow could remain.

Droplets of rain clung to the gnarled branches of the apple tree in the courtyard. As we stepped down from the cart, my hallwoman Olwenna rushed to greet us, her hand over her heart.

I'd sent a messenger ahead with news of Angharad and Rhys, along with instructions for our arrival, for I could not bear any questions. But the look upon her heart-shaped face spoke tomes. "You are here now, m'lady. All will be well."

"Thank you, Olwenna."

Her eyes traveled the faces looking back from the wooden slats of the prison cart as it trailed in behind us.

"The messenger did not say how many, m'lady."

"We will make do. Thank you for your preparations, you had so little time."

"Aye, m'lady, and we were all more than willing. The stable is ready, it is all as you asked.'Tis not the first time we've welcomed those in need, and I'm certain it won't be the last."

Olwenna spoke of the Britons who'd been wounded in the Angle massacre. They'd flooded Cadzow's gates when I was but a girl. Olwenna had come to us years after that, but it was a tale none in our land could ever forget.

"Let us open the cart and get them settled quickly. I will be in to aid shortly," I said.

The prisoners were frigid and starving; some would have wounds. Their leader, Gwenddolau, had been fostered here at Cadzow, and was much beloved. My servants at Cadzow would provide Gwenddolau's people excellent care.

I motioned Eira, Aela, and the children into the hall. The rain had soaked Torin and his men on the half-day's journey by cart.

"Come," I said. "I will show you to your quarters."

"You needn't in the rain," Torin objected.

"Not so. I am your host."

Soon they would sleep in the hall by the hearth, as befitted my guard, but two of Torin's men were yet strangers, and I did not wish them so close.

They followed me through the courtyard, but as I lifted the latch to the hut kept for our guests, my breath caught. For a moment Maelgwn sat at the table, hunched over a map by candlelight, dark hair falling over his eyes. I blinked, and the room was empty once more.

"Is something the matter?" Torin asked.

"No. Only a ghost." I stepped into room. "They will come directly to light the hearth and bring some tapers. As you can see, there are very few warriors left here—we've little need under Tutgual's protection, but you shall meet all those at Cadzow in the stables, if you will aid us there?"

"In tending the prisoners?" asked one of Torin's men, astounded.

"Of course, m'lady. We are at your command." Torin pinned him with his eyes.

"Good, then." I smiled. "I shall see you there shortly."

I met Aela and Eira in the stables. Cyan and Gladys, too, wished to help. If only my husband could see them.

Look, Rhydderch. See how your children tend the victims of your war.

It was true, what I had said to the king. Cadzow was bare bones.

In the years since I'd wed Rhydderch, our presence at my childhood hall had dwindled. Strathclyde's borders were kept by men unafraid to bloody their swords, and no lord or chieftain from within dared raid the wife of Tutgual's son. But my servants here were loyal beyond compare. There could be no better place to shelter Gwenddolau's people. And here at Cadzow, I could await word from my brother. Until then, I could only pray that he and Maelgwn yet lived.

I buried Brant's head at the foot of an oak. It towered just beyond the rampart, where he and Brodyn had so often stood guard when I was a child. As I packed the last of the earth and straightened my back, I could have sworn the branches of the leafless tree rustled in the wind, as if with a sigh.

CHAPTER 24

Angharad

Kingdom of the Picts
25th of October, 573 AD

The fleet sailed north, or so Thomas said. Angharad's bandages had fallen away, but she had no more need of them. The days passed like water. With each approaching vessel, the eyes of the Picts traveled to their weapons.

Brother Thomas studied the stars. "It seems the fleet means to keep a wide berth from shore. Likely to avoid Angle vessels as they travel up the coast," he said.

On that first eve, before sleep, the Pictish commander with the fish upon his brow cut short the arms of a thick woolen tunic and offered it to Angharad. It gaped at the neck but fell neatly to her wrists and dropped down to her ankles, keeping her warm. The next day, upon seeing her stumble in its bulk, he unbound the rope at her wrists to use as a belt, then perched on the oar bench beside her. His eyes were the blue of a northern sea, and they were fixed upon Brother Thomas.

"Tell me. Is that priest your father?" he asked.

"You do speak my tongue!" Angharad exclaimed, rushing on in relief. "Sweet Gods, what a blessing! My name is Angharad, daughter of Rhydderch. Elufed is my *nain*. Surely you know that the queen of Strathclyde herself is a Pict. There was an unspeakable battle, and I was lost from my uncle, who was training me to be a Wisdom Keeper, and my father did not trade for me—"

The commander frowned. "I asked you of the priest."

"He is not a priest, he is a culdee," Angharad said. "He has been my protector, and he is a friend."

"That may be, but I do not keep with priests."

He sat in silence a long while, considering Brother Thomas, who sat bound at the stern, arms wrapped round his knees. Then the commander turned, rattling something in Pictish to his men. Angharad could not understand, but there was an unsettling change in his tone. The mood on the boat shifted, and two oarsmen stood, striding toward Thomas.

"What's happening?" Angharad cried. "What is it you would do?"

"I told you, I do not keep with priests." The commander's face was grim.

Panic surged as the Picts yanked Brother Thomas to his feet, dragging him to the gunwale of the boat.

Angharad ran to the commander, gripping his arm, but he shook her off, drawing his dirk. "A gift to the sea. When your priest meets Manannan, he will know a true god."

"No! Please, do not hurt him!" she cried.

"Do not watch. Look away," Brother Thomas said.

Angharad could not bear it, not one more death. Tears sprang as she clutched the commander's tunic, dropping to her knees. "Please. He is all that I have!"

The commander looked down at her. The hard line of his jaw softened. "You should be thankful I do not strike him dead where he stands. But I am not unmoved." Angharad dared not hope, but perhaps the Pict was not absent of a heart. He sheathed his dirk with a gallant gesture. "He may swim if he likes. Let Manannan choose his fate."

"But I cannot swim," Brother Thomas said.

The commander raised a brow. "Then perhaps your god will teach you to float."

"Please. I have sworn to protect her. I cannot leave this child until I have delivered her home," Thomas said.

"The child needs no advocate here."

"Keep me as a captive, then," Brother Thomas declared. "Surely you can fetch a fair price for a Christian at market."

"You believe you are valiant. You are not the first man to choose slavery over death."

Thomas strained against his captors to stand upright. "Say what you will, but surely some payment is better than none. Drown me and you will have nothing."

The commander glanced down at Angharad, still at his feet, then shook his head. "So be it."

The men dropped Brother Thomas, and he fell in a heap.

"Thank you," Angharad said, rushing to Thomas. "Thank you."

That night, Angharad was given a sheepskin for warmth. When she spread it over herself and the culdee, the commander gave a hard look but did not take it away. She took to peering at the commander when he was not looking. The depths of his eyes held a nobility that spoke of honor. Unlike Brother Thomas, the commander could not sense her. When he chided an oarsman, he clapped the man upon the shoulder, and the two men became boys before her eyes. They were swimming across a clear summer river. They were jabbing at each other with short wooden swords. Angharad did not understand why it was easier to see when she looked at the Pictish commander. But she was glad for it. She began to think he was not so terrible after all.

"What is your name?" she asked him. "I would know what to call you."

For this, she earned a frown. "My name is not yours to keep," he said.

"What do you mean? Why ever not?"

"We *Cruithni* are not like you. There is power in a name. You give away your name and so give away your power. I will say no more about it."

Angharad smiled, but the commander's frown only deepened.

"Why do you smile?" he demanded.

Angharad only shrugged, for she already knew his name. She had asked the water, and it had been given.

The commander's name was Talorcan.

The boat rocked gently, cresting and dropping over the skin of the waves as it followed the fleet. The Picts moved with such ease and pleasure on the water, Angharad felt safe. Sometimes she imagined she had buried the nightmare of each thing that had taken place since the day of the battle far behind in the fog, and when she wept, the ocean took her tears.

There is no end to the chamber we hold for you. Give them to us. We will take them away.

The next morning, Angharad found Talorcan standing by the prow.

"When autumn ends, the winter seas storm," he said. "Each of these ships carries home booty. This was the last raid we will run until spring."

"Are we traveling to your village, then?"

"Yes, my village."

"How is it you came to speak my tongue?" she asked.

"All of us speak it. We learn when we are young."

"But your other men do not speak to me."

"Simply because we choose not to speak does not mean we are unable. Keep pestering me and you'll find I'll soon forget the way of it, too."

"What is it like, your village?"

"I suppose you shall see."

Angharad frowned, irritated by his answers. For, as if in a dream, she and Talorcan stood there already. She saw mountains and rivers where forts perched upon hilltops like so many eagle nests, and great herds of cattle roamed in thick tawny coats.

Angharad had never seen in this way, the way she was beginning to. Visions came readily, colors shone more vividly. It was as if being among the Picts sharpened her sight. But still all Angharad could think of was home.

"When we arrive to your village," she ventured, "will you summon my father?"

"I cannot speak to your fate. It is not my choice to make."

"But if I am not free to summon my father, I am a prisoner. Is this not true?"

Talorcan looked at her sidelong. "Go make use of yourself and fetch the oarsmen some ale. It will not be long now 'til we come ashore."

A shout sounded, and Talorcan looked up. A vessel was cutting toward them, skirting the edge of the fleet. Another Pictish longboat. The hull was bedecked with round, clunky adornments that jostled and bounced with the waves. As the boat drew nearer, the vessel's commander nodded, and Talorcan lifted a hand in greeting. Angharad covered her mouth in horror as the boat sailed past. More than a dozen human heads were strung along the boat, gruesome in their states of watery decay.

"A scout boat," Talorcan said. "We do not ask questions of vessels that trespass in our waters.

"The men," he reminded her, motioning to the ale barrels.

He passed Angharad the drinking horn, and she watched the scout boat disappearing as she lifted the spout on the barrel. Who were the men whose heads bounced like trophies? Bernicians? Or Dragon Warriors who'd been seeking escape? Ale splashed over the top of the horn, and Angharad closed the spout quickly, wiping her fingers on her tunic. She passed the drinking horn round, and the oarsmen nodded, taking turns at quenching their thirst while their benchmate kept the oar slowly churning. When they had finished, she found Brother Thomas.

"Talorcan said we shall soon be at shore."

"Talorcan?" Brother Thomas raised a brow. "Is that his name? He told you as much?"

"Not precisely," she said.

"Then how came you to know? The Picts do not give their names with such ease."

Angharad hesitated, staring at her feet. "Are you angry?"

"Nay, Angharad. I would never chastise you for using your gift."

"My mother would say it was not proper to pry. As would my uncle."

Thomas looked out to sea. "I am certain they only mean to teach you how to wield your strengths with honor, Angharad. With wisdom."

"But you do not mind?"

Thomas considered her. "There are some men I know who might say they do not believe in the power of a Keeper to lay down a curse. But I have seen much in my time. You must learn to make use of your gifts, Angharad. They will protect you. But no more curses. You must be careful with the words that you say."

Angharad shivered at the thought of the Bernician woman, the *squelch* of Talorcan's spear as he retrieved it from her eye. "I did not mean for her to die," she whispered.

Brother Thomas saw the look upon her face. "Ah, Angharad. Who is to say? If you are sorry for her suffering, that is what matters. Do not puff yourself up. There are much larger forces at work. We are each of us quite small and unimportant. Even you. You remind me," he said, gazing down at his bound wrists. "There was a great man named

Patrick who spent much of his life as a slave. He was once a man of Strathclyde—perhaps you have heard of him?"

Angharad shook her head.

"Well. He was taken by the Scots to Scotia, the Westlands. He spent many winters among them. And though he was in bonds, he brought light to many people. If that is my path, I would not regret it."

The bellow of a horn sounded from one of the boats up ahead.

"Ah," Thomas said. "We must be arriving to the firth."

Two timber towers upon stilts kept watch, one on either side of the gray harbor's mouth. As they entered the firth, merchant ships and longboats waited at anchor. A few huts dotted the shore, earthen roofed roundhouses built out of stone, dead grasses like hair sprouting above wooden doors, and on little spits of sand sat round-bottomed coracles, stacked by their fishermen like beetles in a heap.

Soon Angharad spied a bustling quay, built at the head of a sandy crescent beach. Shouts of children echoed from shore, where fishermen tossed scraps to hovering gulls, looking up as the fleet returned from the sea.

"What place is this?" Angharad asked.

Brother Thomas looked round. "I cannot say for certain, but I think it is Dùn Déagh."

Angharad clung to Thomas as the oarmen guided the boat gently into the quay and women and children raced toward the ship. The raiders drew in their oars, tying off with efficiency, their movements betraying what their faces would not.

Home.

"Come," Talorcan said, taking up Brother Thomas's bonds.

Angharad's heart was a fist as they stepped from the boat, her legs feeling wobbly after days upon water. The Picts stopped to stare while Talorcan hurried his captives through the crowd, the dock planks thundering beneath so many feet. Laughter sounded over the cry of swooping gulls as the raiders embraced their families, but they all turned to watch as Angharad and Brother Thomas passed, their eyes fixed upon his tonsure and the brown hood he wore—that of a monk. A woman with white hair stepped forward and spat, her spittle flecking Angharad's cheek. Angharad recoiled, wiping her face. "Why do they despise him so?" she demanded, but Talorcan did not answer.

They followed a narrow road that led from the quay into a broad swath of woods. More stone huts with turf roofs sat here among the trees, and as the Picts retreated, ducking into their homes, only a cluster of children remained, running alongside the strangers in checked tunics and rich dresses of warm wool.

"Where do you take us?" Angharad asked, tugging at Talorcan's short gray cloak.

This time he turned. "I would have rest from my journey. We will stay with a friend. Tomorrow I will take you to see the chieftain. He must be the one to decide your fate."

"And what of Brother Thomas?"

"I will leave for Ceann Mòr on the morrow. It is the last fair of the season. We trade our slaves there."

The children were singing and poking Thomas with a stick. Angharad opened her mouth to protest, but Talorcan said, "Hush now."

They'd reached the wicker enclosure of a farmyard, and the children ceased their taunting to swarm round, watching as Talorcan reached into his satchel and drew out a handful of treasures. Pottery bits and speckled pebbles, swirling white shells. He sorted through his collection with a matchmaker's gaze, placing them in the children's open palms. When the last trinket had been taken, the children ran off, fists clamped round their treasures, and Talorcan muttered something in Pictish under his breath.

They pushed through the wicker farm gate. Across the neatly kept yard, pigs lolled in a pool of afternoon sun, while goats chomped on their hay, yellow eyes frisky. The bee box lay dormant, but Angharad could feel their furry amber bodies, their black eyes growing sleepy in the pockets of their hive. The need-garden still burst with good autumn crops—parsnips and knobbly white carrots. Wild onions waved their fingers in the wind. Beyond the stone hut, Angharad spotted an elder tree and another kind of garden. Yarrow stalks had browned, but it brought to mind Cadzow, and the sight struck her with longing. "A healer lives here," she said.

Talorcan only nodded, then turned to Brother Thomas. "You do not speak," he said.

A woman called a greeting from beyond the hut door, and as Talorcan opened the door, a dirty little terrier burst over the threshold, wagging its tail, frantic with barks. As it chased round Angharad's legs in tight circles, her mouth somehow remembered the shape of a smile. She squatted to stroke him and was rewarded with licks, but the terrier's breath was like moldered clothing.

Inside, the air was dense, smelling of stew. A woman with red hair bound in a plait stood before a cauldron. She looked up as they entered and set down her spoon, sizing up her visitors. Her eyes were green and spaced wide, like a cat's. Flames or waves curled along either side of her neck. Talorcan said something, and the woman spoke back.

"Talorcan," Angharad asked softly, "what did she say?"

"I told him you look like a Briton," the woman said. Her mouth turned down at the corners. Looking like a Briton was not a good thing.

"Oh," Angharad said, looking down at her feet.

"Is it true, then, you're a princess?"

"Yes. Or . . . once I was. I was training with my uncle to become a Wisdom Keeper."

The woman tilted her head. Angharad looked back unabashedly, only to be struck by the feeling that she had been poked from inside.

Then the woman frowned and turned back to her soup pot, tossing in a handful of herbs. Angharad's stomach twisted in hunger.

"Does the chieftan know she is here?" The woman spoke in Brythonic for Angharad's benefit.

"Yes. I sent word I will bring her on the morrow."

"And then you are off?"

Talorcan nodded.

"Very well. You may sleep there, princess." She gestured to a thick pile of skins beside the hearth, but from her tone, she might as well have added "you dirty grain rat."

"With my friend," Angharad said.

The woman cast her green eyes distastefully at the culdee. "He can bed with the pigs. And if you don't favor that, princess, you may bed with the pigs as well."

Angharad felt Brother Thomas behind her, urging her to let well enough alone. She was so very hungry. She would give him a fleece to ensure he kept warm. The woman stirred the cauldron one last time, portioning stew into wooden bowls that Talorcan carried to the nearby table, moving aside a collection of dried plants. When the woman handed him the fourth, their eyes met, and the woman gave a slight shake of her head.

"The priest eats outside," Talorcan said.

Brother Thomas went willingly as Talorcan took up his bindings and shackled him to the pig enclosure. "Be thankful you do not have to fight them for your food," Angharad heard Talorcan say, as the pigs caught the smell and began thrusting their snouts against the wall. Angharad looked down at her stew guiltily, but her body was an animal, raging to eat.

The stew was thick with hunks of beef and little medallions of white carrot, and there was hot bread and slabs of creamy golden butter. The woman poured heather mead into three ceramic cups, dousing Angharad's with a generous splash of water. Talorcan and the woman ate in silence awhile, watching her, before the woman spoke up, setting down her spoon. "You called Talorcan by his name when first you came in. How was it you came to know it? There is no chance you heard it on the boat—our men are most careful amongst strangers."

Angharad swallowed her stew, wondering if she should tell the truth. She did not know this woman and did not like how she'd prodded her insides. But something about the farm felt like a dream. And the woman was a healer, or at least she seemed to be so.

"The sea told me," she said.

"The sea."

"Yes."

The woman smiled at Talorcan. "It seems your god was quite ready to betray your confidence," she said. Talorcan was not amused. "Tell me," the woman went on, watching Angharad's face. "I know you are but a girl, and far from your home. But you must know there are others who share your gift. Women. Here among the First People, you are at the beginning of it all. Our temples are among the oldest and most far famed in the land. I could take you to meet such women. There is a temple at Fortingall, not far from Ceann Mòr."

Talorcan shot her a look of warning. "The girl is a Briton and a noble. The chieftain must decide."

"Elufed is her *nain*; you told me yourself." The woman's look was full of meaning. "We may not call this child a Pict by custom, but the blood is in her."

"She is valuable. We can trade her. I'm certain he will agree."

"Oh? And I believe he'll agree with me," she said, green eyes lit with challenge. "She is valuable in ways you cannot measure."

Their bickering made Angharad's head spin. "I want to go home!" she cried.

The woman frowned. "You are a child. You cannot know what you want."

Angharad could no longer contain the frustration and helplessness that stormed within her. She let out a scream, primal and ear-shattering, full of all of her pain. In the silence that followed, the two of them looked at her, startled.

Brother Thomas shouted from the farmyard, "What's happened? Angharad? Angharad, answer me!"

Talorcan's face darkened, and the woman lifted a hand to settle him. "Go and tell the priest the child is all right," she said.

Talorcan muttered but did her bidding. The woman came round the table, sitting beside Angharad. "You need healing beyond any I might offer," she said.

Angharad did not look at her. Her bottom lip began to tremble.

The woman reached carefully, tipping Angharad's chin so that she might not mistake the look upon her face. Sadness.

"You need healing," she said again. "And I know you do not wish to be parted from your priest."

"He is my protector," Angharad said. "He has sworn to help me find my father."

"He will be sold. There is no changing his fate," she said firmly. "But the women I speak of—the Samhain fair is not far from their fortress. Come with me there. They can help you. You carry a great burden, princess. If you do not learn how to wield it, I assure you, you will break."

Angharad looked down at the thorns yet embedded in her hands, black specks of memory mingling with her blood. "I want my mother," she said. She was tired, so tired, like a salmon battling upstream. She shook her head, unable to draw herself up from the sinking she felt.

The woman spoke gently. "If you were training to become a Keeper, princess, you gave up your mother long ago."

A tear trailed Angharad's cheek.

"Come upriver to Ceann Mòr," the woman continued. "At the very least, it will give you a few days longer with your friend. You will be able to see what becomes of him. Stay here and you will never know."

Angharad looked up. "These women you speak of, you say they might help me. But could they not also help me return to my home?"

The woman looked at the table as if considering how to answer. "Yes," she said at last. "If you go to them, I believe they will help you find your way home."

Just at that moment, Talorcan returned, tossing the woman a weary look.

"Let him come in, then," the woman said. "We need not have put him out like a flock hound."

"He ate, did he not? Leave it at that," Talorcan said.

"As you say." The woman took the bowls from the table and set them down for the terrier to lick.

"Why do you hate Christians so?" Angharad asked.

"Why do you not?" the woman replied.

"Brother Thomas came to my aid. He is a wise and just man," she answered.

"Yet it was Christians who raised war in your kingdom. Now Uther Pendragon is dead."

"Do not speak his name as if you know him," Angharad said angrily. "I saw no Picts come to our aid."

"And why should we? We have our own troubles. And we have our own way," she said. "We do not need Christians shadowing our hut doors, telling us our wrongs and what to believe, as if theirs is the only true way." She took up the stew bowls from the floor. "It grows late. Help me clean the dinner bowls. And you might also clean yourself."

She lifted her brows as she passed Angharad the stack of wooden bowls, as if it were Angharad's fault she had not bathed since before the battle. Angharad followed her just behind the hut, to a place where a stream flowed between moss-covered boulders. The woods were shaded in the purple light of evening, and the sound of the water soothed, but the chill stung her fingers as she bent to clean the bowls, and she thought of Brother Thomas bedding with the pigs.

Angharad cleaned herself as well as she could bear with stream water and brought Brother Thomas a fleece from her pallet, which Talorcan and the woman grudgingly let be.

The pallet was soft as butter beneath Angharad's cheek. The terrier curled into the crook of her knees as the woman moved quietly about the hut, tidying while Talorcan undressed. It seemed he and the woman shared a bed. He climbed beneath the skins, and soon he was sleeping. The woman glanced at the bed, then came to kneel beside Angharad.

"Have you thought about what I said?" she asked. "Tomorrow Talorcan will bring you before the village chieftain. I know his mind well. I can assure you he is not fond of Tutgual, your king."

Outside, the wind rustled the branches of a nearby tree. A whisper urged her. *Go.* Angharad searched the woman's eyes. There was truth there, and comfort. Growing suddenly warm beside the hearth, Angharad wiped her face with her sleeve. "Why have you banked the fire so?" she asked. "I can scarcely breathe."

The woman looked at Angharad, curious. "Would you like me to open the door?"

Angharad was about to answer yes, she would, when she glanced at the hearth. It raged no more than it had a moment before.

It was the woman who burned.

"I wish to go upriver," Angharad said.

"Very well. I will speak with the chieftain on your behalf. Good night, child."

"Angharad," she said. "My name is Angharad."

The woman made a quick gesture, tapping her fingers twice to her breastbone as if by rote.

"Why do you do that?" Angharad asked.

"You trust me with your name. This is how we acknowledge it. If one gives you his name whilst you are here, you must do the same in return." She showed Angharad again, tapping the place above her heart.

"In my kingdom, we give our names to be well mannered."

"It is not so here. You should be careful whom you give your name to. But I will not abuse it."

"And will you not give me your name in return?"

"My name?" she asked. "I will leave that to you. Perhaps you might ask the sea."

"No. Not the sea."

"No? And why do you say so?"

"Because you are not made of water," Angharad answered.

The woman shrugged with a smile, turning toward bed. "Good night, Angharad. Rest well."

Angharad stared at the fire, pillowing her hand beneath her cheek. She would ask the fire the woman's name. Surely it would tell her.

For when Angharad had looked into the woman's eyes, all she had seen were flames.

CHAPTER 25

Lailoken

Caledonian Wood
Kingdom of the Selgovae
January, 574 AD

I stood, waiting. Watching for a sign. And then I heard a sound. A rumble in the direction of the wood. I swiveled, seeking its source. There, beyond the loch, a trail snaked through the forest.

Follow.

I knew I must.

Each step felt like a league. It was not winter here, and the canopy of leaves snuffed out the light, turning the forest into a dim stretch of twilight. The air grew cold, or was that my body, somewhere beyond myself? Each time I came to a twist in the path, I listened for the sound, and the soft rumble drew me on, until at last I came to a hut, half hidden in shadow.

Hearth smoke beckoned, sifting through the thatching. Who or what waited within? I am not ashamed to say I felt fear, but no knowledge comes from comfort. I pushed open the door.

The hearth blazed, yet I felt no heat. Beside it, a man sat upon a woven mat, legs crossed at the ankles. He looked up, and I saw his dark hair was shorn in a tonsure. His piercing eyes were kohled. It was the Keeper of the Falls.

I bowed my head in greeting. I was in his land now, the land of the dead.

He gestured to a waiting mat. He looked somehow more youthful here, his face less lined, eyes less threatening.

I sat opposite him. An earthenware pitcher sat beside a mortar and pestle on the mat before him. I watched as he reached for the pitcher, pouring its liquid into two cups. "Drink," he urged, passing one to me.

I took the cup but did not sip it. He smiled then, understanding that I knew his ruse: one cannot eat or drink in the land of the dead if one wishes to return.

"My body lies bound in the Bull's Sleep. I cannot tarry. But I wish to know why I was drawn here," I said.

The Keeper nodded and shifted the mortar and pestle closer so he might begin mixing whatever substance lay within. It was a fine blue powder, the color of storms.

"Ask me," he said, bending his head to his task. Tipping a splash of liquid from the jug into the mortar, he worked the pestle, creating a paste.

"Why was I drawn here?"

"That is not the right question."

"Who are you?"

The Keeper did not look up, only continued in his mixing. "You waste time you do not have. Ask again."

Frustration flared. I looked at him, thinking. Searching. Attempted again. "Why did you take your own life?"

At this he looked up. "I did not only drown."

"Your answer makes no sense."

If he had leaped from the hilltop, as Archer had said, he would have died from the fall. He would not have drowned. "Assassination. That is that what you speak of."

The Wisdom Keeper scoffed. Shaking his head, he trained his eyes upon the fire, his hand working the pestle as if I were no longer there at all. But I would not be so easily dismissed. I sat in silence as he leaned closer, peering into the flames. His eyes widened then, as if finding a vision.

"They are rebuilding the fortress," he said. "I see a great wall of stone. You stand on one side. I stand upon the other. Listen to me. Listen! For I cannot speak plain. We must cut them down without mercy, we must paint trees with their gore. We must hunt them like wolves through the dark of the wood. Again, and again, and *again* they will come. But hear me, my brother. They must not pass through!"

The Keeper fell back, his hands still.

"You speak of your days, Brother Keeper. Not of my own," I said carefully.

He opened his eyes, pinning me. "Your days are my days. Soon you will see."

A rich, earthy tang came from the mortar, a scent I knew like my own—woad paste for battle. The Keeper beckoned, and I did as he bade, waiting. Mortar in hand, he dipped three fingers into the paint. I felt the cold silken trail as he reached to mark me, forehead to nose.

Then he looked at me, and I understood.

I am going back to war.

The thought set me to flight. For the hut around me had gone, and quite suddenly, I found that I stood in the middle of a vast and ancient wood.

It was early morning, and the low rumble had returned. I had followed it, unknowing. Now I saw its source.

A legion of men moved like a channel of water through the forest. The thunder of their boots shook the saplings, but the rumble came from the sledges they dragged, carrying their weapons of war ever deeper into the forest.

The Angles are coming! I heard someone shout. And in the next moment, a hail of arrows sailed in a punishing rain. But these men were not Angles. Not any I had seen. These men wore red cloaks and plumed helmets, like soldiers of Rome.

I looked for the Keeper, but men were racing now, taking shelter behind trees. They shouted out orders, preparing to fight.

Wake up, wake up! someone called from the trees. I ducked as arrows pierced the man beside me and he fell to his knees.

Wake up! one of the men shouted with a curse.

I jerked as some force took hold of me, yanking me to the surface through too many depths.

"Wake up, you cock wart!"

I shot up to sitting as if plunged into ice, blinded by dark. Gasping for breath, I thrashed and flailed, not knowing my own bonds.

There was a man in my cell, shaking me from sleep. "Quit struggling!" he said crossly. But how could it be? I knew well that voice. "Diarmid?" I asked.

I ripped off my blind. There he stood in the light of the fire, but I would not be fooled.

"You are dead," I said. "And I am still dreaming."

He leaned in close, peering into my eyes like a hoot owl, then slapped angrily at my cheeks.

"Ow!" I protested.

"I'm not dead, you dullard," he said, crossing his arms. "And just what were you thinking, taking the Bull's Sleep with no one to wake you?"

"I had no choice."

"No choice? Is that what you say? Lucky I came, that's what you were. A little while longer and you would have been dead."

"I was not dead," I replied, yanking the bonds from my wrists. "And I wasn't yet through!"

Diarmid paced the little cell, waving dismissively. "Fine, then. Some greeting I've had, too. Traveling all night, the sky pissing snow. Where am I to bed? This place isn't fit for a rat."

I crouched beneath the roof, untwining the last of the rope from my legs, and then straightened. We looked at each other.

"You're here," I said, blinking.

"Aye. That I am." He tried to stand proud beneath the weight of my gaze, but Diarmid was stooped now, one eye gone milky and unseeing.

"We took you for dead."

Diarmid's eyes filled. He brought his hands to his head.

I do not think I had truly cried, not until then.

I went to Diarmid, gripping him tightly beneath my chin. My sobs came out heaving as I clutched the man I'd thought gone—my teacher, my friend. Diarmid wept, too, until our grief sank back on its tide. Then, wiping his unseeing eye, he said, "Fuff off, then. Holding me like a baby."

My chuckle was cut short by a fiery stab shooting up from my feet. Wincing, I bent.

"Winter's bite," Diarmid said. "We had best get your boots off and see what's left of your toes."

"How did you find me?" I asked as we sat close together, fumbling with my boots.

"I found the men first. Maelgwn said you'd come here. Kept mumbling on about some blasted curse. Then I knew right where he meant."

"I'd forgotten you spent time here as a boy," I said.

"Not too far flung. I once knew these hills well. Though I do not like the presence here." He looked accusingly round the cell, and the hairs upon my skin bristled. "I would be mindful what you say."

"Ha," Diarmid scoffed. "I fear no shades."

"This Keeper," I said, "his workings are shadowed, but I will tell you I think he is more than a shade."

I gestured for my satchel, and Diarmid tossed it at my feet. From my medicines I drew a small handful of stag moss to crush over the flames. Breathing in the smoke, I felt the plant do its work, closing the passage between this realm and the other.

Diarmid rooted through my satchel, mumbling. "I'm half starved. What've you got to eat, then? Nothing. I figured as much." He reached for his own satchel and pulled out a loaf, a parcel of cheese, and some salted game. A skin of wine.

"And where did you pilfer that?" I asked.

"Why, Archer, of course."

"He gave me no such things."

Diarmid shrugged. "You were not fostered by a Selgovian aunt as a lad."

"Give it here." The wine had warmed by the fire and tasted of the sun-drenched soil of Gaul. "Oh, that's fine," I said, savoring the path it took down my gullet. I took another draught, then returned it. "So," I said. "How came you here?"

Diarmid's face shifted. I could still hear the clash and roar of battle as if we yet stood on the ramparts, but those of us who were left, we burned to remember even as we bled.

"I suppose night had fallen by the time I awoke," he said. "The smoke stirred me, thick in the air. They'd built pyres beneath the ramparts and struck them alight. My skull felt as if pressed. The world was a blur of darkness and light. I'd been struck by sword and by spear. I had not thought I would live. But I had tumbled downslope, into the shelter of bushes. Now they were searching for survivors to run through with their pikes. I heard our men cry, but what was I to do? I stayed there and blessed them. I saw each of them home."

He looked down, rubbing the tears that had splashed on his knuckles. "I made my way north, traveling by night. When I got beyond the burning, a widow took me in. Some of my wounds had soured by then.

It took many weeks before I was healed. But soon as I was, I struck out
to find what was left of our men. The Selgovae, they have watchers
in the wood, and they knew of the woman sheltering a wounded man.
They had a rough way with questions, but they soon brought me here."

"And did you see any others? Was there any word of Eira or
Angharad? Any word at all?"

His milky eye shifted. "No news, I am sorry to say."

Talk of the battle only stoked my fire to seek justice. For Angharad
and Rhys. Gwenddolau and Eira and Brant.

"Your eye." I gestured. "Can you see from it at all?"

"The other does me well enough," he said, inspecting my foot.
"And I'd say it's a mite better off than your toes. You'll lose two off
this foot. The others might stay."

The third and fourth were shrunken, burnt black like decay.
Diarmid bandaged my foot with a nod. "The Cailleach took them.
That was her price. No visions come in winter without her de-
sign. Now, Lailoken. Tell me your tale."

I told him of our retreat through the forest, of finding our way to
Old Man Archer. The wolf and the boar. The Keeper and his cloak.

"Arrows in the wood. It was this battle I saw, a battle with the Angles, though I did not know its name. There is a blindness that rides
on the tails of that army. A nothingness. It is a place beyond which I
cannot see." Diarmid's words were ominous in winter's dark.

"Angles. Romans. Both seeking land, both seeking power, that's all
the same. I still cannot say how it concerns the Mad Keeper."

"And did he seem mad?"

"Nay," I acknowledged. "Perhaps no more than me."

Diarmid leaned back upon his elbows. "Romans, Romans . . . it
does bring to mind the tale of the Lost Legion."

"Which tale of the Lost Legion?"

Diarmid sighed. "Many generations ago, in the time of Agricola, the Ninth Legion of Rome was the most loathed in all the land. It was they, by the thousands, who'd marched north from their fortress at Ebrauc up through Partick, raping and burning and pillaging as they went. Well, the Selgovae bore the brunt, and they never did forget it. Forty winters passed, and they fought all the while.

"Then one day, the Britons rose up. A new ruler sent the Ninth Legion up to quell it. North again they marched, into the wood. Five thousand strong they were, marching through the Caledonian Wood, through the land of the Selgovae. But this time they would not rape and burn. For they disappeared into the Deep, never again to be seen."

"Disappeared?"

"The Selgovae took them in the forest. Spread their gore upon the trees! And the Romans at their fort in Ebrauc were none the wiser. Had no blessed idea where their men had gone."

"What do you say?"

"I *said*, they spread their gore upon the trees!" Diarmid said with delight.

"Those were the Keeper's words. But I told you as much."

"Nay, you didn't," Diarmid said. "But that's how the tale goes, all the same." We were silent a moment before Diarmid spoke again. "Keep it in your vest," he advised. "Visions don't come for naught. You will understand its meaning when the time comes. That is always the way."

"There will be war with the Angles, that much I know. We must be united or we all shall be dead. And yet I cannot stomach it."

Diarmid's face soured. "United with Rhydderch."

"Aye. An impossible confederation. Dragon Warriors. The Selgovae. Gwrgi and Peredur, too. None could turn their head for fear of a blade in their backs."

Diarmid stared into the flames. "The beast of war consumes many hosts. It was with you on the day you rode out to Sweetmeadow. It was with the men rushing our ramparts. It will be with the Angles when they march against us, too. It feeds on ambition and fear, jealousy and hate. And it cannot be fooled—it is old as man himself, our companion, our shadow. Our master, if we allow it. For with its power, we can bring kingdoms to their knees. We can obliterate entire peoples. Its only demand is that we do not ask questions."

A shiver traced my neck. "I fear I am a host it knows too well."

"Host it when you must," he said, "but do not let it consume you."

"You are a wise old bird."

Diarmid only shrugged. "So some might say."

I pressed the heels of my hands to my eyes. "We were the protectors of our island. I believed in our cause. I have given my life to it. I do not know now what I should do."

"Lailoken, the battle Emrys began is not over yet."

"Perhaps not for others. But it is over for me. The Britons believe they are stronger with Gwenddolau dead. They have severed their spear hand in fear of its power. Let the Angles come. Let the Britons of Ebrauc and Strathclyde and the warriors of Rheged wage their own war."

"And what would you do?" he asked.

I thought on it, nodding. "I would make these woods a refuge for those among the persecuted who yet honor our ways. We will build our own army, an army of Stags. We will stand with the Selgovae to keep their wood safe. We will strike Rhydderch and Tutgual in retribution for their war. Those of us who remain will answer the slaughter brought upon us at Arderydd. When the snows melt and spring comes, the lords of Strathclyde shall hear my reply."

CHAPTER 26

Languoreth

Cadzow Fortress
Kingdom of Strathclyde
26th of November, AD 573

The last of the blackberries had long since shriveled. In the days that passed, I paced the forest in the company of Eira and Gladys, and with Cyan, on occasion, when the mood struck him.

One clear day, I looked north and saw the mountains in the distance were capped white with snow. The next morning, I woke to the rasp of a crow.

The bird's call had invaded my dreams, for in the pillowing fog between waking and sleep, I'd been dreaming of black feathers falling from the sky.

"You seem troubled this morning," Eira said, entering my chamber to help me to dress. It was strange to allow it, knowing she was noble, but she did it with such comfort that she'd set me at ease.

"Someone is coming," I said.

"How do you know?"

"Did Lailoken speak much of Cathan?" I turned to look at her.

"Yes, of course. Your father's counsel and his teacher."

"He was significant to me as well," I said, though the words did not touch it. "Crows warn me of visitors ever since his death."

"He was assassinated by the bishop Mungo," Eira said. "The same man responsible for Lailoken's scar."

I was with him, I could not say. I blinked away the memory of Cathan hanging from a tree.

"The visitor," Eira said, as if to divert me. "Who might it be?"

"Rhydderch," I said, surprising myself. But speaking the words, I knew they were true.

Eira looked away. Her hair was coming in nicely, fair at the roots. Though her face had healed from its memories of violence, the rest of her would never forget.

"I knew I must face this, but I did not imagine how it might feel," she said.

"Nor did I." Together Eira and I sat down upon the bed. We needn't speak it—that my husband had brought battle and dealt death to so many we knew, that if he hadn't failed to find Angharad, she would be with me, and Eira would have fled. That she need never have encountered Gwrgi again.

"I do not like that I shall have to pass you off as a servant," I said. "Can we not consider telling Rhydderch the truth?"

"No, not yet. Please let me say when." Eira did not look at me. Her voice was tight as she stared straight ahead. "And what if Rhydderch has murdered your brother?"

I closed my eyes. "No matter what else he has done, he could not do that."

"And what if he has?" She took my hand now, seeking my gaze.

In all these days, I had never truly questioned that my twin was alive. I had wrung myself with worry, I had been sick. But Lailoken and I had entered this world of the living together. I was so certain of our bond, I reasoned I would have felt it had he left me.

But what if he were gone?

If Lailoken was dead, and by Rhydderch's hand?

"I must go tell Olwenna to make ready for guests," I said.

I stood and crossed my chamber. I felt Eira stiffen, the bond we had forged turning to lead. But I was not finished. I turned at the door.

"If Rhydderch has harmed my brother, he will wish he were dead."

I gathered my son and daughter close as we waited in the courtyard, Cadzow's gates thrust open, listening to the nearing thunder of horses and the discordant bellow of horns. Power rode this way. I felt it like a moon tide. The sounds stirred my blood, my breath coming short. And then the men were upon us, streaming through the pasture, my husband riding at the helm of fifty mounted men. These were the scouts—the cleverest and most skilled among Rhydderch's retinue, tasked with scouring the hills and valleys of Gwenddolau's kingdom for the past fortnight and a month, tracking and killing any survivors who'd fled. Behind them trailed a pack of dogs.

Now I would serve them Cadzow beef and fill their stomachs with mead as they sat at the table where Lailoken and I had laughed and bickered over bannocks. Among their battle-hard faces, Rhydderch's lean, muscled frame was as familiar as the whorls of my own fingers. He rode between two banner men. The dark beard he kept so neatly trimmed crept down his neck. His brown hair, threaded with gray, was overlong and tangled by wind, and his expression was searching; he had not yet seen me.

Eira and Aela stood behind me. It had been easier with Rhydderch gone, making him into a monster. But then his gray eyes locked upon mine, and I saw the cost of Tutgual's war.

The men on horseback slowed their mounts as they filled the courtyard in a flood, their boots blackened with blood and battle mud.

Rhydderch did not smile at the sight of his two living children, only swung his legs swiftly from his horse and gathered them into his arms, breathing in their smell. When at last he released them, we stood looking at each other, our hands uncertain at our sides.

"You've come home." My voice was unnatural. I went to him dutifully and he gripped me too tightly, burying his face in my hair. Then, before I knew it, he had set me back so he might look at me. All I could not speak before his men passed over my face.

He opened his mouth, but I cut him short. "Come, you must be worn through. Get your men into the warm. We have food in the great room and bedding for all."

Rhydderch nodded and motioned to his men, and together we guided them into the hall.

I kept busy in seeing to their comfort. After we'd eaten, the men dusted off the old instruments in the hall, wincing and laughing at the tired old strings. But the songs they sang were solemn, and as evening fell, I could see they yearned for nothing so much as to return to their homes, to their own lovers and kin.

"May we speak?"

I looked up to see Rhydderch before me, offering his hand.

"Of course, we must." I rose from my seat.

In my father's old chamber, the fire crackled and the room flickered with the light of a single oil lamp. Before us the bed loomed, and the air was thick with all that lay between us. Rhydderch went to the sturdy oaken table to tip the wine amphora, pouring two cups, extending one to me. His face was expectant. "Please, Languoreth. Drink. For we must find a way for you to forgive me."

"For which act must I forgive you first?" I scoffed. "Waging war upon my brothers? The death of our son? Or perhaps the disappearance of our daughter?"

Rhydderch stepped back. "So you blame me for all. I knew it would be thus. Will you not let me speak?"

"Speak, though I cannot feign I will trust whatever you might say. Your quest for kingship has corrupted you. You are no longer the man I once knew."

I might well have struck him.

"How could you think I would not attempt everything in my power to save Angharad? To protect our own son? You sit by the warmth of a fire, safe from blades and spears, whilst you lay down judgment like some sort of jurist. You knew this path would not be gentle. Kingship does not come without sacrifice. You swore to stand beside me no matter the cost. Well, you have been brought to challenge, Languoreth, and once again you have fallen short."

I shook my head, trembling with rage. "It is I who has fallen short? How dare you? I am a shade because of you! Everything I love has been taken from me! And now you ask—no, you *demand*—forgiveness? No, I cannot forgive. I would sooner have died than have lost my own children. I have nothing left to give."

"And were they not my children, too?" Rhydderch slammed down the cups. "They slayed the man I sent to trade for her, or did you not know? They left his body lying at the foot of their rampart. I searched for my daughter on that battlefield even as I took blow after blow to protect my own son! And I have been searching for her since!"

Never before had Rhydderch raised his voice. He took a breath, his shoulders sinking. He looked suddenly quite tired, then. Tired and aged.

"They slayed your bargainer?" I asked. "But there must have been some mistake! They never would have done such a thing."

"I tell you, a corpse was their answer. And what was I to do? Defy my father? Give way to Morcant, that he should be named tanist instead? Languoreth, I had no choice."

"There is always a choice!" I said. "Do not play at being helpless. You abandoned a girl of nine winters to one of the bloodiest battles we have known. You led my son into war against his own uncles. It is I who have been helpless, stuck indoors weaving spools into grief, as I wonder what has become of our daughter and how my son's life did end!"

"I cannot say how it happened. Each man in our war party understood they must bring Angharad to me. They were to find her, and not my men alone. A united army of Britons!"

"Perhaps you are not the commander you think. For it was Gwrgi who found her, and where is she now? What has become of her?"

Rhydderch did not move. "What is this you speak of?"

"Aye, Gwrgi found our child! You turned your face from Sweetmeadow, and look what has happened!"

"How came you to know this? If Gwrgi found Angharad, he would have delivered her up. He would not have dared—"

"You have no idea what Gwrgi has done."

"Languoreth, I beg you, speak plain!"

"Our daughter escaped him, so Gwrgi said nothing. Our daughter was not harmed. But now she is lost once more, and no closer to home. The rest is not my story to tell."

Rhydderch went to the bed and sat, closing his eyes. "Dear God. What have I done?"

It was a strange sound, Rhydderch's cry. Strangled and boyish. I stood a moment, stunned. The sight of his ruin caused a caving in me, like rock into water. I went to him and sat beside him. He dropped his head to my lap like a child, wrapping his arms about my waist. "I could not save them. I could not save them," he wept.

I knew his pain because it was my own. We carried twin hollows in our hearts, Angharad and Rhys. Lord and lady of one of the most powerful kingdoms in the north, yet we could not protect our son from death. We could not even find our own daughter.

Rhydderch's tears subsided. We sat, wine in hand, our empty eyes fixed on the fire. After a while, I spoke.

"I claimed your prison cart. Your share of Arderydd's booty. Gwenddolau's people are in our stable, even as we speak. Any who do not wish to earn their keep at Cadzow, I intend to set free. You must handle Morcant. I do not care how. Can we agree?"

Rhydderch looked at me sidelong. "Well enough. If it please you, I will agree."

"Your brother made a trophy of my cousin's head. He carried Brant to Partick upon a pike."

"I am so sorry, wife. I did not know." His voice was tender.

"I buried him in the woods."

"I did not see him take it. I never would have allowed it. That you must know."

"It does not matter. He is home now." I blinked. "Angharad would not have been there to begin with had I not insisted she become a Keeper. It was I who asked that of you, and you conceded."

"I conceded because there was nothing better suited for her," he said. "We cannot give up hope that Angharad is yet alive. I had to return, Tutgual commanded it. But there are men yet searching. They will find her."

"They must. Oh, please, Gods, let them find her." Then I spoke aloud the thought that haunted me still. "You left me a prisoner. You left without a word."

Rhydderch looked at his hands. "I could not face you. I knew you would be angry. I knew you would feel betrayed. I knew the look upon your face would have knocked the battle from me. And I worried, then, I could not fight. Did you not wish me to return?"

He looked up, gray eyes searching mine. There was no cave distant enough to bury my answer.

"You hunted my brother," I said, searching him in turn. "I must know. Did you find him?"

Rhydderch looked away. I waited until I could not. "Please, speak!"

"Aye. I found him," he answered.

"And does he live? Is he harmed? Did you harm him?" I demanded.

Rhydderch threw up his hands, demanding my silence. "If you had any idea . . ." He shook his head. "Your brother lives. Or did so, some days ago."

"How do you know this?"

"One of my men stumbled upon a boot print. A single print, in the middle of the Caledonian Wood. But he was an excellent tracker. He followed a trail of bent twigs and instinct to a cave, stopping just short of their watchman. He left before their warrior caught wind of him and reported to me. Nine men. Your brother was among them."

"And what did you do?" I heard my voice rising. "What happened then?"

Rhydderch's jaw tightened. He glanced at the door, lowering his voice. "I killed him. I killed my own man."

I sat in stunned silence. It was not an act I'd ever imagined my honorable husband was capable of. "I—I do not know what to say."

"Say nothing. It is done. My men believe it was by a Dragon's hand."

I wanted to ask whether he had done it for Lailoken or done it for me. But what did it matter? I could see how it ate at him. How he'd never be free.

"I am sorry," I said. "But I am so very grateful." I reached for his hand. Rhydderch entwined his fingers in mine. "I cannot reconcile Tutgual's blood flowing through your veins," I admitted. "I cannot help but fear it will someday corrupt you."

"That may be so. But I also have within me the blood of my mother, the First People. Everything I have done has been in the hope of eventual peace. But peace is impossible when our kingdoms cannot unite. War with the Angles may be inevitable, and you know as well as I that Gwenddolau would never agree to fight alongside his enemies. He had to be deposed."

"You never gave him the chance."

"Indeed I did," Rhydderch said gently. "When he visited Cadzow. He demanded an ally without bending his knee. I will make it right, I swear it. Your brother must stay awhile in exile. Until my father is gone. But when I am named king, I will seek Lailoken to be my counsel."

"But he is of the Old Way."

"We will face it when it comes."

I thought of the nine in the cave. Was Maelgwn among them? He was to become the next Pendragon if Gwenddolau fell. Surely the men would have boasted if they'd taken his head.

"And what of the Dragons? The ones who remain. Have they not suffered enough? I would see you grant them relief from exile, too. They are good men, husband. They have supped at our table."

"They are men who leveled their blades at my neck. And after this battle, they would do so again."

"Let us leave it for now. I am so very weary."

I passed Rhydderch my cup, unable to press him. We lay back upon the bed, yet in our clothes. I had borne him three children. We'd been wed nearly twenty winters. I was not sure he would touch me, nor if I'd welcome it. But there is something that stirs from so familiar a touch, the safety of habit, the promise of pleasure. I returned Rhydderch's kiss when he put his mouth to mine. We so seldom kissed. If it were not for my certain knowledge of his lips, he could have been any sad champion returning from war. So I met his eyes and offered up what healing I could muster. His passion simmered but never boiled over; he had learned my body as well as any of his weapons. I felt release and slipped behind it. After a while, we stilled.

Rhydderch slept. I lay awake as I so often did, gazing at the thatch.

I berated Rhydderch for his betrayal even while I had betrayed Rhydderch first.

Our very marriage was built upon my betrayal. That I had lain with another man. Before Rhydderch and after. I had borne Maelgwn's child and passed him off as our own. And yet I had never felt guilt strike me before, for love was not wrong.

Outside, beyond the courtyard, was the pasture where I had first seen Maelgwn. When I stood near the cattle, I could envision it still— the day the Dragon Warriors had first galloped through our gate.

Maelgwn's green eyes had pinned me in place. *You.* As if with surprise.

Now I understood Maelgwn and I had known each other before, in some distant time, for our draw was undeniable. To live without knowing him was unconscionable, no matter the price.

And then, once I had known him, once I had felt him, I could not turn away.

Take it, Ariane once told me. *Do not give it up.*

I'd found no such recognition in Rhydderch's steady eyes.

Fondness. Respect. A great deal of warmth. But though he professed it, not that sort of love. Now Rhydderch startled in his sleep, and for a moment it looked as if he were gripping a sword.

I must try harder, I told myself. *I owe him my love.*

Togetherness was our bargain. Allegiance until our end.

CHAPTER 27

Angharad

Dùn Déagh
Kingdom of the Picts
27th of October, AD 573

Angharad had already finished breakfast by the time the woman returned. Talorcan sat at the table, chewing stormily on a bannock, when she gusted through the door, her terrier at her heels. She wore a sumptuous fur-lined cloak, her fiery hair neatly plaited. Over the tattoos on her neck she'd clasped an impossibly heavy torque. It was not gold, like so many torques Angharad had seen. Thick links of silver bound her neck in a chain.

Their argument was a whirl of strange words in a torrent, but Angharad needn't understand Pictish to know the root of their strife. The woman held more power than Talorcan, and Talorcan felt unmanned. Angharad pondered whether or not she should tell them, but instead snuck some bread and cheese for Thomas, hoping they would discover it themselves in time.

"I am going with you," Angharad told Brother Thomas, crouching at his side by the pigs.

He ceased his chewing and looked up. "No, Angharad, you must stay here. The chieftain, he will arrange—"

"I told Muirenn I would go, and I won't change my mind. She's been to see the chieftain. She's arranged it already."

"Muirenn?" Thomas looked baffled.

"Yes. The woman with the fiery hair."

"She told you her name?"

"Not precisely."

Brother Thomas was not amused.

"You said you would not chastise me. Why are you looking at me so?" Angharad frowned.

"Because I worry for you, Angharad. I worry very much. Travel any farther into this land, and you might never return. You do not understand the vastness of Pictland. Mountains and lochs never ending, from here all the way to the foot of the northern sea! Seven kingdoms, with countless lords and chieftains beneath them. Here at Dùn Déagh, this is only the beginning."

Thomas's words were built to frighten her.

"Muirenn says there are women here. Women who will help me go home. If we accompany Talorcan, she promised to take me there. I would stay with you, Brother Thomas, as long as I may."

She said the last with such vehemence that the culdee fell silent. Inside the hut, Talorcan and Muirenn still traded words.

"If you would travel with me awhile longer, Angharad, it will bring me great comfort," Brother Thomas said.

"Then I shall," she said, but her eyes fell to his bonds. "I don't know what I shall do without you."

"We needn't think about that yet," he said. He bowed his head. "In the beginning, it is always hard. The mystery takes us in hand in ways we cannot understand. But we must never stop listening, Angharad. That is how we learn to believe. All will be well. We must believe in that, together."

*   *   *

Talorcan sat in the bow of the currach as his men powered the boat up the river Tay.

Muirenn perched beside Angharad, her terrier upon her lap.

Muirenn. That was the name the hearth flames had given, but Angharad dared not use it. As they navigated the river, Muirenn's eyes darted often to Talorcan, and Angharad knew she felt exposed to injury, naked as a new root.

"He is unhappy you woke early and went to the chieftain," Angharad said.

"You speak your mind freely, princess," Muirenn said, then softened. "Perhaps I should have waited, but I hoped to avoid a spectacle." Her eyes traveled to Brother Thomas, who sat bound at the stern of the currach.

"A spectacle? You mean to say your chieftain might have harmed him?"

"Some matters are better settled away from the gaze of our people, that is all. Our chieftain is protective of our ways. We have seen what happens when people open their ears to the silver tongues of outsiders."

"But he heeded you. The chieftain granted your request. Is this why Talorcan is angry?"

"I have stolen a chance for him to parade his priest, and he is sore from it."

Angharad screwed up her face. "I do not think that is why."

"Is it not?"

"No. Talorcan wishes to prove himself to your chieftain. Most men wish as much, only Talorcan seems to wish it even more."

"You are very curious for a little girl." The heavy silver torque round Muirenn's neck caught the light as she turned to glance at the stern of the boat, and Angharad finally understood.

"I think it is because the chieftain is your father."

"Curious and clever." Muirenn raised a brow, and her approval felt sweet as honey.

"Well, I hope he won't be angry for long." Angharad reached to stroke the terrier. "You seem stony at first, but your heart is soft as petals, Muirenn." She looked up carefully, tapping two fingers to her chest.

Muirenn blinked. "Well done, princess." She gave a little smile, looking out over the water. "Stony but soft. Such is the way with many women who have given themselves to the goddess."

"Your goddess lives in fire." Angharad tried it out, as if to make sense of it.

"My goddess *is* fire. But perhaps not in the way you think. She has many names and many faces—but it is we who give her masks. We are so small, you see, and she, so very vast."

"But I saw no masks or faces. I saw only flames. And then I heard a whisper."

"Yes, princess. That is the way."

Angharad looked at the river. "Sometimes I fear I will never find my way home."

"Do not fret," she said tenderly. "You must remember that when you are a child of the Gods, every moment you are finding your way home. If that is what you truly wish, I have no doubt the Gods will deliver it, Angharad."

The wind and the slap of water against the hull slipped them into silence a moment, then Angharad's eyes fell again on Muirenn's torque. "Your torque is different from any I have seen," Angharad said. "You are a noble, and yet the links—they appear so heavy and thick. Ours are slender and made of gold. As mine was."

"Have you lost it, then?"

"I didn't lose it. It was taken."

"Thievery is always punished. Perhaps someday you shall see it re-turned." Muirenn reached absently to the metal at her throat. "My torque is forged from Roman silver. There is a story behind it. Would you like to hear?"

"Yes. I love stories."

"Very well. Long ago, our kings wore torques of the finest gold. The *Cruithni* prospered, our people multiplied. But then one day there came a red tide. Romans. We watched as it washed onto shore in crimson capes and plumed helmets, with spears and broadswords and great tools of battle unlike any we had known. Our vast island began tipping, as if into the sea. Thousands upon thousands were dying in the wake of this tide. The high king in the north worried for our peo-ple. He gathered three ships to carry himself and his bravest men in search of a treaty. He swore his allegiance to Rome. The high king returned, his boats weighed down with silver, and with a promise of peace.

"In return, we had only to watch as the tide came for all others who stood up to fight. Britons and Scots. Rival Pictish clanns. These were our enemies. Years passed, one after another, and our lords and high king amassed hoards in tribute from Rome. But when next the Roman emissaries came, they brought silver in exchange for our men and our boats—for we possessed some of the best warriors who navi-gated these waters." Muirenn hesitated, her fingers tracing the links about her neck.

"Then what happened?" Angharad asked.

"Our men, once skilled and fearless, returned to us haunted, if in-deed they returned at all. Our enemies came in secret to treat with our king. They looked at each other, noblest among the *Cruithni*, now hollow and thin, broken from war. By this time, we had seen what Rome truly offered—annihilation or servitude. They desired a kingdom with no bounds, and we were their slaves. Then one night a priestess had a dream. We must fight, or the Romans would consume us, they would swallow us whole. She brought her message to the king. The *Cruithni* rose up and brought battle to Rome. Much blood was spilt, and many lives were lost, but at last we drove them from our borders and our seas.

"The priestess, however, worried that memory is short. She did not wish the *Cruithni* to ever forget. So she demanded the Roman silver that had turned us to slaves be melted down and fashioned into torques. Yes, the chains are heavy. And so was our burden. We wear them and are forever reminded what it cost to be free.

"This torque has been worn by the chiefs of Dùn Déagh ever since. When I was chosen by council as my father's successor, the torque of my ancestors was given to me." Muirenn sat back.

"You will be the next chieftain?"

"Yes."

"Are you a warrior, then? Can you also fight?"

"Yes, I can fight."

"Why do you call yourselves the *Cruithni* when all others call you Picts?"

Muirenn made a hiss at the word. "Pict is the name the foreigners gave. We are the *Cruithni*. The First People."

"And what ever happened to the priestess?"

"Well. The priestess went back to her village so she might train more priestesses. So that if a time came once more, when they were needed, they would be ready. But the high king was grateful for her vision, for without it, he would never have had the power to bring all the tribes together. In thanks, he gave her a fortress high upon a hill at the mouth of a sacred glen. The glen was the beating heart of his kingdom. And the fortress of the priestess stands to this day."

"Is it true?"

"It is true. And it is to that very place you are bound. It is a place very few Britons ever shall see."

Brother Thomas had been listening in silence and spoke. "I have heard tell of this place. The Crooked Glen of Stones. It is said a magnificent old yew grows there, far below the fort."

"You shall certainly never see it, priest. Your journey ends at Ceann Mòr. Talorcan will fetch a price for you, and that will be that."

"Why must you be so cruel?" Angharad said.

Muirenn scoffed. "Why? These men of Christ trespass upon our land and bring chaos to our people. They say we are full of *sin*." She spoke the word as if it were bitter. "They declare there is only one god—their god—and that all others are false and without power."

"Yes. But Brother Thomas is not that way."

"They are all that way. There was a time when we would open our gate and invite them to speak, for such is our custom. There were even kings in the south who chose to follow their way. It brought a crumbling of their clanns. They cannot make peace with our druids. They want wealth, and land, and protection, but what do they offer? Nothing but strife." Muirenn tilted her chin, fixing her gaze up ahead.

Angharad closed her eyes. The crooked glen. A deep place. Buried in time. A place few Britons shall ever see. And now Angharad traveled there, to the place where the priestess from Muirenn's story once dwelled. It sounded like something from a Song Keeper's tale.

All around her, Angharad could hear the river as if it were singing. Louder here than ever before. The Tay was a channel of dark water, deep and full of darting fish. Its song was soothing Talorcan. The river nestled between undulating hills, where the trees were lit yellow and orange like so many flames. The air smelled of earth and tasted of rain. Angharad felt the push of clouds racing overhead and their will to become water. She felt an otter kick from an underwater rock and glide beneath the water's skin, sleeker than any vessel.

If such things were made of the gods, Angharad wanted more.

She worried for Brother Thomas, an enemy here. And yet it was if the river cast a spell. The trees along the water were bowing. This river was gentle, a most ancient mother. Tatha was her name. She whispered that she'd been born on the slopes of *Beinn Laoigh*, that the *Cruithni* born to this land were her children. Could Angharad, then, be the river's child, too?

Keep him safe. Let Brother Thomas stay by my side, Angharad prayed.

The river breeze tickled the wisps of hair at her neck. Muirenn had washed and plaited it for her. Angharad looked down at her crimson wool dress, a gift from a villager. Angharad had followed dutifully as Muirenn had taken her round, procuring a pair of leather booties from one family, wool stockings from another, a linen undergarment, and at the last, a fur-lined cloak.

Angharad had wondered why the villagers gave such beautiful things with such generosity. Now she understood that the chieftain's daughter had asked them to do so. Nonetheless, the people had not begrudged her. What they gave, they gave freely. They did not speak the same tongue. But as the craft carried on swiftly upriver, Angharad began to feel an unusual sense of home.

Perhaps it was the blood of the *Cruithni* awakening within her. Though the *Cruithni* themselves might not count her as such, Elufed's blood was in her. But while she knew her *nain* was a Pict, she did not even know from which kingdom she'd come. Elufed did not speak of it.

Angharad knew she had been taken from her family when she was terribly young. She'd been in Strathclyde now far longer than she'd ever been in Pictland. Angharad had studied the map in her lessons, her fingers traveling the vellum up, up, up. But now she could feel the mass of land stretching beyond them. She looked at Muirenn. Surely there had been Britons who'd traveled here before, for they'd had the good sense to make maps of it. She thought of the map Rhys kept in his chamber, rolled out upon the table, how she had perched on his knee to study it. Her heart twisted when the memory struck, but the river was certain.

Do not worry, child, the river promised. *I will help*.

Angharad looked up as they passed a towering stone slab at the water's edge, carved with a hulking warrior painted in bright colors and gripping a spear. His leg shot out midstride, as if he were patrolling the land. The boundary marker of a new chieftain or king.

They passed currachs carrying all manner of goods. And where the footpath to Ceann Mòr snaked along the river, Angharad caught glimpses through the trees of snowy white sheep and heard the deep moan of cattle being driven to market. Fields of emmer and barley were already deep in their rest, and when the gruff call of a raven sounded, Angharad realized it would soon be Samhain.

"What day is it?" Angharad asked, turning to Muirenn.

"The day before market day." She answered Angharad, but her eyes were set upon Brother Thomas.

CHAPTER 28

Angharad

The river Tay narrowed, twisting like an adder. Black boulders rose from the water, tufted in green moss even in autumn, and ancient trees lined the riverbanks, trunks skirted with river grass. Everywhere great hills broke the crust of the earth, baring steep shoulders. They drifted past a retinue of tattooed *Cruithni* bearing spears, watching the boats traveling the river, and Talorcan nodded in greeting. Fields of sheep and crops gave way to a speckling of neatly kept huts along the riverbank. And as the river narrowed further, Muirenn pointed. "Look there," she said.

High on the hill, a fortress brooded. The hall was a muscular work of stone topped with a tightly thatched roof, a pair of red banners rustling in the breeze from either side of the entrance. Angharad squinted. They carried the symbol of the boar.

"That fort belongs to Bridei, the high king," Talorcan said. "He holds many forts throughout the land."

"His banners fly only when he is within," Muirenn said.

"The high king is here?" Angharad asked.

"Yes. He comes to collect his rents and stays through Samhain. He often buys slaves at the market. The high king of the *Cruithni* is wealthier than any king of the Britons. He is richer even than Tutgual. It is fortunate Tutgual rules beside a powerful *Cruithni* wife."

"Then you know of Elufed? You know of Tutgual's queen?" Angharad asked.

"Only from stories," Muirenn said. "Whispers in the trees."

"She never would speak of her upbringing. I do not even know the name of her tribe."

"Names, names. You are too hungry for names," Muirenn said.

Angharad shifted away, drawing her arms about her chest. Who wouldn't wish to learn more of their *nain*? Angharad had never imagined she would find herself here. But now that she was a hostage in Pictland—for though Muirenn had not spoken it, what else could she be?—Angharad found she knew nothing at all.

She clung to her anger round two bends in the river, but as the fortress fell behind them, they breached the mouth of the river, and Angharad released her struggle with a sigh.

"Ceann Mòr," Talorcan said.

A loch stretched before them like a great pool of silver. The river wind had dropped, and the skin of the loch was a glassy reflection of hill, sky, and mountains of cloud. Crannogs perched on the water, their thatched roofs like paps, boats tied below them while more drifted by.

"Beautiful, yes?" Muirenn leaned in. "This loch is a trick; it plays with the eye. It would seem that it ends, but it stretches quite a long way."

Angharad followed her gaze to the far end of the loch, where hills became mountains, their peaks disappearing in high banks of cloud.

Talorcan jumped from the currach and helped drag it ashore, then lifted Angharad out, placing her gently on her feet. His foul mood had lifted. He led Brother Thomas to a log on the flat, pebbled shore, tossing his rope, a grudging invitation to sit. Tents and cookfires crowded the shore, and beyond them, a wicker fence stretched for storing livestock. People nodded in welcome as Talorcan and his men erected the tents, then carried the contents of the currach inside.

Angharad sat beside Thomas, the market on her mind. Children raced past with wooden swords in their fists, or ran by in droves, jostling a leather ball with their sticks.

"Perhaps you should join them," Muirenn said, coming up from behind. "I could speak to them for you." Angharad shook her head. She had no desire to play. Muirenn looked at her, scratched her head as if thinking. "Very well. Come with me, then, princess. I will show you the market."

Angharad glanced at Thomas, and Muirenn sighed. "Angharad, your priest is better left here. Talorcan will mind him, believe me. He'll do nothing, I promise, to endanger his profit."

Thomas nudged her from his place on the log. "Go, then, Angharad, I shall be here when you return."

Angharad accepted Muirenn's outstretched hand. It was strong and warm in Angharad's. Past the cluster of tents, merchants set up their wares within stalls, their sturdy wooden carts for sleeping and goods. As Muirenn's auburn hair caught the late-afternoon light, Angharad thought how similar it was to her mother's—wavy and thick, the color of acorns. She squeezed her eyes shut, imagining, if only for a moment, that it was her mother's fingers clasping hers instead.

My mama loves me. She is trying to find me.

"Careful or you shall trip," Muirenn warned, breaking the spell. Pottery and perfume oils. Wooden bowls with smooth swirling grains. Beautiful bratts woven in a myriad of checkered fabrics, to be wrapped for warmth and pinned to drape over one shoulder. Carved figurines. Tapers. Little dolls sewn from cloth.

They walked for a while past the long stretch of merchants. Flute carried beneath light fingers over the race of a drum. But such merriment felt hollow, and Angharad's vision blurred with missing her home. Muirenn drew her to sit beneath the branches of an oak, her catlike eyes solemn in the shifting afternoon light.

"I was younger than you when I left my own mother, you know."

The flames upon her neck had already become part of her to Angharad, but her eyes fell on them now. They whispered of secrets.

"Are you a priestess, then?" Angharad asked.

"I might have been. Oh, how I wished it were so. When a priestess came to visit my father, I begged her to take me away. I clung to her robes. It was very difficult, the training. I missed my father and mother, and at night I felt most alone. I would lie awake and try to remember my mother's face, but as winters passed, I began to forget. Then one day I realized I could recognize my mother's face when I gazed at my own.

"That was the day that I became my own mother. And then I became a child of the goddess. After that day, I was never alone."

"And yet you returned home. So you might be with your family?"

"No, little princess. It was not my choice to make. Someday, perhaps, I shall tell you my story."

Angharad closed her eyes, trying to press her mother's face into her heart. "I miss my mother so badly, it feels as if my heart bleeds."

"Someday, Angharad, you shall see her again."

Children gathered at the feet of the musicians, twirling in dance. It had been so long since Angharad had seen something resembling joy. The warmth of the people hummed like a hive. Muirenn placed her arm around Angharad's shoulder. "You know something?" she said. "You are not so terrible, even for a Briton, and a princess, at that. Come. I smell honey bread. I wager you have yet to try that."

The morning of the slave market dawned, and Angharad woke with a pit in her stomach. She sat beside Thomas, refusing a plate as Talorcan and Muirenn ate their breakfast.

"Angharad, you must eat," Thomas said. She shook her head, but he caught her eyes with a sad smile. "Those who are wise know better than to travel on an empty stomach," he said. Angharad burst into tears. "Think of the story of Patrick," Thomas said. "Do not be afraid. I am not afraid."

Angharad covered his hands with hers. Then came the ominous pound of a drum. No, not one drum, many, echoing over the loch from the fortress on the hill.

Talorcan appeared above them, a razor in his hand. "Your hair." He gestured as one of his men sloshed over a bucket full of water. Thomas's hair had been shorn in the way of a holy man, but in the days they'd been traveling, his tonsure had become overgrown. Talorcan meant to shave it to fetch a better price.

"Do it, then," Thomas said, bowing his head.

Angharad sat in silence as Talorcan wet Brother Thomas's scalp, plunging a hunk of soap into the water to make the shave smooth. When he finished, he wiped the razor clean on the corner of his tunic, then stretched out his hand in a peace offering, to help Thomas stand.

The culdee looked at him a long moment. Then he accepted.

"Come, then," Talorcan said.

Muirenn emerged from the tent and eyed the soapy bucket, her hair coiled into a nest at the nape of her neck. "He could have had one of his men do it," she told Angharad, falling in beside her.

The morning was cloudy, with a bite to the air that sank to the bone. Merchants and marketgoers looked up as they passed, some gazes lingering, others moving quickly away.

The river had promised, *I will help.*

Remember the river, Angharad thought.

Tutgual had told Angharad there was no room for kindness when dealing with slaves. *There is no servitude without fear*, he had said. *Do not look to your mother. Her softness will earn her a knife in the back.*

Some nights after feasts, servants would go missing. Angharad remembered lying abed, closing her eyes, as fighting and laughter roared from the hall. On those nights, her mother came early to sleep. Soon her soft singing was all Angharad could hear.

Brother Thomas had been free under his temple of trees. But he'd chosen to help Angharad, and look what she had done. Cursed the Bernician, and they were taken by the *Cruithni*. Now the people round them stared, and Angharad glared into the crowd. "Why must they watch? Surely not all here are rich enough to purchase."

"They are curious to see people from faraway places," Muirenn said. "And near places, too. The raiders often bring slaves from Dalriada, enemies who bring us nothing but war. They take Pictish wives and dishonor their treaties. Dalriadan slaves fetch a very good price."

"And what about priests?"

"Priests do just as well."

Angharad reached out, taking her hand. "Muirenn, you are wealthy. Buy him. Please? Can you not use his aid on your farm?"

"Angharad, no. Do not ask me again. And do not use my name for things you do not understand."

Angharad tried to yank away, but Muirenn pulled her close. "Walk by me, Angharad. Else they shall think you, too, are for sale."

Angharad did not want to walk beside Muirenn. She did not want to do as she was told. The line of people ahead slowed as they approached a wooden platform. Upon it stood the first batch of slaves. Ropes, chains or collars, bound wrists and feet. They awaited their fate as their flesh merchants stood close, keeping watch on their quarry.

Tightening his hold on Brother Thomas's rope, Talorcan forged on, leading him like a bull to the slaughter to join the other slaves.

"No, wait. Please, wait!" Angharad pushed after them, but Muirenn gripped her.

"Angharad, you mustn't. You have said your farewells."

Thomas looked over his shoulder, finding her eyes. *Peace. Be at peace.*

As the priest climbed the platform, jeers erupted from the crowd. Angharad stood mute while children snacked on hazelnuts. And then the hazelnuts fell from their fingers as a warrior's voice called out. The answer came in a chorus, a deep and guttural *huh!* as if the wind had knocked in a kick from their stomachs.

A line of people trailed down from the fort. At the center strode a man who looked like a king.

"Bridei mac Maelchon, high king of the *Cruithni*," Muirenn said.

A purple-checked bratt was draped across his broad chest, pinned at the shoulder with an exquisite silver brooch. His robe was crimson, embroidered in gold, falling to his ankles, where intricate leather tooling adorned the straps of his calfskin shoes. He was bearded, his hair a mix of silver and black.

The *Cruithni* stretched out their hands, smiling, their faces tilted as if welcoming the sun.

Upon the platform, Talorcan pushed Brother Thomas down upon one knee, and Muirenn guided Angharad gently to do the same.

The high king wore the thick silver chain of legend, but his appeared even heavier than the chain about Muirenn's neck, for King Bridei's bore the weight of all Pictland.

A group of richly dressed men—petty kings or chieftains—followed next, but there was one man who did not walk within the neatly formed line. He strode next to the king, his long legs keeping him nearly one step ahead. His graying hair was shorn, save the thick length of hair he'd bound like a horse tail running down his back.

A Wisdom Keeper.

"Who is that man?" Angharad whispered.

"Briochan, the king's counsel," Muirenn said. "He is a powerful Wisdom Keeper, beloved nearly as much as Bridei himself."

Briochan's eyes skimmed the crowd like a flat rock over water, but when they fell upon Angharad, they caught.

His eyes were the color of oak wood, and when they touched upon hers, Angharad felt suddenly as if she stood in a fog—heady and disoriented, as if she no longer knew which way was earth and which way was sky. She tried to shut herself away too late. Or perhaps it was senseless. But then, as quickly as she'd felt it, Briochan moved on.

The high king and his retinue took their place, and the first man was thrust forward. The slave market began.

A boy with pale hair and angry eyes. A pair of girls who seemed sisters. A man in midlife, beside himself, weeping. Their eyes carried their stories. Angharad could not bear to look. She turned instead to the retinue of the king. Beyond Briochan and Bridei, a regal old woman caught her eye. She stood so motionless she might have been an effigy. Her silvery hair was plaited and coiled atop her head, set with a pair of delicate bone combs. Her eyes were serene, the color of winter. Something in her features felt like an echo.

Muirenn, it seemed, had noticed the woman too, for suddenly, the chieftain's daughter appeared less like a woman and more like a child.

"Who is she?" Angharad asked.

"The priestess of Fortingall," Muirenn said.

"Is that the very woman you have brought me to see?"

Muirenn looked uncertain. "I did not imagine she would be here, I meant to bring you to her fortress. She has not attended the Samhain market in many a winter. Her daughter has always come in her stead."

Suddenly, Angharad did not care, for only one figure stood ahead of Brother Thomas now. He would be next.

"We do not have to stay. We can return to the tent," Muirenn said.

"I will not leave him."

She shrugged. "As you say."

Bridei seemed distracted. But then a young woman was pushed forward. Her hair was greasy and unclean, but beneath its curtain, her face was pleasing—light eyes, a straight nose. Angharad heard "Dalriada" in the torrent that fell from the slaver's mouth. Briochan, the king's counsellor, looked up. Leaning to Bridei, he spoke low words in his ear. Bridei lifted a hand. The slaver nodded, then smiled. The deal had been done. Bridei's man came to collect the woman as the payment was settled. She looked at the king, her face pale with dread.

"She is Dalriadan. She should feel fortunate. She could be dead," Muirenn said with disdain.

Angharad heard the echo of the man who'd taken Eira. *Now she is our Pendragon whore.* But now Talorcan strode forward, pulling Thomas behind him.

Voices that had been jeering dropped to a whisper. The atmosphere felt eager, as if slaving were sport. Brother Thomas squared his shoulders. Angharad twisted her fingers, trying not to weep, for she would not see Thomas any more distraught.

Talorcan began speaking. Angharad tugged Muirenn's dress. "Tell me what he says."

Muirenn listened, bowing her head. "He says, 'This man before you is a priest from the south, a priest of the Britons.'"

Talorcan paused, his eyes flicking to Angharad before he continued.

"What does he say now?" Angharad demanded.

Muirenn's face shifted. "He says the priest is a forest dweller. He would do well with a gentle hand."

"He would do well not to be sold here at all!" Angharad said. But the bidding had begun, the crowd come alive. Talorcan moved from bidder to bidder as the *Cruithni* haggled over the priest.

Then Bridei mac Maelchon lifted his hand.

Talorcan stepped back, lifting his brows in delight. But before he could agree, granting Bridei his prize, the priestess stepped forward, laying her hand on the king's sleeve. Bridei startled and turned to acknowledge her. The priestess shook her head. Bridei stepped back with a bow, and the priestess came forward, pressing a leather purse in Talorcan's hands.

Talorcan nodded. The deal was done.

"I do not understand," Angharad said.

Brother Thomas looked astounded. The old woman faced the crowd, Brother Thomas's rope in hand. No one uttered a sound.

Satisfied, she turned, and four warriors fell in beside her as she descended the platform with Thomas in hand.

It had been many long winters since Britons had given up sacrificing men. But Cyan told her stories of Picts beyond the border who drowned men in pools, or cut out their entrails, leaving them for dead. Now Brother Thomas had been bought by a priestess. Twisting from Muirenn's grip, Angharad ran.

"Stop! Wait!" Angharad cried, ducking and scurrying through the thick of the crowd. "Stop!" she cried, and at the sound of her voice, the old woman turned. One of the warriors caught Angharad by the collar of her dress, holding her at arm's length as the priestess strode near.

"And who is he to you, child?" The priestess spoke in Brythonic, her gray eyes inquisitive.

"He is my friend!"

"Angharad, please." Brother Thomas looked pained.

The priestess seemed startled. "What . . . what is your name?"

"Angharad." She straightened. "I am daughter of—"

"Release her," she commanded. The warrior dropped his hold. "I know who you are." The priestess looked at her as if seeing anew. "Come forward," she said. Angharad obeyed her uncertainly. The woman's hands were like ice as she lifted them to Angharad's cheeks. The priestess murmured in Pictish, tilting Angharad's face to the light. "Can that be you?"

Angharad felt the tremble of age in the old woman's fingers as the priestess gazed deeply into Angharad's eyes.

"Oh, no. Oh, my child," she said.

But even as she gazed, Angahrad gazed back. A skinny little girl, handed to a man upon horseback. She had pale golden hair and eyes the color of shadowed snow. In Angharad's stomach, the feeling of being rent in two.

"You are Rhydderch's child," the priestess said. "Elufed was my daughter. You have her eyes, my daughter's eyes. How is it you came to me?"

Just then Muirenn burst breathless through the crowd. The priestess looked up, eyeing her, and nodded. "Ena," she said.

"Eachna, my lady." Muirenn bowed, but beneath her reverence was the hardness of rage. "We did not expect you at market. I was bringing the child to Fortingall."

"It does not matter. I am here now. The river. She called me."

A shiver traced Angharad's arms. *Hennain*. Great-grandmother. The priestess was her family. Tears gathered in her throat as Eachna drew Angharad close. She smelled of flower water and heather.

Eachna smoothed her hair. "You must come with me now. I will keep you safe."

Amidst the warriors, Thomas stood with a smile upon his face.

"Unbind him? Please," Angharad said.

But Eachna drew back, shaking her head. "No, child. Not yet." The priestess spoke to Muirenn. "Ena, you are welcome, if you would come."

The chieftain's daughter seemed to consider it a moment, then frowned. "No. I will stay. I meant only to bring the child to you. Now that task is done."

Angharad looked between them, feeling even more the child. Muirenn had known that Eachna was her *hennain*, yet she hadn't said a thing.

Muirenn stepped forward. "So, then. I must say farewell."

"Why did you not tell me?" Angharad's voice sounded small.

"You will be safe now, princess. That is all that matters." She bent to embrace Angharad, whispering into her hair. "Eachna will care for you. So much awaits there. But be mindful not to lose your way in her Fortress of Dreams."

"Come, Angharad," Eachna said abruptly, taking her hand. "You shall ride upon my horse."

At the foot of Bridei's hill, Eachna's horses waited on their tethers. Lady Eachna mounted a stormy white mare with surprising grace as one of her guards lifted Angharad, placing her before Eachna in her saddle. Thomas trailed behind them, his rope knotted to the pommel of a warrior's horse.

"It won't be long," Eachna said. "A quarter day at most. Rest, child, while we ride. I can feel you are worn through."

Her *hennain's* hands rested easily on the reins as they turned onto a narrow road that skirted the loch. Eachna was slight, but her arms circled Angharad like those of a great mother bear.

"Are we going to Fortingall?" Angharad asked.

"Yes, child, to the White Fort, my home, at the mouth of the glen. While we travel, I hope you might tell me how you found yourself here."

Angharad had lived lifetimes since the blackberries had spilled from her hands. She did not know how to speak of it. Not to someone who cared. As if she could sense it, the priestess covered Angharad's hand. "There, there, child. There is time. I understand."

It had happened so quickly. The battle and the blood. Gwrgi and Eira. Brother Thomas and the Bernicians. The curse and the Picts. The river and trees had whispered their promises, then risen in a fury to wash Angharad away.

Now Eachna was here.

Angharad twisted back in the saddle uncertainly, searching for Muirenn. The chieftain's daughter stood watching them depart from the edge of the field, nearly out of sight.

"Muirenn," she called, though Angharad did not think she could hear.

But Muirenn tilted her head at the sound of Angharad's voice. Lifting her hand to her breastbone, she reached to tap two fingers over her heart. Angharad's eyes filled. She lifted her hand, tapping two fingers back. Muirenn smiled, nodding.

But her fingers wandered, restless, to the chain around her throat.

CHAPTER 29

Lailoken

Hart Fell, the Black Mountain
March, AD 574

In the weeks that followed my Bull's Sleep, winter closed in. Diarmid and I returned to the huts at the foot of Black Mountain. Winter's grip was deadly, sealing the passes. I had already given the Cailleach two of my toes, so there was little to do but idle by the fire and devise a way to decimate Tutgual's fortress at Clyde Rock.

It might have seemed impossible to anyone untouched by madness.

But as Maelgwn enjoyed saying, perhaps I possessed exactly the right amount. "It is an excellent riddle for your prodigious intelligence," he said. "For it possesses sheer rock cliffs and a triple set of ramparts. The watchtower on the eastern crag can spot an approaching vessel leagues away. A death trap lies between the second and third rampart, and we are without arms, boats, or men enough to do it."

Clyde Rock was a tidal fortress, commanding the salt waters of the Firth of Clyde. A symbol of Tutgual's power, it had been the pride of the Britons since time out of memory. No traveler could enter the rivers Clyde or Leven without paying Tutgual richly. This meant it also possessed rich coffers.

Perhaps it was true—no enemy had managed to breach its ramparts in living memory.

But that only made it all the more enticing.

"Are you in agreement then, Maelgwn Pendragon?" I asked.

There had been a spark, but suddenly, Maelgwn was solemn. "And what of Languoreth?"

"I would never risk her! We will warn her, of course. She mustn't be anywhere near. She or her children."

"But you would make her a widow?"

I met his eyes. "If my sword should fly, who would still my hand?"

Maelgwn did not have a chance to answer, for Diarmid, who'd been eavesdropping, lifted his head. "Well, you aren't going without me!"

"Lend your Sight if you're so eager. For I've nearly figured out a way, but we are in need of an ally. One to provide arms, boats, and men."

"I would've searched after it days ago. You never asked."

The look I gave him was exasperated.

"Just you wait. We'll have a look, then." He took up the fire iron and rose stiffly to bank it, adding more fuel. "Fire scrying isn't my favorite, but it does in a pinch, eh?"

Once the flames were roaring, he sat down and gestured at Maelgwn. "Bring me more ale."

Maelgwn and I played at *fidchell* while Diarmid sat drinking, eyes half closed as he stared into the fire. Such a long time passed, I was certain he'd fallen asleep until he gave a loud "Hah!" and threw back his head with a laugh.

I glanced at Maelgwn. "I don't know if I like the start of this."

Diarmid recovered himself, wiping a tear from his eye. "Oh, it is perfect. But you shall never believe me."

"Test me," I said.

Diarmid put his hands upon his knees, leaning in. "Aedan mac Gabrahn."

"Aedan the Scot?"

"Aye."

Maelgwn considered it. "King of Mannau. Plenty of ships. Plenty of men—"

"The deadliest warriors I've ever seen!" Diarmid cut in.

"And when have you seen them?" I asked.

He waved a hand. "In tales, in tales, but it's all the same."

I had a friend in Rheged who I knew could get word to Aedan mac Gabrahn. Aedan's kingdom of Mannau was just north of Partick, and neither I nor any of the others here dared venture through Strathclyde. But the Song Keeper Taliesin was the Song Keeper of Urien of Rheged, the man who had fathered Eira. Taliesin would know the Song Keeper of Aedan mac Gabrahn. Our bonds as Keepers were built to subvert the will of kings in times such as these. I would use the brotherhood of the Wisdom Keepers.

One of Archer's men carried a message to Rheged.

And this was how, soon as the snow melted from the passes, and the rivers began to run high, turning the season to mud, Diarmid and I left the others at Black Mountain and went to find Taliesin upon his boat at Rheged's quay.

"I never did ask what it was exactly that you saw in the fire," I said to Diarmid as we left our hired horses at the stableman's in Rheged and strode along the quay.

We were wearing dull cloaks with large hoods lent from two of Archer's men, so that we might look like Selgovae. They used this port often, so we did not seem out of place.

Diarmid looked at me sidelong as we turned onto the docking. "What I saw in the fire? Whatever are you on about?"

"You were staring at the fire, then shouted, 'Aedan mac Gabhran!'"

I must have spoken too loudly, for at the sound of the king's name, people on the quay dropped their sacks and trunks, turning to the water in alarm.

"A jest, a jest," I said in apology. I bowed my head to hide beneath my hood.

"And can't a Seer have an idea, or is that only you?" Diarmid asked. "It was a good one, at that. You hadn't thought of it. Look!" He pointed, eager to change the topic. "Here we are. He said the vessel had a red and white sail, did he not?"

Taliesin was speaking idly with other three men in the belly of the boat. He glanced up as we neared, but he did not call out my name. It was a busy passage, the Sea of Rheged, and I was dead or an exile. My scar made me readily recognized, and with his staring, milky eye, Diarmid the Diviner did not precisely blend in.

Taliesin gripped my arm as I stepped aboard the boat. "Well met, old friend. It is good to see you among the living. But you have grown thin."

"And you have grown rich," I quipped, nodding to his boat and his brooch—silver and garnet, with more jewels besides. He would have laughed in the days when he and I had first met, both of us traveling north to train as young Keepers. But his broad mouth did not smile, and his brown eyes were sad. He greeted Diarmid, helping him settle comfortably, then nodded to the men manning the boat.

"They are trustworthy and well compensated. They shan't say a word. Come, brother. We shouldn't tarry. I'd see you to Barsalloch before we endanger your head."

We set sail along the coastline, west and then north round the point, taking some sustenance and talking of the war.

Aedan mac Gabrahn had agreed to meet. And Taliesin had offered his own sea fort as a middle place. Our allegiance to our kings might've seen us on opposite sides, when Urien came against Gwenddolau in the Battle of Arderydd, but there was little we would not do for a fellow Keeper in need. As a counsellor, I fought. As a Song Keeper, he'd borne witness, his principal task to mark the valor of his lord.

As the boat cut through water, we traded lines as we once did, this time composing our song of the war. It soothed us, I think, to return to shared habits. It helped us understand what had become.

"The slaughter was terrible, shields shattered and bloody," he began.

I tried my own line. "Swiftly came Maelgwn's men, warriors ready for battle, for slaughter armed . . ."

"A host of spears flew high, drawing blood from a host of strong warriors . . ."

"A host fleeing, a host wounded—a host bloody, retreating." I stopped and fell quiet, looking out to sea.

We reached the cliffs of Barsalloch just before sundown, and I stepped from the vessel to help drag it ashore. High above the flat, pebbled beach, gorse sprouted from cliffs littered with fat, grazing sheep. Taliesin led the way as we mounted the steep path up to the fort, drawing ahead quickly as Diarmid puffed.

"Don't walk so quickly," he called from behind.

I glanced over my shoulder. "If you're all out of wind, you need only say."

"Me, out of wind? Ha." He caught up, lowering his voice. "We shall see who runs the faster when Urien of Rheged sells us to Strathclyde."

I shook my head. "Taliesin is a brother of the robe. He will not give us away."

"That's what you think."

"And tell me, old friend, did you see this in fire?"

"Nay," he said, solemn. "I saw it in the sea."

We passed a midden pile of shellfish being picked over by shorebirds, then passed through the gate. Five little huts nestled within the rampart's enclosure.

The fortress, I knew, had been a gift from the king. So perhaps it should not have surprised me to find Urien of Rheged sitting at the table when Taliesin ushered me in. Well, that and the fact that Diarmid had warned me.

The king looked up as we entered, and Taliesin spoke low. "You must trust me, Lailoken. All will be well."

"Urien, King." I bowed my head deeply and Diarmid did the same, though he kicked at my heel when he straightened, making his point.

The king of Rheged was gray-haired with green eyes and dressed in rich, patterned cloth. The thick twist of his torque glinted beneath oil light. Urien of Rheged was an honorable man. I'd met him before, even counted him a friend. Now, when I saw him, I saw only Eira's father. Yet the king did not know his daughter had lived. Then there was the fact that he'd come against us in war. I understood, out of necessity, why he had taken Rhydderch's side. Our cause was futile. He could not refuse. But since being besieged by my sister's own husband, I did not much trust in honorable men.

I threw a dark look at Taliesin, and Urien shook his head. "Save your anger, Lailoken. I intend you no harm. Come in, then, and sit."

We did as he bade, taking a seat upon the bench.

"I heard Aedan mac Gabrahn has agreed to come meet. If two men of interest meet in the bounds of my kingdom, I will hear all they might say."

"Only fair," I allowed, looking round the hut. Only two men kept watchful eyes on the king. With Taliesin's three, that made only five. Still, I was glad I'd asked Maelgwn to keep to Black Mountain. If anything should happen, I knew he'd carry on.

"So." The king motioned, and a man brought us wine. "You are not dead. And neither am I. Aedan mac Gabrahn won't arrive 'til the morrow. How, then, Lailoken, shall you and I pass our time?"

It was quite pleasant, in the end. We drank and we dined. Taliesin and I recounted stories from our youth. He stood up and performed a song, most affecting, called "*Cad Goddeu.*" The Battle of the Trees.

"I'd have a word, Urien King," I said, before the night ended too soon.

He nodded and beckoned. The other men withdrew.

I was not certain how to tell him all that I knew. So I told Urien what mattered most for him: that his daughter, Gwendolen, had not in fact died. But that now I could not know if she yet lived.

"The details are a story not mine to tell," I said. "But I would have you know I am enamored of your daughter. I am reclaiming my power, and I hope I might find her and make her my wife."

Urien sat back, stunned. "How do you know that this servant is truly my daughter?"

"It doesn't much matter to me whether she is your daughter or no. But I believe all she has told me is true. And should she tell you what has befallen her, I have little doubt you shall believe her, as well."

"And you have no idea where she's gone? Or what might have happened?"

"She promised to meet me in the Selgovian lands. My men and the Selgovae search for her still."

I knew that I loved Eira. I knew that I missed her. But I hadn't any idea how difficult this would be—sitting across from the man who had made her. Seeing, in him, the slope of her nose.

"I must get some rest," I said, and stood.

"I must thank you, Lailoken," Urien said. "It seems I relinquished my claim long ago, but if I should see her, I should like her to understand I never meant any harm to befall her."

Urien drained his cup and looked down at his hands. Flexed them into fists, as if testing their strength. "Gwrgi of Ebrauc," he said, looking up.

I nodded. I knew precisely what he meant.

* * *

Aedan mac Gabrahn was not a man who appreciated being surprised by the presence of another king.

But once all was settled—and blades put away—he clapped Urien on the back and sat down by his side. "You are counsellor to a shattered kingdom, Lailoken. You are lucky I've come."

"And why did you agree?" I asked.

His hazel eyes were deep-set, his curly hair the color of dark leather. "Because I like you—though I cannot say I much know you."

Aedan's easy way of speaking belied his deeper machinations. Aedan the Wiley, he was called by the Britons. As a boy, he'd eaten his first meat off the tip of a knife. His ambition was insatiable. He spoke Goidelic and Latin. Brythonic, Pictish, and Greek. And if he saw reason, he'd just as soon cut off your head as he might grip your arm.

He was shorter than I imagined. Yet somehow more frightening.

"Aye," I said. "My kingdom was shattered, and I would take my revenge. I wish to bring horror to the men of Clyde Rock."

Aedan sat back, lifting his brows. "You wish me to aid you. You and what others?"

"Nay. I'll not touch it," Urien said.

"Seven men, plus him." I nodded to Diarmid, who winked his milky eye, leaning in.

"Is it true as a lad, you had to spar for your supper?"

Aedan's mouth twitched with amusement.

I pressed on. "I know the mount well. May I tell you my plan?"

The king of Mannau sat rapt as I detailed the way of it. I could see it enticed him—the impossible raid. I also knew how much Aedan disliked Tutgual. And how very much he liked booty.

"There will be white cattle wintering from my family's own stock," I said. "The granary and kitchen house will be weighted down with food. And the coffers will be heavy—they'll just have collected spring rents. The booty will be yours. I'd only hire passage in."

Aedan's gaze was piercing. He turned and glanced back at the bench, where sat his three men. He'd not introduced them when he entered, and they'd moved to the wall to sit wordlessly behind him.

But now one of the men met Aedan's eyes with a nod. His reddish-blond hair was curly and kept from his face by a thin strip of leather. His arms were muscled and covered in fine reddish hair. He possessed the same deep-set eyes as his father. Though not hazel. Blue.

"Artùr, my son," Aedan said. Then he turned to Urien. "King of Rheged. You'd watch Britons die?"

Urien was unshaken. "That is a question better put to Lailoken."

I could not see any judgment in his eyes, but it stirred my anger all the same. "Aye, I am most happy to watch Britons die. For it was these Britons, without cause, who brought war upon me. My brother, my cousin, my nephew, my warriors. All dead. And I—Strathclyde's son? Tutgual and his sons believe their might indestructible. I will pile the walls of their fortress with their dead."

Aedan mac Gabrahn was watching me with a measure of respect. "'Tis a shame you were not here for this meeting," he said to Urien.

"It did not happen on my land."

"You have been more than fair," I said.

"On this occasion only," Urien said. "Do not attempt such a thing again."

Aedan mac Gabrahn gave a sniff of satisfaction. "We'll do it," he said. "The thirteenth of April. It'll be a new moon. Dark on the reaches for landing the boats."

We finalized our plan. And with that he was gone.

CHAPTER 30

Angharad

The White Fort
Glen Lyon, Kingdom of the Picts
28th of October, AD 573

They followed the road beneath a white autumn sky, where clouds bellied low over undulating hills. The horses plodded steadily around the western slope of Bridei's fort to the ford on the river Lyon. On the far side of the grassy bank, a wood of elm and oak stretched, and nearer to the river, bony fingers of birch. A herd of tawny cattle with thickening winter coats grazed between the trees. But as they drew closer to a clearing ahead, the snowy mare beneath them tensed, and Angharad caught sight of a constellation of standing stones.

Eachna reached to stroke her horse's neck. "She feels the spirits that lie sleeping. Tamed horses do not like such places. The spirits are strong and make them uneasy."

The gray boulders were ancient and smooth, sloping like melted wax into the land. Something within the quality of the rock caused them to shimmer ever so slightly, even in the cloudy haze. Her *hennain* leaned forward in the saddle so she might better see Angharad's face. "Do you remember this place? Your blood remembers."

A *place of threes*, Angharad thought. For indeed there were three clusters of worn stones mysteriously placed in the clearing. Beneath them, Angharad could feel her ancestors dreaming.

Eachna urged her horse onward, nodding at the settlement up ahead. "Fortingall."

Angharad craned her neck. Roundhouses with thatched roofs were nestled against a hill that arched like a whale's back. There were bee houses, need-gardens, and healing gardens, too. Wicker pens held sheep for wool and goats for milking. But what drew Angharad's eye was the round stone wall standing at the center of all else. A magnificent yew grew within the low stone enclosure, its graceful arms only beginning to thicken with age. Nearby, a simple rectangular temple stood with a peaked thatched roof.

"Brother Thomas spoke of this tree," Angharad said.

"It was given by those whose ash bones rest in the field," Eachna said.

"And the fortress?" Angharad pointed halfway up the eastern rise of the hill, where a rampart emerged out of the trees.

"White Fort, in your tongue. It has belonged to the priestesses of Fortingall for countless winters now. The high king provides men to keep it, men such as these." She gestured to the men on horseback. "They are honored to protect us, but they keep to the fort lest we bid them come down, for we have little need of protection. No clann among the *Cruithni* would dare ravage this place."

Angharad glanced back at Brother Thomas, and his blue eyes were reassuring. Muirenn had promised Eachna could help her find her way home. But her *hennain* had not yet spoken of this. She had wondered at Angharad's journey but not asked after Angharad's mother or father. She spoke only of Elufed, as if Angharad's own parents were nothing at all. Now the sight of huts with warm fires stirred Angharad's longing.

"Lady Eachna?"

"Yes, child?"

"I must send a message to my mother and father," Angharad said. "They must know I am safe. They will send someone to fetch me."

Eachna nodded. "Of course. We shall make it so, if that is what you wish."

"I do wish it. Please! I fear they believe I am dead. Please send a messenger. Send a messenger this day!"

"It is too late to ride out today. I will send a man at first light. In the meanwhile, you may tell him what you wish to convey."

"Oh, thank you," Angharad said. She imagined how it would feel to rush into her mother's arms. The smell of her. But they had been spotted, and figures began to emerge from the huts, girls in gray dresses of varying ages, bearing markings of adder and deer, horses and hounds. Birds of all sorts. Their faces were radiant, curious, expectant. She heard one of them call in a crane's whoop, and more women gathered until all stood waiting at the stone wall that encircled the yew.

"Lady Priestess!" The younger girls rushed to her, hugging her legs, patting Angharad's foot where it dangled over the horse's flank. Eachna clapped her hands with a smile that creased her face into its worn pathways, and she dropped lightly from the saddle. Angharad did the same. The littlest girls raced round and round, touching Angharad's dress and smoothing her hair like so many tiny mothers.

"I told them you are my blood daughter, and so you are their sister, for all these are my children."

Angahrad felt a pang of jealousy. Eachna was her *hennain*, and she'd only just found her. But just as quickly as they'd clustered, the women caught sight of Brother Thomas. An older woman stepped through, stormy eyes fixed accusingly on Eachna, and for a moment Angharad startled. Elufed?

No, but the woman carried an echo of Elufed. High cheekbones and a long, straight nose. Gray eyes. But her hair was ashy, where Elufed's was gold. She strode forward, issuing a stream of what could only be rebuke before throwing up her hands and stalking back into a nearby hut.

The women were silent.

"Fetla, my blood daughter. Elufed's elder sister," Eachna said, watching her go. She murmured something dismissive in Pictish.

"What did you say?" Angharad asked.

The priestess turned to her frankly. "It is a saying we have here at Fortingall. Too many hens, not enough cocks."

The women ate a light supper of bread with goat's cheese and honey. Eachna kept a man posted outside the stable but saw to it that Brother Thomas was made comfortable within. And at evenfall, Fetla gathered the women to sing to the tree.

Angharad marveled at the transformation as Fetla looked tenderly upon the tree. Winters fell away. Her voice was clear, a silver bell, rising and falling in a melody that haunted, raising the hairs on Angharad's flesh.

It was a sad song, she decided. A song of remembering.

Later, Eachna went to sleep early, and Fetla came to perch upon Angharad's bed. "May I look?" she asked, gesturing to Angharad's hands.

Angharad nodded and Fetla uncurled her fingers, examining her palms. In the hearth's semi-dark, she saw the places where Angharad's skin had sealed over thorns.

"Thorns. *Cartait*," Fetla said, touching them gently.

"*Cartait*." Angharad tried. Elufed's sister nodded. "Fetla?"

"Yes."

"Do you know of Muirenn?"

"Yes. She was here at Fortingall once. Lady Eachna told me Muirenn brought you to us."

Angharad nodded. "I heard Lady Eachna call Muirenn by a name I did not know. Is Muirenn not her name?"

Fetla thought a moment. "Ena. It is the name she was given. It means 'little fire.'"

"She did not seem to favor it."

Fetla only smiled. "Ena is fire, and Lady Eachna is water. The two do not mingle well."

She smoothed the sheepskin keeping Angharad warm and brushed her fingers along the center of her forehead. It was as if her touch held a power, for suddenly, Angharad felt every moment of the past many days. Her body was so very weary.

"That's enough then. Sleep now."

The warrior rode off the next morning, carrying Angharad's message with him to Strathclyde.

"I know you are eager. But it is a very long journey, and winter is nigh," Eachna warned. "You must be patient and wait. I am certain your mother and father will come for you soon."

"I will be patient, I swear it." Angharad wrapped her arms around Eachna's waist. "*Hennain?*"

"What is it?"

"How was it you came to the market? Yesterday at Ceann Mòr . . . you said the river spoke."

Eachna took Angharad's arm gently, tilting it up to expose the underside of her wrist where slender blue veins trailed beneath Angharad's skin.

"You need only to look at your own flesh, little bird. We are made of water. Rivers of red run through our body. Is it so strange we should hear them?"

Angharad shook her head. It was not strange at all.

"Tatha, the river, spoke, and I knew I must visit the market. There I saw the priest and understood what must be done. A priestess is not skilled because she is all-knowing. No such person exists. A priestess is skilled because she learns to hear the language of the Gods—they speak in a tongue of whispers. I have been a child of the Gods for many winters, and even I did not imagine to find my own flesh and blood there. Perhaps I should have supposed, for the Gods delight in surprises. I listen, and I trust I am a child of the Gods. That is my teaching."

She said the last as if ending a prayer. For now, that was all that Eachna would say.

The tongue of whispers. It was a tongue Angharad knew. She had listened, and it had led her to the land of the *Cruithni*. It had pulled her to this woman, her own blood, who knew the secrets of her gift when Angharad did not. Now Angharad only hungered to know more.

But it frightened her even as it continued to draw her in. For if she continued to obey it, she did not know what she might become. Already she found herself forgetting Brother Thomas. And when she remembered that he waited in the stables, she felt a hot rush of shame.

"I still cannot understand why you bought Brother Thomas. You have no plan to . . . hurt him, do you?"

"You mean string his innards from our old tree?" Angharad's eyes widened, but Eachna only chuckled. "Oh, yes. We know what the southern folk say."

"It is only, you have bought him. Can you not set him free?"

Her *hennain* tilted her head. "Is that what you wish?"

"Yes. Oh, yes, Eachna. Please."

"And you would have me free him right away?"

"Please." Angharad nodded.

Eachna studied her a long moment. "Then perhaps you will be pleased to know your priest is already gone."

"What?" Angharad froze. "What can you mean?"

"I have already granted his freedom, on the condition that he leave at first light."

Angharad blinked, her stomach sinking with regret. "I did not have the chance to even say goodbye."

"Come," Eachna said, gathering her close. "All wounds heal in time. I only hoped to spare you the pain of farewell. He has food enough, and travels with my blessing. No *Cruithni* shall harm him. You have my word."

"But—"

"You asked for his freedom, and I have granted it. There can be no men of Christ here. Surely my own blood would know that."

Angharad felt adrift without Thomas, no matter what Eachna might say. She walked to the stable as if to ensure he was gone. Eachna's gray mare was the only friend to be found.

Outside the stable walls, the women were chanting or praying or sitting in lessons. Angharad looked down at the thorns in her hands.

"Wounds left unhealed turn and go sour."

Angharad looked up to see Eachna watching from the stable door, a wooden cup in her hand.

"They are healed," Angharad said quietly.

"Those are not the wounds I speak of. I have seen behind your eyes. The horrors of war leave wounds far more insidious than marks upon the skin. The memories bore into not only the body but the mind and the heart, carving wounds we cannot see. The festering is more than most men can bear. It will kill you in the end. Ena brought you here not only because you are my blood but because this is a place of healing. We must cast out your terrors. I would help you, if I can."

Angharad sat very still. "Will it be painful?"

"It is always painful to remember your horrors," she answered evenly. "But it is nothing a child like you cannot withstand."

Her *hennain*'s words frightened her. Angharad had bound all of the suffering—hers, Eira's, the Dragon Warriors. She had learned to slip out of herself when the memories became too much to bear. But she had begun to realize that nothing in her power could truly make them abate. Now Thomas was gone. It was all too much.

"Do you know what today is?" Eachna broke the silence.

Angharad shook her head.

"It is the eve of Samhain," she said. "And there is a place I would have you visit. But the choice is yours. Nothing can heal if the soul is not willing."

"What sort of place is it?" Angharad asked.

"A powerful one."

The hunger returned. It would not fade away.

"I will go." Angharad stood.

"Good." Eachna nodded. She handed Angharad the empty wooden cup. "You must travel alone. But never fear, little bird. I will tell you precisely what you must do."

CHAPTER 31

Languoreth

Cadzow Fortress
Kingdom of Strathclyde
3rd of April, AD 574

Cadzow came awake beneath the touch of my hand.

We'd stretched our stores through the winter, each of us licking our wounds. But as the woods sprang with spring flowers and curling fern fronds, the hall breathed new life, as if it had been sleeping.

As I strode though the chambers I'd known as a child, the air somehow felt lighter, even when my heart sank with waiting for word of Angharad or the men.

Rhydderch's scouts had wintered near the wall and yet combed the land. Still no one they encountered had seen any sign of my daughter. Lailoken had been seen taking shelter in a cave with the last of the Dragons. If Rhydderch's scout had seen them, who else might have discovered the place where they lay?

I felt a shameful relief when Rhydderch rode off with Cyan, leaving Cadzow to the women again. To keep safe his tanistry, he dared not keep too long from Partick.

And as the storm season faded, restoring a measure of predictability to our seas, Rhydderch sent word that he and Cyan had left the capitol to reside at Clyde Rock. Here Cyan could pick up his learning of tribute and merchants, treaties and trade.

Eira's hair grew in the color of sun, and no longer did she darken it, for here she was safe. Gladys stayed with me to learn the running of a hall, watching how Gwenddolau's people brightened our hamlet in returning to their trades. Millers and cloth dyers, weavers and crop hands. Some stayed at the hall, pledging their loyalty in exchange for my care. New grooms and herd keepers who'd tended Gwenddolau's beasts found healing in tending those that dwelled here.

I was checking the need-garden in the courtyard when I heard the sound of a cart approaching, and a few moments later, the gate guard called up.

"A merchant, m'lady. He comes bearing salt."

"We have no need for more salt," I answered. "Olwenna has seen our store fully stocked."

Hearing my voice, the merchant replied, "My salt comes from the *Bavarii*, far across the sea, and this sack I bring from their most ancient mine. I would not wish to leave without offering you a sampling, if it please you, m'lady."

I straightened. There was a warmth in his voice, and it was oddly familiar.

"Let him come through," I said. I had been waiting and waiting for a messenger to come. I could not risk turning one away.

I waited on edge as the gateman searched and then admitted him, and the traveler and his cart rolled through the gate. He wore the hat of a merchant to cover his fair hair, and his mustache had been trained in the manner of a Gaul. A full beard grew below it, further disguising his face, but I knew his eyes well—it was Fendwin the warrior, one of Pendragon's men.

His eyes touched on mine as Torin's men appeared from the grounds, ensuring I was safe.

"A salt merchant has come. Clear the kitchens, if you will? I would do my tasting there."

Eira would know him. I could not risk her emotion giving Fendwin away. She sat in her chamber, working at her stitching. "Fendwin has come," I said.

Eira dropped her bone needle, her hand flying to her lips. "Sweet Gods, but how?"

"He comes as a merchant. We must keep him safe."

She nodded and stood, following close behind. My guard had cleared the servants and left. I'd never been so thankful for a warrior's lack of interest in cooking.

"I would see this salt merchant," Eira said.

At her voice, Fendwin turned, hands falling to his sides. Though we had the kitchens to ourselves, he kept his voice to a whisper. "Eira, here? How can it be?"

"There is too much to say." She went to embrace him, and then he stood back at arm's length.

"You are alive and well. Thank the Gods it is so. Lailoken and the Selgovae have been searching since autumn. When winter came, we feared the worst."

"Yes, I am well," she said. "Now tell us of the men."

Fendwin's face darkened. "Nine of us live. Some women and children, too, under Selgovian care."

"Who yet lives?" I demanded. "Who?"

"Maelgwn and Lailoken. Myself and old Diarmid are among the surviving men."

I felt the air rush from my lungs. Maelgwn, my love. Maelgwn yet lived. I felt the presence of his token in the pocket of my dress.

But Eira's blue eyes were full of concern. "And the women and children?"

"Dreon and Rhiwallon's wives. Some of their kin."

Eira stepped back. "But . . . what of the others? What of all the others?" Her voice rose in alarm, and I reached for her hands.

"There may be others yet, Eira, who found refuge in another land."

The look upon Fendwin's face told a darker tale. But we had so little time.

"Tell me where you are in hiding," I said. "Perhaps there is a way I can send provisions to you there. Perhaps we can visit—"

I felt Eira's spirit rise at the thought of it, too. But Fenwin shook his head.

"I will tell you where we have settled, but you must keep away. No provisions, no messengers. Do you understand?"

To know where they were but be kept away? It was a torturous bargain, but Eira and I both knew why it must be made.

"A chieftain named Archer shelters us in the great wood. We are warm and provided for. We can last there, if need be. When the time comes we will send for you, and you can visit us there."

Eira and I nodded. But Fendwin glanced away.

"What is it, then?" I asked. "Is that not why you've come?"

"I am glad to give tidings, but no. I fear I've come with a warning. The Dragon Warriors have recovered our strength in more ways than one. Keep yourself from the sky mount. In ten days hence, when the light of day comes, there shall be prophesy."

The sky mount—Fendwin could mean none other than the fortress of Clyde Rock. Sweet Gods. Lailoken meant to raid Tutgual's fortress.

"He's gone mad. It is too dangerous! And you cannot manage it alone," I whispered fiercely.

"We will not raid alone, but I cannot say more. Heed me, I beg you. I have risked my own hide to come. For I do not wish any more of your children to be harmed." Fendwin's tone was frightening.

"Blood after blood. This is his wisdom, Uther's great counsel? My husband and son are within Clyde Rock's walls. Tell them they must wait!"

"Ten days, Languoreth, and it will be done. For our allies will raid whether we join them or not."

"Oh, Lailoken," I whispered. "What have you done?"

Fendwin took up his salt, eyeing the door. "I must go. Forgive me. I fear I have lingered too long."

I nodded. "Yes, of course."

"Keep safe," Eira said. "Tell Lailoken . . . Tell Lailoken I shall wait."

Fendwin looked to me for a message, but I could only shake my head. I should have sent kind words to my brother, or to Maelgwn, to express my gladness they lived. But this? This?

I knew the Dragons might have their revenge. But they did not attack Ebrauc. Lailoken attacked Strathclyde, his own home!

I felt then just how deeply the betrayal of Arderydd had wounded him. I thought I had known.

I'd known nothing at all.

"Fendwin," I said, and he turned at the door. "Thank you for your warning. And risking yourself to come."

Fendwin nodded. For a moment it seemed he wished to say more, but he bowed his head and stepped from the kitchens, waving farewell to my guard.

Ten days.

Eira and I looked at each other. "Languoreth, you must know that if you send warning, Lailoken and the others—they will all die."

I expelled a breath. Now, either way, it was I who must betray. Would that I could set Tutgual upon his rock to await his own doom while removing to safety all those I loved.

How could I summon Rhydderch and Cyan out of harm's reach without causing the slaughter of my brother and his men in return? What of Elufed and Rhian? I sank my head into my hands.

"Don't despair, Languoreth. We have some time yet," Eira said. "We will pool our wits. There must be a way. I promise I shall help you keep Cyan safe."

She did not mention Rhydderch.

I knew then Eira wished Rhydderch might get what he deserved.

I took the path through the wood toward my mother's old healing hut.

I could imagine only one thing that would bring them from danger without giving the raid away.

The hinges groaned as I lifted the iron latch and stepped into the dark, fumbling to cast open the small wooden shutter. Stale air mingled with the smell of pine resin and decaying lovage. I blew dust from ceramic jars of bearberry twig and stag's-horn moss.

"I hope their properties are not depleted," I whispered to the half-empty room.

The plant I sought would not grow until midsummer. I would have to rely on what scant supply I'd set aside before the turning of the year. Too little and it would not affect me. Too much and it would stop my heart. I tucked the wolfsbane gently into the hidden pocket of my gown, and my fingers brushed my little green ring.

I thought of Maelgwn and my brother standing beneath Caer Gwenddolau's ramparts as they witnessed the slaughter of their men.

I thought of my son.

I knew there was no other course that might achieve the right ends.

There would be slaughter. Blood after blood, and now, in my failure to stop the raid, the blood would wet my hands. But Cathan had once told me all leadership was blood.

And this was not revenge. What Lailoken sought was justice.

Rhydderch must not know. He must never know.

Latching the shutter, I ducked from the healing hut, closing the door behind me.

I told Eira alone what I planned to do.

Together we kept awake trying to figure a way we might warn Rhian and Elufed. It was impossible. They were at Partick, I knew, not at Clyde Rock. I could only pray that they'd stay. Anything I did could mark me a traitor, and I did not want my children to have to suffer my death.

The wolfsbane's effects would be immediate, and the journey to Clyde Rock was nearly a full day downriver on favoring tides. Knowing as much, I waited seven days, fear gnawing at my stomach. What if I delayed my sickness too long? What if they did not come? What if Rhydderch sent Cyan, but pressing matters kept my husband to the rock?

At last it came time to prepare the wolfsbane. I took little more than I would give to one who truly needed it. But it struck quickly, making my insides burn and my heart race, then falter, in my chest.

The pain was worse than I imagined.

A feeling of dread overtook me as I doubled over, getting sick in my washbowl. Aela must have heard and came in search of me, only to find me leaning over the bowl upon the floor, my body in tremors. Her face blanched. "My lady!"

"I'm unwell," I said. "Tell Torin to send for my husband. I want my husband and my boy."

"You need a healer," she said.

I nodded and waved her off. "Please, Aela. Just do as I say."

Do not die. Don't you dare die, I commanded my body. Time altered. Eira came with my guard, lifting me to my bed. Sound came in waves and absences. My body was weak now, but within it, my spirit was a mountain. The plant was not my adversary. The plant would deliver a blessing: my loved ones would not die. And so I became a servant to my sickening. Days slipped away, but it could not have been more than three sundowns later when at last I heard Cyan's voice.

"Mother?"

I opened my eyes with effort. Safe, he was safe. But my boy's face was stricken. I could scarcely lift my arm. What use was this body if it could not soothe him?

"Come." My voice was a rasp from beyond the veil.

Cyan took my hand, and I then saw Rhydderch standing behind him. Strathclyde's future king.

Safe.

Rhydderch came and placed his palm gently atop mine and Cyan's. It was cool from the out-of-doors, and it brought me comfort.

"How long have I been ill?" I asked.

Rhydderch blinked as if to clear his thoughts, his face lined with worry. "I cannot say. We came as soon as we got word. Two days, it has been, since you fell sick."

Relief washed over me. Tomorrow it would be done.

"Stay with me," I whispered.

"We will stay. Rest now. Only rest," Rhydderch said.

I let my eyes close.

There were deeds I would carry to my grave.

This was one.

CHAPTER 32

Angharad

The White Fort
Glen Lyon, Kingdom of the Picts
Samhain
31st of October, AD 573

Angharad followed the footpath as Eachna had instructed.

It was the eve of Samhain and the thinness was unsettling. She could feel the yawning gap between this year and the next, the eagerness of the dead to make themselves known. Trees knit their fingers in a tunnel overhead, and she spoke to them as she walked to ease her sense of dread.

I am the daughter of Rhydderch and Languoreth, she told them. *Even now a messenger travels to Strathclyde. Any day they will come for me. Any day I will go home.*

The branches rustled in the wind. Low clouds raced. Angharad spotted the ford Eachna had told her of and took the path down to the water, stepping carefully over water-slick rocks.

I was the foster child of Lailoken. Memory kicked, the Chi-Rho marked upon doors, and the sting and choke of charred, bitter smoke.

She thought of the bright-hearted people of Cadzow, whose huts lay scattered in the fields and woods around the fortress, her mother's

kin. How long until torches came seeking them, too? She tried to picture her father, but he felt like a stranger.

I am a blood daughter of the Cruithni, she ventured.

It felt like trying on one of Elufed's fine dresses, sleeves and hem
pooling.

She thought of Briochan, Bridei's counsellor, and the curious sensation of wandering in fog.

Her mother had told them tales of an isle west of Gaul, where nine
priestesses dwelled who could raise terrible storms or calm an angry
sea. It thrilled Angharad to think Britons once knew such mysteries. Now she wondered if the Britons might have learned such secrets
from the *Cruithni*.

A mother otter with her kit scurried over a fallen log. The flowing
river was soundless, creating an eerie silence, but in thinking of the
spirits of the river, Angharad no longer felt afraid. She encountered
no other person; not a single currach passed her by. It was as if she
moved within some strange sort of dreamtime. It was colder here, in
the heart of Pictland, and fewer leaves fleshed the trees. Winter would
soon entomb these great hills in snow.

It will be quite beautiful, she thought. *It is a pity I won't see it.*

The path that ran along the river Lyon became a cowherd's trail.
It ambled through pasture before skirting along the bottom of a hilly,
wooded glen and dropping onto a rocky streambed, where Angharad
had to pick her way over boulders.

Eachna had promised she would know the waterfall when she came
upon it. And as her ears picked up the rush and chortle of running
water, she came at last upon the falls.

She stopped a moment, listening.

Water tumbled in a series of cascades from a cataract up the
wooded hill, where hazel and birch rose from a steep bed of boulders

speckled silver with lichen. The roar of the water was like the churn
of the firth in a summer storm, unaffected by wars and the worries
of men. It felt like a secret, the way the pools at its feet were quietly
breathing.

The river it gushed into was a dark channel the color of steeped
roots, too deep and swift to cross, save at the ford Angharad had tra-
versed downriver.

She closed her eyes, seeking permission, as her uncle had taught
her. A presence drew near, exploring in return, but then withdrew. It
was older than the trees, and if it did speak, it was not in any tongue
Angharad knew. Yet she sensed she had not been given the right to
trespass. She stood a moment, watching the white tumble of water,
uncertain she would be able to complete the task Eachna had set
for her.

Always they come here, always they are seeking, the water seemed to
say in a sigh. Angharad felt a little shameful, for she, too, had come
seeking.

She had come seeking three stones. A round stone. An oblong
stone. A stone in the shape of a triangle.

She did not yet know what their purpose would be, only that
Eachna had bade her fill the wooden cup with water from the falls,
then collect three stones, placing them in the cup, for the water
was important. But Angharad dared not do this without the water's
permission.

She sat upon a nearby boulder. Wrapping her cloak around her
knees to ward off the cold, she inhaled a deep breath of freshwater
spray.

They come seeking because you clean them, she told the water. *It isn't
your fault you're magnificent. You are a god. You cannot help your nature.*

She was not certain the water welcomed it, but the way it fell
from its mossy shelves was so graceful and not altogether unkind, so

Angharad decided she would offer her own nature to the waterfall in a quiet series of rememberings. Splashing in the river Avon in the shadow of her mother's fortress, spinning with her arms out beneath Cadzow's trees. Days on end following the tracks of wild creatures. Pressing her ear to her father's chest to hear the pulsing of his heart.

She did not mean to remember all the things that came after— leaving Cadzow upon her uncle's horse, warriors scaling the fortress walls, bloody spears, vacant eyes, the sound of Eira screaming. The memories were punishing, delighting in her suffering. Water fell from the height of the wooded glen, beating against rock.

She looked at the pool at the base of the falls. It had not grown or shifted, not to any mortal eye, yet suddenly, the water seemed to open the circle of its arms, as if inviting her to peel off her clothing and plunge into its icy embrace.

But that's mad! It wants me to swim, Angharad thought. *It is Samhain and nearly November.* Surely she would freeze.

She looked round, wondering if she might trust it, for some water spirits were known to be devious, delighting in luring people to their deaths.

At first glance, the pool was not deep, but the waterfall was commanding, its wildness complete. It neither tricked nor made promises. But then Angharad realized the rocky bottom of the pool was a trick of the eye. In truth, beneath the layers of earth and of stone, the pool was bottomless. An entrance to another world.

Yes. Travel deeper, something urged. A voice? No. A Knowing.

She followed, and the veil between worlds dropped away.

The spirits of the falls circled the pool, though she could not see them when she looked with her eyes. Only through the mist in her mind could she begin to make out their shapes. Long and lean, made of water and of light.

Fear raced through the cracks in her. They could take her if they wished. It was Samhain. Boys and girls were stolen with alacrity this time of year. These spirits were ancient and far more powerful than she. Eachna had promised Angharad she had nothing to fear. How could her *hennain* have sent her here?

She spun round, certain something stood, breathing at her neck.

You are not real, Angharad said. But it was. And it was not. Heart racing, she glanced to the river path, wondering if she should scramble back over the rocks the way she had come. But she was weary to the bone of weeping, of feeling afraid.

"I will not fear you," she shouted over the roar of the water. "Do you hear me? Angharad of Strathclyde is not afraid!"

The pool was breathing. The waterfall stood vigil. Angharad's voice was carried away by the impatient rush of water.

Would she dare to step in?

She felt the glen beyond, vast and vacant. Angharad clenched her jaw, stripping off her clothes.

Her skin met the air and turned to gooseflesh as she edged toward the pool, testing the water. Minnows darted, and the water swallowed her pale white feet in a thousand tiny needles. Rotted leaves and a silky layer of silt made the stony bottom slick. She took a step farther. The jolt of cold was so blinding that for one blessed moment, Angharad's noisy and haunted mind tipped, blackness sloshing out like an overfull bucket.

Plunge, the waterfall seemed to beckon.

Plunge, it commanded. For only then might she clean her spirit of its sludge.

Angharad took a breath before she could question it and dunked beneath the surface.

The cold slapped the breath from her lungs, her skinny body convulsing. But beneath the water's skin, she felt scarcely the weight of a fish scale. The roar of the waterfall muted to a whisper. Cold seeped through in a liquid fire of blazing light.

So much sorrow.

So much death.

It was possible she would never be entirely free of it.

But she understood, in that moment, the gift this water god offered.

A new beginning.

Angharad found purchase on the slippery bottom and pushed, bursting through the surface with a gasp. Her body was shaking, her skin tight. The water came only to her navel here.

She stood, looking across the river, the waterfall at her back.

The trees stood in sharper relief, as if cut by a smith's tool. She had not been dragged into the nether world, though she felt its invitation pulse beneath the leaves and silt that swirled at her feet. Her hair was wet and smelled of stream water. She felt bright and at peace.

Angharad wanted to linger in the newness, but her body kicked, demanding survival. She scurried to the boulder where she'd piled her clothes, drying her wet body with her cloak before dressing. It was only as her shaking subsided that she was reminded of her task. She'd been given so much, she hesitated to ask. *May I?*

Angharad waited. A breeze ruffled the pool, and the boughs of a young oak in the streambed bent as if to nod.

Angharad bent to fill the wooden cup with water and found her three stones quickly.

Head. Body. Heart.

Dropping them gently into the cup, she pressed her fingers to her lips in thanks.

The presence of the place retreated. Angharad wondered when she might visit again. There would be time yet, she told herself, before her mother came to fetch her away.

She would be thankful for each day she had among the priestesses of Fortingall, for she did not know if she should ever return. And Angharad had so many questions—questions that women like Eachna and Fetla alone might answer.

She found the women in the temple, circled round the hearth in silence, palms resting in their laps.

Eachna looked up as Angharad shut the temple door behind her. "Come," she said.

The Samhain fire had been lit in the hearth. The air was thick with waiting and smelled sweet and herbaceous, like dried herbs and bracken. A mat of reeds lay beside the hearth, and Eachna gestured for Angharad sit. "Do you wish to be whole, then, Angharad?"

The priestess's wintry eyes burned with fire. The women waited, eyes closed. Fetla was watching.

Before this day, it seemed impossible. The thorns had bedded too deep. But the waterfall had opened her, and this small stretch of land buried in the hills felt a world apart from weapons and men. Something within Angharad was shifting.

"I wish to be whole," she said.

"And have you the stones?"

Angharad offered up the wooden cup. Eachna drew them out carefully, reserving the water and cup, as the women began to hum a deep and haunting tune. Taking up the tongs, Eachna scattered the hot, glowing wood, smoothing the coals into a bed and laying the stones upon it. The song of the priestesses swelled until the stones glowed like dragons' teeth.

One by one, Eachna removed the pebbles from the fire, dropping them into the wooden cup. There was a hiss of steam, and the water crackled. Eachna peered into the liquid, lips pressed tight with concentration. But as the round pebbles dropped, water sizzled up and out of the cup, splashing onto the hearth's edge and nearly scalding Eachna's leg.

"Heart and body suffer, but worst off is the mind," Eachna murmured. "Lie back and close your eyes."

The hearth fire warmed Angharad's skin as Eachna knelt, placing her hands upon Angharad's feet. But it was something other than the hearth that warmed the priestess's hands, for slowly they grew hot, like Angharad's cheeks when she was struck by fever.

A pulsing came, a heartbeat. It traveled in waves from her feet, up Angharad's skinny legs, and into the trunk of her body, gentle as water.

Water can carve away even rock, her mother used to say.

Beyond the temple walls, the yew tree was listening. Angharad felt its roots beneath the temple floor, cradling them all. Roots below, the priestess above. But as the waves from Eachna's hands traveled through Angharad's body, they built, filling her small vessel to the brim. Now the waves were met with resistance as Eachna shifted, placing her hands upon Angharad's stomach. So much had roiled there. She felt nausea rise and churn like a kick in the gut. The pulsing persisted, soft but unrelenting. Angharad felt the swift prick of sweat and rolled onto her side just in time to be sick. She scrambled to her hands and knees.

A bucket came beneath her. Angharad heaved and heaved. The humming kept on, making her head swim, and she wanted to shout at the women to stop, but she was a slave to the convulsing of her insides as they turned themselves out.

Eachna's hands were on her back, and Angharad tried to swat them away, but Eachna would not remove them. Fetla held Angharad's hair, her voice coming low in her ear. "Give it back, Angharad. Give it back. This is not yours to keep . . ."

Spit it back upon the beast.

Was that Fetla who spoke, or a whisper from the tree?

The roots of the yew were holding her up. The roots of the yew would drink Angharad's poison. The sacrifice of the tree moved her to tears. Tears and vomit fell into the bucket. The pulsing was going to break her. To free her.

But Eachna had not yet reached her head.

"Breathe, Angharad," the priestess said. Then she moved her hands to the back of Angharad's skull.

A piercing came like that of a spear through her eye. Angharad screamed, thrashing with pain. She wailed and wept, but her *hennain* did not remove her hands from her head. Angharad broke apart. Fetla gripped her shoulders.

She knew, in her way, the priestesses of Fortingall were battling the beast.

She knew they would not stop until she had recovered body, mind, and heart.

The pulsing came again and again. And then, gradually, the vomiting ceased.

The bucket was cleared away.

Angharad was empty.

She collapsed, boneless, onto her stomach. Her lids were so heavy. The temple floor held her up. The pulsing was there. It came now from innumerable hands pressed upon Angharad's body. Her arms and shoulders. Knees and chest. She gave herself over completely to their care. After some time, the sensation stopped.

The hands were gone. Their humming had ceased, and the silence stirred her.

Then Eachna's voice came. "Open your eyes, little bird."

Slowly, slowly, the women helped Angharad to sit. The temple felt watchful. Beyond the thatched roof, high overhead, the night sky was breathing.

Angharad felt the reed matting beneath her skirts, her legs stretched out before her. She felt the priestesses gathered round in the sort of stillness that follows a great storm.

"Open your eyes, little bird," Eachna said again. "You have been dreaming, don't you see? Only now are you coming awake."

CHAPTER 33

Lailoken

Tutgual's Fortress at Clyde Rock
Kingdom of Strathclyde
13th of April, AD 574

The currachs moved silently through the night water.

The sky was moonless as the tide traveled inland. The wind was at our backs, pushing us closer to the behemoth black rock.

Eira had found her way to Languoreth. I did not know how. But now I knew she was safe. She had sworn she would wait.

So now, I must live.

We'd sharpened our swords and readied our spears. Fendwin had polished his dirk. I watched Artùr coil and uncoil his rope three times about him now, as if for luck, securing his grappling hook at the back of his hip.

We'd been preparing for the raid for several days, and that sort of thing tended to bond men completely. Perhaps it was because the Dragon Warriors and the men of Mannau were more alike than we were different. We both believed wit and brawn were of equal importance. I'd grown fond of the way the Scots got things done.

"I always thought the cliff looked great fun to climb. 'Tis a shame you have to do it in the dark. The view from the top is magnificent," I said.

I thought Artùr allowed a hint of a smile, though I could make out only the whites of his eyes. He and his men had painted their faces to merge with the rock. "Next time, perchance," he said.

Ten men to climb and overtake the might of a fortress. But one hundred more were divided between these eight small currachs and the rest of Aedan's fleet, awaiting our signal a short distance out in the firth. By the time Artùr and his men reached the cliff top, it would not yet be daybreak, but Strathclyde's sky would blaze with our own brand of fire. Artùr and his men would steal into the uppermost level of the fortress and set the roof of Tutgual's great hall alight.

This is how our raid would begin.

I'd watched Artùr train as our men tarred the currachs black. He was deadly with his blade. His spear throws toppled targets. He excelled at swimming, bested his brothers in footraces and in hand fighting, and had committed several good poems to memory (which he recited with reverence when given enough drink). Not to mention he'd grown up climbing the crags of Mannau's cliffside fortress for fun, so he could pick his way up a sheer rock face as if he weighed little more than a feather.

I'd gladly try my hand at fatherhood were I guaranteed a boy such as Artùr.

It seemed to defy both fairness and reason, but Aedan's five sons were all rather like that. The king of Mannau, his lands pressed by enemies on every side, had bred a strange race of godlike warriors.

Rhys came to mind. I turned to look out over the black sheen of water.

Aye. But there is the difference, I thought. Rhys excelled at weapons, but he did not favor war. Artùr thrilled for it.

This was the difference between life or death.

I heard the low murmurs of warriors praying to their gods, but I had not returned to mine yet. I was not yet ready.

"Ho, now, we've drawn close enough," I said.

We drew water with our oars, easing the boats beneath the trees overhanging the river. Now was the time for the climbers to disembark. The tide would carry them upriver as they swam.

Aedan rested his hand upon his son's curly head. "Artùr, take care."

"Aye," Artùr said. His deep voice was calm.

I watched as he and his men slipped over the edge of the currach into the frigid, salty water. The cold would burn, make their bodies seize up. But their strokes were sure and silent as they made their way across the expanse, disappearing from sight as they neared the base of the rock. We had spoken many times about what would come next.

Grip your way up the vertical face that rises above the river Leven.

At the top of the cliff, use your grapple to pull yourself up, over the rampart.

The grass below will be soft and thick—they will not hear you land. Here are the kitchens, the well, the smithy, and two guard huts. Silence the lookouts first. Then on to the hall.

A scattering of men will be asleep in the dark, drunk on mead. You must be quick, or their death cries will raise the alarm. There will be oil lamps and torches. Light the thatching of the hall.

Tutgual's men will come racing up from below to put out the flames.

The fire will signal Aedan's fleet. The fire will signal us, waiting in the small patch of wood.

Two men must unbolt the outermost gate.

We will be there, knocking. Let us come in.

The climb was our only uncertainty. So we waited in our patch of trees to rush the lower gate, our currachs pulled ashore and hidden with brush.

The stars faded. Just as first light was threatening to dawn, I saw it.

Fire licked crisply across the thatched roof of the hall, carried on the wind. We listened for cries of alarm from the guards.

"Steady . . ." Aedan's whisper was hoarse. And then he said, "Now!"

Beyond Clyde Rock, his fleet was racing through the water.

We crouched low as we ran our way through the wood. Then we lifted our shields, bursting through the forest and into the clear expanse.

A watchman's warning was garbled as Artùr appeared on the platform behind him and slit the man's throat. I watched as the guard dropped, thudding lifeless on the grass. Tutgual's men would have heard the alarm from below. I did not envy them the moment they realized their fate.

"Quickly," I called to the men. "They've made it down to the gate!"

The clash of swords rang through the fiery dark, and suddenly I was thrust back into Arderydd. There—wasn't that Gwenddolau's war cry? There I stood, praying Angharad made it safely to the warriors below. There I crouched, holding Rhys as his body gasped and choked.

I did not have to summon it. Battle rage came upon me. I only obeyed it. Yanking my sword from its sheath, I charged the gate with a yell as the men of Mannau opened it from within.

I nodded to Artùr and his foster brother, Cai, as they stepped back from the gate, slashing my sword into the weak place between shoulder and neck of the first guard I saw.

Blood spattered my armor. The guard screamed in pain.

He looked at my face. I saw recognition dawn before the light left his eyes.

"Aye, *Lailoken!*" I shouted. Come! Test me. Who would die next? Blood after blood.

You. Eat my blade. Choke upon my justice.

My hands were slick with blood upon the oar, but we rowed swift and steady, powering the currach as one while we looked back at Clyde

Rock. Black smoke billowed. The ramparts were painted in blood. I
had raced up to the hall, even as it burned, in search of Tutgual's body.
The king's chamber lay empty. But it did not so much matter.

Soon Stratchlyde and beyond would hear of our raid.

Or, rather, the raid of Aedan mac Gabrahn. For it was right that
the fame should belong to Aedan.

I would not be remembered. No man of Tutgual's had lived to tell
the tale.

And as the bewildered villagers from the settlements along the
water stood safely on shore, the wind picked up. The men of Mannau
hoisted their sails. There was no mistaking the fleet of Aedan mac
Gabhran. Aedan journeyed on to win the throne of the kingdom of
Dalriada from his brother, Eoganan. Now he claimed two kingdoms,
Mannau, and Dalriada in the west. The battles of Aedan and his men
had only just begun.

But Arderydd had been answered. And Gwenddolau's breath came
like a sigh.

Aye. Rest now, brother. It has been done, I told him. *Now your spirit
may at last dwell in peace.*

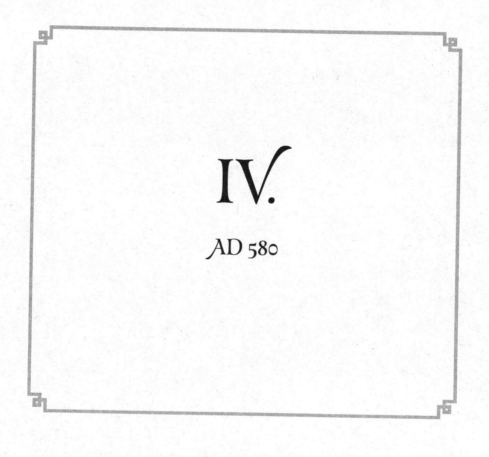

IV.

AD 580

CHAPTER 34

Languoreth

Fortress on Clyde Rock
Kingdom of Strathclyde
2nd of June, AD 580

"Tell me the story of how you came to be Tutgual's wife."

I stood with Elufed on the exposed black shoulder of rock below the guard hut, looking out over foamy whitecaps on a gloomy summer sea. In the six years since the raid, the hall and huts had been rebuilt. June was proving a farce of summer, and we were wrapped in our cloaks. Soon the whip of wind would penetrate wool, skin, and bone, and we would be forced to return to the dimly lit hall, where the air was close, smelling of sickness.

Tutgual was ailing. He had never ailed before. But I had learned never to hope.

Elufed's eyes were a reflection of the water, churning and gray. The queen did not care to speak of her childhood. In fact, she seldom had. But there was something to this day—the wet smell of kelp and soil and salt, this sloping rock where we so often stood, a place apart, where no one else might see or hear.

The swans had returned.

And I had seen a nostalgia in her eyes when she looked upon her husband, helpless and prone, the papery skin of his cheeks scarlet with fever.

"I was a child in a place of dreaming," she began. "And my mother a woman of great wisdom and import. I never knew my father. It was like that, among women. Men did not matter. If a woman wanted a child, she took a lover—sometimes a warrior, sometimes a king. And then one day a Briton came upon horseback with a torque upon his neck. I did not speak his tongue, but I knew him for a lord, and I could tell from his eyes he was looking for my mother. His eyes were hungry and vacant as a ghost's. He was searching to discover who he might become. I led him to our settlement, and he stayed for three nights. When the man departed, my mother sent me with him."

"And you went of free will?"

"Not precisely."

I did not want to imagine. I did not want to press. So I asked instead, "Did you not wonder about your father?"

"Tutgual became my father—he became all things. Father, husband, lord. And I knew, if I wished to survive, I must become all things to him. And so I have done. Perhaps you find that strange."

"I do not think it strange," I said. "I quite understand."

"There was a yellow-haired guard who smiled kindly upon me," she mused. "One of my mother's lovers. But he rode off to war and never returned. Another guard came in his place. Always it was so."

Elufed fell quiet, and I knew that was all of her story I would have on this day. Perhaps someday the queen would say more.

"I must return to the hall and look to my husband," she said.

"Of course. And Rhydderch will soon be arriving from Partick. I'll stay awhile longer and watch for his boat."

Elufed nodded. She took a few paces, then turned. "Yes. Stay out awhile, Languoreth. The sea air truly does you much good. It is easy out here, to think of what one might become."

Elufed's eyes held mine. It was a look another would not notice.

I watched her wind her way down the path, past the old well and the kitchen house, and climb the steps to the place where the great timber hall stood proud upon the hill.

I puzzled over her meaning. *What one might become?*

I thought of the old king, his lungs laboring with fluid, his priests burning camphor and letting his blood. He asked me for a remedy some days ago, though he sent his priests to watch me prepare it. Ever shrewd, he was, and the mixture had done him some good—even his men of Christ had said as much. They could not know how my fingers yearned to pinch from my little jar of nightshade.

I could not be blamed now, if his health should falter.

Now his queen bade me linger while she went inside, and I understood what Elufed meant to do. I was not the only woman on Clyde Rock with knowledge of plants.

I had waited so long to take Tutgual's life.

But Tutgual's life was not mine to take.

Death took the king swiftly; he dropped first into a sleep. It was a gentler end than he deserved. But his queen—though stone on the outside—possessed a kind heart.

Rhydderch had been the king's chosen tanist. It was a strong motion in his favor, but it would not make him king. Now the Council of Strathclyde sat shut within the great room of the hall on Clyde Rock, deciding our fate.

The boats had been ceaseless as the petty kings and chieftains, Wisdom Keepers and priests of the council, came from all across Strathclyde to view the body of the king. It was not to be removed until the new king had been chosen. The deliberation lasted less than one day.

"It shall be Rhydderch," the queen assured me. "It was always meant to be."

I looked worriedly at Rhian, who was sitting beside me. But she was not distraught at the thought of Morcant being passed over. Rather, her blue eyes filled with hope as she turned to me. "When you are made queen, I wish to join a nunnery. Make it so, Languoreth. I cannot abide another day."

I reached for her hand. When the doors of the great room opened, we stood. Elufed stepped back.

The councilmen flooded out, departing while the tide was yet favorable. But not before stopping before me and inclining their heads.

Bowing to their queen.

I blinked, disbelieving, as if stepping into sun.

Had this not been the plan of so many since I was a child? Cathan and Ariane. My father. Elufed. Now, at forty winters, I was at last queen.

As each petty king or chieftain, Wisdom Keeper or priest, stepped near—meeting my eyes, bowing his head—the meaning of my position dawned with more light. Their eyes filled with a constellation of feelings as each looked at me.

Already it had begun. For they wished me to see precisely what they thought of me. Admiration. Resignation. Happiness. Hesitation.

I—Languoreth of Cadzow—was the new queen of Strathclyde.

There is no ceremony in Strathclyde for a woman who becomes queen.

I stood on a platform before a sea of people at the Gathering Place in Partick, not beside Rhydderch but watching from a short distance away.

We were both dressed in the purple reserved for only the most noble to wear.

Rhydderch swore his oaths to Christ and the land with great feeling under the watchful eyes of Father Natan. The torque of Tutgual was fixed upon his neck.

The torque of Elufed was clasped upon mine. But I swore no oaths.

It was not always that way. Long ago, among the Britons, there were tribes who called queens their main sovereign. It was they and they alone who made pacts with the Gods. That was before the Romans came. By the time I was born, queens were wives of kings.

But that did not mean we did not have power.

I swore no oaths. It didn't trouble me; in fact, I found it quite freeing. For though I was queen, I was somehow less bound.

And I knew precisely where my allegiance lay.

After all the feasting and the toasting and the dancing and the smiling—oh, the smiling that must be done!—we slept as if we had been craving sleep for winters.

The next day, we when we woke, we took breakfast in our chamber, just Rhydderch and me.

His gray eyes were happy and touched on me with pride. "Yours is the first petition I shall hear as king," Rhydderch said with a gentle bow of his head. It was not like him to be playful. I was not quite sure what to do.

"Are you quite certain you are prepared?" I asked.

"I know to whom I am wed." He smiled. But then he reached for my hand. "Tell me what you think needs righting before we begin."

"Very well," I said. "I would first speak about Morcant."

"Aye. You will be pleased that even I do not think it wise to keep him in Strathclyde, but I have not yet decided what I should do."

"I have given it some thought. Morcant is bullish, and his retinue strong warriors. He delights in fighting—so I would say put him to good use. Strife continues with Bernicia in the east. Why not arrange a marriage between Morcant and a daughter of the Gododdin?"

"Morcant is already wed," he said.

"He is a danger to you here in Strathclyde. Who knows when he might try to come against you? And Rhian has been unable to give him any children. You are too shrewd a man to be blind to her bruises. Busy him with adversaries and find him another wife. One more suited to his temperament."

"I do not think he will set her aside."

"Rhian wishes only to enter the church. Surely, if Morcant knows no other shall have her . . . ? I have heard Caw's youngest daughter is strong-minded, and of course her father is a Christian chieftain of both wealth and good influence. He will approve of Morcant—it is a powerful match to be aligned with the brother of the king. And Caw is loyal to Strathclyde. He would never betray you."

I could feel his mind turning. "Please, Rhydderch," I said softly. "I fear he may kill her."

He pushed away his plate. "Then there is nothing to consider. It will be done."

"Thank you, my king." I exhaled in relief.

"And the next?"

"I should very much like to keep Torin as captain of my guard."

"Very well. I approve. But he must select double again the number of men who now guard you, and those warriors shall be subject to my approval. It is important you are safe," he said. "You are beloved by half the people and disfavored by the other because you are crossways of their god."

"That I know," I said.

And then Rhydderch straightened. "And now, I think, you would ask me about your brother."

A look passed between us. Lailoken had been in exile for seven long years. And in all this time I'd been forbidden to see him, I had been waiting for this very moment to come.

"Do you remember your promise?" I asked.

"Yes, Languoreth. I swore to you that when I was made king, I would ask your brother to be my counsel and so bring him home. I intend to keep my word."

My mouth suddenly went dry. "Please. Go on."

"It seems that Lailoken has amassed a great following somewhere in the wilds of the Caledonian Wood. I know you have not visited him, but I believe you may know where," Rhydderch said.

"I do not know where, precisely, but I have some idea."

Lord Archer, Fendwin had said. I had never forgotten it. I would have disobeyed Tutgual's decree in a moment and sought him out sooner had it not been for Fendwin's warning that I would only bring danger to the door of the Dragon Warriors.

"Take Torin and your guard. Go in secret—we must keep his whereabouts safe for the time being—but tell Lailoken I wish for his counsel."

I would take Eira, of course. Rhydderch knew of her handfasting with Lailoken, and we had long since given Eira her own lodgings. She must know right away. Rhydderch's eyes were warm in offering this long-awaited gift. But gifts from men in power always came with a price.

"I am not ungrateful, but how do you mean to accomplish this? He is a man of the Old Way. You will curry too much upset with all your Christian lords."

"You are right," he said carefully. "And this is why I would send you to meet with Lailoken. For we cannot bring one man from exile without also bringing another."

"Whom do you speak of?" I closed my eyes, for I already knew. It was the look upon Rhydderch's face. The shadow of guilt. Of resignation.

Mungo.

"You cannot consider it," I said.

"Lailoken has gathered a following. These past years Mungo has built a monastery at Hoddam, and he has done the same."

"A place of zealots, no doubt! Do you not remember what he and his followers have done? Desecrated a hill holy to the Wisdom Keepers. Assassinated a rival priest. Robbed my father's granaries. Scarred my brother's face. Murdered Cathan, head Wisdom Keeper of Strathclyde. Mungo has been our enemy since Lailoken and I were children. And now you would have me and my brother play a role in inviting that wickedness back in?"

"Languoreth, the Angles are massing in Bernicia. By all accounts, they soon will attack, and still my people are divided. If Strathclyde is to remain a land of the Britons, I need the retinues of each and every petty king and chieftain in this land. They must all come together at the side of the high king. The divide has only grown greater in the years my father was in power. Now we must show them a new way, you and I. If we cannot envision it, who else shall try?"

"Find another Christian," I said. "Surely there must be one. Why not Father Natan?"

He sighed. "The Christian lords have already come to me. They demand Mungo."

"He has seen to it! Can you not see? He has visited them in private!"

"Yes," Rhydderch said. "Mungo has returned. That is the fact of the matter. It was my father who exiled him to pacify the people of the Old Way, and now my father is dead, and we must pacify the people of the New. It is Mungo they want. We have no choice but to bring him into the fold."

I shook my head. "Who is commanding whom? Do you rule the lords of Strathclyde, or do your lords rule you?"

"I swore an oath to the land and all its people, no matter their faith. I will not disregard it. Your brother took up arms against Strathclyde. He is privileged to be granted an opportunity to return home."

"I am going to be sick," I said.

"I pray you recover quickly, as you must be hale for your journey."

I lifted my head. "You do not ask, then. You command."

"Yes," he said. "I command."

"And how do you mean to control him, the man who murdered my father's counsel, who raised a mob against my father, a king? I watched Cathan choke and go blue as he swung from the bough of a tree!"

"I have not forgotten what he has done."

"A man who murders Keepers, and you would set my brother in his path?"

"Yes, Languoreth, I would. For Lailoken is one of the few men I believe capable of helping us control him. I hear Wisdom Keepers from Scotia gather to hear him speak. I hear tales of pagan warriors massing in the wood."

"Do not use that word. You have never before used that word. Am I now your *pagan* wife?"

"Apologies." He bowed his head. "I hear it used now far too freely."

"It stinks of Rome, and of small-minded, capital-dwelling zealots. They have called the people of Cadzow as much. Or didn't you know?"

"I am aware. And I do not think it right. But Christians must feel they, too, have a voice. I ignore the Christian lords at my peril. I would keep Mungo close. I would benefit from his ambition. Let him convert those who wish to be converted. We have always been a people who safeguard our freedoms. Christians, too, have their right to choose. The path is now forked, Languoreth. You must make way for change."

"I will seek out my brother and ask his return. But you, husband, must be prepared for what this shall mean. Lailoken and Mungo in the same court? One will end up dead. And as long as I have breath in my body, it shall not be my brother."

"Believe me, wife. I understand what I ask. Please. Go to the Caledonian Wood and relay my message to your brother. I have spared his life once already. Now I offer him yet another. Tell Lailoken not to be a fool."

CHAPTER 35

Angh" ## Angharad

The White Fort
Glen Lyon, Kingdom of the Picts
March, AD 580

The grinding of the quern stone sounded like the ocean. Not the lazy slap and tumble of fair-weather waves, but the low and scouring churn of a winter sea. The stool beneath Angharad teetered as she reached into the sack of grain to sift another handful into the mill. The light half of the year was beginning, but the sun was still a lamb upon shaky legs. Angharad stopped to wrap her shawl more tightly around her before gripping the wooden handle again.

Turn, turn.

Change was coming. The air of the mill shed was with thick with it. Did Angharad summon it?

She did not know her own strength. This was what Fetla said.

Eachna was made of water. Wind and weather pushed water about. When Angharad visited the waterfall, it reminded her again.

Why do you show me this? she asked, but received no answer. She did not understand it. Angharad was not unhappy. Her days were a circle, just like the turning of the heavy quern stone. Waking. Prayer. Calling in and graining the horses. Porridge. Instruction. Contemplation. Grinding grain into flour. Tending the need-garden. Always, Angharad was listening, for that was what she'd been taught. The women of Fortingall listened, for they were students of the many tongues of spirit. And in listening, Angharad had grown wise, Fetla said.

Far wiser than her sixteen years.

In this way, seven winters had passed since the siege that had become known as *Cad Arderydd*. The Battle of the High Lords.

Her mother and father had never come for her.

The messenger had returned, his expression bearing the shame he knew awaited an unwanted child. Eachna relayed her mother's reply: Languoreth had wept for joy upon hearing that Angharad lived. She could scarcely believe Angharad's rare fortune. She wished nothing more than for Angharad to continue her training with the priestesses at Fortingall until she earned the title of priestess herself.

Angharad knew when her mother was young, she'd desired to become a Keeper. This was the reason Angharad had gone with Lailoken, in part. Because she saw the mark of her mother's wound and sensed if she could achieve what her mother could not, her mother might finally feel whole.

Eachna had held her the many nights she'd cried, murmuring words of love and healing. Angharad had not forgotten about the life she had lived before, in Strathclyde. It was only that Eachna had taught her how to release it, how to bless it. Fortingall was a holy place. A place of ritual and vision for young women with strengths to come into their power. In the evenings, by hearth light, they recited their kennings. This was the place the Picts came to dream: A mother who'd lost a baby and wanted another. A man without use of his legs. They slept and woke to tell Eachna of their dreams, and Eachna divined their meaning. Eachna laid her hands upon them and gave them healing.

Angharad knew how to prepare the dreaming draught. She'd learned the meaning of birds and their flight, but such things were thick-footed and clumsy. Angharad did not need a dreaming draught to aid one who was troubled—she need only peer into their eyes. And why commit to memory what a sparrow hawk dipping west foretold, when one could simply ask the sparrow hawk itself?

When she said as much to Eachna, the old woman merely nodded, as if this was something about Angharad she always had known.

Since then, though Angharad had not yet been made priestess, Eachna brought her to administer those in search of cures. Now that Imbolc had come and gone, and the light half of the year was upon them, more people were arriving. Even now there were ten. Last summer the high king, Bridei, their patron, had arranged for the building of a new hut.

With the gifts given in thanks, they wanted for little now. Eachna had sent two women to the market some days ago, and they'd returned with fine cloth for new robes.

In seven winters Angharad had never left Fortingall—she wore the robes of a novice. But she did not miss the broader world, for all worlds were visible when she closed her eyes to dream.

"Angharad."

The voice stirred her from her thoughts, and she turned to see Ora, a fellow novice, standing at the door.

"There is a woman here, a stranger. She is asking to see you."

Angharad's pulse quickened. After all this time, she still imagined that someday her mother might come. "A woman? What does she look like?"

Ora wrinkled her nose. "Dark hair. Fair skin. She wears a blue cloak."

Angharad hid her disappointment. "I don't know any such person."

"Well, she's come, and she's waiting with the others." Ora looked guilty.

"What is it?"

"I haven't yet told Eachna. The woman asked to speak only to you. She waits in the first cell of the nearest hut."

"Ora! Very well, I am coming. But you must go and tell Eachna. We do not harbor secrets."

Ora hurried off as Angharad stood and brushed the last dusting of flour into its sack. A gust of wet wind assailed her as she closed the door to the mill shed. The weather had shifted. Angharad could smell snow coming from the north. She stopped hurriedly to take up the feather that blew against her skirt, holding it between two fingers so as not to damage its appearance. Owl. How curious. She would add it to the big wooden box she kept next to her bed. There were hundreds of them now—robin and raven, kestrel and dunnock.

Her mother had once told her that feathers were signs of her love. But in listening, in growing wise, Angharad had learned a feather in her path was nearly always an omen. She glanced uneasily at the three circular huts where guests dwelled in their seeking.

People came in need, asking for her. Word had traveled that Angharad had Sight. Likely this woman was no different. Yet Eachna was renowned for her abilities. It was strange the woman wished to see Angharad alone.

The dreaming huts were candlelit places of whispers. Angharad lifted the latch quietly so as not to disturb the ailing. Within their little cell, they would be resting or in prayer, perhaps even dreaming.

A fire burned in the center hearth pit. She glanced at the seven small chambers to ensure all was well before reaching to slide the woven reed panel that served as a door, stepping into the first cell. The room was lit by a single oil lamp. Angharad could see the outline of the woman perched upon the simple wooden bed, still wearing her cloak, but could not make out her face.

Angharad slid the door shut behind her, squinting as her eyes adjusted to the dim. "Hello." She greeted the woman in Pictish, the tongue that came most readily.

"Hello." The woman's answer was low and perfunctory.

"Ora tells me you've asked to see me, but I am not yet a full priestess, so I have summoned our Lady Eachna."

"I wish you had not done so. I wished to speak to you alone." There was displeasure in her voice.

"You wish to speak to me?" Angharad asked. "Do you mean to say you have no ailment?"

"I have no ailment." The woman stood. "I have come to discuss a matter of much importance."

She stepped into the light, and Angharad saw two sapphire eyes fixed steadily upon her. She had dark hair, nearly black, and skin pale as moonlight. Her face looked familiar, as if Angharad might have seen it in a dream. But so often these days she was dreaming, and most dreams were not her own.

"Are you a messenger, then, sent by Strathclyde?" She heard the excitement in her own voice even as she felt shamed by it. Strathclyde was no longer her home. Eachna was her mother now. The wound had been healed and she would not reopen it.

The woman tilted her head. "I am a messenger of sorts. But not from the place you imagine. I am a Wisdom Keeper. I have come from the north. I would speak with you about your training."

Angharad took a step back. "My training has been done here, these past seven winters, under the careful tutelage of my *hennain*, a most renowned Seer. I am only one winter away from earning my place here as priestess."

The woman opened her mouth, but just then the reed door slid open and Eachna stepped in, her damp white hair curling about her face like a fury's. She seemed taken aback at the sight of the woman, her eyes flickering with surprise.

"Eachna." The dark-haired woman bowed, but not deeply. Eachna came to stand beside Angharad, and as she did, Angharad sensed a strange feeling emanating from her *hennain*.

Fear.

"What brings you here?" Eacha's back was straight as a rod.

"I have come about the girl."

"And now you have seen her. Angharad is hale, she prospers. Fortingall is the child's home."

"She is no longer a child. She is a woman now." The dark-haired woman spoke to the priestess, but her eyes were upon Angharad. "You say she is hale, but I do not think this is the case. You have not done right by this child, Lady Eachna, and it has come to our attention. Aside from that, she has outgrown you. You do her a great disservice in keeping her here."

"Not done right by this child?" Eachna's voice was shrill. "My own blood. Did I not keep her on when her mother desired her to stay here? Do I not love this girl as if she were my own? I have trained her as well as any high priestess might."

"Nay, Eachna. You have kept the truth from her."

Angharad turned to her *hennain*. "What is she speaking of?"

"You overstep your bounds," the priestess warned.

"Save your curses, Eachna. I do not fear you. Will you not tell her, then? Or are you too fearful to offer her a choice?"

Eacha stood stone-faced as the woman waited, then huffed with impatience. "Very well. If it must be so. Angharad, did it not seem strange that your mother did not desire you to return to Strathclyde with all haste when she heard you were well?"

"Stop, I say!" Eachna commanded, but the woman carried on.

"This woman made you a promise many winters ago that she would send word to your mother and father that you were safe in Fortingall. Yet no message was sent."

Angharad sank back, astonished. "But the warrior . . . I watched him ride out. I saw him return—saw the look upon his face!"

"The warrior was sent to feast with Bridei and journeyed no farther than his fortress on yonder hill. Your grandmother wished to keep you here at Fortingall. I understand her coffers have grown quite full due to your Sight."

Eachna stalked toward her, indignant. "How dare you say such things? You know nothing. Do not heed her, Angharad. These Keepers from the north have slippery ways of speaking. Her tongue is deceitful; it will spin you false."

"Be mindful how you speak to me, Eachna," the woman said. "Whispers on the wind. You cannot conceal your deeds. I have it from one of your own. And now that all Tayside is talking of her, I cannot imagine you thought to conceal her for long."

Angharad rounded upon her *hennain*. "Is this true? You never sent word to my mother and father? Tell me, is this true?"

Eachna thrust her chin proudly. "Everything I have done, I have done so that you might become who you are destined to be. Search yourself, little bird. Who would you be if I had left you broken? I healed you with my own hands. What might have become of you had you returned to your home? You never would have left your mother and father again to carry on with your training. You cannot deny the gift you have been given. Do, and it will consume you. I did not give you a choice, Angharad, but I gave you your life."

"You lied. All of this time . . ."

Eachna frowned. "Long ago, I gave Strathclyde a daughter. And with your arrival, the Gods saw to it a daughter was returned. Your place is here, with me."

"Nay," the dark-haired woman said. "Your mother never would have left you had she known you yet lived."

"And what do you know of my mother?" Angharad asked sharply.

"I was her counsel many years ago."

"Now I know you are false. My mother had no counsel," she replied.

Something flickered across the woman's face. Sadness, or perhaps surprise. But she guarded herself closely, and Angharad could not read any further.

"Enough," Eachna said quickly, sliding back the reed door. "You have seen the girl. She is well. We have no need of you. You will leave."

"You have no power here, Eachna. Not in this," the woman said.

Angharad looked between them, anger boiling. "I am not your gaming piece!" she shouted.

No messengers had been sent. Eachna had deceived her. The betrayal stung like a hornet's barb, and Angharad's eyes blurred with tears. She could hear no more. Before either woman could utter another word, she pushed past Eachna and ran from the hut.

She heard her *hennain* call out for the guard as Angharad raced past the bewildered faces of her fellow novices, across the half-frozen field, and into the hut she shared with Eachna. Objects clattered to the ground as she yanked her belongings from a wooden shelf and threw them into her trunk. She thought in a frenzy where she might go.

Home?

She could scarcely recall it. A faded dream.

There was Bridei's Tayside fortress, but what fate awaited her there? He was Eachna's patron. He would only send her back. No, Angharad decided. She would strike out on her own.

She snatched two spare woolen robes from their hooks on the wall and then, fastening her cloak over her shawl, grabbed her trunk and dragged it out the door.

Up ahead, Mother Yew was a smear of emerald through her tears. The tree, the waterfall, and Fetla. Those were the things she would mourn the most.

The trunk was not overheavy but was cumbersome, scraping and dragging over the mucky earth.

"Angharad, what's happened?" one of the priestesses called out. "Where are you going?"

The women of Fortingall stood beyond the tree's enclosure in alarm as three warriors came jogging, spears in hand, answering Eachna's summons.

Eachna's wrinkled face was bent in a scowl as she strode from the dreaming hut, the dark-haired woman following behind.

"Eachna, this is not the way," the woman warned.

But Eachna would not hear it. Her cheeks were tinged red. She did not favor rash behavior. She did not like that Angharad had made a scene. Now all the priestesses were watching.

"Angharad, stop," Eachna commanded.

Angharad did her *hennain*'s bidding out of habit. But Eachna had lied.

"Where do you think you are going, child? Stop this foolishness," her *hennain* admonished her.

Angharad swallowed, gripping her trunk. They all stood there now, the priestesses and novices of Fortingall, watching.

"You cannot leave. I forbid it," Eachna said. But there was pain in her command.

"I cannot stay, Lady Priestess."

How her *hennain* seemed shaken by the cold formality with which Angharad used her title. Eachna stepped forward, taking her hands. "There is so much more I might teach you, Angharad. Your mother and Elufed, your own *nain*, they will never taste the world of spirit that awaits you here. Do not be swayed by this woman. Stay with me. You are my blood daughter. Fortingall is your home."

"Let the girl make her own choice," the dark-haired woman said.

"You have broken the bounds of hospitality, coming here to take my child," Eachna said.

"You have stolen this child, and I have spoken with Bridei."

Eachna scoffed. "With Briochan, more like." She turned to her men. "Take her to the boundaries of my land, and do not depart until you have seen her gone."

Yet the warriors did not move.

The dark-haired woman nodded to Angharad, her blue eyes calm. "Angharad? Is this what you wish?"

A soggy March wind gusted, stirring the priestesses' hair as they stood before the great tree. Angharad set down her trunk and went to stand before Eachna.

The old priestess lifted her hands to Angharad's face, her stormy eyes watering with tears. Angharad looked deeply into the blackness where Eachna's heart crouched, cradling its wounds. Eachna was so powerful, but now Angharad realized just how twisted she had been by fate: she gripped too tightly things she did not wish to lose.

"I wish to go alone," Angharad said gently. "I will find my own way."

"Go, then," Eachna said at last. "You are free to leave—you have never been a prisoner here."

But she spoke more for herself than to Angharad, it seemed. The old woman straightened, smoothing her wiry white hair. "Someday you will be grateful for all I have given you," Eachna said.

Her *hennain* was so elderly. In two winters, Eachna would be gone—Angharad knew this. And she did not wish to leave with bitter words on her tongue. "I am grateful now," Angharad lied.

She bent to pick up the handle of her trunk. Though it was not heavy, its weight felt immeasurable.

"I will take my leave," the dark-haired woman said. Bowing to Eachna, she drew up the hood of her cloak and started off down the narrow, mud-furrowed lane. Something tugged at Angharad. An urging. A whisper. She looked after the woman, wondering. But Fetla called out her name. "Angharad, wait!"

Fetla was hurrying past the great yew and through the enclosure's wooden gate, her face tight, her slate-colored eyes fraught with distress. In her arms she carried a wooden box. "Your feathers," she said.

In her haste, Angharad had forgotten them. Fetla extended the box and Angharad took it, clutching it beneath her arm. She felt the presence of the birds like a blanket. "Thank you," she said.

Fetla nodded, her stern expression wavering. Her gaze trailed after the dark-haired woman. Leaning in to kiss Angharad, she whispered in her ear: "Follow her."

Angharad drew back, questioning. Then she understood. Somehow this was Fetla's doing. The arrival of this stranger. She wondered how Fetla had discovered her *hennain*'s deception and when. Perhaps she had only just learned.

That was what Angharad chose to believe.

Angharad embraced her fellow sisters, then bent to carefully set the box of feathers in her wooden trunk. The wind kicked up, changing direction. It seemed nearly to push at her back as she followed the muddy boot prints the woman had left on the road.

Follow her, Fetla had said. But Angharad was uncertain. Only a little while ago, she had been grinding grain. Now she was running from home. She felt like a bird flushed from the bracken, heart skittering in her chest. She crouched to drag her trunk along, its metal fittings caked with mud.

Dark clouds were mounting. She would not get far before being overtaken by the weather. She had not been practical. She had not been thinking. She spoke Pictish as if it were her first tongue, and no one dared trouble a priestess. But she was a girl of sixteen winters without the robes of a priestess to protect her.

Up ahead the woman in the blue cloak turned, as if only realizing someone was behind her.

I am not following this stranger, Angharad thought. *She and I only happen to be traveling in the same direction.*

The dark-haired woman stopped at the boulder marking the fork in the road and paused, looking about. She leaned her head from side to side as if to crack the bones of her neck. Angharad reached the boulder only to find the woman had settled her slender frame against it and drawn out a small apple from the deerskin satchel she wore across her shoulder. She ate it in slices off the tip of her knife.

"Hungry?" she asked, offering a crescent.

Angharad shook her head.

"A storm is coming," the woman said.

"Yes."

"What are your plans, then?" The woman's pale face was expectant. Curious.

"I do not know." Angharad looked at her warily. She was a Seer blind to deception. Hadn't the waterfall tried to warn her? Eachna was made of water. Wind and weather pushed water about. But who was made of wind and weather? This woman who stood before her now? Angharad still did not understand. She knew only that she had wanted so badly to be mothered, to be a child, to be loved. And Eachna had wanted to heal the wounds of a daughter she had given away too soon.

All these years, her *hennain* had concealed her, used her for her own ends.

The dark-haired woman wiped her small blade on her cloak, sheathing it at her belt. "You may walk a ways with me, if you like."

"Where do you travel?"

"To the Orcades."

"But you do not speak like a Pict," Angharad said. "You have a funny way of speaking. As if it is not your native tongue."

The woman laughed, a deep, silky sound that belied her narrow frame.

"You find that funny?" Angharad frowned.

"It is only that you remind me of your mother," the woman said. Then she grew serious. "I dwell in the Orcades, though I was born across the sea. But my story is mine to keep."

"I have heard of an isle of priestesses in the north. It is said they can raise storms."

The woman turned to her. "We wear the robes of the Cailleach, as many priestesses do. But as for our secrets, unless you should decide to come with me, I am sorry, Angharad. Those, too, are mine to keep."

"The way you say my name . . . you speak as if you know me."

"I have told you already, I once counselled your mother."

"Before I was born to her."

"Yes."

"And why did she never speak of you?"

"I believe when I left, it made your mother quite sad."

"Well, then, why did you leave her?"

"I told your mother when I agreed to be her counsel that I did not answer to women and men. A woman of the Gods remembers to listen. Always she knows when it is time to leave."

"I agree it is so. And that is precisely why I have left." Angharad stopped to yank her trunk over a protruding rock. They had come to the river. Ever since arriving at Fortingall, Angharad had felt as if the river had drawn her there. When she visited the waterfall, it beckoned as if to hold her, soothing her in its cold and weightless embrace. But now Angharad felt no such pull. It was as if the river had released her.

The woman frowned at Angharad's trunk. "What possession can you carry in that impossible box that is so necessary?"

"Things I have collected over many seasons," Angharad said, tugging it determinedly. She looked at the woman from the corner of her eye. Angharad could not dispel the sense of familiarity. She had seen this woman before.

But where?

And then, in a flash, it came to her. The vision she'd had as a child in the woods, after the battle. The dark-haired woman had been walking in morning mist, wearing a blue cloak.

Please help me, which way? Angharad had begged.

The woman had directed her into waiting danger. And yet, had the dark-haired woman truly led her astray? Or had she been summoning Angharad since her long journey began?

Angharad's skin tingled. Soon it would rain, the icy sort that brought phlegm and fever if one was exposed overlong. And the woman came from the north. Could she be one of the weather workers Angharad had heard of in legend?

"You said you came to speak to me about my training," Angharad said.

"Yes. There is a place for you, if you would come. I can see you are gifted. But there is still much you might learn. I am only a messenger. You may ignore your summons. That is your choice. I would not tell you what you should or should not do. But we do not have long before the storm sets in."

Somehow Angharad felt the woman warned of more than just weather.

"You could always return home," the woman said. "I imagine your mother loves you very much, and she has been deceived most terribly."

Angharad considered it. The path was forked. Seven winters she had been away, and so much had changed. There had been a time when all Angharad wished was to return to her childhood home. But she was not the little girl she once was. The cord to her mother had long since been severed. Angharad was a woman now.

"If I go with you, and I do not feel it is right, am I free to leave?" she asked.

"What a funny question," the woman said. "We are always free."

Angharad was intrigued by this woman. She loved her mother. And she would return. But somehow Angharad knew this was not that day.

"Very well. I shall go with you."

"I am gladdened to hear it." Her tone was wry. "Yes, you are very much like your mother. You make nothing easy."

"Nor do you," Angharad countered. "For you have left me to drag my trunk on my own, and you have yet to even tell me your name."

The woman stopped, her lips tugged into a smile. "You are right," she said. "My name is Ariane." She bent to grip the other handle of Angharad's trunk. "Come, then, child. We will carry it together."

CHAPTER 36

Angharad

Woodwick Bay
Orcades
Kingdom of the Picts
2nd of June, AD 580

It had taken nearly three weeks to reach the Bull Fort, Bridei's citadel at the northernmost point of the Land of the Picts. As they sailed beyond the fort, there was nothing but ocean.

But then, in the distance, a new world of islands sprang up before her eyes.

"What is the head priestess like at Woodwick Bay?" Angharad asked. "For I will admit I am nervous to meet her. Can she summon storms and scatter fog? Does she know many curses? Can she help heal the sick? Is she kindly or stern? Does she strike with a rod when giving her teachings?"

Ariane frowned, thinking. "She never uses her power without purpose, like any good priestess. She has never used a rod upon novices because she has never been given cause to. She is proficient in healing enough to teach others. And I am certain she knows curses, but she casts them only at young girls who arrive asking far too many questions."

As they'd traveled, Ariane had explained that the king of the

Orcades was Cendalaeth. Cendalaeth was the patron of all the sacred settlements on the islands, of which there were seven.

"The settlement at Woodwick trains priestesses for the six sacred sites and beyond," Ariane said. Pledged to Cendalaeth were several chieftains who yet inhabited their ancestral isles, which were scattered both near and far, out to sea. All the lords, including the king, paid tribute to Bridei. "It is much like the rest of Pictland," she said, "only our little kingdom is floating."

But the Orcades were not like the rest of Pictland.

It was a place of deadly swirling whirlpools and whole islands inhabited by nothing but birds. Great beasts called whales sometimes washed up upon the beach, and the main island was largely without trees and exceedingly flat—the only real mounds upon it being hills of the dead.

As they came up the eastern coast, arriving at Woodwick Bay, Angharad found she was utterly enchanted. The beach curved to meet the water like a waning moon. The shoreline was rocky and heaped with green and purple kelp, but beyond it the goddess had turned fickle, tossing up fat banks of wildflowers that spilled onto swaths of lush green grass. Warriors kept watch here, bowing to Ariane as she and Angharad carried the trunk, following a neatly kept path into a beautiful old wood.

Roundhouses and a temple dotted the forest floor. Women came out to greet them, much like at Fortingall, yet all wore blue cloaks, just as Ariane did. And as they caught sight of Ariane, they brightened, or straightened, or grew suddenly reverent, dropping their heads in a bow. "Welcome home, Lady Priestess," they said.

Angharad turned to Ariane, gray eyes widening. "You told me you were only a messenger."

"Yes, that is true."

"Yet they call you Lady Priestess."

"What is a priestess if not a messenger of the Gods?" Ariane asked, looking at Angharad expectantly. She smiled as they neared a tall young woman with dark hair and amber-colored eyes. "Here," Ariane said. "This is Catrin. She will show you where you will sleep."

Spring passed into summer, and Angharad scarcely thought of Eachna's betrayal or the women of Fortingall she'd left behind. Wood-wick became her new family—not only her sisters, all nearly as skilled as Angharad, but also the warriors and their families whom Cenda-laeth had settled in the broch a short way up the beach.

Their task was the care and protection of the Daughters of the Cailleach training at Woodwick Bay.

It was a flat white morning in June when the women went out to gather kelp for the sheep, for they had a break before the afternoon teaching, and they always found delight in seeing what the storm tide had turned up. The waves lapped gently. But they soon lost one another, buried in cloud. Fog had rolled in, thick as a blanket.

Now the blue-cloaked figures of the other novices were shadows flickering at the edges of another realm. Angharad smiled, delighted to be blind to everything around her. Always she was seeing. Now she could only feel. She stretched out her hand as far as it could reach, and her fingers disappeared into the unknown. *Anything could emerge from out of this mist*, she thought. Gods or monsters. The isle could have come loose from its roots. It could be drifting out to sea even now, a vast and anchorless boat.

She walked to the shoreline, where water lapped at her leather boots, peering into the white. And then suddenly, slogging out of the thigh-deep water, appeared a man. Angharad went still. He was mus-cled and dressed for war, a golden torque fixed at his throat, his eyes the color of the sea and looking at Angharad as if she might be a selkie.

Manannan? she thought. But this was no god. This was a man of flesh and bone stumbling from the ocean, seawater clinging to his curly reddish-blond hair. He blinked. Then one of the priestesses cried out. "Raiders!"

Screams echoed in the fog as the raiders thundered out of the blinding mist, crashing their boats ashore. The watch horn at Wood-wick Broch blasted in return, summoning more men as the warriors plunged into the white, weapons in hand. There was a moment when all was eerily quiet. Then the bay erupted into chaos.

"Watch yourself!" one of the guards shouted, colliding with Angharad, sending her out of harm's way.

Angharad skidded onto her bottom on the rocks. She and the raider from the sea looked at each other as if suddenly remembering their parts. She shouted a curse at him. He glanced at her, then leveled his weapons, eyes set upon the guard, dirk in one hand, sword in the other. The two men circled each other from a distance, testing and feinting. Sizing each other up. The raider raised a brow at the guard, shaking his head slowly, as if in warning.

Her guard charged. It happened so quickly that Angharad did not even see the blow. Only blood spilling on sand and the guard's eyes blinking in surprise before he crumpled at her feet, going still. She screamed, grabbing hold of her wicker basket and swinging it at the raider's head as he lunged at her.

"I am a Wisdom Keeper! We are not to be harmed," she shouted. Frowning, he reached to grab hold of her, and she lashed out, thrashing and kicking. They tumbled onto the rocks, the raider's bulk falling on top of her, and Angharad beat at his ribs, struggling to break free. Then Angharad heard the raider exhale as if he'd been kicked. He cursed and leapt to his feet, leaving her prone upon the rocks. A spear pierced his torso, thrust by a warrior somewhere in the fog. The raider's face hardened as he gripped the wood, yanking the spear from his side and flipping it toward the guard running at him, impaling him in the throat.

Run, you fool, her instinct commanded. Two guards lay dead. But her legs would not obey her. The raider dropped to his knees, his face in a grimace.

Angharad's mind raced. "Your lord is wounded!" she called out, scrambling to her knees beside him. This man was a noble, and likely their leader. If she saved him, they might spare the priestesses from harm.

The spear had pierced his armor, and blood was already darkening his tunic. "You are losing blood quickly. We must get you to the settlement," she said, pulling back his armor to better see the wound.

"Leave it!" he shouted, struggling to get up. Pictish was not his native tongue.

"Stop struggling. You make it worse," she snapped, reaching for his arm to help him stand. She hoisted his arm over her shoulder, gripping his wrist. He smelled of sweat and seawater. "Sweet Gods, you are heavy," she grunted as he leaned upon her shoulder.

In the fog, Angharad could see only a few paces ahead, and she sucked in a breath as she stepped on the body of a fallen guard, his fingers curled into the earth as if he'd been crawling along the ground.

"Stop this madness. We are Keepers. Are you blind to our robes? Tell your men not to harm us. Tell them now!"

The raider only frowned. Angharad turned to look at him in disbelief, jabbing her elbow into the seeping source of his wound. He gave a strangled cry, glaring at her sidelong, but shouted something in Goidelic.

He was a Scot, then. A Westman.

"There, 'tis done! We will not harm you," he said.

Angharad shook her head as she dragged him along the beach,

body after lifeless body appearing in flashes of suspended horror from the fog.

Dead, dead, all of their guard, dead.

"These warriors were our friends," she admonished him. "They were only doing their duty."

"What man is not duty-bound?" he answered.

Angharad scoffed, searching the whiteness for Ariane. Straining, she caught sight of her standing nearer to the trees, where the fog had begun to shift, moving off to sea.

"Are you hurt?" Ariane demanded.

Angharad shook her head. "But this man is wounded, and he is their lord," she said.

"Take him to the temple. I will be there shortly," Ariane said.

As a sudden gust of sea wind thinned the fog over the rocky crescent of beach, Angharad made out thirty men or more, sodden from the sea, plundering the fresh corpses of the *Cruithni* on the beach.

"You Westmen are monsters. You show no respect."

"Now, that isn't true. We show them the same courtesy they offer us."

Angharad pulled him along the path as his men surrounded the priestesses, ushering them in a line toward the settlement in the wood.

They arrived at the wooden temple, and Angharad slipped from beneath his arm, offering no more aid.

"Enter," she said, nodding to the temple door.

As he stepped into the room, she forced him to meet her eyes. "Why have you come?" she demanded.

The raider looked back, defiant. Incensed, Angharad searched him.

She saw boats, many boats, charging fast across the water. Blood at the broch that belonged to King Cendalaeth. Bodies strewn everywhere.

"You raided Cendalaeth's broch," she said in alarm. "Tell me. Is the king dead?"

The man did not answer, but something told her it had been by his hand.

"Bridei will kill you for this," she said.

The man pressed his hand to his wound. "Not if I kill him first."

It was the way that he said it. His eyes told a story, but Angharad did not wish to search him any further. They would treat his wound and then he would go.

"Artùr." A tall, dark-haired warrior strode forward, stopping at the sight of the raider and his wound.

"Artùr," Angharad echoed, eyeing his torque. "You are the son of Aedan the Scot! King of Mannau and Dalriada?"

The man gave a perfunctory nod. Artùr did not seem pleased that Angharad had known him. But who did not know of him? Aedan and his many sons, the men of Gabrahn, were among the bitterest enemies of the *Cruithni*. Bridei had killed Aedan mac Gabrahn's father, begetting a blood feud.

Now Artùr stood before her. And Angharard had aided him! What in the name of the Gods had she done?

She scarcely had time to consider it before Ariane stormed through the temple door and the men drew their swords.

"How dare you lift your weapons in such a place?" she reprimanded them. "Sheath your blades and do not raise them to me again."

They looked to Artùr and he said, "Go on, do as she says."

"Who else among you is wounded?" Ariane demanded.

Artùr's face reddened when no others came forward. Angharad felt his deep stab of shame.

"You have forced a sanctuary here, but I will grant it only for the wounded," Ariane said. "Two men may stay with you. The others must go."

Artùr glanced at the dark-haired warrior. It seemed they could understand each other without speaking.

His brother, Angharad thought.

"I need only one man. Cai will stay."

The warrior nodded.

"Cendalaeth is dead," Angharad said. Ariane closed her eyes a moment, then opened them, eyeing the men. It was dangerous, each moment they lingered. And they could not shelter thirty men at the temple. There was no place to hide them.

"Our king is dead, and your boats are full of plunder stained by the death of our people. Have your men bring in our dead before they depart. And you will not forget the kindness we have shown. Do you understand?"

Artùr met her gaze. "Aye, that's fair. I'll give my word."

The raiders worked hurriedly to carry in the dead from the beach, then gathered round Artùr as he spoke in low tones. With the fallen *Cruithni* laid out, the priestesses began washing their wounds clean, scarcely looking up as the raiders strode from the temple and set sail back to Dalriada, leaving Artùr and Cai behind.

"Remove your armor and tunic and lie upon the table," Ariane instructed Artùr, then turned to Angharad. "You will help tend him," she said.

"Surely I am of better use elsewhere."

"Cendalaeth is dead, and we shelter his murderer," Ariane replied. "Even now all the warriors of the Orcades will be scouring the coast. I need you to tend him because you are gifted at all you turn to, and we must see him gone."

"Of course. I will do it," Angharad said. She pressed a linen to the wound to try to stanch the blood, and Artùr winced. "You. Cai," she said. "Press the wound while I fix a poultice."

Ariane nodded. "Good, then. I must go quickly to the broch. The women and children will be frightened, and they deserve to know of the dead."

The dark-haired warrior Cai did as Angharad bade while she prepared a poultice of fern root, bog myrtle, and moss, then packed the wound.

"Little more than a graze," Angharad said, though it was quite grisly. "You are lucky it did not pierce deeper. You would surely be dead."

She had scarcely wrapped the clean linens over Artùr's shoulder and round his ribs when Catrin burst through the temple door. "Bridei's men! His warriors are coming!" she said.

The priestesses who yet tended the dead looked to Angharad in alarm. She cursed, yanking off her blue robe and thrusting it at Cai. "Here, put this on. And you"—she turned to Artùr—"lie there and feign the death I wish had found you."

Artùr frowned but lay flat once more, eyes closed in a semblance of eternal sleep.

"Draw up your hood." She motioned to the priestesses. "Cai. Turn your back to the door and help me tend him."

Just then the temple door opened, and three of Bridei's men strode in. At the sight of the dead scattering the temple, they stopped, tapping two fingers over their hearts.

"We would find the men who have done this," Bridei's man said. "Did any see which direction they fled? Did any stay ashore?"

"Nay," Angharad said. "They pushed off from the bay; we saw nothing more as we were tending the dead. Their families will soon come, and we would have them cleaned so as not to frighten the children."

"Well enough." He nodded. "But you are now without guard. Men from the mainland will arrive in five days' time. Can you keep safe enough 'til then?"

Angharad nodded.

The man looked round the oil-lit temple. "We will leave you to carry on your prayers for the dead," he said. And ducking in apology, they left.

Artùr and Cai kept motionless until the warriors' footfalls retreated. Then Cai offered his hand and pulled Artùr to sitting. Angharad steadied her breathing.

"Why did you land on our shore? Was your lust for blood not satisfied by your slaughter at Cendalaeth's broch?" she asked.

"We were separated from our fleet in the fog on the Eynhallow Sound. We wouldn't harm priestesses, despite what you think," Artùr replied.

"Oh? But you will chase them like hounds?"

"I didn't wish to have villagers summoning the guard. If you hadn't screamed, I wouldn't have chased you."

"Who would not scream at the sight of raiders appearing out of the sea?"

He looked at her a moment, then tipped his head as if conceding her point.

"Come. You cannot stay here. The families will soon come to sit with their dead." Angharad led Artùr and Cai to the hut she shared with Catrin. "I suppose you must stay here, unless our Lady Priestess says any different. Catrin and I will bed elsewhere."

"I would not send you from your beds," Artùr said.

"You are not well enough to travel," she told Artùr. "A journey by boat may kill you. There's no helping it now. Stay here. We will bring food when we can."

The next morning Ariane sent Cai to aid in the washing to earn his sanctuary while Angharad returned to change the dressing on Artùr's wound. Her fingers were cold, and he stiffened as they brushed against his bare chest.

"Aye, go on, then," he said, and Angharad unwound the linen. Artùr's torso was impressively muscled, and she tried not to notice the smoothness of his skin beneath her fingers as she gently removed the dressing.

"How many winters are you?" Angharad asked, curious.

"Twenty-two. And what of you?"

"Seventeen."

"Ah. Seventeen." He studied her. "You ken my name, yet you've not told me yours, Lady Priestess."

Angharad looked up. "I'm not yet a priestess. I am only a novice."

"Lady Novice?" He squinted at her, waiting.

"My name is mine to keep," Angharad said, though not unkindly.

He allowed a smile. "My father's first wife is a Pict, as are two of my brothers. I ken their ways well."

"Is this why your father wars against Bridei? He would have one of his own sons upon the throne?"

"We war against Bridei because he is a pestilence. He murdered my forefather, Gabrahn, and does not cease in raiding our land. He wants Mannau for his own, and Dalriada, too. Until Bridei is dead, we will never know peace."

"And what would you do with peace when you and your family are so crafted for war?"

Artùr considered it. "I cannot say. Study the Songs, perhaps."

Angharad laughed, then regretted it. "You would study the Songs?" she asked carefully.

"Every lord studies them, but Songs cannot win a kingdom."

"Stories are a different sort of survival," Angharad said.

"Aye, I agree."

"I've brought a clean tunic," she said, passing it to him. "It belonged to one of our guard."

Artùr nodded in thanks, but Angharad's eyes lingered on his bandaged wound as he pulled the tunic awkwardly over his head.

"It was my fault, wasn't it?" Angharad asked. "Your wound. You were sheltering me on the beach. I didn't realize, but you were trying to shield me from all the flying points . . ." She trailed off, waving her hand, and Artùr's mouth turned up at the corners.

"Nay. The spear may've struck me wherever I stood."

Angharad shook her head, meeting his eyes. "It would have struck me. I should have thanked you."

He lifted a brow. "Go on, then, I'll wait. I've nowhere where else to be just now."

"Thank you," she said earnestly.

"Aye." He cleared his throat. "Well."

Cai stole a fisherman's boat by night and hid it in the brush. Over the next few days, Angharad and Artùr fell into a comfort as she visited the hut to tend him. But as the day approached when Bridei's men were due to arrive, Artùr's wound was not yet healing as it should.

"Each time I come in, you are pacing," Angharad said. "You must do as I say and lie back and rest or you will not be sound enough to journey home."

Artùr looked up as if he'd forgotten Angharad was near. She felt the confinement in him, his frustration. He was frantic as a caged beast.

"I can take it from you, if you'll let me," Angharad said softly. "So you might find some sleep."

Artùr stopped pacing, his eyes on hers. "How?"

"Come. Sit before me."

Artùr sat upon a stool. Now that he was so close, Angharad wished she had not offered. It would link them, she knew.

But Artùr could not heal if he would not rest. Angharad took a steadying breath and lifted her hands, looking into his eyes.

As their gazes met, a sensation passed through her, a rush or a quickening, as if she had drunk too much ale. She looked away.

The sensation was penetrating, unsettling, awakening. It was too strong. Too much. But the path Angharad walked was a crooked one, and she knew better than to see this man, Artùr, as only a man. *Look deeper*, she told herself.

Her interest in Artùr distracted her. She understood then that the goddess had sent this man so that Angharad might learn to better command her own skill. This was why Ariane had demanded she tend to him.

"Close your eyes," Angharad said.

Artùr hesitated, and Angharad realized Aedan's son did not have the luxury of vulnerability. She had encountered others like that, mostly warriors, mostly men.

She would have to show him the way.

Angharad placed her hands gently on either side of his head. The goddess was a mother tending to her child. A priestess's body was merely a vessel. Artùr's lashes settled upon his cheek at her touch, his breath growing even. When Angharad next looked down, Artùr the little boy sat before her. His eyes, though closed, were blue pools of innocence.

Look how the world had worn him.

Now he had a spear wound in his side and armor leathering his heart.

She drew it into her body, the discomfort rocking her in waves. She yielded to it, allowing it in.

Artùr let out a sigh. He opened his eyes, looking into hers. "Thank you, Lady Priestess," he said.

She smiled. "I told you, I am only a novice." She risked a glance at him, then said it before she might take it back. "Angharad. That is my name."

"Angharad," Artùr said. His voice was quiet, and Angharad was taken aback by the tenderness beneath it.

Linked. She had known it. There was nothing for it now. Their gaze held new meaning.

"Where did you learn that skill, Angharad?" Artùr asked.

"From a priestess in Fortingall, but also from my uncle. When I was a young girl, I left my mother and father to train with him," Angharad said. "He used to take the tears from me, some nights, when I was weeping."

"He was a Wisdom Keeper?" Artùr asked.

"He was. Lailoken was his name."

Artùr looked at her, blinking. "Lailoken, you say?"

"Yes. But then I was lost from him, and . . ." Angharad bowed her head, the weight of it too much a burden after Artùr's strong healing.

But Artùr's face was full of wonder. "Angharad! Of course! You're Lailoken's young niece," he said.

"You know my uncle?"

"Aye," he said. "I ken your uncle well."

"And he is yet living?" she asked, astounded.

"Aye. And he's never forgotten you. He speaks of you all the time."

Angharad's head was spinning. "However did you meet?"

"Have you not heard of the raid on Clyde Rock?"

"What raid?" Angharad's eyes widened. Her mother and father! Her brother and her sister! "Tell me. You must tell me, Artùr!"

"Aye," he said calmly. "The raid of Aedan mac Gabrahn on Clyde Rock? It's been six winters since, but your uncle aided in it. That's how I came to know him. I'm sorry to be the one to tell you."

Six winters ago! Eachna had never told her, even if she'd known. "Please, I must know. Were any of my family harmed?" she demanded.

"Ach, no." He frowned as if to reassure her. "Warriors all."

Angharad nodded, mind racing. "And where is my uncle now?"

Artùr hesitated. She could sense her uncle's whereabouts were a secret he kept close. She looked at him, beseeching. "Please."

"Well enough. Your uncle is in exile in the Caledonian Wood. He's settled on the land of a chieftan called Archer, should you ever need to find him."

"Thank you," she said.

"Aye."

Silence fell between them as Angharad let settle all Artùr had said. A raid on Clyde Rock—what else might have happened in the years Angharad had been away? She'd felt at peace with her decision to train at Woodwick Bay, but now, for the first time, she began to wonder if it might not soon be time to return home. "Artùr?" she asked quietly.

"Yes, Angharad?" His blue eyes looked almost hopeful.

"If you should see Lailoken again, will you carry some words from me?"

He bowed his head. "Aye."

"Tell him . . . tell him that I love him. And that I do not blame him. And . . ." Angharad searched. "Please tell him I hope to someday see him again."

"I'll tell him," Artùr promised.

Lailoken had avenged Arderydd. But her poor mother, to be caught in the midst of so much bloodshed. Angharad blinked a tear, and Artùr reached gently to brush it from her face.

"I've upset you. Perhaps I should have held my tongue."

"Nay. I'm glad you've told me. 'Tis only it seems so strange that you and I have met. And that you would know my uncle. It seems almost . . ."

"Fated?" The playfulness in his tone belied the heaviness of his gaze.

"Everything is fated in one way or another, is it not?" she answered.

"Aye. I suppose it is." Artùr considered her. "You're lovely. Do you know that, Angharad?"

She did not know how to answer. She opened her mouth to speak, but just then the door to the hut opened, and Ariane appeared with Cai.

"Artùr, the boat is ready. Are you hale?" Cai asked.

Ariane turned to her. "What say you, Angharad? Is he ready for travel?"

Angharad blinked, returning to herself. "Yes. Yes, I believe so."

"Aye. I'm feeling well enough now," Artùr added.

"That is fortunate," Ariane said, "for we've just gotten word that Bridei's men will arrive here by day's end."

Angharad's stomach sank. Artùr looked at her a moment, but Cai stood, impatient, and she felt Artùr's armor envelop him again.

"Aye. We'll endanger you no longer. We've taken too much of your kindness already. We're grateful for your hospitality."

Ariane nodded, passing him a sack of food.

It was better that Artùr go, Angharad reasoned. His presence tested her, and the pull she felt to him left her scattered and distracted. But Angharad had surmounted the challenge and helped him, hadn't she? She gave thanks for that. And had he not landed here four mornings ago, she might never have learned of her uncle.

Angharad walked him to the door and Artùr stopped, turning.

"I'll give your message to your uncle," he said. "He'll be joyed to receive it."

She was too aware of Ariane and Cai standing close. All she could say was "Thank you. I wish you safe travels."

But Artùr took her hand, brushing her knuckles with a kiss. "You've healed me, Lady Priestess. I will never forget it."

CHAPTER 37

Lailoken

Grey Mare's Tail Falls
Kingdom of the Selgovae
13th of June, AD 580

I was standing at the foot of the waterfall, training with my blade. The pounding of the water was deafening, its spray beading my beard in a thousand tiny pearls. He came readily now when I called him, the Keeper of the Falls. When you are in exile, time is an enemy, unless one learns to make it a slave. Pain and adversity were my tutors. I exposed my body to such elements the likes of which few others could endure.

I no longer wanted such things as Lailoken the man would want.

I lost my taste for meat, for its flesh tasted only of death.

Initiates came from Scotia.

Let them come, I said.

Let them come, Archer agreed. For Aedan mac Gabrahn sent word of a Gathering across the sea at Drumceatt. King Aed had outlawed Wisdom Keepers with the support of a priest named Columba.

Send your brightest minds, then, to me, I said. Whisper on the wind that a haven awaits. Come to the forest. Come to *Suibne*—the wild man—I will take you in.

CHAPTER 38

Languoreth

Grey Mare's Tail Falls
Kingdom of the Selgovae
13th of June, AD 580

Eira and I had been traveling for days by the time we reached the waterfall with my men.

We'd found the chieftain called Archer in his hall, only to have him direct us a half day farther into the Caledonian Deep.

"Go to the Mare's Tail," Lord Archer had said. "You'll find your brother there."

So we rode to the place where a ringed stone wall stood upon a little mount, all that remained of an old Selgovian fortress. A sliver of white water cascaded down an impossibly high cliff, and I searched the vast landscape, feeling the land's thrumming power.

"Keep back, Torin," I told him, turning to my guard. "We don't wish to send him running."

I am shamed to say that neither I nor Eira knew my brother at first when we spotted him beneath the falls. I am shamed to say I thought, *Who is that madman, spinning beneath the water's spray, wrapped in pelts?*

He was thin—too thin—and his once neatly kempt hair had gone bushy and wild, threading down his shoulders in tangles and plaits. He was training with his sword. I had seen him work the weapon a thousand times. But now, as Eira ran to him, he rounded with a wary sort of rage. Seven long years my brother had been hunted.

And then recognition dawned. He blinked in disbelief.

His eyes were a question. *Can it be you?*

His blue eyes trailed past Eira to where I stood. *Can it be you?*

A keening escaped me as I ran to him, as Eira ran to him, and the three of us collided, tears streaming.

But it was no longer just me and Lailoken now. I stepped back to give space for his love. He and Eira spoke hurriedly, their faces together, holding each other's cheeks. Then my twin came and drew me to him.

"I am sorry, I am sorry," I said, my words muffled by his pelted shoulder. "We could not come until now."

"I knew you could not." He drew back, holding me at arm's length. He searched my eyes as if to find the story of the past seven winters, even as I searched his. I saw wisdom there, and suffering. A new kind of strength. He smiled and gestured to the twisted gold torque at my throat. "Pretty," he quipped. "Was it a gift?" But he was yet waiting.

"Come." I beckoned Eira. "Let the three of us sit."

We settled on some boulders at the water's edge, warm from the sun.

"Tutgual is dead. Rhydderch has been named king, and I am now queen," I told him.

"Aye."

"You knew this?"

"Aye. I hear much from this place in the forest. You might be surprised. I will admit I did not think to see you here at the falls."

"Then you knew I was coming."

"Your caravan is difficult for a scout to miss. You do not travel in small company, Languoreth. But I am so happy for you, sister. You are the queen our people have waited for. Our father would be proud." His blue eyes were filled with warmth.

"No, no. Don't you see, Lailoken? I have come to bring you out of exile. I and Eira. Rhydderch wishes for you to be his counsel. We have come to bring you home!"

"But this is my home."

I shook my head. "No, brother. How can you say that? Your home is with me, in Strathclyde, where it has always been."

He frowned. "Strathclyde has not been my home for quite some time."

Eira, who'd been listening, reached to touch his bearded cheek. "Lailoken, I think you are a man much changed."

"If that is so, then change was much needed," he said. "I answered the death of my kin. Everything I have done since, I have done in search of some sort of peace."

She took away her hand, and it settled uncertainly.

"Brother. I am offering you freedom. Freedom to come home. Is that not what you wish? Is that not what we have waited for these past seven years?"

"At what cost?" he asked.

"Very well." I knit my fingers in my lap. "At great cost. For Mungo, too, returns from exile. And the Christian lords of Strathclyde have demanded his place as Rhydderch's counsel. You and Mungo would offer counsel together."

His blue eyes went wide. And then he laughed. He laughed with the wild abandon of a madman, his hand to his stomach.

"I cannot say I share your humor," I said when he ceased.

"No," he agreed. "Your humor has left you. For surely you might've seen what folly this is."

Eira frowned. "The man I knew would have been eager at the opportunity to quell Mungo's influence. This is what your sister and Rhydderch offer, Lailoken. That and your freedom."

"My love, they offer me shackles. Here I am free. Rhydderch seeks me out to quell the worries of the lords of the Old Way. And he fears Aedan, king of Dalriada and Mannau, a man I now call a friend, along with his son Artùr. He would use me to his ends. Mungo—" He gathered his mucus and spat, then turned, looking at the empty path behind him. I watched his eyes trail to the top of the falls. "Come," he said. "You are weary from your travels. I would take you to our village. You will see what it has become."

But he stopped when we strode toward my guard. "I'll not lead a caravan of Strathclyde's soldiers to our door. Pick one man, and make it one you trust. The rest must wait at Archer's."

"Well enough," I said. "Torin?"

Torin nodded and I climbed astride my horse. Lailoken mounted Eira's mare, helping her sit before him. Wrapping his arms round her waist, he led the way along the trail.

We had not spied any huts from the forest road. As the rest of my guard followed back to Lord Archer's hall, we turned at a silver birch, following a herd path that twisted and folded in upon itself. Lailoken took one way and then the next in a manner that left me utterly disoriented until the path suddenly widened, becoming one trodden by many feet.

It was a boot print in mud that summoned thoughts of Maelgwn. Could one of these prints be his?

I had bent my mind and my heart to loving my husband. I had tried to push Maelgwn from my mind, dismissing the fact that finding my brother would very likely mean seeing my love once more. But now, as we drew closer to the place where the Dragon Warriors had sought refuge, I felt all the more a traitor for becoming another man's queen. It had been eight years since Maelgwn last touched me, yet I still carried the ring in my pocket, still found myself brushing my thumb against my fingers as if some trace of him lingered there. He had been with me always, a shade in the shadows of my chamber, unseen by any but me.

Lailoken spoke of freedom. How lucky my brother was. There was no freedom for me. Not while Maelgwn yet breathed.

Soon we saw huts. Some ramshackle, some neatly kept, built with what pieces of wood and nature's gifts as could be spared. Lailoken called out a greeting, nodding at the men and women who came out of their shelters. There were dozens of them. Possibly hundreds. And though they beamed at the sight of my brother, their faces went stony as I passed slowly by.

"Why do they look at me so?" I whispered as we drew ever deeper into the forest.

"Because you are wedded to Rhydderch," he said. "The new Christian king."

"They do not understand the path I must tread."

"It has been treacherous to them. Which is why they look at you so."

"Do not speak to me about treachery, Lailoken. I have lost both a daughter and a son." And he'd no idea what Eira had endured.

"Aye." Lailoken bowed his head. "Aye."

We rode awhile in silence.

The wood thickened. Broad-trunked oaks and fat towering pines. And then at last we came to a pasture at the foot of a mountain. Clouds choked the crevasse that led up into escape, drawing a cloak over the hilltops. It was beautiful. Beautiful and desolate.

"Did you ever have to flee?" Eira asked, and Lailoken followed her gaze.

"Once or twice. In the beginning, we climbed the valley each day, those who were able. We had to gain strength. We had to know we could climb faster and with surer feet than any who sought us from below."

The thought of it struck me, and I wanted to tell him how a day had not passed when I had not thought of him, thought of them all.

But then, up ahead, I spotted a little farmstead. There at the mouth of the valley sat two thatched huts of wattle and daub, encircled by an unassuming earthen bank, their only protection a wall of sharpened stakes. Goats milled, grazing on new spring shoots. Beside the stream, a *fulacht fian* had been dug out for cooking, garment washing, ritual, and bathing, the squat dome beside it covered in skins.

And then, like a trick of the eye, warriors stepped into sight as if dropping from a hidden realm. They appeared from behind boulders or the boughs of a tree. From behind Torin's horse came two men I would have sworn a moment ago had not stood there. They came, too, unhurried, from the doors of the huts.

I had steeled myself all the way to Black Mountain to show the warriors strength rather than weakness. But now, as they stood, shoulders back, looking at me in silence, I was overcome. Proud and noble men, persecuted. Hunted. Dishonored. Survivors of a forgotten kingdom.

The last of Pendragon's men.

My fingers flew to my mouth and I swallowed a sob. But their eyes were full of distrust. Did they not know how I loved them? Did they not understand where my loyalty lay?

"Stop," I said to Torin. "Stop here." I dropped from the horse and walked to the fence.

Let them see me, I prayed. *Help them see the honor in which I hold them.*

Lailoken lifted his hand, gesturing to the men. "You recall Diarmid the Diviner and, of course, Fendwin."

I smiled and clasped both their hands. "It does me much good to see you. I am so glad you are hale."

And then I heard his voice, the one I had so longed to hear, unaltered by time, unaltered by circumstance.

"Welcome, Languoreth of Cadzow, queen of Strathclyde."

Maelgwn stepped through the cluster of men. There were no new scars upon him—only the familiar little crescent that cut into one dark brow. But his black hair had grown long and fell loose past his shoulders. He stopped before me and his men waited, watching.

Maelgwn bowed ever so slightly. Then, eyes locked upon mine, he dropped down to one knee. One by one, the Dragon Warriors followed. I could no longer hold back my tears.

Maelgwn stood then and nodded, turning to his men. "We have waited many long winters. Now, at last, our queen has come home."

CHAPTER 39

Languoreth

A time long ago, Malegwn and I spoke of running away. Boarding a boat out of Rheged and sailing off. This now was a taste of the life we might have had—friends gathered round a hearth telling stories, the touch of a hand at the passing of a cup, our eyes catching each other's when we laughed. I had tasted it before, in the moments we'd stolen. I had buried the memories like acorns in the crevices of my heart. For a little while, there in the huts at the foot of Black Mountain, the rest of the world felt so far away. Then I turned my head, and the terminus of my torque poked the hollow of my throat. I looked at Maelgwn and mourned for all the years of a life unlived. One we might have—in some other dream—dwelled in together. He looked up from across the hut, sensing my shift like a change in the weather.

"Aye, that's a lovely tune," Diarmid grumbled to the Song Keeper plucking her *cruit*. "You'll soon have us dashing our heads against rocks."

"Torin." I set down my cup. "I would speak with Maelgwn Pendragon."

Torin nodded and stood to summon him, picking his way over men seated on the rush matting upon the floor. Maelgwn leaned forward, his green eyes upon me as Torin spoke.

"You would speak with me?" he said, closing the space between us.

"Yes, if you do not find it a trouble."

His brows drew together at the nerves in my voice. "Come, the other hut is at your disposal."

"I will follow," Torin said, for it would not be seemly.

But I had already beckoned my brother. "Lailoken will come. Will you keep watch outside?"

"If you wish it," Torin said.

The hut was littered with skins for sleeping and smelled of men. Lailoken ducked through the entryway and nodded at us both, then sat upon a chair, turning it to face the door to give us what privacy he could. Malegwn drew two stools side by side, then reached for a hunk of wood to toss onto the hearth.

"The fire," he said. "We must give a care not to let it die out." But his eyes held more meaning. Awkwardness fell between us, and I felt like a child. For all the absence we'd sustained, embers had burned between us. But now, after the battle of Arderydd and the seven long years of exile, after Rhydderch's ascension to the throne and my queenship, seeing Maelgwn only made me more aware of the toll this endless and disorienting battle between duty and love had taken on the both of us. I loved him. I longed for him. But I was so very weary. I no longer wished to be that careless young woman, consumed by an impossible love and dreams of running away.

My place was in Strathclyde, at the center of a kingdom. I had a duty to my people, and the trial of my days had only just begun.

"You look well," I said, sitting, smoothing my skirt. "I worried over you. I worried you had been injured, or worse."

"Aye, I am hale."

"I am sorry . . ." A look passed between us. Sorry my husband had brought war to them, that they had spent these past seven years in exile, that I had been unable to see them sooner, that now my position would forever keep us apart. He read my face, and I saw the shift and roil of my emotions reflected in his eyes.

"You sent warning at great risk to yourself. I swore to you I would protect your daughter," he said. "I failed you. I am sorry. It seems we were all tasked with things we could not do."

He straightened then, a formality entering his tone. "And you . . . you look well. Your new station suits you."

"Thank you." I bowed my head. His stool was close enough to mine that our knees rested against one another. It was dizzying, his nearness. It had always been so. But perhaps that was due to the fact that it had always been forbidden.

"Rhydderch has asked Lailoken to be his counsel," I said.

"And Lailoken has yet to make up his mind," my brother spoke up from his chair.

"If he would agree," I went on, "would you indeed be able to spare him?"

It was a ridiculous question. It was Lailoken's choice to make, and queens did not ask. But I could not find my way to the root of it. Not yet.

Maelgwn crossed his arms over his broad chest. "It is most considerate of you to ask, my queen. But you know you needn't."

"I always knew that, should anything happen to Gwenddolau, you would become Pendragon. Now you have, and Lailoken is your counsel."

"Come, Languoreth. Both you and I know I rule over nothing. Not any longer."

"You rule the hearts of these men. That much is evident. And what of the hundreds of people who have flocked here to live with you in the wood?"

"Fair," he acknowledged. "That is an honor, for they are remarkable people, and my men are remarkable men." He cleared his throat. "Our scouts bring word that the Angles are massing in Bernicia."

"Ours hear the same."

"'Ours.'" He nodded. When our eyes met, I saw sadness in their depths. "I knew this would come. I think I have always known. Have I lost you, then?"

I had not expected him to ask so forthrightly. I had not thought to feel as I did. We looked at each other, Maelgwn searching me. Me, searching myself. I could not do it any longer, undergo this guilt and this torture. There had been too much suffering. There had been too many things I had lost.

Maelgwn's hands rested upon his lap. I reached carefully to cover them in mine, and his eyes closed at my touch.

I made myself say the words.

"I will always love you," I said. "But I cannot bear the weight of that loving any longer. There is too much at stake. This must be done."

He opened his eyes, and I saw his hurt. "There were so many days I imagined you here before me," he said. "I imagined it a thousand different times, this first touch after so long. After surviving all we have done. Never did I imagine that you would say this."

I pressed his hands, fighting to keep my voice steady. "I have lost my daughter. My son. I have lost you, over and over again. I cannot do it any longer, Maelgwn. It breaks me."

He was quiet a long moment. Then he straightened, easing his fingers from mine. "I understand," he said.

"I am not certain you do," I said, begging him to see. "For so many years, you have held half my heart. Battle is coming, unlike any we have seen. I am needed by my husband and my people. I must mend my spirit and hold it intact if indeed this war is to be won."

"No, Languoreth." He stood. He was not angry, but his olive skin looked pale in the hearth light. "I do understand. All this time, I had given you the whole of my heart. And you suffered in torture, giving only one half."

My conversation with Maelgwn left me nauseated and reeling.

I woke the next morning feeling desolate. I'd worn myself thin arguing with Lailoken over Mungo until the wee hours. I was slated to stay, as the journey had been tiring, but I could see how my presence pained Maelgwn. I could feel how it yet ripped at me. I would leave today and stay somewhere along the road.

Eira found me as I was leaving the hut.

"Sister, I am going to stay," she said. "Lailoken and I, we have been too long apart . . . I must have more time. There is so much we have not yet discussed."

"No, no, you needn't explain." I took her hands. "Please know that I am so truly happy for you. It is only that I am so very preoccupied with my own worries. Stay. I had imagined as much. With any hope, I will see you quite soon."

"Yes, I hope it is so." She nodded to Lailoken, who was striding toward the hut. "For I, too, have spoken with your brother. Will you tell her, then?" she asked him.

"Aye." He came to stand before me. His humor was gone, and in its place the solemn resolve I had prayed to see. "Tell Rhydderch I will meet him," he said. "But it cannot be here. I will not risk any lives."

"I think that is wise. Let us meet at the fort of Dùn Meldred in two weeks' time. It is more than a day's travel north by foot. You could have come from anywhere."

"Meldred is a Christian."

"Yes, and I've considered it. There cannot be a more advantageous point to meet. Meldred will feel the import in holding such a gathering on his own land. He may be a Christian, but he is young, and you should impress upon him your influence. Mungo will insist on being there, I have no doubt. But I will travel with my own retinue. I will wait for you there."

"Well enough. A fortnight."

"Keep safe, brother."

"And you, sister."

As Torin and I followed one of Archer's men back into the forest, I turned one last time, looking up into the cleft of the valley.

Maelgwn was nowhere to be seen.

I straightened my shoulders and fixed my eyes on the road ahead, leaving the settlement of the Dragons behind.

CHAPTER 40

Angharad

Woodwick Bay
Orcades
Kingdom of the Picts
22nd of June, AD 580

Angharad dreamed that night of a man in a cloak made of feathers. He stood atop a towering waterfall. There were mountains all round, and she could feel the lochs and streamlets nestled in their depths. The feathers of his cloak—jackdaw, raven, owl, hawk—rustled in breaths of wind and mist that kicked up off the water.

"What place is this?" Angharad asked.

But the man did not answer. She looked to where his eyes were set. In the distance, a great forest stretched, covering the earth like a rich emerald cloth.

He lifted his arm to point, but Angharad saw nothing—only leagues upon leagues of river, trees, and sky. She tried harder. She reached out with her unseen fingers, the ones that helped her to sense all of the things that lay beneath.

The forest was breathing.

Beneath the oaks, wolves trotted over leaf litter. Wild boar dug their spear-pointed feet into the earth, churning it up. Yet all was not well. There was something in the distance, something stirring that caused the wolf and the boar to lift their heads as if trying to catch a scent on the wind. And then Angharad heard it coming, like hoof-beats, ominous as the pounding of a death drum.

She did not see the beast, but she could feel it; she sensed it in the way of the wolf and the pig, in the rank breath that puffed from its nostrils, the insatiable hunger that twisted its face.

The beast was the size of fleets.

The size of legions.

Its influence crossed oceans and far-flung lands of forest or ice or grass, ancient and vast. She saw in flashes the horrors it had wrought, spanning the length of mankind's memory.

It fed its young off the hearts of wicked men.

There are yet forces upon this earth more powerful than you, Angharad told it. *You are not older than the weather. You are younger still than mountains. You do not command all.*

She realized too late that she should not have spoken. For the beast heard her and lifted its great head.

"I cannot stay here," she said to the man beside her, with a dawning sense of dread.

But the man was no longer there. He was plummeting down the gash in the hillside, arms outstretched, as if he thought he might fly. Blood bloomed in the water below, where the shattered body of the man in the feathered cloak now lay, dreaming with the dead.

Angharad woke, her skin clammy in the dark.

She remembered the cool touch of her mother's hand upon her forehead when she was a child and woke from night terrors. *'Twas only a dream . . . Close your eyes and practice your numbers,* she would say.

Only a dream. There had been many a time in Fortingall when she had wished it were so. She had peered into the cracks of so many women and men.

Angharad went to the hearth, squatting to touch a reed to the embers to light her nearby taper. But even as the wick caught, casting a small but reassuring beacon, she felt ill at ease. Guarding the light with a cupped palm, she stepped from the hut she shared with Catrin and counted the paces she walked in the dark.

One, two, three, four, five, six, seven.

The taper lit Ariane's pale skin as Angharad stirred her gently from sleep. She sat up suddenly, alert as any watchman. "What is it?" the priestess asked.

"War is coming," Angharad said.

"Tell me."

"I dreamed of a beast with no body. It scours, ever hungry. It came before Arderydd. Now it comes yet again."

"You speak as if this beast had retreated only now to return," Ariane said, wrapping her blanket round her as she swung her feet over the edge of her bed. "War is ever lurking. It is we who let it in." She looked up. "Who has let it in?"

Angharad closed her eyes. "I cannot say. It came in a dream. But I could not see the threat itself. What use is a warning without understanding?"

"Dreams are visions, and those who send them do not delight in speaking our tongue. You were raised in a world of dreaming, Angharad. You must trust you will find the answers you seek. Tell me of this dream."

Ariane listened as Angharad told her of the man in the cloak. Of the wolf and the boar.

"There was a time not so long ago when Wisdom Keepers wore such cloaks," Ariane said.

"Keepers, you say?" Angharad asked.

"Yes. There was a Song Keeper who wore such a cloak to enable him to wing to the world of Annwn and so bring back his tales. Diviners used them for their ends. Men and women adept in their dreaming. It enabled them to fly."

Angharad saw blood blooming in water. "I do not think it was so."

"Very well." Ariane tilted her head. "If that is what you believe."

"The man leapt from the falls to his death."

"And what did he do before he leapt?" Ariane asked.

Angharad searched her memory. "He only pointed to the forest."

"No, no. That is not what I mean." She looked at Angharad as if considering something. "If you should dream of him again, perhaps you will see."

Angharad's head ached. "Why must spirits always communicate in riddles? At least elements speak plain."

"You know the meaning," Ariane insisted. "Tell me the simplest thing. What did you feel?"

"Fear," Angharad said. "I felt terribly afraid."

"Why?"

"Because the Angles are coming for those I yet love. They will come through a great forest, attacking the Britons. First the Gododdin, then Strathclyde." Angharad spoke as if trying out the words. She looked at Ariane. "The great forest I saw . . . it must be the Caledonian Wood. Artùr said that my uncle was there."

"Angharad, I think it is time you returned to your mother," Ariane said.

"Yes," Angharad agreed, searching the glowing heat. The flame flickered. Then she knew.

"Yes. It is time," she said. "I want to return. But I do not think we are meant to travel alone."

Dùn Déagh was just as Angharad remembered it.

As they followed the narrow path up from the quay, entering into the shelter of the forest, where sturdy stone huts were nestled and children trailed behind them, eyes wide as eggs. She had come here first as a child herself. Lost and alone, save the company of Brother Thomas, whom she had never again seen and would never forget. Now she returned, nearly a priestess, accompanied by Ariane and their small retinue of men.

"What is it?" Angharad asked Ariane. "You're thinking of something."

"It is only that I wonder why a Pictish chieftain would ride out in aid of the Britons."

"She is not only a chieftain," Angharad said. "She was an initiate of Eachna's once."

Ariane raised a brow.

"It shouldn't be far now," Angharad said as they mounted a steep hill.

The hall was more an imposing hut than a wooden feast hall like that of the Britons. Windowless and built of drystone, it had a turf roof and a sturdy wooden door.

Four warriors stood waiting with spears in hand, wearing summer cloaks. As they caught sight of the priestesses, they bowed their heads, and a stocky warrior with a twisting serpent tattooed upon his neck opened the door to admit them. "We received your message. Our lady is expecting you."

The hut was spacious, the rectangular hearth pit enclosed by the same artfully stacked drystone. Herbs hung from the thick beams of the roof. Two enormous wooden chairs sat side by side at the far end of the hut, where Muirenn and Talorcan sat robed in their finery, regarding her.

"Greetings, Princess." Muirenn smiled. "Though I can see you are a princess no more. You are a priestess now, or nearly so? And a woman fully grown. Tell me, then. Did you find your way home?"

"Lady Muirenn," Angharad said, tapping the place above her heart. "And Talorcan, my lord. Thank you for welcoming us."

Talorcan's eyes smiled at the sight of Angharad, even if he might not allow his mouth.

"You do not travel with Eachna," Muirenn observed. "Who is this in your company?"

"I completed my training in the Orcades. This is my teacher, Ariane, head priestess at Woodwick Bay."

"Welcome," Muirenn acknowledged her. "Come, sit. You have come in much haste. Tell me why you've returned. What would you ask of me?"

Angharad took a breath. "The Angles are bringing war to the Britons. And if we do not help them, all of us will die."

Muirenn and Talorcan exchanged a look.

"Explain," Muirenn said.

"You once told me the legend of the silver torques of the *Cruithni*," Angharad began. "The Romans desired a kingdom with no bounds, and the *Cruithni* had become their slaves. Then, one night, a priestess had a dream. If the people did not unite to fight, the Romans would swallow them whole. The *Cruithni* united and rose up, vanquishing Rome."

"Yes," Muirenn said, waiting.

"The priestess went back to her village so she might train more priestesses. So that if a time came once more, when they were needed, they would be ready. Can't you see, Muirenn? Eachna of Fortingall is my *hennain*. I have trained at Fortingall. I share the blood of that first priestess. Now it is I who have slept and dreamed. The Angles of Bernicia are coming. I cannot yet say when, but I know we must travel to the Caledonian Wood. That is where the battle will begin."

"Angharad, I have seen evidence of your gift. And I cannot deny how fate led you to Fortingall. Nor can I deny your bloodline. But this is not my battle. Why should I risk lives to aid Britons? Besides, there are many lands that lie between Dùn Déagh and Bernicia. Unless they should come by sea, they would have to conquer many Britons before they were any threat to me."

"And I tell you if you aid the Britons now, you will help save not only yourselves but all the people who dwell in the north. The chain you wear round your neck is forged from Roman silver, to forever be a reminder of what it cost to be free. This is what it costs to be free."

Muirenn looked at Angharad a long time. "And say I lend my retinue. What do you propose?"

"I would propose we leave on the morrow. Even then I worry we may be too late."

"What if I am wrong?"

Angharad spoke softly to Ariane as they sat with their cups later beside Muirenn's fire. But Angharad had no stomach for food or drink. She set her cup down so she might work on her cloak. The rhythmic piercing and bonding of needle and horsehair through the delicate hollow shaft of the feather, wrapping, securing each gift just so, soothed her ragged nerves.

"What if you are wrong?" Ariane echoed. "Muirenn will be angry. She has summoned her *teulu*. Tomorrow we will travel south with her men. To reach the Caledonian Wood in the south, we must pass through the lands of the Gododdin. They are no friends of the Picts. Now Muirenn must ask permission to march through their kingdom, to join the Britons in a battle that does not yet exist."

"It feels impossible. We do not even know what the Bernicians may be planning." Angharad rubbed her eyes with the backs of her hands. She had not slept before their journey by boat, and now her eyes felt gritty, as if full of sand.

Ariane reached somewhat awkwardly to cover Angharad's hand with her own. "You have set the cart rolling, Angharad. It rattles fast now, down a steep hill. It will only pick up speed before this is all through. So enough of this foolishness. Finish your cloak and be done with it. Acknowledge your power. For too long you have mistrusted it. For too long you have given it away. Now you must claim it."

"What if I am not ready?"

Ariane looked across the hut at Muirenn. "And do you believe Muirenn was ready when that heavy torque was fixed upon her neck? Or your mother, for that matter? Yes, Angharad. The yoke of destiny is heavy—but it does not ask more than we are able to give. Follow it or shrink from it. The choice is yours. But if you refuse it out of fear, you will never become the woman you are truly meant to be."

"I am asking them to leave their land, to risk their lives," Angharad said.

"Yes. That is what you ask. And they have made their choice." Ariane's voice was steady. "I have seen it come to pass a thousand times, and always it comes to this. Each one of us must choose what we believe. Do you believe you have a gift, or will you toss it away?"

Angharad secured a new feather shaft to her cloak. "You bring to mind something my mother would often say: *We do not always have the choice we would like, but we always have a choice.*"

Ariane smiled.

"Why do you smile so?"

"It is only that your mother is very wise. I shall be glad to see her again."

"You told me once that my mother was sad when you left. You spoke of fate and the Gods and listening. But you had counselled her as a child and seen her become a young woman. Did you not love her?"

At the mention of the word, Ariane's mouth turned down in disdain. "In the place I come from, we do not speak of love in this way."

"Rather like the Picts, I suppose." Angharad looked across at

Muirenn and Talorcan. But Angharad could read Ariane as one looked at clouds and understood weather.

Ariane had loved Languoreth very much. And now Ariane had devoted her life to Angharad's training.

"Is it finished, then?" Ariane gestured to the garment in her lap.

Angharad looked down in surprise to find that, indeed, her work was at last done. She had become so accustomed to her fingers affixing feathers to her great bird while she sat, nearly dreaming, that she hadn't even noticed she'd just tied off the thread at the hem of the cloak. The last feather covering the cloth belonged to a crow, black as beginning.

"I suppose it is done," she said.

"Have you put it about yourself yet?" Ariane asked, knowing Angharad hadn't.

"Tomorrow, perhaps. I'd only sully it now." She set aside the cloak.

Later, the atmosphere in Muirenn's hut was somber as everyone drifted in search of sleep, but Angharad sat awake by the fire.

Behind a woven reed screen, Muirenn's servants had laid out two spare bedrolls. Ariane already lay there, sleeping. But thoughts of war kept Angharad awake.

Tomorrow they would begin their journey into the land of the Britons.

They were marching toward a battle that had not yet begun, hoping Angharad's vision would not lead them astray.

The thought of war was a terror that threatened the peace Angharad had worked so diligently to reclaim, ever since the battle of Arderydd, waged by her own father.

Angharad's legs threatened to buckle from exhaustion. She sighed and stood, moving across the hut to find her bedroll.

But as she began to lie down, she saw something other than a sheep's fleece covered her makeshift bed. Her fingers searched and touched feathers in the dark.

Upon Angharad's bed, Ariane had spread Angharad's feather cloak.

I am only a woman of seventeen winters, she told the Gods, willing them to hear as she refolded the cloak gently, tucking it aside.

As Angharad drifted into slumber, the creak and crackle of turf blazing in the hearth were as ominous as war carts.

The warriors in the hut rolled over, dreaming of blood in their sleep.

CHAPTER 41

Languoreth

Dùn Meldred
Southern Kingdom of Gododdin
27th of June, AD 580

The fortress of Meldred was a desolate, silent place. Another world from the lands of the Selgovae.

It is the trees, I realized as we drew nearer to the fort. Meldred had butchered large swaths of wood in fear of invaders, and in so doing, he'd fashioned a haunting expanse. Still, a burn ran through, and the pastures were green with the richness of summer. Men could not conceal themselves in such low-hovering plants as heather and myrtle, so those also yet thrived, and the scent of their blossoms caught on the breeze.

Perhaps it was I who was desolate, for I knew what waited within.

Mungo, with his guards and his company of monks.

And then there was Meldred, a young lord of Gododdin. His father was Lot, his mother was Ana—daughter of Aedan mac Gabhran. Both mother and father were of the Old Way, but Meldred had married a daughter of Caw, one of the most devoted Christians of Strathclyde.

I held no fondness for Meldred's wife, Cywyllog. I had met her at court. And though she was kind to Rhian, she was cold to me. After all, her family was enamored of Mungo. There was no one in all of

Strathclyde who did not know of the feud between Mungo and my family. How uncomfortable for them that I was now queen.

The hills of the fortress were folded close, like two hounds sleeping side by side. The more distant hill arched higher than the front mound, where the fortress was built. I felt eyes upon me and looked up at the guard tower perched high atop the back hill.

Aye, I am here, I wanted to call out. *The unclean Lioness of Strathclyde.* I had heard what they said of me, the staunch supporters of the Christian way.

"Do not eat 'til I taste it first," Torin warned, his eyes trailing to the wooden hall peeking overtop a towering oaken rampart.

"They would not dare," I said. "I hold far too much sway. We need each other now, they and I. Never fear, Torin. I shall set it all right."

Cywyllog stood waiting in the sun. Her servants, at the sight of me, all dropped to one knee, but Cywyllog's bow was abrupt, only what was required. "My Lady Queen."

"It is so gracious for you to host such a Gathering," I said, reaching warmly to clasp both her hands. Snow melted in sun. That was the way of things. If only by outer appearance.

Cywyllog was a dun-haired beauty with thick brows and acorn-colored eyes, slight in stature but quick in wit. "My children," she said, gesturing to a boy and a girl who clung to her skirts.

I nodded kindly and looked to the hall. "And your husband. Is he not at home?"

"Oh!" Cywyllog made a show of looking well shamed. "Meldred and the bishop must yet be inside, speaking of holy things. So enraptured are they, they must not have heard our Lady Queen's horses."

An insult, not to be met by the lord of the hall, but I gathered a smile. "We must look to your good husband's manners, for soon his king shall arrive, and then what would we do?"

I pushed back my light riding hood and adjusted the exquisite golden torque that gleamed at my neck, leveling her with my gaze. *Careful*, my look said.

For a moment Cywyllog seemed nearly nervous before she brushed it away. "Come, then, Lady Queen. We have prepared this little hut for you, nearest the hall. You will, I hope, pardon its roughness. We were not expecting any such visit. We have done what we can, what with warriors, monks, and Wisdom Keepers alike all arriving to stay."

"I am certain I'll be well suited," I assured her, ducking through the door. A bed, a hearth stacked for lighting, a bowl with well water to wash.

She had entered, but now paused and turned. Beyond the walls of the hut, I startled at the angry barking of dogs. "Apologies," she said. "My husband keeps his hounds in the enclosure nearby. I will instruct the hound master to keep them quiet during your stay. In any case, I am sure you will want to wash away your journey. Have you traveled very far? And with no trunks along with you—no trunks at all?" Her dark lashes blinked, but her motives were clear. I had arrived with only six riders. As she was hosting, she was most certainly privy to the fact that my brother would soon be here, and no doubt she expected I had visited him in hiding. She wanted to know where the settlement lay.

"I have come ahead of the king only to be sooner reunited with my brother. They will arrive in haste and with all my belongings. I have no need of washing, but would be admitted into your hall."

"Of course, my Lady Queen. Without further delay."

All stood at once as I strode into their great room. It had been bright in the sun, and in the moment before my eyes became accustomed to the dim, the figures rising from fleece couches and chairs appeared shadowed and sinister.

"Your lady assures me you were deaf to the sound of our horses," I said as Meldred came forward, bowing his head.

"It is as my wife says, Lady Queen. I pray you accept my apology, for I assure you, your presence is most welcome. I was speaking with the bishop." Meldred stepped aside. Mungo stood before me, brown eyes piercing and bearded face stern.

"I was not aware he had regained such a title," I said, alluding to his exile. "But if all goes well at this Gathering, counsellor of Strathclyde may be his to share. Greetings, Kentigern."

Mungo gave a cursory nod. Time had not been kind—the gaunt features that made him appear skeletal had only stretched the more taut. I heard he oft fasted, depriving himself of food, yet never failed to eat in the company of kings. His desire to eschew his practice in order to please those in power made it all the more insulting that he would not make himself supplicant to me.

When I was young, I had thought him simply vile. But now I'd grown wiser. I understood the danger of Mungo to be something far worse. Mungo believed himself to be one of Christ's holiest men. It was his very devotion to his god that drove him to illogical and violent acts. My brother and I alone, it seemed, had borne witness to his menace. He'd delighted in my fear of him when I was but a child and had encountered him trespassing on the slopes of Bright Hill. He had desecrated a site sacred to my people. He had murdered his rival, Brother Telleyr. He had incited a mob to scar my brother and steal my father's grain. He had hired assassins to murder Cathan, our most beloved friend.

How it must pain him now, that I was Strathclyde's high queen, and that the end of his banishment rested upon his ability to make peace with me and my brother. No. It was Mungo who suffered. I would not allow him to injure me now.

Mungo and his monks ate with reserve but supped nonetheless. I watched Melred, the deft son of a king, playing at both sides of the gaming board, neither Old Way nor new. I watched Cywyllog, in all other ways the clear sovereign of her hall, gaze at the exiled priest with the honor and reverence an initiate gave to one's master.

I made my excuses far before sunset, Torin and I following the servants back to the hut. I'd rather sit with Torin for company. Soon Lailoken would be traveling in darkness along the Thieves' Road. He would arrive before sunrise and keep hidden until Rhydderch was spotted. Only then would he come.

And I, for my part, had lasted more than a moment in the company of Mungo. Once I had imagined the very act of seeing the man would flatten me. Though he still turned my stomach, watching him for an evening had inspired a new idea altogether.

"Torin," I said as I lay down my head.

"Yes?" he asked, averting his eyes, laying out his bedroll facing the door.

"I do not think it so ill now to have Mungo at court."

"Is that so?" There was surprise in his voice.

"No, I do not. For I have been thinking. Surely we can find a man worthy of trust who might be persuaded to take up the hood of the monk."

"You wish to spy upon Mungo." Torin thought a moment. "It cannot be a warrior from your retinue. He would never be believed."

"Of course. I agree. But then who? If only we could find a youth already in training. Brother Telleyr would have delighted in selecting such a man. If only we had known . . . We were fools not to think of spies and treachery. If we had, Brother Telleyr might have died an aged man."

Our minds turned in silence, mine rather sadly. Then Torin spoke. "There may be just such a man who dwells in the wood beyond Partick, though he is not young. He is a culdee, and I have heard some visit him for wisdom, though he is mostly occupied with the carving of crosses."

"Thank you, Torin. When we return, I will visit him there."

We had been unprepared for Mungo's maneuverings, my family and I. Each torturous act had arrived, more unexpected than the last.

But I would be outmaneuvered no longer. The Lioness, they called me. Then a lioness I would be.

CHAPTER 42

Lailoken

Dùn Meldred
Southern Kingdom of Gododdin
27th of June, AD 580

I lay on my stomach in the grass, watching the torches of the guard tower flicker in the distance.

Their voices carried in the dark, drunk and inattentive. I contemplated somehow getting myself over the rampart and finding my sister, so that I might sleep at least a short time before the day's unpleasant events began.

I had thought long about what I might do should I ever again lay eyes upon Mungo. There were many nights when I was young, a boy of nearly sixteen winters, when the blisters from burning shut the open gash upon my face filled with liquid and I woke in the night crying out, my fists clenched with rage.

Mungo was a zealot, dangerous and irrational.

I was to share a counsellorship with this man?

I spent time in contemplation. But I needed no Bull's Sleep to divine that I would rather be a wart on a cock than allow that man any measure of power. And the only way to ensure that Mungo did no harm was to accept Rhydderch's terms. Once I returned to Strathclyde, the way forward would be clear. He had his Christians, yet I had an equal faction of Britons and Scots, Wisdom Keepers and warriors all, brutally punished for worshipping in our ancestral way.

The sun rose.

I foraged some bilberries, keeping from sight. Then at last I heard the horn from the watchmen. There was Rhydderch's standard, followed by the new king himself and a retinue of nearly eighty men. I stood and stripped, rolling up my tunic and stuffing it in my satchel and donning instead the freshly sewn robes of white given me by my sister.

It had been seven winters since I had worn the white robes of a Keeper. In that time, I had been a warrior, a seeker, a wild son of the wood.

I was all those men still.

I stood at my full height. The warrior at the front of Rhydderch's guard barked out a warning as he spotted me.

Lifting my hands in a gesture of peace, I looked once more at the tower and the fortress ramparts with a sigh.

Then I strode slowly downhill, the unseen shades of my fallen brothers following solemnly behind me.

CHAPTER 43

Angharad

Dùn Déagh
Kingdom of the Picts
25th of June, AD 580

Muirenn's fleet of twelve warships set sail at dawn. With twenty-four warriors at oar in each vessel, it made a force of 288 men. In two days' time, they would dock their boats at the port of Din Eidyn in the land of the northern Gododdin.

"I am grateful to you, Talorcan," Angharad told him.

The warrior frowned at her Pictish, answering in Brythonic. "You would be wise to keep your gratitude. To even reach your Caledonian Wood, we must earn entry through Gododdin lands. I sent messengers ahead to plead our passage, but the Gododdin are rich and warlike, and not always clever. They may kill our messengers just for the pleasure of it."

"They will not slay the messengers." Angharad continued in Pictish. "They may be proud, but they cannot be foolish enough to turn away warriors who seek to help their people." She paused. "Why do you insist on speaking to me in Brythonic? I speak Pictish as if it were my first tongue."

Talorcan raised his dark brows, making the fish etched into the skin of his forehead seem as if they were laughing. "Seven more winters. Then you might speak like a *Cruithni*."

"Seven, you say?" Angharad asked.

But Talorcan's humor had faded in the shadow of their task. "We must hope the Gododdin have faith in your cause," he said. "We will need provisions along the way. The Caledonian Wood is at least three days' travel south by foot." He risked a glance at Angharad. "Tell me. In your vision of this war, did you see victory?"

Angharad looked to the dark, cresting water. "I cannot command my visions as such. I understood it to be a warning. The rest is uncertain."

"Perhaps there is no certainty," Talorcan said. "Picts aiding Britons. Such things are beyond thought. Perhaps even the Gods cannot fathom it."

At this Angharad could not help but smile. Just then Talorcan looked past her shoulder. Muirenn, who'd been walking the length of the ship, came to stand beside them, watching the water companionably. After a while, she turned to Angharad. "You never told me why you left Fortingall," she said.

"Eachna lied to me. She betrayed me. You warned me that day when she took me away."

"I feared Eachna had forgotten how to be pure in her service to the Gods," Muirenn said. "She had also dashed my dreams of becoming a priestess. It broke my heart. Only now do I see the truth of it. The people of my line have been called yet again. Had I stayed beneath the yew at Fortingall, I would not possess any warships to lead. And had you returned to your mother when you wished . . ."

"Eachna should have given me a choice," Angharad said, hearing her own anger.

"You were but a child. Torn by war and alone. What would you have chosen?"

Angharad fell quiet. She thought of the cloak of feathers she had folded in her satchel. Its bulk was cumbersome, the weight of its wool oppressive.

"Do you not find it so very heavy at times such as these?" Angharad asked, gesturing to Muirenn's torque.

Muirenn touched it, her fingers tracing the place where the silver links met with the fire inked upon her throat.

"No, Princess," she said. "At times such as these, I remember how all the days it felt heavy in the past are the very days that have made me grow strong."

CHAPTER 44

Lailoken

Dùn Meldred
Southern Kingdom of Gododdin
28th of June, AD 580

The warriors brought me to Rhydderch, still mounted upon his
horse.

"Brother." Though I bowed, my voice spoke another tale. One of
betrayal.

"Release him. He is no prisoner," Rhydderch said, swinging down
from his horse. As he made to come toward me, his men gripped their
weapons, ready to protect their king, but Rhydderch lifted a hand,
bidding them stay back. We looked at each other, and I remembered
the look of vengeance I'd seen flash in his eyes on the battlefield.
Only now did I wonder: What had he seen flash in mine?

"You must know, all this time I have conspired to bring you back
home," he said.

"Aye. I know what you have done. I'm grateful," I said, the last
rather gruff.

"I lost a daughter and a son." Rhydderch stood erect, eyes matter-
of-fact. But I'd known him long enough to hear the sorrow in his tone.

"I could not save them."

"An impossible task," he allowed. "If we are to reunite, I must know all can be forgiven."

"And I must know you will heed me as your counsel."

"I swear upon all the Gods I will honor your counsel. I trust you beyond measure. Help me, Lailoken. Strathclyde will soon stand on a sword's edge. I would have you at my side."

"Then all can be forgiven," I said.

"Good." He smiled. "For I have brought you a horse."

Rhydderch gestured, and one of his guard emerged from the center of his retinue, leading the reins of a powerful gray mare.

I stroked her smooth cheek. Her eyes were calm and deep as a well. "Thank you. She is magnificent," I said, pulling myself astride.

Rhydderch climbed back upon his own mount, and together we guided our horses back onto the fortress trail. I felt the weight of boulders lifted, yet we stood at the foot of a mountain that threatened to crush us all the same.

"Before we arrive," I said, "one more question, and this is most earnest."

"What is it?" Rhydderch turned, gray eyes wary.

"You expect me, then, to step forth into the same hall with Mungo without cleaving open his head with my sword? Just so I understand."

"Yes."

"Impossible."

I had tethered my loathing, at least for now. I meant only to lighten Rhydderch's mood, as I'd once been able.

But Rhydderch did not smile, only looked at me sidelong. "It is good to have you returned, brother. Please do not cleave open Mungo's head. You will beget a civil war."

"Only jesting," I said. Then added, "But I cannot swear I won't curse him."

* * *

We arrived at the fortress, and Languoreth and I embraced as if we had not seen each other in seven winters. I greeted Meldred and Cywyllog, whose eyes were too eager. I said nothing to Mungo. I did not have the opportunity. The moment I opened my lips to speak, Meldred's watchman came hurrying through the door.

"What is it?" Meldred asked.

"There are beacons blazing on the hills."

"What news do you hear?"

"The Angles of Bernicia," the messenger said. "Archers, spearmen, footmen by the thousands. They are marching northwest along the old Roman road to lay siege upon Din Eidyn."

Rhydderch cursed. "I thought we might have more time. Their king, Hussa, has only just taken the Bernician throne! How can he have gathered such a force so quickly?"

Languoreth's eyes mirrored mine across the great room. The Angles of Bernicia were coming for the Britons. Sweet Gods. We were not prepared for this war.

Arrows in the wood, Diarmid had said.

At last I understood. The Keeper of the Falls had shown me. There was an old Roman road that yet ran through the forest; the Ninth Legion would have taken that road to crush the Britons in his time. Now Hussa, king of the Angles of Bernicia, traveled it to crush the Britons in mine. He had shown me a triumph in the wood.

The Caledonian Deep. It must begin there.

"We must waylay the Bernicians in the Caledonian Wood long before they reach Din Eidyn," I said.

Those in the room looked at me as if I were mad.

"We must ride north to Din Eidyn!" Meldred said. "They will need every man they can muster there. If Din Eidyn should fall, we will all be lost."

Languoreth's skin had gone sallow, but Rhydderch must have seen my expression. "Tell me what you know."

"It was a dream, a vision, but the Bull's Sleep does not lie. Thousands beyond belief marching the old Roman road through the Caledonian Wood. If we attack there, we stand a chance at survival."

"And if we muster all of our forces to Din Eidyn?" he asked.

"The battle I saw did not take place at Din Eidyn. It was in the shelter of the Caledonian Deep. If we do not engage them there, I fear all of us may die."

Even as I spoke, my thoughts were racing. If what the Keeper of the Falls had shown me was truly coming to pass, each moment we tarried was a moment wasted.

"We must summon allies beyond our imagining," I said. "And we must summon them in great haste."

But each lord had his own plan.

Rhydderch signaled his man. "Send out the scouts. We must know their precise number," even as Meldred called out, "Summon my men. We will ride to the aid of our brethren at Din Eidyn."

"We will not survive if we cannot act together," I said. "The Bernicians depend upon our discord. Do not give them what they seek, Meldred."

"Silence!" Mungo's voice rang out as he lifted his hands. "I must call for silence. Lailoken claims we must waylay them here? I heard tales of his lunacy, brought about by war. My king, your proposed counsellor is not of sound mind. We cannot stand against an army of such measure."

"Tell me, then, Mungo. What is your plan?" I challenged.

Our eyes locked in loathing as Rhydderch strode between us. "I would have a word with my counsellors." His voice was hard. "War comes this way. I must know from you now: Can you set aside your differences? Quick now, and tell me true, for you breach this pact at your peril," he warned.

"I agree," I said.

Mungo's dark eyes were placid, as if untroubled by storm. "Yes," he said. "I offer you my hand."

We gripped each other's arms. I wanted to pummel him.

"Good," said Rhydderch. "Now tell me, Bishop, what would you propose?"

"We must not abandon our fellow Britons in their hour of need," he said. "I am in agreement with Lord Meldred. We must keep Din Eidyn from capture at all cost."

"The Bernicians expect us to ride to Din Eidyn! If we strike in the Caledonian Wood, we can finish them before they should even reach Din Eidyn. At the very least, our attack would give the northern Gododdin more time to prepare. But we need allies." I turned to Rhydderch. "We must send your three fastest riders. One must go to Strathclyde to summon your army. The second must go north to Mannau, with a message for Artùr, son of Aedan. And the third must ride south, to Urien of Rheged. I will muster my men along with the Selgovae. They know the Caledonian Wood better than any."

"Artùr and Aedan raided Clyde Rock," Rhydderch said. "They would sooner run a blade through my back than come to our aid."

"I am your counsel now. If I summon Artùr, he will come. You forget, too, that Meldred and Artùr are kin. Artùr will come with his cavalry to help the Gododdin."

"Aye," Meldred said. "Artùr is my uncle. We will tell him that I, too, request his aid."

Mungo nodded his assent.

"Well enough, then," Rhydderch said. "While we wait for the scouts' return, we will finalize our plan."

CHAPTER 45

Languoreth

Dùn Meldred
Southern Kingdom of Gododdin
28th of June, AD 580

War.

       I'd watched in silence as the news dawned on the men gathered in the hall and plans for a coalition were made.

The Angles of Bernicia would have to travel in great number to use the old Roman road. Theirs would be a long march northwest to Din Eidyn. And while the first part of their journey began in their own kingdom of Deira, as soon as they entered the land of the Britons, they would be exposed. It seemed the Bernician king, Hussa, counted upon our division. Upon the past feuds of our kingdoms preventing us from becoming a united force. Upon the Selgovae granting the Bernicians passage through their great wood in exchange for an offer of peace.

And so my thoughts fell to Ebrauc. Neither Rhydderch nor Lailoken had mentioned them. My hate for Gwrgi was a burning pyre, but sweet Gods! The Angles were coming. Even I could see we needed Ebrauc's blades.

I caught the sleeve of Lailoken's robe as he moved to the table, drawing him aside. "And what of Ebrauc, Brother? Surely they, too, must come to our aid."

"I did not summon Ebrauc, with good reason."

"I know there is bad blood. You cannot know how much I loathe him—"

Lailoken spoke low. "I burned Gwrgi's men alive in the forest. I strewed their arms and legs from trees. If I see him, I will kill him, and all will be undone."

"Do not be foolish, Lailoken. You fought them. You know they are fierce. Men are men, and we are in need of them."

My brother's blue eyes turned stormy. "There are things you do not know of, Sister, things I cannot say. But Gwrgi slipped my grip more than once and will not do so again. The next moment I see him will be his last."

"Lailoken, I swear to you, I understand. You must know, Eira has told me all."

Sorrow replaced the fury in the depths of his stare. "Then you know, if I see him, what I must do."

"Gwrgi's day will come, I swear by the Gods! But we cannot let hatred keep warriors from our ranks. Between the north and south of Ebrauc, they stand to muster nearly one thousand men. Come, Lailoken. You have taken leave of your senses!"

"No, Sister. But should I see him, that is precisely what I might do," he said.

"Lailoken." Rhydderch beckoned from his seat.

"Please," I said. "Summon them. Rhydderch may be king, but I am your queen. Do not let your loathing blind you to good counsel."

Lailoken did not answer. I hoped I had moved him. I watched him sit down beside Rhydderch, bowing his head as the men began to speak. I could see the new wisdom born in Lailoken from his ashes of torture and pain. Mungo was trial enough for us both. Now I had advocated for Ebrauc to take up our fight. But I, too, had suffered and burned and emerged forever changed. This moment demanded everything if we wished to survive.

I settled beside the fire, trying to stifle my frustration. Cywyllog spoke, and I did my best to engage her. After all, she was our hostess, and it seemed we would be thrown together here until the battle was done. Then, from the table, Rhydderch stood to summon a fourth rider. My brother's eyes found me and gave a nod. Ebrauc. It would soon be done.

It was long into night by the time Rhydderch and I had a chance to speak. We knew rest would be needed in days to come, but not a soul slept that night, keeping awake for the scouts to return. They returned just before dawn, the horses ridden until their coats frothed.

The Angles of Bernicia were coming. They marched at great speed toward the land of the Britons along the old Roman road.

In their ranks were some ten thousand men.

"I would stay with you," I told Rhydderch. "I am not afraid."

"Nay, Wife, it is not safe. I would have you west, behind the ramparts of Clyde Rock."

"But you will meet Hussa's forces over three leagues away. The fortress will be out of harm's reach. I beg you. I have been shut away while those I loved rode to battle before. I will not allow it again."

"And who will rule Strathclyde," he asked, "if I am dead?"

"Surely not me, Husband. The council would not have it, as well you know. Your brother Morcant, more likely, and we cannot have that. You are the middle way. The only way. So you must fight and return, Rhydderch, for we cannot lose you."

"And I cannot lose you. Please," he said. "Go. The queen should be in Strathclyde."

I took a step nearer, tilting my head. "Come, Husband. I am not blind to the truth. If we should lose this battle, it will not matter where I might be. For whether it be the next day or several days after, there will soon be no kingdom of Strathclyde left to rule. Please. Let me stay. Let the people know Strathclyde's queen is with their king."

He reached to sweep a wisp of hair from my face, and I saw he did not have the life force to argue it any further. "As you wish, Languoreth. I can see you have made your choice. I will not dispute it."

"You will be quite safe here," Cywyllog said early the next morning. "They shall have to cut their way through nearly half of Gododdin first. And Meldred has summoned his Swineherds to protect us here at the fortress."

Her servant moved the bread close in an offering, but I had no hunger and waved it away. "His swineherds? Does your lord have such confidence in the men who would mind his pigs?"

Cywyllon smiled. "Ah. You shall see. We in the fortress shall have nothing to fear."

Warriors of some sort, they must be. But why they were so called, I could not say. "I do not worry for myself. I worry for our men."

Cywyllog bowed her head to concede my point, though I did not think her concern extended much beyond her own kin.

"You should worry, Lady Cywyllog," I told her. "For the great battle of the Britons has already begun. We must fight to remain masterless, or soon all will be dead."

All through the night, warriors had been bolstering the ramparts.

For two days, men poured into the fortress from the countryside: tenant farmers and millers, tanners, woodworkers, cowkeeps. Eira led a small company of women and children from the Caledonian Wood to join us at the fortress for safekeeping. But even the servants of the hall were fitted with weapons. And on the eve of the second day, I saw the arrival of a small band of men.

They were not more than thirty in number, traveling by foot in thick leather armor, each with a wolfhound trotting by his side. Their animals were sleek, their dark eyes unfriendly. These were not hunting dogs; these were dogs of war.

"The Swineherds of your lord," I gathered, looking at Cywyllog. "But where is their quarry?"

"They seek their quarry at our command," Cywyllog said. They brought to mind the Fianna, men who gave service to their lord for the summer, then lived off the land in the lean parts of the year. Wolving, it was called. But such men were heroes of old Westmen's tales. These men's eyes were too savage to inspire such regard. Perhaps I had underestimated the ambition of Meldred. His holdings and his retinue might have been modest, but he had drawn warriors, and from the look of them—rather like the warriors of Mannau—these warriors came from a variety of clanns.

"What do you know of these Swineherds?" I asked Torin as he came to stand beside me.

"Outcasts and unwanted sons," he said, following my gaze.

"And what else?"

"Each man, when his place is earned, is given his own hound."

"Of course," I said. "I heard Meldred's dogs. He keeps them in an enclosure beyond the hut where I sleep."

"They are rough," Torin allowed, "but they will help keep you safe."

"Oh, I do not doubt it. But I would like to learn more about them, all the same."

"As I can," he said.

"How many men in all have come?" I asked, looking out over the crowd.

"One thousand from Strathclyde. Another thousand from Strathclyde march north to fight at Din Eidyn. Urien comes this way with nine hundred men. One thousand come from Ebrauc."

"How many have the Selgovae?"

Torin exhaled. "I cannot rightly say. Their kingdom is vast, and they keep to themselves. Less than one thousand, I'd say."

"Four thousand men to stand against ten thousand."

"Aye," Torin said. "It seems that is our fate."

Warriors and tents covered the pastures beyond the hillsides. We'd had no word yet from Aedan or his son Artùr. Even with Ebrauc, we were still not enough.

I looked to the sky, the summer sun nearly overhead. Even now the men were striking their tents to march for Pebyll. They would camp this night near the path of the Angles, who were due to reach the settlement by morning. I had kissed my brother when he left to muster his forces in the Caledonian Wood.

Now Rhydderch came to stand beside me, taking my hand. "Would that you had gone to Clyde Rock," he said.

Torin had become my shadow. He would stay behind with a small number of my guard in case our men should fail and the Angles break through. I turned to him now. "Torin, will you pardon us?"

He nodded and stood at a distance, averting his gaze.

"Well, I, for one, am glad I was not whisked away to Clyde Rock," I said. "It cheers the warriors to see me. My brother will soon fight in the distance. Eira is here. My tenants are just arrived from Cadzow to fight for their queen."

"We will depart shortly."

I turned to Rhydderch, placing my hands upon either side of his face. It frightened me to see him this way—bleary-eyed and disheveled from lack of sleep—and now an ominous tone had crept into his voice.

"When Boudicca raised her rebellion against Rome, everyone thought it an impossible task," I said. "They, too, were outnumbered. But the tribes came together to fight for one cause. Now, for the first time in ages, the Britons have set aside their differences. The very men you slaughtered at Arderydd fight for us now, out there in the wood. This will not be the end. It cannot."

"Aye, love. But Boudicca's rebellion failed."

"This battle will be different. You were given this role with good reason. And tomorrow you must fight harder than ever before, for I will not lose you. The Britons cannot lose you."

He closed his eyes, covering my hands in his.

"You know. They say the Iceni queen was a diviner, with long tawny hair. Perhaps I am Boudicca returned." My words were soft, but I could not muster a smile. "Perhaps tomorrow is the day we will at last win Boudicca's fight. Rome. The Angles. This army that marches is just a beast by another name carrying the same bottomless stomach. Slit open its belly, Rhydderch. The beast shall not have us."

A blast of the horn sounded, summoning the men.

"That's it, then," Rhydderch said.

My chest tightened. "So soon?"

I leaned into him, and he wrapped his arms round my waist. As we kissed, his mouth lingered a moment on mine as if he hoped to remember. I reached into my cloak and took out a sprig of ivy I'd plucked that morning, tucking it beneath his armor where it might cover his heart. "May it protect you, my love. Gods keep you safe."

He bent to kiss me again. "I love you, Languoreth. You bring me such strength."

"And I love you," I answered.

Hand in hand, we descended from the rampart into a world of chaos. My ears filled with the barking of dogs and the chanting of men: warriors in their kin groups singing their songs, the low tones of Mungo and his priests chanting their prayers. My thudding heart threatened to shatter the cage of my chest. But I raised my chin high, meeting our men's eyes as I walked among them, offering words of encouragement.

They were ready too soon. Torin and my guard stood watch beside Meldred's Swineherds at the base of the outer rampart.

Rhydderch turned, lifting a hand in good-bye.

I bit my lip, battling tears. For within that farewell, I felt each man's farewell. That of Maelgwn, Fendwin, Diarmid, my brother, that of every miller and boatman, every farmer and herdkeeper. It was the summoned sacrifice of so many of our people marching headlong into an unknown fate, their faces grim, mouths set, determined.

Only when the last line of men disappeared from sight did I duck behind the hut and retch in the summer grass. I wiped a hand across my face, knuckles white.

Now there was nothing to do but wait.

CHAPTER 46

Lailoken

The Caledonian Wood
Kingdom of the Selgovae
30th of June, AD 580

> *We go in the name of the Gods*
> *In likeness of deer, in likeness of horse,*
> *in likeness of serpent, in likeness of king.*
> *Stronger am I than all persons.*
> *The hands of the Gods keep me,*
> *The love of the Gods in my veins,*
> *The strong Spirit bathing me,*
> *The Three shielding and aiding me,*
> *The hand of Spirit bathing me,*
> *The Three each step, aiding me.*
> *Keep watch upon our hunt that we may return.*

I looked up from our prayer to the Morrigu, goddess of war. The Dragon Warriors' heads were bowed beneath the forest as they whispered now their own words of protection. But this day we hunted no boar.

It would soon be night, and this day, we hunted men.

The sky through the canopy was fire and ocher smeared by gray cloud. I thought I caught the acrid smell of smoke on the wind from the huts I knew were burning as the Angles of Bernicia marched toward the Caledonian Wood.

One thousand Selgovae waited throughout the great forest, hidden among the trees. We men of Pendragon were only eight in all. But another 160 in our retinue were Keepers fled from Scotia when Keepers were outlawed, men who'd settled in the forest. We Dragons had trained them, and together we made a new brotherhood: the Army of Stags. I had no word from Artùr, but I knew he would come. If he'd received my message and ridden like wind, he and his cavalry might join us within the day.

We would strike like lightning and disappear into the forest. A force the size of the Angles clung together like a hive, but the workers on the outside were exposed. An army of ten thousand men possessed a long and vulnerable flank.

I thanked the Gods at seeing Maelgwn as he appeared among the warriors in his battle armor, saving me from my thoughts.

The men fell quiet, eyes on the Pendragon, hands upon their spears.

Now it began—the pounding of our wooden spears against the soft earth.

Huh. Huh. Huh-huh-huh. It was a guttural sound, our chant. A sound for a kill.

Huh. Huh. Huh-huh-huh. It was a chant that recalled each battle we had fought. A chant that summoned our fury for every scout who'd ridden out and not returned, for every finger the Angles had sent when they captured our men, for every house we'd seen burned, for every woman who'd been raped, for every babe they had killed. The horrors, we had fought them—fought them for years, even while other countrymen turned away their gaze.

It was right that it was us here now, in small number at the beginning of the great fray. For we had fought, and we had killed. And we were still here.

Huh. Huh. Huh-huh-huh. We had chanted a thousand times on mornings we rode out to victory. On the morning of Arderydd when we witnessed a slaughter. Now our chant was both a summoning of our strength and a summoning of our dead.

Huh. Huh. Huh-huh-huh.

Maelgwn stood upon a boulder, lifting his voice. The warriors watched him, hawklike, never stopping, only softening their chant.

"Seven winters ago, we came to this forest broken, bloodied, and in need of shelter," he said. The warriors' voices rose up in chorus.

Long may we honor the courage of the dead.

"But we did not merely subsist in anguish, forever mourning our brothers. We chose instead to honor them, here! In the trees of this very forest. We built instead a refuge for Song! A place to keep Wisdom. A place to tend the hunted and the wounded, where we may yet honor and give sacrifice to the Gods who sustain us while zealots burn the huts of the innocent even as they say *amen!*"

The warriors roared and Pendragon nodded, meeting the eye of each and every man.

"We carried the bloodied body of Uther from beneath the ramparts. I watched him choke and wheeze on his death. On this day, the very men who slaughtered our brothers beg for our aid. And I, Maelgwn Pendragon, will not turn them away. I will not say to the Christians that I refuse to fight. Because on this day we fight to protect the lives of every Briton! Here in our new land, where the Selgovae have sheltered us, the Angles are coming, and I will not let them take our lives. I will not see our people enslaved! On this day we hunt! On this day we punish! On this day we fight!"

The cry from our men carried through the forest.

"*Yaaaaaaahhhhhhhh!*" came the echo from the Selgovae, perched in the trees. My breath came fast. Every leaf and branch stood out in relief. I felt the thunder of the Morrigu chase through my veins. And then, far above the canopy, I heard a new cry.

I looked up into twilight in search of the source. There, above the forest canopy, a golden eagle was circling.

Gwenddolau's bird.

Uther, you are with us. Now we cannot lose.

Night dropped its mantle. The Caledonian Deep was our tunnel to travel along the flank of the Bernician army unseen as they marched ever deeper into the wood. On soundless feet, we moved past oak and elm, burn and streamlet, slipping into overhangs and hollows. We had no need of light—we needed only our senses.

We waited while they stopped, settling at last for the night. I heard thin voices speaking a thin tongue. Tonight we would strike and kill them in their sleep. Tomorrow we would strike while they were on the move.

Quiet fell, and their men at watch paced with shoulders back, too proud in the dark.

The snap of a twig. The nervous whinny of Angle horses.

Could they not feel the whites of our eyes upon them in the dark? Did they not sense the danger?

Soon you will be dead.

Maelgwn lifted his hand. *Do not strike yet.*

Closer.

Steady.

Strike now.

* * *

That night we were the terrors of the Caledonian Wood. Over three hundred we must have killed, in five different raids. By dawn our bodies were but shells, but the blood on our armor was not our own.

The Bernicians who had seen the dead would speak of it in their thin tongue with low voices.

Sleep with open eyes.

It is true what they say about the Caledonian Deep.

But we needed more men. None of us had slept, up all night butchering Angles, scaling trees like squirrels or racing like stags through the great wood.

Now we were isolated from our own hive, a horde of Angles between us and Rhydderch's army, with no way of sending word. How far north did Hussa's army stretch?

Discouragement threatened. No matter how many we slayed, too many yet lived.

And then, not long after we had returned to our camp, we were stirred from our rest by the rumbling sound of horses.

"Weapons!" I called out.

But these riders were not Angles. Cheers rose up as Artùr came speeding through the forest at the head of nearly two hundred cavalry. The men of Mannau.

"Well met!" Maelgwn lifted an arm in greeting.

"Our infantry follows," Artùr said. "They will stand with Meldred. We will join them at Pebyll."

"We are grateful," Pendragon said.

"And you've come in good time," I added. "It's great fun. Like spearing fish in a pool." I reached to grip his arm only to see blood on his armor.

"A wound, but nearly healed," he explained. "Your niece Angharad was my healer. She trains to be a priestess at Woodwick Bay in the Orcades."

"Angharad?"

Artùr was watching my face.

"I . . ." Words left me. I covered my mouth with my hand. "She lives? And she is hale?"

"Aye. She is hale. And she sends word of her love of you. She hopes to see you again. So do nothing foolish, for I would not see you break her heart."

I looked at him. Could it be? Angharad lived, and Artùr was taken with her. The Gods never ceased to surprise me.

"Thank you," I told Artùr. "And what of the blood soaking your sleeve?"

"Ach, that's Angle, of course."

"When? Riding south?"

Artùr shook his curly head, his blue eyes lit with humor. "Did you not notice my late arrival? We rode first to Trimontium, in the east, to sever their supply line."

"Begging your pardon?"

"Aye." Artùr's face split into a smile. "It only made sense. Well, lead on, then." He drew up his reins with impatience. "We cannot have Dragons stealing all our sport."

CHAPTER 47

Angharad

Din Eidyn
Northern Kingdom of Gododdin
28th of June, AD 580

The warriors of Din Eidyn could spare no provisions, for they were preparing for war. But they granted the *Cruithni* trespass through their lands, and they shared with the Picts a warning. "Travel the old Roman road a few leagues for speed, but then you'd do well to keep off it, lest you encounter the Bernician army. Tell any who question you our king has granted you passage."

Talorcan nodded at the Gododdin general, who then added, "You must hold us at no fault should the Bernicians set fire to your boats."

Talorcan turned to the quay, eyeing the boats with the look of a father leaving his child. Muirenn touched his arm. "Come, then, my love. There's no help for it now."

Angharad, too, looked back at the boats. For that was where she'd left her feathered cloak. It was only going to hinder her, she reasoned. And it had been a rather silly thing, after all.

As Muirenn and her retinue of nearly three hundred men took up their weapons and shields, the Britons who'd flocked to the fortress of Din Eidyn for safety emerged from behind its ramparts to watch them pass in awe.

"Mother, look at the priestesses!" Angharad heard a little girl exclaim.

"Hush! Don't look them in the eye," her mother commanded, burying the girl's head in her skirts.

Angharad's own people did not know her for a princess of Strathclyde. How could they? That child was no more. Angharad had lived just as long as a Pict as she ever had as a Briton. But now, for the first time, she saw herself as she appeared to a Briton's gaze: a northern priestess in a blue cloak with stern kohled eyes and coiled red hair, and when the sleeve of her cloak caught in the wind, the birds that had been needled up her arm seemed to nearly take flight.

Ariane hummed a strange tune, gazing at the sky.

As they left the Gododdin capital of Din Eidyn and began to follow the old Roman road, Angharad observed the state of her body.

Fear. Her chest was tight with it, her belly weak. Its only desire was to convince her that she must fear for her life and the lives of the people who now walked beside her. But her mind searched and reclaimed something deeper.

Trust.

She had been taught by circumstance to rely on it. Now, again and again, she returned to it. The old road they marched had been built for war by Rome. It was straight and unbroken as far as her eyes could see, leading into the heart of an impossible battle. Angharad scarcely knew how best to hold a blade.

Yet, looking at her boots, she reminded herself that the road she truly walked was the Crooked Path. It was a way of mystery and whispers, of twists and turnings that had delivered her here. It fed her, like a mother. When she saw and understood the workings that guided her from another world—the greater world—nothing felt so exhilarating.

For in seeing and understanding, Angharad became free.

The countryside was vacant as they continued south. Every tenant and villager had either been summoned to fight or hid within the safety of their nearest hillside fort. Some of the hut doors hung open, and Angharad saw tunics and cook pots strewn over bracken-covered floors. They had gathered their possessions and livestock in much haste.

The *Cruithni* stopped to sleep, then took to the road again before dawn, rested enough with oats in their stomachs. Despite the warning, the *Cruithni* had been hesitant to leave the old Roman road before they must—they would have to rely on unknown paths in the forest and could not travel nearly as fast. But then, just after sunrise, a shape in the sky caught Angharad's eye. Dark brown with white flashing and a wingspan greater than the height of most men. Ariane noticed it, too.

"Look!" Angharad pointed. "A golden eagle."

She watched its path as it soared and dipped, tipping west over the woods. "Gwenddolau's bird," she whispered. She had nearly forgotten. Diarmid had kept them in the temple. "We must leave the old road now," she told Muirenn.

Muirenn had spoken little since their march, save to bolster her men, and Talorcan looked uneasy, traveling through a foreign land by foot rather than by sea.

In a quiet moment, when they stopped at a burn, Angharad approached her. Muirenn looked up.

"Do you regret that you've come?" Angharad asked.

"No, Angharad. I do not regret it, whatever should lie ahead. I chose a life of listening. And though Bridei may think me a fool, I could not turn away." Muirenn smiled a little, then bent to clean her hands. "It is only that, since we have left our boats, my ears have gone quiet without the sound of water, and the men are eager for a plan. They feel vulnerable in this land."

"Soon we will reach the Caledonian Wood," Angharad said. "The Gods will be waiting. They will show us what to do."

"Let us hope you are right." Muirenn stood and stretched, then called for the men to keep moving. "The Gods await in the Caledonian Wood," she said. "Come, then, and follow me. We will meet our fates there."

CHAPTER 48

Lailoken

The Caledonian Wood
Kingdom of the Selgovae
1st of July, AD 580

My body ran with sweat. I'd given my gray horse to one of my men. Not a breath of wind stirred the trees, and we had been running through the forest all morning. We'd had them. I'd felt their fear. We'd divided into packs that ran the length of their flank, nearly six leagues in all, striking out of the forest, leaving bodies behind. They did not know where we might next strike. And then, from across a great distance, came the blast of battle horns. The sound was hideous and discordant. The sound let loose a panic I had not known still lived in me.

An echo of Arderydd.

I stopped and bent over, breathing. Cursing. Seven winters gone by, yet the blare of the battle horns thrust me calf-deep in mud once more, slipping, hearing Dreon cry out in agony as a spear thrust between our shields, piercing his thigh.

I beat at my head, trying in vain to summon my battle frenzy, but my fingers were trembling. Somewhere in the distance, a new war had begun.

"Lailoken!" Artùr's voice came, and I returned to myself to see him mounted, gripping the reins of a second horse. "For you," he said.

I blinked to clear my vision, for I was caught between worlds: the horror of what had been, and the impending horror of what had yet to become.

We had painted the trees with their blood. Now we must ride to face them in an open field. Now the Angles of Bernicia would come at us in swarms.

And yet here was Artùr, frowning as he looked down upon me, eager to ride. Even now Rhydderch's sword was raised. Even now the men shouted. Even now the Angle archers let rain their arrows as the cavalry charged, shattering bones. This was not Artùr's battle, though his mother was a Briton. And yet. Here Artùr sat upon his black horse.

"Yes," I said. Gripping the saddle, I yanked myself astride. I kicked the horse into a run and made three bellows of the horn at my belt. If this was the last battle I should ever fight, let it be with the last of the Dragon Warriors. Let it be with my Army of Stags. If this was the last time I would punish with my sword, let me say yes.

Yes to freedom.

Yes to honor.

Yes to death.

Theirs or my own.

We hastened toward Pebyll, where Strathclyde and Rheged had already begun their fight. We had lost some warriors. Some ran on foot, those upon horseback charging ahead. But brush clogged the forest trails, and low-hanging branches seemed to appear out of the ether, flattening us to our horses' backs or making us yank our mounts to a halt.

"Enough," Maelgwn called out. "We must take the Roman road."

It was foolhardy, pursuing an army of more than nine thousand men at a canter down the very road where they stood in pitched battle at some unknown distance ahead. The Bernician scouts would see us, no doubt. By the time we reached them, Hussa's men would be turned back upon their body to form a new head like a hydra, ready to face us even as their pitched battle raged on at their northern reach.

So be it. There was no more retreating into the safety of the wood.

I crashed through the tree line at the edge of the forest. But the road was not empty. By instinct, I jerked back on my reins, preventing my mount from colliding with another man's horse. Whinnies echoed as both our mounts reared, and I saw a blur of red and black as I swung my blade at the other rider's neck. The rider blocked it, swinging his own sword. Our eyes met.

I had run headlong into Gwrgi of Ebrauc.

I let out a cry of rage.

All I wanted was to kill.

Our swords clashed with such force it jolted our bodies, nearly sending us both from our horses. *A good idea*, I decided. Righting myself, I lunged at him, dragging him tumbling from his horse. Gwrgi's sword dropped from his hand as he hit the ground and I pinned him beneath me, slamming the pommel of my blade into his cheek. No, that wasn't right. I wanted to use my fists.

Again and again I struck him, blood coming with each strike, until Maelgwn's voice came from somewhere outside me, shouting, "Lailoken! Stop this at once!"

Gwrgi's lips stretched into a bloodied smile as I lifted my head only to find myself surrounded, a thorny garden of spears at my throat.

Maelgwn and the cavalry from Mannau emerged from the wood, weapons trained on the men of Ebrauc who surrounded me. "Draw back your spears!" Maelgwn warned them.

Gwrgi took advantage of my distraction and slammed his fist into my jaw. It knocked me just enough to the side that he rolled from beneath me and stood, eyes wild. "Come, then, Lailoken. I've waited so long. Be my first battle kill. I would begin with a Dragon today."

I wanted to murder. I would finish him with my bare hands.

But if I struck him, our retinues would fall into battle with each other. And we could not afford it. I threw back my head with a growl of frustration. A fraction of a moment and I might have caved in his head. I could not be blamed. Such things happened in the chaos of war. But now we'd been stopped. Farther up the old Roman road, a battle raged, and our allied men were bleeding with every moment we delayed.

"You are wasting time. Tell your men to fall off," I told Gwrgi.

He considered me unhurriedly, as if, somewhere up the road, his fellow Britons were not dying. If Gwrgi and his brother had ridden with all their men, they were nearly one thousand in number, a fact I believed, to judge by the endless stream of mounted men. He was thinking they could kill us all. None would be the wiser.

"Aye, you could do it," I acknowledged. "But I swear to you, we Dragons do not die easily. We will take your men with us, as many as we can. And Artùr, just there? His father is king of Mannau as well as Dalriada. Aedan loves his sons. I do not think it would be wise to try to slay him."

In the distance, four blasts sounded from the battle horn. It was the signal Rhydderch and I had spoken of. Panic struck.

"Four blasts from the battle horns signals our retreat," I shouted. "We must get to them now!"

"Ride," Gwrgi conceded, leaping back upon his horse. "Ride, I said!"

We charged along the old Roman road, and I leaned over my mount, urging it faster on, until the sounds from the battle raged about my head, and then we were upon it, our momentum carrying us like a tidal wave as we crashed into the rear of the Angle forces, running down their footmen beneath the hooves of our horses.

"Yaaaaaahhhhhhhh!" I lifted my sword, hacking the unsuspecting backs of the Angles who were racing to pursue the Britons in their retreat. But then a double blast bellowed above the fray. This horn belonged to the Angles, warning of our attack. I sucked in my breath as the vast horde before us stopped and turned to face us.

Perhaps it was battle madness, but as they lifted their weapons and charged, they were indistinguishable for a moment from a giant black boar. I was standing motionless in the river, waiting for the beast to charge. And then, with an earsplitting battle cry, the Selgovae burst from the forest, Old Man Archer first among them, his eyes wolfish with war.

The boar and the wolves. Aye. I saw it now.

"Here come the wolves," I shouted in the face of the Bernician warrior, who turned as I rode him down, cleaving his weapon arm off at the elbow. But now the Bernician archers were loosing their arrows, their points piercing Selgovae flesh, embedding themselves in the trunks of the Caledonian Wood.

I wiped my eyes clear of the armless man's blood only to block a spear thrust to my leg with the thick of my shield. Deadly points sailed from everywhere, each seeking a home. I roared out in pain as an arrow pierced my other thigh, its barb tearing deep into muscle. I knew better than to yank it. Gritting my teeth, I snapped the shaft, leaving the barb inside.

I swung my weapon in the rhythm that came from beyond thought, the one fueled by hate and elemental survival, lifting my head to try to catch sight of our men as they battled in the fray. Maelgwn and Archer had drawn tight their men, pinching the Angle forces upon two sides now, the rear and the flank. Ebrauc's and Artùr's men were entangled close by, battling with me in the thick of it.

I sensed the shift before it came, the turning of the tide. And not in our favor.

And then the army was swelling back upon us, the men roaring their fury. Artùr picked up the measure of his attack as three men charged him at once, having caught sight of his breastplate and torque. Infantry and horseback were not a sustainable pairing. Our legs were too vulnerable. But to dismount—we would be swallowed. It was an almost certain death.

"Artùr!" I shouted. "Artùr! Fall back and come round! Fall back and come round!"

He'd felt the shift come, same as me. We had to pull back and circle about, for thundering along the distant flank was the Angle cavalry. If we did not beat them out of the fray, they would hem us in from behind, trapping us against their infantry with no hope of escape. The horse beneath me had grown tired; I felt the clumsiness of his legs. I lost sight of Maelgwn even as Fendwin and I signaled our men to withdraw. Even as we shouted, Dragon Warriors were cut down all around us.

There are too many, I thought. *This has all come undone.*

Where was the second set of blasts from Rhydderch's war horns?

At the first signal, Rhydderch and Urien were to retreat, leading the Angles beyond the battlefield and over a short rise, where the land on the other side formed a vast bowl at the foot of Dùn Meldred. At the second signal, Rhydderch's men were to turn and reengage just as our cavalry came round. The Angles trapped within the bowl would be forced to battle Britons who stood on higher ground, with our cavalry closing in from behind.

At last the horn's bellow echoed between the hills, and I let out a whoop.

"Finish this fight!" Fendwin cried as we ran through their cavalry, cutting them down. I glanced over my shoulder as I crested the hill.

Bodies were everywhere, piling up as living and dead were trampled underfoot. But we had divided them—half their men were locked in combat with the Selgovae and the bastard warriors of Ebrauc on the battlefield. The other half had charged Urien's and Rhydderch's men in pursuit. Now Artùr's men and the Army of Stags pushed the Angles downslope, even as Urien's army turned to engage the Angles in a tremendous clashing of blades.

We no longer battled a force of ten thousand men. We had forced Hussa to split his army.

With our warriors clashing together, it was impossible to say exactly how many Angles we still faced, but it looked from this height to be only half his army. The other five thousand marched on to Din Eidyn. Gods be with the Gododdin there.

I could see Meldred's fortress now. I felt Eira and my sister beyond its timber walls. I spun at the sound of an approaching horse only to find Maelgwn, face bloodied but otherwise intact.

"Shield," he said, motioning to his face.

"Arrow," I replied, gesturing to my leg.

The sun was choked by dark clouds. A summer storm was coming. But Maelgwn's gaze, too, had fixed upon the fort. Rain and storm bolts were the least of our worries. If we should fail, Dùn Meldred would be overrun.

"We cannot let her die," Maelgwn said.

Together we charged into the fray.

CHAPTER 49

Languoreth

Dùn Meldred
Southern Kingdom of Gododdin
1st of July, AD 580

The rain was a thunder of pounding fists.

The army had fallen back to the foot of the fortress. The men had closed us in the great room at the sound of Meldred's battle horn, rushing out into the storm to join the fortress's last defense.

I went to sit beside Eira and the women and children from the forest.

"Take my hand?" I asked her. There was such strength in her grip. She had survived so much. Down below, I heard the Swineherds whistle, sending out their dogs. I heard them snarl and growl, the anguished cries from ripping flesh. I heard the squeal of hounds meeting swords. I heard a hundred deaths piling at the foot of the rampart.

The Angles were coming.

What a prize I would make. Strathclyde's queen. I would kill myself first.

"Let us sing," I said, in an effort to quiet the children.

Cywyllog had collapsed and was rocking to and fro, praying with the monks, but the fear upon her face showed she'd found no satisfaction.

I bent my mind to my own prayers even as I sang. The names of all those I loved who battled below on the grass.

CHAPTER 50

Angharad

Dùn Meldred
Southern Kingdom of Gododdin
1st of July, AD 580

Angharad lost sight of the eagle as they followed a cattle trail through a wood and up into the hills.

Show me, show me, Angharad begged. But nothing more came into sight. She was just about to stop when they heard the ominous blast of battle horns.

"This way," Ariane called out. They moved toward the bellow of horns, picking up speed.

Too late, they were too late.

Angharad cursed aloud. Soon the retinue was at a run, racing over hidden pastureland and mounding slopes of heather as they drew closer to the war being waged on the other side of the hill.

"Keep from sight at the hill's crest," Muirenn warned her men. "I would see where things stand."

"Angharad, you must be careful," Ariane said as Angharad crept to the hilltop to peer over the edge. A fortress stood on the far hill. And stretching in the distance beyond it, she saw the emerald canopy of a forest.

"The Caledonian Wood," she said.

Down the hillside below her, a vast and sunken place in the earth, swarming with death.

It took her without warning, her fear of what she might find as she scoured the heaving mass of men and clanging metal in search of shields and standards.

Rheged.

Strathclyde. Angharad's breath caught in her chest.

"My father is here," she said, and for the first time, Muirenn looked concerned.

"You must promise you will stay here, or you will endanger us all. I cannot be preoccupied with keeping you safe."

Angharad met Muirenn's eyes with a nod. "I have no place on a field of battle," she acknowledged. "But your ancestors are with you."

Muirenn kissed her cheek, then drew out her sword. Angharad felt strange, as if a storm gathered inside. Perhaps it was the *Cruithni*, for their blood was like water, and ever since they neared the hilltop, Angharad had felt their blood beginning to rise.

"The Britons are outnumbered," Talorcan said. "Even with our swords."

"Yes. But look. Here comes their cavalry. And there! The Britons beneath the fortress have turned round to fight. Now is the time, Talorcan. We will attack from this hill and hem them in." Muirenn turned, lifting her voice for all her retinue to hear, her heavy silver torque catching in the light. "Talorcan is right. The Britons are outnumbered. But we are not two hundred eighty-eight men. We are two hundred eighty-eight *Cruithni*! And we do not come here to fight for the Britons. We come here to fight for ourselves. For if these vile men triumph today, next will they come for our people! Next will they come for *our* families! Today they will not triumph!" Muirenn shouted. "On this day, we will water the field with Angle blood!"

The battle roar of the Picts sent a shock along Angharad's spine.

They were in hiding no more. She took Ariane's hand as Muirenn and her men propelled themselves down the hillside, the fury of their war cry making the men below stop mid-strike.

A horn sounded from beneath the fortress ramparts, and within the mass of tangling bodies, each side summoned their men to face a new fight.

For a moment, it was as if the battle had frozen in confusion.

This was not their war. Who had these wild, painted warriors from the north come here to fight? But then Muirenn reached her first Angle and, with one swift move, ducked to sever the tendons in the backs of his legs with a single strike.

"*Yaaaahhhhh!*" she cried. The Angle man dropped, spasming upon the ground.

The sight of the Picts sprinting downhill, dispatching Angles left and right, brought new life to the Britons. The warriors lifted their spears, faces fierce with fury and eyes filled with hope. The very earth shook with the rise of their battle cry, a roar of welcome and thanks that summoned forces greater than any could understand. The battle snapped back into motion. As Angharad watched, one of the *Cruithni* took a cluster of arrows to his chest.

"Pray with me," Angharad said.

"Yes," Ariane agreed. "But first, it is time at last that you wore this." She reached into her deerskin bag and drew out the folded bulk of Angharad's cloak.

Angharad stepped back. "But I left it aboard the ship," she said.

"A mistake you will not make again. Come, Angharad, and don it. You are a novice no more."

Angharad fastened the cloak about her shoulders. The feathers stirred in the growing wind. Ariane looked to the darkening sky. Angharad reached for her hands. They lifted their intertwined fingers to a sky full of gathering cloud, chanting a charm of protection.

Charm for the Britons.
Charm for the Picts.
Charm against arrow,
Charm against sword.
Charm against spear,
Charm against peril.
Charm against harm in this field of battle.

It began in monotone as Angharad and Ariane swayed upon the hill, arms lifted to draw down the power of the sky. Angharad squeezed her eyes shut to block out the blare of battle, for words had no power if one did not believe. They chanted the words again and again, 'til the words were a circle without beginning or end and their voices became vessels, deepening in tone. *Charm for the Britons. Charm for the Picts . . .*

Angharad rocked as the wind whipped her hair.

The air of the battlefield crackled with the promise of lightning and thunderous rain, and though her lips did not cease in their chanting, deep from the place within whispers, Angharad summoned her, calling out her name.

Cailleach Bheur.

There was such vast power sweeping above the fields, even the golden eagle had taken to its nest to brave the coming storm. Angharad reached out with her senses, letting the storm blow through her body. Her head swam with pulses, and still she drew it in.

Charm against arrow. Charm against sword . . .

She was not big enough to contain it. The force breathing beneath her was a frenzy. A bringer of chaos. A loud rumble of thunder made her open her eyes. And then the gray-black sky burst open, drenching every warrior on the battlefield to their marrow in an instant.

"It is only a summer storm," Ariane said. "Do not be afraid."

They chanted on.

Rain beat on their heads. Down on the battlefield, men's faces ran in rivers of blood.

"What have I done?" Angharad whispered, her hands flying to her mouth. The soil had been churned up by the boots of thousands of men. Now that soil became slick as an eel's belly. Men slipped and scrambled, ankle-deep in mud. "Oh, what have I done?"

Ariane's voice was stern. "You can do nothing the Gods do not grant. Look now. The Angles scramble and slip—they cannot gain purchase on the slope beneath the rampart."

It was true—she could see if she squinted in the rain. They had slowed in their attack, and the Britons took advantage, sending their spears sailing even as unseen archers let fly their rain of arrows. Angles were falling back in heaps, wounded or dead.

And then Angharad saw him as he mounted the crest of the distant hill.

His hair was plastered with water as if he'd stepped from the sea. He bled from his brow, and as he pushed his mount over the rise, he pivoted sharply in his saddle to slash at the men who pursued him.

Artùr.

Goddess above, what was he doing here?

And there beside him was Cai.

Protect him, protect them, she begged, tipping her head to the storm.

The field below was an ocean of dead bodies. The rain pounded down. There were more Angles lifeless than there were yet fighting.

Angharad felt their fear.

Your beast has abandoned you, she thought into the wild whipping of the storm. *All there is left to do is flee.*

As if they had heard her, a blast of a horn sounded the Bernicians' retreat as the men clawed from their death pit, fleeing on foot or kicking their wounded horses to find refuge in the Caledonian Wood.

Artùr and his men swung round on their mounts, taking off in pursuit.

Talorcan struck down Angles as they scrambled to race from the battlefield, one after another. Bodies piled at the ramparts of the fortress. Archers in brown cloaks, some of whom held blades, followed the Angles unhurriedly, to finish them in the wood.

The worst of the storm had assailed them, and now, as the dark clouds swept north, the rain lessened, becoming little more than a finicky mist. Below on the battlefield, the warriors stood, weapons still gripped, surveying the field of the dying and the dead.

Silence reigned.

And then, as they looked to one another, Briton and Pict, their shoulders sank in relief. As whoops of victory rose up, smiles creased their bloodied faces.

"They've done it." Angharad turned to Ariane. "They've done it." She threw herself into Ariane's embrace.

"Come now, Angharad of Strathclyde," Ariane said, smoothing the feathers of her cloak. "Your homecoming awaits."

CHAPTER 51

Languoreth

Dùn Meldred
Southern Kingdom of Gododdin
1st of July, AD 580

I sat alone on a pinewood bench, eyes closed and hands clasped. My body was wrung out. I could not push the hand of fate. I could only sit and let the images of those I loved fill the blackness behind my eyes, trying not to jump at each new blast of the battle horn.

And then, just when I dreaded the worst of my own fears, I tilted my head, suddenly listening.

"Do you hear that?" I asked sharply.

The monks across the room looked up from their prayers. Cywyllog blinked. "I hear nothing."

"Precisely." I stood, hurrying to the door.

"Do not open it!" Cywyllog commanded.

I lifted the bolt, throwing the door open wide, and the room was flooded with the echoes of cheers.

I raced outside and climbed the platform of the inner rampart, un-prepared for the sight that met me below.

So many dead.

"Oh no. Oh no, please . . ." I whispered, scurrying down, pounding upon the door of the inner rampart, shouting, "Let me out! Let me out!"

The men did as I said, and the look I gave them was one of wonderment and trepidation. We had won. We had done it.

Yet who had survived?

I ran down the hill, slipping, my dress caking with mud, tears choking my voice, as I gestured for Meldred's men to cast open the outer gates.

The warriors were coming now, so many wounded. Blood, mud, and gore obscuring their faces.

"Rhydderch? Rhydderch?" I cried, my voice sounding panicked as a child's. Gripping the arm of the first man I could reach. "Have you seen my husband? My brother? Have you seen the king?" The men shook their heads, and as they poured past, up into the safety and dry warmth of the fortress, I reached the battlefield and stopped, struck by the horrors that lay at my feet. "Rhydderch! Lailoken!"

Maelgwn, my heart yet longed to scream. And then, in the distance, a most curious sight caught my eye. A retinue of strange warriors, walking slowly across the field. They wore gray hoods. Their hair was plaited, the look upon their faces grim. Mud darkened their bodies in the places they were exposed, but I could see beneath the smears of earth that animals had been pricked into the surface of their skin.

"Picts," I said aloud. At the front of their clann strode a man with black hair and two fish upon his face. And beside him, three women. Rain bedraggled all, save the one who was tall. She wore a cloak that fluttered in a thousand fingers as she moved. A cloak made of feathers. She stopped at the sight of me, standing stock-still, and I squinted to better see her face beneath her hood.

Who was this mysterious woman? Had it been she who had summoned the Picts?

A pale arm emerged from her cloak as the retinue she walked before stopped, and I saw a trail of birds upon her wrist as she reached to push back the hood of her cloak. Her mass of tawny hair was bound back in coiled plaits, some of which had come loose, falling about her freckled face. Her gray eyes regarded me. Then her voice came, carrying across the field of the lost, the field of the dead.

"Mother."

It could not be.

It could not be after all these years.

"Angharad? Angharad," I cried as I burst into tears, hands covering my mouth as I ran, stumbling, not fast enough, over dead bodies, nearly slipping and falling as I fought just to reach her, yet the beautiful young woman stood motionless. Why did she not come to me?

"Angharad!" My voice was a wail, as if she were some apparition who might just as easily disappear. I stumbled over the lifeless leg of a fallen man into the space before her, and we stood, eyes searching.

"Oh, my love. Oh, my sweet." I closed the distance between us, clutching her to my breast as if she were yet a child, the relief of the solidness of her body in my arms overwhelming my senses. "Oh, my love." I rocked her, my hands moving in disbelief to her hair, the curve of her back, her face as I drew back to look at her. "You are alive," I said. My voice was weighted with as much heartbreak as wonder. "How have you come here?"

Speak. I wanted to shake her.

She had only called out my name.

Speak so I will know you are real and not some trick of the Gods.

But who was I to demand of her, I who had given her up? I who had forsaken her? The eyes that looked back into mine were those of the child I once knew, but they held the look of a stranger. My heart fractured to shards in the cavity of my chest.

She thought a moment, her acorn-colored brows drawing together in a frown. "I suppose it all began with a dream."

"Will you tell me? Please. I want to know all. But you have been in battle. Oh, my love. Come back to the fortress."

I gripped her hands, unable to release her. But I had been so shocked at the sight of my daughter, so suddenly returned, and in the midst of such a place, that I had forgotten her company. "I am sorry; forgive me. I am entirely overcome. Please. You are most welcome. Follow me back to the hall." I looked to them now, my face full of gratitude, and my eyes caught on those of the dark-haired woman who had been standing beside my daughter all the while, unnoticed.

"Languoreth," the woman said, with a slight bow of her head. She had never been one to paint her emotions upon her face. Her face, that same delicate complexion like the underbelly of a leaf, her unflinching blue eyes, not a gray hair upon her head and hardly a wrinkle upon her skin.

"It cannot be." I stepped back, looking between the two of them. "Ariane?"

She smiled then, a thing I remembered was once quite a rare sight, and a flood of emotions threatened to drown me. Disbelief. Joy. Sadness.

Anger.

I sucked in a breath. There was too much here. Too much. I needed time for us all to speak. And Rhydderch. Lailoken. I could not bear the thought they might not have lived to see Angharad returned.

"Come." I nodded to them all. "We are still sorting through the living and the dead. There will be plenty of time for speaking once we have found those who remain."

CHAPTER 52

Angharad

Dùn Meldred
Southern Kingdom of Gododdin
1st of July, AD 580

The hall of Meldred was full to bursting, though Muirenn and Talorcan kept clear of the far end of the great room, where the priests dined.

Angharad could not keep her eyes from trailing to the faces whose memory she had battled so long to keep. The graceful sweep of her mother's brow. Her father's eyes, a wintry reflection of her own, tracking each movement she made as if she might slip from the room. He had wept when he held her, but she had difficulty summoning tears.

It had been so long.

She could not offer her parents the child they had lost, the little girl she knew they yet wished her to be. And as her mother met her eyes across the room with a hint of a smile, she saw its edges were touched with sorrow.

Angharad felt out of place here. With Ariane, among the Picts, was where Angharad felt most at home.

Wind and weather. The waterfall had told her Eachna was made of water. *Wind and weather push water about.* Now Angharad had begun to understand something of herself. But she was only at the beginning. She knew she could not stay.

Artùr had not returned—he and his men, along with the Dragons, had finished the Angles in the wood, and Artùr had begun his long journey back to Mannau. She realized, though it did not matter, that while she had seen him, Artùr had not even known Angharad was there.

But there was Eira. And Lailoken sat beside Angharad, his strong hand pressing hers in reassurance as he adjusted the poultice Ariane had bound to his thigh. And there were many yet in need of healing. Angharad and Ariane and Languoreth had tended the wounded, side by side.

Angharad's knowledge already surpassed that of the woman who had borne her. "A priestess." Her mother had looked at her in wonder. "Angharad, you astonish me."

But this overwarm room of warriors and queens, petty kings and chieftains, was deafening with its thousands of unspoken voices. Angharad's senses felt burned by wind and by lightning, and now the inner voices of the Britons cried out far too loud. That one was thinking of his wife. That one was envious of her father, the king. Maelgwn Pendragon, sitting by the hearth, may have had his thoughtful green eyes trained on the fire, but they strayed in stolen moments, lighting upon her mother.

Her uncle turned as if she had spoken her discomfort aloud. "It is only for a short time," he assured her. "On the morrow, most shall ride away." He bent his sandy head in a bid for her gaze. Angharad looked at him. "Do you know what I would say?" he asked.

It calmed her to search him. Like slipping into her cloak.

"Yes," she answered after a moment.

He nodded then, more to himself than to Angharad. "Well, then," he said. "We have spoken it all."

CHAPTER 53

Lailoken

Grey Mare's Tail Waterfall
Kingdom of the Selgovae
September, AD 580

I had woken that morning at the foot of Black Mountain, unable to recapture my dream. There had been a woman there. A stranger. A girl to whom I'd been speaking. There had been a longing vast as a range of mountains.

The dream echoed its importance, tugging at my memory. Somehow I knew it might return if only I visited the falls.

I stood long, gazing up at the snowy cataract, thinking of the Keeper of the Falls. And then I sensed him, as if I had the ability to summon him, though I had discovered, of course, it had been the Keeper of the Falls who had truly summoned me.

He is more than a shade, I thought. *He is a god of place.*

I had thought it a myth that in the days of Rome, Wisdom Keepers had given their lives in an effort to become gods. Perhaps it was because the way of accomplishing such a feat had been lost. But now I understood that the Mad Keeper had not been driven to his death by any loss of his senses. He had given his life in an effort to protect his people from the coming of the Ninth Legion and, in so doing, had become a God of the Falls. He had returned to warn me of the Angles, and so it would seem he had given his life not only to protect the Selgovae but to protect us all. Perhaps he had not returned; rather, he had never departed. His tale was one of patterns, of beasts that die back or are slaughtered but never truly fall away.

Now I sensed his footsteps, measured, trailing after as I followed the goat path back downhill, settling to sit in the little gray cell built for dreaming within the old wall of stone.

Close your eyes, I thought I heard him say.

I took a breath and did as he bade, feeling myself dropping deep, then deeper again.

I pushed aside thoughts of how I must soon return to Partick.

How we had won a battle, but now surely faced many more to come. The Angles had failed to take Din Eidyn, but returned now to Bernicia and to Deira to regather their strength.

Soon war would come again.

Deeper, the Keeper said. *Close your eyes, and I will tell you a tale.*

There were temples once. They dotted the land like pinpricks into veins, tapping into the power that thrummed beneath the land of the living; the land of the dead. There, within the temple walls, you would sleep in a cell and dream in darkness, and when you woke and spoke of owls whose eyes burned yellow in the black, of plunging beneath the deep gray waters of a loch, the Keeper would ponder and tell you its meaning.

There were star trackers once, who lifted their eyes to winter skies within circles of stone. They sang songs of summoning, and through the long, hollow halls the ancestors came, forgetting their earthly ends of ash or decay. They came to bear witness, to bind our treaties. On Samhain, when the days stretched thin, they came to sit at the table and dine with the children they'd borne. They came to be remembered.

There were temples once, you were telling the girl who had come, for she was trying to remember. But the girl sat beside us as if we were not there. She walked a land vacant as a desert, a land of shades and blowing grasses. She walked and sought the places where temples once stood, but for too long they had lain altered, neglected.

For too long, the ancestors of the girl had been sleeping.

You were weeping for them, then. All the lost children. Rocking beneath the wave of their sorrow.

A thousand times, and a thousand times again, they will come searching, calling your name. In distant times, they will summon you.

And because of your sacrifice, you will hear them.

You will hear them and return.

And they will remember.

Myrddin, they will cry out.

Myrddin.

ACKNOWLEDGMENTS

Across the pond, I'm grateful to John Hume at Moffat Wigwams, who shares a love of history and inspired me to write about the Ninth Legion. Thanks to the Armstrong family for their time and generosity of spirit. To Teresa Johnston, for her friendship and excellent fact-checking of the flora and fauna in this book, and Glenn Gordon, for his expert guidance and good company. Thanks to James of Mheall Cottage near Dunadd for being a wonderful host in Argyll. On the Isle of Lismore, I'm grateful to Robert Smith and Iris Piers of Explore Lismore, and to Ina MacColl, Barbara McDougall, Jennifer Baker, and all the people at the Lismore Gaelic Heritage Centre for their time and wisdom, and for the use of their wonderful library. You were right: it can't be done in two days. I hope to return so I might do your stories justice. Thanks to Caoimhe Ní Ghormáin at the Library of Trinity College Dublin for pointing me in the right direction. I owe a huge debt of gratitude to Mr. Alexander McCulloch and his family in Gatehouse of Fleet for their warmth, hospitality, and interest, and for the time Mr. McCulloch took to show me around Trusty's Hill. I'm not through with Rheged yet! Samantha Cooper, owner of 23 Enigma in Glasgow, shared her wisdom. In Fortingall, I'm grateful to the Fortingall Hotel and the gracious landowner who directed me to the "White Fort." As always, I'm indebted to the National Museum of Scotland, Historic Scotland, and my friends at Chatelherault

Country Park, who I hope haven't forgotten me. Thank you to Kyle Gray for brunch and good times whenever I visit. And last but never least, thanks to Adam Ardrey, whose nonfiction books *Finding Merlin* and *Finding Arthur* are required reading for any who enjoy my novels.

In the US, I feel so fortunate to be published by VP and executive editor Trish Todd at Atria, who has believed in my writing from word one, and brought these books into being with the magnificence that is her standard. Your wisdom and support make all the difference. Thanks also to senior vice president and publisher Libby McGuire, VP of independent retail sales Wendy Sheanin and the incredible sales team at S&S, Isabel DaSilva in marketing, and my publicist Megan Rudloff. A big thank-you to production editor Benjamin Holmes for his patience and professionalism in pulling everything together, and to David Chesanow, who has ruined me for all other copy editors with his attention to detail and desire for excellence. Thanks to Fiora Elbers-Tibbitts for her grace and kind attention to this book.

To Faye Bender at the Book Group, the sort of agent one tries to dream up but doesn't know how until one meets her. I'm so glad to have your guidance, acumen, perspective, and support. A huge thank-you to Bruna Pappandrea and the team at Made Up Stories for their enthusiasm and support in developing *The Lost Queen*. And to Jennifer Kent, whose vision is unlike any other. Thank you for diving in with equal parts genius and care. To Flora Hackett at William Morris Endeavor, for connecting with me and Languoreth. We're so happy to have you.

Thank you to the good people at Simon & Schuster Canada for making such beautiful editions of my books, and to Simon & Schuster Audio for bringing my stories to more readers, especially those who love to hear Toni Frutin say pretty much anything in her Scottish accent.

To my family, friends, and Tribe, who have shown me so much

love and support, especially in the past two years as I worked so hard on this book. You fed me, encouraged me, exercised me, listened to me, hugged me, watched my son so I could write, and made me laugh when I needed it most. I hope you know who you are, and how special you are to me. You lift me up. I couldn't have made it to the finish line without you. I'm so lucky to be loved by you. But a very special thank-you goes out to Linda Johanson, mother, confidante, and creative sounding board. I'm so thankful that out of all the mamas in the world, I got you.

AUTHOR'S NOTE

In her day, Languoreth of Cadzow was one of the most powerful women in Scotland. Today, you'd be hard-pressed to find a native who has heard of her.

How could a woman of such influence be wiped so effectively from the collective memory of her own people?

The answer to this question lies in the nature of the warrior-king society of early historic Scotland, in the enemies Languoreth made in her lifetime—men of a new patriarchal religion that sought to subvert the matriarchy that had held sway in the British Isles for well over a millennium—and in the explosion of her brother Lailoken's reputation, which would transform him, over time, from flesh and blood into a fictional icon: the wizard we know today as Merlin.

Languoreth's husband, Rhydderch Hael, was a Briton who ruled the kingdom of Strathclyde from approximately AD 580 to AD 614. Scholars acknowledge Rhydderch's history, along with the figures he encountered, men like Aedan mac Gabrahn, Columba of Iona, Urien of Rheged, and Mungo, also known as Saint Kentigern. They know the children descended from Rhydderch and Languoreth's union, who surface in medieval Welsh Triads, saints' lives, and king lists.* Languoreth is named as the wife of Rhydderch in the twelfth-century *Life of St. Kentigern*, and her memory is preserved in the fourteenth-century *Red Book of Hergest*. She's remembered as Rhydderch's adulterous queen in a piece of Glasgow folklore called "The Fish and the Ring."

These mentions amount to more early medieval "press" than can be claimed by any one of Languoreth's female contemporaries, yet scholars still declare Rhydderch a historical figure even as they relegate his wife to the realm of fiction—if they mention her name at all.

Of course, I am not unbiased. I've devoted a decade of research to Languoreth and Lailoken's history with the sole intention of resurrecting the people I believe inspired an ancient yet enduring legend.

The Forgotten Kingdom, the second book in the Lost Queen Trilogy, brought unique challenges, including the study of three additional cultures: the Scots of Dalriada, the Picts, and the Anglo-Saxons. Characters were roaming the length and breadth of Scotland, which meant the introduction of new flora and fauna. I also had to piece together two very different historical battles, the records of which are scant: the Battle of Arderydd and the Battle of the Caledonian Wood. Throughout the process, I noted things I wanted to share with readers so they, too, could explore the truth behind the fiction.

The Battles

The Battle of Arderydd, one of the most violent and least remembered civil conflicts in Scottish history, took place in the year AD 573, according to the *Annales Cambriae*. Pitting Languoreth's husband against her brother and Lailoken against his young nephew, it tore her

---

*King lists are medieval genealogies preserved through oral tradition before being written down. They admittedly veer into the world of fiction, as later medieval rulers in Wales sought to bolster their pedigrees by attaching themselves to heroes of *yr Hen Ogledd*, "the Old North."

family apart. The ramifications are discussed in a "Dialogue between Myrddin and His Sister," in which Myrddin's sister states that she lost both a son and a daughter. It was difficult enough to write the death of Rhys, so I allowed Angharad to survive and embark upon a journey of her own.

Both William Forbes Skene and my colleague Adam Ardrey believe Arthur and Aedan mac Gabrahn played a role at this battle on the side of the victors. But this is something that has given me pause.

There is no mention of Aedan mac Gabrahn's involvement at Arderydd in any surviving text that deals with the battle. Skene argued the nearby "Arthuret" Hills carry a memory of Arthur, which might prove his victory at Arderydd. And while Adam Ardrey suggests that Aedan might have sided with Rhydderch to gain support for his claim to the kingship of Dalriada, I've come to a different conclusion.

First, I don't believe Aedan mac Gabrahn needed Strathclyde's support to take the throne of Dalriada, a situation that came down to its own civil war between Aedan and his half brother, Eoganan. Aedan won, and chased Eoganan into "retirement." There is no record of Strathclyde's involvement.

Second, as a Scot embroiled in his own battles in Dalriada, why would Aedan offer men for a battle between Brythonic kings down by Hadrian's Wall?*

Third, while there is no textual evidence that supports Aedan's or Arthur's involvement at Arderydd, two often-ignored texts provide some compelling clues about the nature of Aedan's relationship with Lailoken: the medieval poem "Peiryan Vaban" ("Commanding Youth") and a Welsh Triad that remembers the "Three Unrestrained Ravagings of the Island of Britain."

---

*The battle of Arderydd was in AD 573. In AD 574 Aedan took the throne of Dalriada. From the chronicles we know Aedan participated in more than one battle against Eoganan in the Argyll area in the year preceding his ascension to the throne.

"Peiryan Vaban" is a rare poem attributed to Myrddin. In it, Myrddin is portrayed as a warrior, speaking to an unknown but powerful youth of the violent revenge "Aeddan" will take upon Rhydderch for the death of Gwenddolau in a battle, presumably at Arderydd.

Then, in the Triads, a memory is preserved of a violent raid upon the court of Rhydderch by Aedan: "*When Aedan the Wily came to the court of Rhydderch the Generous at Alclud, he left neither food nor drink nor beast alive.*" The date of any such raid is unknown, and Lailoken may or may not have been present, but this is the reason I've included Aedan's raid on Clyde Rock in this book.

Other evidence also leads me to believe it unlikely that Aedan formed an alliance with British kings against Gwenddolau. In Adomnan's *Life of Saint Columba*, Rhydderch asks the saint whether he should fear death by Aedan mac Gabrahn's hand. Later, Myrddin is brought from exile to become one of Rhydderch's counsellors, or so the story goes. Myrddin was effectively an enemy of the state, languishing in exile for nearly seven years. It seemed unlikely that sheer nepotism could win him back a place at court, especially given the religious tensions in Strathclyde at the time, which are detailed in Mungo's hagiography. It makes much more sense if Lailoken was able to offer something that Rhydderch could not attain on his own: an alliance with Aedan mac Gabrahn. It was only after 580, when Lailoken emerged from exile, that Aedan mac Gabrahn joined a confederation of Brythonic kings to help fight the Angles of Bernicia.

The Battle of the Caledonian Wood is listed as the one of the Nine Battles of Arthur by Ninnius. For those who want to learn more, Adam Ardrey has written a very intelligent re-creation of it in his book *Finding Arthur*.

The Anglo-Saxon Invasion

The Anglo-Saxon Invasion was actually a series of migrations, battles, and raids that went on for many decades in different parts of Scotland and England. These events took place much later in Scotland than in England, where Romanized towns were conquered earlier and with greater ease. In fact, there is evidence that Clyde Rock was still a Brythonic stronghold well into the eighth century, a date that does not hold with Anglo-Saxon occupation as it is claimed to have occurred in the rest of Britain. In the first two books of my series, we see the beginning of their conquest, one that would push the Britons into the south and west of the British Isles, creating strongholds in Wales, Cornwall, the Isle of Man, and across the channel in Brittany. As the Britons of *Yr Hen Ogledd*, "the Old North," were forced from their ancestral lands to find new homes among their distant kin, they took their stories with them. This is how the legend of Arthur and Merlin came to be claimed by southwestern England, Wales, and Brittany.

Historical Accuracy

I strive to present an accurate portrayal of sixth-century Scottish life, but the post-Roman and Early Historic periods are among the least archaeologically represented in all of the United Kingdom. While my extrapolations are based on archaeological or anthropological evidence, I am neither an archaeologist nor a historian, so I don't doubt there will be argument over some of my choices, and I've likely made some mistakes.

In central and southern Scotland, halls were most often built from timber with thatched roofs, which burned easily during raiding and war, or rotted away, leaving little more than postholes. Many Scots lived in huts of wattle and daub that had changed little since the Iron Age and left almost no trace. New structures were built on top of these sites by conquering peoples and subsequent generations, further obscuring any archaeological record. In recent years, archaeologists have created some well-rendered digital reconstructions of sites, and I've referred to these whenever I could.

Iron Age stone brochs had multiple levels, as did Roman buildings built on Scottish soil. We do know from the postholes that hall beams were massive, and I believe such posts could certainly have supported an upper level. Given the lofted roofs of halls, I suspect ladders or stairs might have been used to make the most of space.

In this book and the last, Partick is a walled city. There's no evidence of that as of yet, and walled towns were more prevalent in the years that followed. However, when I imagined Languoreth as a girl approaching the town for the very first time in *The Lost Queen*, the walls were there, brooding, with guards atop, so here I'm guilty of creating a scenario not fully grounded in fact. This is a novel, after all.

There is written memory of a market or fair in Kenmore at Loch Tay that occurred around July 26 until the beginning of the twentieth century. I've shifted it to October to suit my needs.

Language

In *The Forgotten Kingdom*, it's the Picts who protect their names, but in reality it was likely a convention of Britons and Picts alike. As a culture that lived and remembered via oral tradition, the Britons occupied a world in which the spoken word held tremendous power, and names were sacred. It's also evident that there were titles as well as more intimate family names, probably used just among kin—for example, Uther Pendragon versus Gwenddolau. In the author's note for *The Lost Queen* I talk about the origins of Lailoken's name and its transformation into Myrddin, pronounced "MEER-thin."

The Britons and the Scots were part of a cultural group that spoke similar languages, so, for lack of a better term, we refer to them both as Celtic.

We don't know what language the Picts spoke, but the Venerable Bede listed it as distinct from that of the Britons, Scots, or Angles. It is now more commonly thought to have been related to Brythonic. Still, very few Pictish words survive, so I've used one wherever I could. *Cartait*, mentioned in King and Bishop Cormac's *Glossary*, which dates from around AD 900, means "pin" or "thorn."

I've used modern Welsh words (*hennain, taid*) in places because the Brythonic or Old Welsh versions have been lost, and I wanted to honor the language as I was able. Throughout, I've substituted Gaelic words where Brythonic or Old Welsh words are lost or unknown—*Cailleach*, for example. Thus, the languages in this book are a bit of an artistic re-creation. I apologize to any native speakers for inevitable errors in my re-creation of the linguistic diversity of the time.

Regarding place names, I tried to balance historic integrity with accessibility for readers. Sometimes I opted for ease of pronunciation: Partick is modern, Pertnech is old. Other times, one word was chosen over another, more accurate word to lend a more relatable sense of atmosphere. *Aye*, for example, is a form of assent used in Scotland today, possibly originating in the sixteenth century, which makes it technically non-Brythonic, as well as a thousand years too late for use in my book. However, one word for yes in Welsh is *ie* (pronounced "Ee-ya"). Given that the two languages are related, I felt that *aye* sufficiently captured the spirit of the expression and how it might have been used.

Fortingall is modern, while Dùn Déagh is an older name for the modern-day town of Dundee. Today, the Crooked Glen of Stones is called Glen Lyon. Ceann Mòr refers to modern-day Kenmore at the head of Loch Tay.

Occasionally, I integrate lines of epic poetry directly into dialogue.

"When the light of day comes, there shall be prophesy" comes from "Peiryan Vaban" (translated by J. K. Bollard in *The Romance of Merlin*).

Angharad

Triads were used by Celtic storytellers as mnemonic devices. They were effectively groupings of three—the three savage raids, the three bravest men—that served as an index to a collection of stories banked in their memories. Named as one of the "Three Lively Maidens of the Island of Britain" was "Angharad Ton Velen, daughter of Rhydderch Hael." That Angharad is mentioned in a triad suggests there was once a story about her, but it has been lost. "Ton Velen" translates roughly to "tawny waves." Historian Tim Clarkson speculated that the poem or tale "may have been composed by a bard at the royal court of Alt Clut, perhaps in the years around 600." He added, "Traditions of uncertain reliability, preserved at Glasgow Cathedral in the twelfth century, identify Rhydderch Hael's wife as Languoreth, Queen of Alt Clut. This lady, who may have been a native of the Hamilton area, was presumably Angharad's mother."

Unfortunately, we know next to nothing about her, so aside from her name and relationship to Languoreth, Angharad is largely my invention.

Myrddin in Exile

In the little town of Moffat, there exists folk memory that Myrddin took refuge nearby after the Battle of Arderydd. In poems attributed to Myrddin, Rhydderch is mentioned as an adversary trying to hunt Myrddin down and kill him, and Myrddin complains of the hardships of hiding deep in the Caledonian Forest after fleeing from the battle. During his exile, it was said that Myrddin went mad, something we might recognize today as PTSD.

I believe Nikolai Tolstoy was the first author to place Myrddin's

exile at Hart Fell, located in the Moffat Hills. When I visited the site, I made what could be a remarkable discovery.

Literal readings of the poems in the Myrddin cycle have led many to believe that Myrddin lived at the spring itself, thigh deep in snow, sheltering beneath an overhang of rock. But in 2017, I visited Hart Fell with Scottish mountaineering guide Glenn Gordon, and I noticed intriguing marks on the Ordinance Survey map. Near the base of Hart Fell were the archaeological remains of a burnt mound, as well as what looks like a raised ditch and possibly hut circles.

Burnt mounds, or *fulachta fiadh*, were man-made outdoor pits where heated stones were used for cooking, washing, and, some archaeologists believe, ritual bathing. Water from a burn was diverted and heated with the rocks to boil meat or, if covered with a wicker frame and animal skins, make for a wonderful way to bathe and keep warm in cold weather. They originated long before the early medieval period, but some were still in use in Lailoken's time. As the son of a petty king or chieftain, Lailoken would have been used to the comforts of hall life, a fact he bemoans in the exile corpus. Though there's no way to know the dates of the site without further investigation, I find it difficult to believe Lailoken would have sheltered under a rock during winter when there might have been a perfectly serviceable settlement at the base of the hill itself. The view from the burnt-mound area is quite good—one could see men approaching from a great distance and retreat up the hillside if needed.

Historical Sites

Clyde Rock (also known as Dùn Breatainn, Alt Clut, and Alcluith) is known today as Dumbarton Castle. It boasts the longest recorded history of any Scottish stronghold and is lovingly maintained by Historic Environment Scotland. "The Beak," where some early medieval buildings might have stood, was leveled in the seventeenth century to house a powder magazine, but fragments of glass and jewelry dating to the sixth and seventh centuries were discovered at a site below.

To help protect this incredible historic location, rock climbing is prohibited, and any damage to the mount is a criminal offense.

Any archaeological remains of Cadzow Fortress are likely buried beneath and beside the ruins of a later medieval castle. The grounds have been wonderfully preserved by the people of Chatelherault Country Park in Hamilton, including the woods that Lailoken and Languoreth walked, and you can visit the mysterious Roman earthworks nestled in an ancient stand of oaks.

The site of the Battle of Arderydd is on private land. What remains is a Norman-era motte-and-bailey fortification built on top of a much older site, dating to the early medieval period or even the Iron Age, but to my knowledge it's never been excavated.

You can find the Grey Mare's Tail waterfall and the Tail Burn Fort outside of Moffat. The Iron Age bank and ditch were built approximately two thousand years ago. Some archaeologists believe it was a purely defensive site, while others argue that it must have possessed some ritual significance. The curse and the Keeper of the Falls are my invention. Wild goats roam the landscape, and it's stunningly beautiful. If you visit, please keep to the trails, and stay safely away from the mouth of the falls.

The Caledonian Wood once covered an estimated 1.5 million hectares, or about 3.7 million acres, across the whole of central Scotland. It was home to lynx, wild boar, elk, wolves, bears, and many other animals. The Romanized citizens living below Hadrian's Wall in the first century AD believed the forest beyond the wall was full of shades (ghosts) and rife with man-eating beasts. As of 2018, the wood is undergoing an estimated £23 million "re-wilding" in order to remove nonnative pine plantations and reforest it with native trees like oak, elm, and Scotch pine.

At Fortingall you can visit the ancient yew. It's believed that, prior to the establishment of the monastery, it was a pre-Christian site. My description of the bark does not come from touching the tree, which is prohibited. The residents of Fortingall are grateful for the care and respect of visitors.

The Picts

Little is known about the Picts, who, during the sixth century, controlled much of Scotland, from north of the Firth of Forth up to Orkney. They left behind an impressive class of stone carvings, but there are still far more questions than answers when it comes to where they originated, what language they spoke, and what became of them.

Bridei is a historical Pictish king who warred with Aedan mac Gabrahn, and the chronicler Adomnan mentions his head druid, Briochan. Talorcan is a Pictish name, while Muirenn, Eachna, and Fetla were invented for this book. There is controversy regarding whether the Picts were really tattooed. Given the parallel significance of tattooing in many other cultures, I decided to make use of the concept. I was inspired by Osprey Publishing's books on the Picts,* and the practice was useful to help the Picts develop a unique identity among other the peoples sharing their great island.

Religion

In our modern, technology-obsessed age, it's difficult to truly imagine the ancient mind. Languoreth and Lailoken lived in a time when curses were thought to have power. The natural world was animate, filled with gods and goddesses and spirits of all sorts. The arrival of Christianity did not alter this. Early saints and Celtic druid priests professed the ability to work miracles with equal facility—Columba

---

* *Pictish Warrior AD 297–841* and *Strongholds of the Picts*, Osprey Publishing.

and Mungo included. The collection of prayers and charms to cure all sorts of ailments found in Alexander Carmichael's nineteenth-century *Carmina Gadelica* is a beautiful testament to the preservation of a very ancient way of thinking and believing, in which the names of goddesses were merely substituted with those of Mary, Jesus, or various saints.

In the years before Christ, Greek chroniclers exploring the British Isles told tales of men or women who professed to be able to control the weather and predict the future. Of course, the belief in "second sight" is one that transcends culture and dates back indefinitely. In lending Angharad's character such gifts, I wanted to show second sight in the way the Celts themselves might have experienced it, both for the outsider and for the person who possessed the gift.

Given that I write about a time that's so archaeologically elusive, with so slight a body of written texts, I can't argue that some refer to my novels as fantasy. But I would ask readers to consider this: If a Christian character in a historical novel believes in the power of prayer and imagines they see a result, the work is still deemed historical fiction. If a pre-Christian character does the same, the work is deemed historical fantasy.

In the years I've been writing and researching the Lost Queen Trilogy, new archaeological discoveries have been made. Ronan Toolis and Christopher Bowles published their findings on Trusty's Hill in Dumfries and Galloway, which they believe could have been the seat of King Urien and his "Lost Dark Age Kingdom" of Rheged. The tenth- or eleventh-century "lost village" of Cadzow was discovered in 2015 beside the busy M74 motorway; and farther north, a handful of new sites have revealed new findings about the enigmatic Picts.

As new information on the Early Historic period continues to be revealed, I hope for a clearer picture of the rich and varied cultures of the forgotten kingdoms I write about.

Stories make no promises of truth—yet through the study of folklore, history, archaeology, and anthropology, I've come to believe that beneath every legend lies a kernel of truth. And so I've followed the trail of Lailoken and Languoreth to reconstruct their paths through the mists of early Scottish history. I'm still traveling that shadowy landscape, searching for the kernels of truth in the stories that remain.